THE
QUEEN
OF
DAYS

THE
QUEEN
OF
DAYS

GRETA KELLY

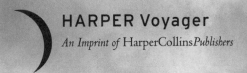
HARPER Voyager
An Imprint of HarperCollinsPublishers

THE QUEEN OF DAYS. Copyright © 2023 by Greta Kelly. All rights reserved. Printed in the United States of America. No part of this book may be used or reproduced in any manner whatsoever without written permission except in the case of brief quotations embodied in critical articles and reviews. For information, address HarperCollins Publishers, 195 Broadway, New York, NY 10007.

HarperCollins books may be purchased for educational, business, or sales promotional use. For information, please email the Special Markets Department at SPsales@harpercollins.com.

Harper Voyager and design are trademarks of HarperCollins Publishers LLC.

FIRST EDITION

Designed by Jennifer Chung
Chapter opener illustrations by Jennifer Chung
Map design by Mike Hall

Library of Congress Cataloging-in-Publication Data has been applied for.

ISBN 978-0-06-324096-4

23 24 25 26 27 LBC 5 4 3 2 1

For Gretchen, Kurt & Karl
There is no me without all of you

THE CITY OF COTHIS
IN THE KINGDOM OF ASHAAR

GRAND CANAL

MIDDLEMARCH

THE DOCKS

1	The Temple of Karanis
2	Cothis City Code Hall
3	Temple of Nananthe
4	The Grand Archive
5	The Summer House
6	The Sunken Gardens
7	Warehouse District

1

BALTHAZAR

Of all the times I'd been arrested, this was the only time I'd gotten pinched on purpose. I reminded myself of this in a vain attempt to keep my spirits up, as I squinted around the dank underbelly of the Cothis City Code Hall. I picked at my ale-soaked trousers, trying to ignore the way the heat from too many bodies made sweat trickle down my back.

Kai's head lolled my way as he shifted on the bench. He exhaled a dainty snore sending a puff of day-old breath straight into my face. I turned away, eyes watering, and stifled the urge to hit him. Kai was my oldest friend, and one hell of a fighter in a tough spot, but the damn fool could be careless as sin. Great Below, what kind of self-respecting criminal fell asleep mid-job? Especially as strange a job as this one was shaping up to be.

Our patron had ordered us to get arrested on this day and by this precinct. It was Kai's bright idea to start the bar fight, and once that thought filled his empty head, he went at it like a raging bull. I ran a hand over my whiskers. At least no one had been injured. Well, permanently.

I felt a mirthless kind of smile hitch my lips as I looked past the dozen sleeping bodies of my fellow inmates, past the brown mud-brick walls etched with the Codes of Law up to the ceiling. There was no artificial light in the cell, for the obvious reason that drunk criminals plus fire equals one big bloody mess. The only illumination came from a shaft of moonlight shining through a metal grate in the ceiling on the far end of the room.

Ostensibly it was there for ventilation, but the almost-summer air was so soupy breathing it in felt like drowning. While the air might have been a touch fresher beneath the grate, the laws of general ass-holery prevented anyone from sitting beneath it: namely that every few hours some jackal-cursed idiot up above would stop there to take a piss.

Through the grate's metal bars, I could just make out the Great Spear shining mockingly in the sky. By the height of the constellation, I knew it was well after midnight. Which meant I'd been in this hole for seven fucking hours. I closed my eyes, letting my head thud against the wall, and cursed the patron in every language I knew.

It was his damn fault I was here wasting valuable time that could have been spent planning. Instead I was stuck in a jail cell, waiting for some legendary fixer. A woman who could kill the empress in front of the whole court and get away with it. A *demon* who could bend the nature of the world—if you were the kind of idiot who believed such talk.

And I wasn't . . . Usually.

Urgh. It was almost insulting. My crew, the Talion, was young, but we were more than capable of stealing some old statue from the governor. Given the personal history we had with the rat, we probably would have done the job for free. Well. Most of us, anyway. But the patron had his own ideas, his own very specific time line, and this one annoying caveat: either the Queen of Days joined the crew, or the job was off.

I sneered as the words rattled around my skull. *Queen of Days.*

The name practically screamed incompetence. And not the kind of incompetence that the real professionals rolled their eyes at and tolerated, because what's one more kid playing in the sandbox to them? It's the kind that gets a person knifed and tossed in the nearest canal.

Except . . .

Except that the stupid nickname aside, the woman got results. She single-handedly robbed the Sala Antiquities Museum three months ago. And last year she breached the Bastion to bust out four men. And the Bastion was in the middle of the godsdamned ocean, an island guarded by a fleet of patrol ships from both the water and the air. She'd have had to scale nearly seven hundred feet of sheer cliff to even reach the prison. And that was after the twenty-some-mile swim across open and unforgiving ocean.

She was good. Damn good. And her insistence that we meet in a jail cell could only mean she was connected to the codekeepers. Well connected too. But who was she? Where did she come from? No one knew.

When my family still ruled Cothis, there hadn't been a single whisper about her. Five years later, I returned home to find people speaking of her in hushed, almost reverent tones. Lunacy.

But it was the kind of lunacy I could use. The kind that wouldn't only get me out of this cell but secure the biggest score anyone in this cursed kingdom had ever heard of.

I opened my eyes, staring at the closed cell door, straining my ears for the sound of footsteps. According to the patron, the Queen of Days would be in these jails tonight. All I had to do was wait, and she would find me.

He'd been characteristically sketchy on the details—one of the many reasons my crew didn't like working for him. But the way he'd arranged all this didn't really matter to me. Afterall a payoff this big was worth the petty indignity of jumping through the old man's hoops. Anyway, he probably had a codie or three on his payroll, too.

I shook my head mirthlessly. The Empress's codekeepers were

supposed to be righteous and true. As upright and just as the Codes of Law handed down to us poor mortals by the god Enkaara so many eons ago. Bullshit. Here in Cothis, many, many miles from the capital and the empress, the codekeepers were hardly better than any other street gang. Just better funded.

Still, I would have given anything to have a codie on the take. Anything to get out of this cell and into some dry clothes. The agony of staring at nothing but a closed door was making me itch. I stretched my neck from one side to the other, coaxing a few satisfied cracks from my spine. The pops were so loud, I almost missed the sound of the door shivering against its hinges.

I turned waiting to hear a key scrape against the lock.

Nothing.

"What the . . ."

I shook my head. *I must be more tired than I—*

My thoughts collided with a wall of silence. A silence that crept out from the darkness beneath the door on a whisper of frigid air that scoured the cell. Impossible. Cothis was never cold. But goose bumps pimpled my skin. My heart beat too loud in my ears as all sound retreated outside. And inside . . . Kai stopped snoring. The men around me went still. Not a single murmur. Not even a breath.

A metal tang electrified the air. There was something primal about it. Like the scent of spilled blood or rotting flesh. It was a smell that should have been identifiable. But what should have been careened face-first into the floor as the hairs on the back of my neck rose in mute horror. Because someone—*something*—was behind me.

Slowly, like dread had filled my joints with sand, I turned.

A figure stood at the far end of the cell. I couldn't make out its—no, *her*—face, but I got the impression of a tall, slight woman. She leaned against the back wall, watching. Assessing. After a moment that stretched into hours, she straightened and stepped into the shaft of light.

Moonlight flashed against the planes of her silver mask. Black

THE QUEEN OF DAYS   5

mesh screened the eyeholes, transforming her face into a floating silver skull. More black fabric covered her body, from her hood to the tips of her black leather boots. But it did nothing to soften her figure as she moved. Looking like a collection of sharp angles, she prowled forward, stepping silently around the sleeping men.

She stopped two precise feet from my knees, tilted her head to one side. "Balthazar Vadalen?"

All moisture evaporated from my tongue at the sibilant sound of my name on her lips. I nodded.

"You wish to obtain my services?"

I managed another nod, the small movement enough to shake words lose in my brain. "What did you do to them?"

It seemed to take her a moment to understand the question, for she paused before looking down at the people around her. Had she only just realized they were there? "They sleep."

"Yes, but how?" My eyes narrowed when she failed to reply. "I need to know that my friend will be all right. Did you use some kind of gas?"

"Your friend is in no danger. He sleeps. When our business is concluded, he will wake."

"Well that's me comforted," I grumbled, trying not to breathe too deeply lest whatever she used on the others start to affect me. And I was sure she'd used something. I was the only person sitting upright—everyone else was either slumped over, like Kai, or laying on the floor. I'd spent enough time with Zee to know that some gases crept low to the ground. Couldn't remember why, but that wasn't important.

I filed the thought—and the hope that Zee could re-create the compound from the traces on our clothes—for later. We were here for business after all. "So, here's the deal, I need you to—"

She made a sharp cutting motion with one hand. "Not here. Come." She turned away, gliding to the door.

I knew the door was locked. Great Below, I'd seen a half dozen men try to break it down, the others egging them on with equal parts hilarity and hope. But somehow I wasn't surprised to see the handle yield beneath her gloved hand. The door slid open on silent hinges, like they obeyed this woman with bated breath and quiet terror.

She floated through the door, her presence tugging at me like I was no more than a dog on a leash. The indignity made me bridle, and I let it bloom into anger. I was tired and bored and not paying attention. She wasn't a demon, just a clever woman who'd probably turned the sewer grate into a trapdoor. I'd assumed she had contacts in the Code Hall. Here was the proof.

I shook my head and pulled myself up, feeling more relaxed—more in control—than I had since I'd gotten arrested. But . . . the idea of leaving Kai behind still made me pause. If the meeting went south, I might need backup to get out of here. Then again, Kai's idea of help wasn't always that helpful, I thought, catching a whiff of my damp clothes. Silently promising to return, I smiled at my still-sleeping friend and walked out of the cell.

The guard station outside was a perfect circle of slimy gray stone with a half dozen closed doors studding its thick walls at even intervals. A rusted iron chandelier with three tiers of lit candles hung over a wide wooden table. Cards and food and half-empty tankards were abandoned on the table's scarred surface. No guards, though. Only the woman.

An unaccountable desire to laugh welled up my throat as she sat at the center of the table. For all that she was dressed like a burglar, she held herself with the dignified air of a noble. With folded hands she looked like she was waiting for a not particularly important meeting to begin. Shaking my head, I took the seat opposite hers.

Something akin to a companionable silence spread out between us, and in the light of the chandelier, I studied her mask. It was truly a masterpiece. Unlike the featureless oval of many a masquerade mask, this was precisely molded to glide over high cheekbones, a long, slightly upturned nose and angular jaw. The metal was etched with intricate scrollwork that accentuated the wide catlike eyes, and the mask's full lips were painted in black lacquer. They tilted up at one corner in the slightest hint of a smile. But the impenetrable fabric hiding her eyes soured the tableau.

She brushed an invisible something from her sleeve and placed her gloved palms flat on the table. "So. Balthazar."

"Please, call me Bal," I said, leaning back in my chair, my stomach clenching as it's uneven legs wobbled.

She inclined her head. "Bal. Why does the Talion require my services?"

I felt a muscle in my jaw tick. "To be honest, we don't."

"Then why are you here?"

"Because my patron—the man who commissioned this job— insisted you join the crew."

She didn't speak for a long minute. "And why does your patron require my presence?"

It was the same question I'd asked before taking the job. The answer still made no sense. "He says that you're to be the 'weapon of last resort.'"

"Ah. I see."

I believed her. Something about the way she said it, the way her posture incrementally relaxed, made it clear that this answer made sense to her. Damn, did I want to ask her why, but the question would have to wait. My eyes swept the chamber, half sure that some codie would waltz in any second now. She might have them in her pocket, but I sure as hell didn't. Time wasn't on my side; I wasn't going to let my ignorance be another advantage she could use.

"And your patron is sure this is the job he wishes to hire me for?"

"He was pretty damn sure," I said, frowning. "Why?"

"There are several conditions to my employment. Two of them are that I will not work for the same person twice. Nor will I accept contracts lasting more than seven days."

Suddenly the jumped-up name made sense. "So that's where the title comes from? Queen of Days?"

"Partially. Yes."

The stilted way she spoke reminded me of an old elocution tutor I once had. She'd been a stuck-up old broad who came from the corporal punishment school of education. It was a real effort not to roll my eyes. "Well, the time frame won't be an issue. As for your other condition? The patron insisted on your presence, so I'm assuming he's aware that this is his one shot to use you."

"And you?"

"What about me?"

"Are you sure that you require my presence?"

I rolled a few replies around in my mouth before settling on, "Yeah. I'm sure. That good enough for you?"

She graced me with a shallow nod. "What is the job?"

I sniffed. "In two days, the restoration of the Cothis temple will be complete," I said, not bothering to hide my distaste.

Each island in the Kingdom of Ashaar had a temple dedicated to their city's patron god. Every few generations, the old one was knocked down and a new one was built in its place, supposedly in veneration of the god's glory. Nonsense, really. It was just a way to employ the faceless masses, keep them off the streets and overworked so they didn't have time to dream of better lives.

"During the opening ceremony, Governor Paasch will consecrate a new idol to the god Karanis. We've been hired to steal the idol during the ceremony, but before it's consecrated."

Her back straightened vertebra by vertebra before stilling completely. It was the kind of readiness that hummed. Like she was the human equivalent of a wire slipped over an unguarded throat.

I smirked, enjoying the feeling of her surprise, and flashed my most feral smile. The plan was as daring as it got, not that my crew couldn't handle the challenge. And if I was being honest, the brazenness was part of the allure. Governor Paasch had ruined our lives. He deserved what was coming.

"Who set the terms for this job?" she asked, her voice rough. "You? Or your patron?"

I frowned, thinking it was obvious: the man who paid me. "My patron."

"Why? Why steal the idol during the ceremony? Why not before?"

The front two legs of my chair hit the floor with a *thud*. It wasn't like these weren't good questions. They were the exact ones I'd asked. But the *way* she was asking them, the intensity with which her voice echoed off the room's rounded walls, put me on edge.

"According to my patron, the idol won't be finished until right before the consecration. Would it be easier to steal beforehand, yes. But he's not interested in an unfinished idol. He wants the real deal. And he doesn't want to wait until after the ceremony."

"Does it not seem unnecessarily dangerous?"

Of course it was dangerous. Crazy dangerous. And yeah, I'd have rather waited until after the ceremony, but, "He's not paying us for easy."

"I wish to meet him."

I exhaled a hard laugh. "He thought you might."

"And?"

"He said you can come with me to deliver the idol after the ceremony. He won't meet you before."

"I see."

"Clearly," I grumbled. "So, are you joining us?"

She sighed, though the mask muffled the sound, transforming it into the papery rustle of moths in flight. She clasped her hands, elbows braced on the table. Her pointer fingers were pressed against her black lips. "I shall."

"Good. We'll cut you in on the take. Five percent for three days of work sound good?" I smiled innocently, ready for the outraged exclamation that would surely follow this measly offer.

"I do not require money."

I felt my brows rise. "Then what do you require?"

"Tell me the names of your companions."

"It's a small crew," I began, rolling with the change of subject even though it made me want to hit something. I had a feeling nothing would be easy with this woman and a spiteful part of me wanted to refuse. *The money, Bal. Just think of the money.* "You saw my man Kai in the cell," I said, nodding toward the open door.

"Kai? Ah, no. What are their full names?"

"Malakai Fanoak, though you'll call him Kai unless you want to start a fight."

She nodded once. "Who else?"

"Zeelaya Agodzi, she's my cousin, and her husband, Edik Agodzi." When she didn't speak, I bared my teeth in a small smile. "That's it. Like I said, it's a small crew."

She watched me for several long moments, saying nothing. Eventually her hands parted in a small impatient gesture. "And? Who else?"

"I told you—"

My words banked as the candles in the chandelier waned. Water pebbled and dripped from the ceiling. Dragged out of earth and stone like the slow breaking of a dam. Tiny teardrops plinked on the table between us as if they were the steady thrum of a clock running out. The walls around me seemed to constrict, squeezing. *Squeezing.*

She knew. She knew about Mira.

Impossible. She wasn't really part of the crew. I never let her do anything riskier than open doors or be a lookout. Never anything dangerous. *She wasn't part of the crew.* My vision flickered as an invisible finger scraped the inside of my skull.

What the hell was happening to me?

"Who. Else."

My lips twitched, moving of their own accord, ready to surrender the name of the one person in this world I'd give anything to protect. I bit down hard, tasting blood in my mouth.

Had the patron told her about Mira? That old bastard—he knew I did everything I could to keep her on the sidelines. Anger raced up my spine, and for one wild moment, I almost walked back into the cell and closed the door behind me.

Then I remembered the payday. Remembered all the good that money could do; the life I could give Mira if we succeeded. But only if the Queen of Days joined the crew. Only if we actually pulled this off.

Through gritted teeth I said, "Miraveena Vadalen."

"Your wife?"

"My sister," I spat. "And if you think you deserve one cent of her cut, you're crazier than you look."

"I told you; I do not want your money."

I smacked my hand to the table, glorying in the pain that danced up my arm. "Then what do you want?"

"Time."

I blinked. "You want time?"

"Yes. A month, to be exact."

"You want a month of our time? And what do you expect us to do in that month?"

"Ah. You misunderstand. I do not mean that I want a month of your service. I want a month of your life. Thirty days you would have lived, which you will now surrender to me."

The Queen of Days demands thirty days. It was like the first draft of a shitty nursery rhyme, I thought with a slight laugh. "You're joking."

She had to be joking. But she wasn't. She was utterly, deadly serious.

"If you agree to work with me, you agree to die thirty days sooner than Creation intended."

She was insane. Utterly cracked. No one could just lop off a month of a person's life. She was no better than some dockside oracle claiming to read the future from a line on my hand and the gold in my pocket. I shook my head, struggling to dislodge a sense of total disbelief. What was she? Why would the patron insist on her participation? It was . . .

A good deal.

No wonder she had a reputation for doing crazy, impossible things. She was impossibly crazy, so risking her life was obviously no great hardship. It almost wasn't fair, negotiating with a deranged person. But Cothis wasn't built on fairness. If all she wanted was an impossible-to-keep promise, the more money for the rest of the crew.

For Mira.

Wasn't an empty promise worth the life I could give my sister? My family?

I shrugged. "All right. Fine. A month of my life."

She tilted her head to the side. "I think there has been another misunderstanding. Apologies. Ashaarite is not my native tongue, and I find it both cumbersome and imprecise. It is not only thirty days of your life which I require, but Kai's, Zeelaya's, Edik's, and Miraveena's as well."

"Not Mira." The words sprang from my lips, splattering desperation on the walls. Hatred rushed through me, twisting and churning. This—this *thing*—wasn't getting anywhere near my little sister.

She studied me quietly for some moments longer. "All right. Would you like to take on her debt, or prorate it among the rest of your companions?"

"I'll take it," I said without hesitation.

"Very well." She extended a gloved hand. "Are we agreed?"

I stared at her hand. Surely she couldn't mean for me to . . .

"I have to agree *now*? For all of them?"

"Yes. You are the leader of the Talion, after all. And my terms are, in my own opinion, rather unusual. No doubt they will be happy to acquiesce to our agreement if it means more money for them in the end."

"No doubt." I sneered as I said the words. The woman didn't know the first thing about my crew. I might lead them, but I didn't make decisions for them. Or . . . I didn't used to.

Until this job.

Edik and Zee were still pissed I'd taken it without talking to them first—and for keeping the patron's identity a secret. Kai was too, if I was being honest. He just didn't want to admit to being angry with me. But Edik was convinced that this job was dead reckless. And when he and Zee found out who the patron really was?

Shit.

The woman before me wasn't the only one who wanted to have a few words with the old man. He had a knack for sending us into the worst kind of danger, which was exactly why I didn't tell anyone he was involved.

I looked past her still-outstretched hand, struggling to find some kind of purchase. But all I saw was the plain stone walls of a jail cell.

"Will the codekeepers be helping us?" I asked, the idea hitting me with sudden hope. "Can you at least make sure they look the other way?"

If she could ensure their cooperation, or at the very least, their indifference, it would go a long way with my crew.

She paused, seeming to consider my question. "No," she said finally, shattering all hope. "Not unless you wish to sacrifice more time."

"Look, Catsuit, I can't sacrifice their time as it is."

"Ah. I see." Her hand dropped. "Then our business is concluded."

She rose, and the light seemed to dim with her. The light and my future.

Mira's future.

If this woman left, so did the job. The payday. Any chance I had at getting Mira into a good school and getting her a home—not just a ratty ship cabin, but a real home—would be gone.

The ghosts of my parents' voices slid through my mind. Their final desperate words begging me to take care of her. Of all of them.

"Wait." My voice was soft, cracking with my resolve. But it was enough to make this demon of a woman pause.

And turn back to me.

Get your shit together, Bal. There's no such thing as demons. Or magic. Just crazy-ass women in costumes.

"Fine. I'll do it. I agree to your terms."

When her hand rose again, I didn't hesitate. I took it, grimacing, as a mosquito bit the back of my neck like a bad omen of things to come. "So what should I call you? Your Majesty Queen of Days?"

I felt her body shake through the shared link of our joined hands and realized she was laughing. "Tassiel."

"Tassiel?" The name rang against something in the deep recesses of my mind.

"Or Tass," she said, "as you seem to prefer diminutives."

"Tass it is," I replied, though my preferences clearly counted for shit today.

2

BALTHAZAR

I shot a kick at Kai's legs, and he jolted awake so hard he almost fell off the bench.

"Great Below, man," he grumbled, pushing his long brown hair out of his eyes. "What was that for?"

"Get up. It's time to go."

"But the woman hasn't even shown up yet," he said through a yawn.

I rolled my eyes. "Yeah, she has. We met, agreed to terms, and now we're leaving."

Hurt flashed across Kai's face. "What? You met without me?"

"If you wanted to be in on the meeting, Kai, you shouldn't have fallen asleep." I smacked his arm to let him know I wasn't mad and nodded to the door. "You want to meet her, or would you rather rot in here for a few more hours?"

Kai shrugged but dragged himself up and followed me into the still-silent guardroom. I heard him suck in a breath when his gaze landed on Tass. His steps stuttered, but I pulled him forward. "Tass, this is Kai. Kai, Tass."

The pair regarded each other for a moment; Kai with his mouth hanging open and Tass with an air of mild curiosity. She looked from me to Kai and back again. "You are kin."

I smirked as Kai's momentary surprise washed away, instantly replaced with a cocky grin. "Not officially," he said, laughing. "Though Bal and I can pass for brothers, he's the last hope of the Vadalen line. I'm just the bastard."

"In every sense of the word," I said, something in me easing at the way Kai's devil-may-care attitude righted the world around me. The precinct underbelly no longer seemed so daunting. Nor Tass so alien. I could almost pretend this was nothing more than another long and drunken night filled with speculation about which of my illustrious line fathered Kai.

Though it could have been any of my uncles or older cousins, my money was on my father. Kai's mother worked in our house, after all, and in truth we *could* pass for twins. We both had the tall frames, wide shoulders, and slightly hooked noses of the Vadalen men.

The only striking difference between us was that Kai wore his dark hair long and unkempt, where mine was shorter, the tips brushing my collar. It was a concession to our long-suffering cousin, Zeelaya. Switching names to pull pranks on Zee had been one of our favorite youthful pastimes.

"Ah, there you are, my beauty." Kai crowed in triumph as he spotted a crate of confiscated clothing beside our cell. He snatched his vest—robin's-egg blue with gold piping—from the top of the pile. Kai shrugged into it before diving back into the crate for his sash— unmistakable in the gloom by its dark purple dye and vermillion tassels.

Made me want to laugh every time I saw him. Though hip-length vests and waist sashes were what passed for fashion in Ashaar, Kai was the only criminal I knew who took to the trend with such rarified zeal. Kai tossed a navy-blue sash at me before looking around the guard station with his lips turned down in disdain.

"Well, how are we busting out of this place? Makes me itch, being down here."

I shot Tass a look as I pulled on my vest, fingers going instinctively to the pocket where I'd left a necklace. One with a pendant of an eye hammered into wafer-thin steel like the icon of a forgotten god—the symbol of the Talion gang. I smiled at the words etched onto the edges: let chaos reign. A motto. An oath.

"Are we going the way you came?" I asked, motioning back to the cell. I had to admit, I really wanted to see the trapdoor she'd rigged up.

"No," she said, sounding slightly confused. "Come this way." Tass turned on her heel and crossed the room toward one of the closed doors. Stopped. She angled her silver face over her shoulder, and I could have sworn I caught the faintest whiff of jasmine. "Your silence will be appreciated."

"Hold up," I said, digging my proverbial heels into the ground. "It's gonna take a lot more than silence to sneak through the precinct. Where's your exit?"

"The front door," she replied as if that wasn't the surest way to get us all shot.

Kai took a half step back. "You know what, I was pretty comfortable back in the cell. I'm just going to—"

"How do you expect to walk out the front door?" I asked, clamping a staying hand on Kai's shoulder. "We'll be seen."

"I assure you, you will not. If you remain *silent*," she said, an edge entering her voice for the first time. But it wasn't hubris. It wasn't the unearned swagger of someone with terminal overconfidence.

This was the flat certainty of a professional at work. All those rumors about her circled back to me. Not just of her breaching the Bastion and robbing the museum, but a hundred other impossible-to-believe acts of insanity pulled off not just here in Cothis, but all over Ashaar.

This woman, whoever she was, was good. Damn good. And if I could manage to shove my pride aside for half a minute, I might just admit she was better than me and my crew. Maybe even learn a thing or two.

So I ignored the incredulous look Kai was giving me and gestured for her to continue. She opened the door as if locks didn't exist and led us down a narrow, poorly lit hall. Branching corridors echoed with angry voices, but that was to be expected in a jail. No guards though. And that wasn't just odd. It was telling. No matter what Tass claimed, she had to be paying off someone in the precinct.

Was the whole place empty? Had all the codies up and decided to go on a smoke break? Was that how Tass expected to get us out the front door?

The answer came sooner than I'd have liked. Following her through the Code Hall's catacomb-like basement, we reached a very familiar set of stairs. Stairs I knew would lead into the bullpen. A space that—judging by the sounds of murmured conversations and shuffling paper—was very much not empty. I gestured upward, giving her an eloquent look of "What the fuck?"

Tass just held a finger to her lips and very slowly pressed her palm to my chest. Warmth passed through her gloved fingers, sinking into my skin for the space of two heartbeats. Like I was a horse that needed calming, I thought sourly, her botanical perfume wafting into my face as she turned away.

But damn it if it didn't work. I was calmer. Steadier. And ready to see what this fixer was capable of. Steeling myself for a fight, I followed.

As we went up, I caught a glimpse of a sturdy iron chandelier, fully lit despite the lateness of the hour. But there was something strange about the light. It was almost too bright, too prismatic. It seemed to catch the edges of my vision and blur. I shook my head, willing the tiredness out of my eyes, but to no avail. The light still shimmered at the corners of my eyes. But I didn't need clear sight to make out the two dozen codekeepers scattered through the room.

Kai stiffened, reaching for weapons that weren't there. He opened his mouth, but I shook my head before he could speak. In the middle of the office, in plain view of so many codies, Tass's request for silence suddenly seemed of deathly importance. As if our silence could stop all these people from spotting us.

And they would, because it must have been the quietest night shift on record—three whole people were giving statements to inspectors, so I understood why they were too busy to notice us. But the rest? No paperwork could be so engrossing that they didn't see us walk by.

Yet walk we did. We followed her steps, up past two desks, right two more, then back three. Left. Right. Forward. Back. Like the office was a labyrinth only she could see, and one wrong step would lead to ruin. Or at least a swift kick in the ass before we got dragged back to lockup. *Who is she? Who is she that she can lead two criminals through the Code Hall without anyone trying to stop us?*

My skin crawled at the feeling of being surrounded by so many codies, but not one looked at us. Their eyes just slid right past Kai and I, hit Tass, and immediately turned down like a rodent playing dead beneath a falcon's shadow. Every. Single. One.

I counted them as we passed: twenty beat codies, six secretaries, a desk sergeant, and four inspectors. A million questions churned in my mind, but my tongue was glued to the roof of my mouth.

Tass's pace didn't increase as she meandered toward the exit. Slowly. So damn slowly. The doors loomed, like in a dream where everything was both close and entirely out of reach. I hated those dreams. Nightmares of uncontrolled fate. My gaze rose to the pale granite wall above the exit, and I found a frail sort of refuge in the familiar words. There, etched in fading black paint, was the Code of Enkaara as given to humanity by the Creator.

Even with my vision blurring at the edges and Tass's perfume clogging my mind, I could have recited the code by heart. In my line of work, it was always useful to know the line of the law; when to toe it, and when to leap right on past.

The pressure in my chest finally eased as we made it through the doors, down the stairs, and into the never-sleeping streets of Cothis. I tipped my head back and gulped down a breath of muggy air before experience kicked in and put me back on guard. I did a quick scan of the streets around us, searching for anyone who might be watching. Only the Temple of Karanis stood guard tonight. A great monolithic blot against the night sky. I scowled at its alabaster walls and looked away.

"Great Below, woman," Kai exclaimed. "Just how many codies you got on the take?"

"Codies?"

"Yeah, codies." Kai's brows rose when this failed to illicit any kind of response from the woman. "Codekeepers."

Somehow she still seemed confused. "That's why we had to meet you in the Code Hall, right? Meeting in the cells is one hell of a way to ensure good behavior." And, you know, guaranteed that if a deal went south no one could follow her home and knife her in the back. "So you have to be working with at least a few codies."

"Oh. Yes . . . but also no." Tass looked to me. "I shall see you in two days' time."

"No. Hold up," I said, catching her arm before she could walk away.

She stiffened under my touch and turned. The air temperature plummeted. The sound of carriages, the incessant call of hawkers faded, eclipsed by the sound of my pulse. I dropped her arm and held up both hands. "Easy, Tass."

She regarded me for a moment. Her shoulders relaxed, muscles uncoiling, like she'd decided not to kill me.

"Come with me," I said as the specter of my sudden and colorful death receded. "Stay with my crew."

"Why?"

"Because in two days we're going to be pulling off the most dangerous job anyone in this gods-cursed city has ever attempted. If we're going to get away with it, we need to work as a team. We can't do that if we don't see you until the day of the job. Stay with us. Learn the plan. Get to know the crew, their strengths, and weaknesses." I shrugged and ducked my head closer when she didn't seem convinced. "They'll need time to get used to you, too."

"Not likely," Kai muttered.

I could've cuffed him, but Tass didn't seem to mind. Eventually she nodded. "Very well. Where to?"

The stars burned brighter with my relief. "I've secured lodging with an old friend."

Kai snorted at this, but thankfully refrained from comment. He and Shasheba had never gotten along and being forced to take her charity wasn't sitting well with him. He would get over the indignity, but I doubt he'd ever count Shasheba as a friend, though admitting as much made my chest ache.

"This way." I led us down one side street and then another, winding away from the center of the city, with its Code Hall and mansions and that eyesore of a temple that shone unbearably bright in the moonlight. I scowled at the ground before forcing my head up and my shoulders back.

This wasn't the first time I'd walked away from the streets that had once been my home and the dreams that went with them. Though Zee and Kai had been back a few times, I'd always refused. Until now. All Father curse me, I wanted to hate this place. I wanted to hate this whole damn island, from the warm turquoise waters of its crisscrossing canals to the seedy underbelly of its many wharves. I couldn't manage it. Even after five years of self-imposed exile, Cothis still had me on tenterhooks.

"Bal?"

The way Tass's voice clung to the vowel, transforming my name into something new, made me smile. "Yeah?"

"What is there between you and Governor Paasch?"

Kai huffed an incredulous laugh. "Where are you from, woman?"

Tass flicked the question away. "Someplace else."

"Must be far if you don't know that story," Kai muttered. "Bal's father was the governor before Paasch. A whole line of Vadalen governor's ruled Cothis for the past . . . I dunno, two centuries, I think." Kai scratched his chin in thought, and then shrugged the effort away. "Doesn't matter. Bal's father, Zanek, was the rightful governor of Cothis. And he was a damn good one, too. It was him who took Paasch under his wing. Taught Paasch everything he knew, not realizing the power-grabbing prick was going to stab him in the back one day."

"What happened?" Tass asked, no doubt sensing that Kai was about to go off on a tangent.

"The gods turned on us." The words slipped out of my lips, darker and deeper than the night around us.

Tass turned sharply to me. "What do you mean?"

"He means that after a few years of bad weather, Paasch riled up every religious idiot in the city and convinced them that Zanek had fallen out of favor with the god Karanis. Pretty soon, the entire city was calling for Zanek to be sacrificed to appease Karanis. All because of a bit of rain," Kai said, spitting to one side.

"It wasn't just 'a bit of rain,' Kai," I snapped, drawing a worried glare from the bent man I was walking past. No doubt going home, I thought, as the scent of fresh orange juice wafted over from his battered handcart.

I forced my voice down before I continued. "It was three years of the worst hurricanes this island has ever seen."

"And that was enough?" Tass asked.

I snorted, watching a gondola filled with Karanis-knew-what float slowly by. "I think you fail to understand what a hurricane means to an island crisscrossed with canals." I stopped at the crest of the next footbridge and pointed toward a line of brick row houses on the other side of the canal. "You see that line of discoloration just below the bottom window?"

"Yes."

"That water mark shows how high the flooding gets during the average rainy season." I moved my finger up, past the top of the first story window, to the very lip of the second. "Three years running, the floodwaters got up to there. Hundreds of people died. Thousands lost everything they ever owned."

Tass seemed to consider this. "And this was a good reason to kill your father?"

"No," I said, my throat closing around the word. "There was no reason—good or otherwise—to kill my father. I'm saying that scared, desperate people will do anything they can to feel like they're in control."

"What of the empress? How is it that Paasch convinced her to look the other way?"

"The empress," Kai muttered, bitter laugh filling the air. "Useless piece of—"

"The empress had only ascended to the throne three days before the coup," I said before Kai got us arrested again for criticizing our glorious leader.

"And there were more pressing issues for her to attend to?"

The dry disapproval in Tass's voice was almost comforting. Almost.

Because, no. No there couldn't have been anything more important than Cothis descending into chaos.

Not even a godsdamned coronation.

"Arisha is a long way from Cothis."

Tass grunted in understanding. "So Paasch had your father killed. I take it the rain stopped."

"Yes." The admission soured my tongue, and for a moment, I couldn't speak. "But not before he had my mother and all my aunts and uncles killed. They would have gone for me and Zee and Mira, but we were still kids at the time."

They did go for us, in fact, the memory of it still too raw to speak of. If it hadn't been for a handful of loyal servants, we'd have all died too. Mira nearly did die when she and her minder got separated from the rest of us. Only the soft heart of a kind stranger had saved her life, leaving her at the back door of our family's summer home before disappearing into the mayhem.

"So this job is your revenge?"

I looked down at the rippling, murky waters of the canal, and for a moment they were filled with blood. I shook my head. "Have you ever lost everything, Tass?"

"Yes."

It wasn't the answer that threw me—a person didn't go as crooked as we had for pasts filled with puppies and fucking rainbows. But the flatness in her voice made me pull up and stop. I looked at her, wishing she'd take the stupid mask off so I could see her face. See that she understood.

"Then you should know that revenge isn't something you take in the dark like a snack at midnight," I said, nodding toward the line of half-drunk fools laughing as they waited their turn at the shaved ice stand. "It's a plan made over years, all the more decadent for the labor it demands.

"Is this job simply about the payday? Maybe for the rest of the crew. But not for me. Stealing the idol, ruining the consecration will make the city wonder if Karanis hasn't abandoned Paasch. If the very god Paasch wielded like a blade against my family hasn't seen him for what he is and cast him aside like trash.

"What Paasch did to us, the lives he took . . . This job doesn't even scratch the surface of what he deserves. The true revenge is coming. This job is just the appetizer." I swallowed. Turned. "Come on. Shasheba's probably waiting."

Someday, I swore to the cracked cobblestone streets, *someday I will take my true revenge.* This was only the first sliver of payback for the lives Paasch took from me and Mira and Zee. *Shasheba, too.* I made the thought a vow as the road narrowed around the mouth of the Middlemarch.

That quarter of the city lay in the heart of the southern island. Like its name suggested, Middlemarch was once all marshland—a sacred space to my near-forgotten ancestors. So naturally, when the steady pace of progress demanded it, the marsh was drained. Hallowed ground be damned.

Temples to the Ankaari, the race of our benevolent gods, were built here in half-hearted recompense. Garishly painted buildings dedicated to the kingdom's many deities dotted the neighborhood. They squatted in between the morose-looking businesses whose facades had long since wilted, as the progress that demanded the marsh's destruction flitted away with the strongest breeze.

Not that it was the worst place in the city. Lamplighters still came at night, and if the roads were too narrow for carriages, they were still wide enough for the worshipful masses.

Masses indeed, I thought with a mirthless smile. Men and women, even a few children—not *all* of them pickpockets—swarmed the neighborhood. Unusual most times of year, this week's consecration made everything a matter of exception. Religious fervor gripped the city, ensuring that all of Middlemarch's many temples were teeming with worshippers, from the great temple of Enkaara, the Father of all the worlds under heaven, and to each of his seven children. Though the patron god of Cothis was Karanis, I couldn't honestly say that any more people swirled around his grand temple in the upper city than any of these temples here in the Middlemarch.

I shook my head, shoving past the swaying, intoxicated fools wandering out of the temple of Zefira, goddess of air. It was easy to believe the goddess could make you fly when her acolytes laced their incense with opium. Made them easy targets for the thieves that swam through the worshippers, too.

Child street gangs had staked out roadside plays to entice freshly befuddled believers, playacting all the creation myths of Ashaar, from the cataclysm that turned our once vast continent into an island chain, to the unending feud waging between the twin goddesses Nananthe and Ruekigal. The playacting was rough and wickedly crude, but people loved them. Laughed so hard they cried, even as tiny hands robbed them blind.

That Shasheba, a daughter of the highest echelons of Cothis society, could end up a priestess in Middlemarch was still something I had a hard time believing. Yet here she was. Her reputation was so ruined for having been promised to me, that this was her best option. Running the Temple of Nananthe, goddess of passion, love, fertility, and, oddly, war. The goddess should strike me down where I stood for having hurt Shasheba the way I had. Lucky me that gods didn't actually, you know, exist.

I felt a bitter smile twist my lips as the temple came into sight. The facade was pretty enough; orangey brick and red-trimmed windows. But the building had slanted over the years, leaning over the road like a drunkard in a slow fall. Little wonder the locals called it the Low Temple, considering it made as much money selling flesh as it did peddling fertility charms and midwifery services.

The common room was still half full by the time I pushed through the slightly warped doors of the Low Temple. Patrons milled about the wide space, flirting with white-robed men and women; Shasheba's acolytes, all but oblivious to our presence.

It was late enough, by now anyway, that all the wealthy patrons had come and gone and the acolytes not currently entertaining were all crowded on a square couch sharing sweet-smelling tabbac from tiny sea glass pipes. Those sitting there did notice us and smiled as we entered—well, they smiled at Kai. He'd made quick friends with the acolytes during our weeklong stay in the attic. Rather too many friends in Shasheba's judgment.

"And that's me off the clock," Kai said, clapping my shoulder with a grin before swaggering off.

As the acolytes made room on their couch for Kai's bulk, I spotted a familiar mess of tightly curled hair wedged into one corner. My vision flashed red. "Hey," I said, my voice coming out sharper than I'd intended. "What are you doing down here?"

Mira turned, her dark eyes narrowing as she scowled. "What? I'm just sitting."

"Mira." I paused, trying to clear some of the anger out of my voice. "You know you aren't supposed to be down here alone at night."

Mira heaved a labored sigh and rolled her big eyes so hard they almost disappeared into her skull. At the ripe old age of twelve, Mira was sure she was all grown up. And if I was going to let her stay in what amounted to a brothel, then why shouldn't she be allowed to look around? No matter how many times I told her it wasn't appropriate and that it could be dangerous, the explanations just bounced right off her.

I swallowed hard and searched the room, as if Zee would appear and back me up. My eyes skated past a long wall of empty birthing and treatment chambers, and up to the second- and third-floor balconies lined with bedrooms. But I couldn't see my cousin sitting in any of the artfully arranged couches and brightly colored poufs, all low lit and overly perfumed. Damn it all.

She and Edik said they'd keep an eye on Mira. Figures they'd let the promise slide. They wouldn't even be on this damned island right now if they had another choice. But given how much shit they were slinging about the job being too reckless, I argued back—in my head—it couldn't be as reckless as letting a twelve-year-old wander around this place alone. I felt my lips flatten into a thin line. "Where is Zee? She's supposed to be watching you."

"Zeelaya and Edik went to sleep hours ago."

My eyes rose, following the frosty, feminine voice to where

Shasheba watched me from the top of the stairs. Her light, lamp-like eyes were hard and filled with judgment. After an agonizing moment of scrutiny, she made her way down the stairs in a graceful sashay of full hips. A woman like that could drive a man to his knees with a single look, I thought. The urge to apologize (for the thousandth time this week) rose to my lips and I had to bite the inside of my cheek to quash it. Whatever Shasheba wanted from me, it wasn't an apology.

"Don't worry," Shasheba said, planting herself in front of me with crossed arms clearly wanting to toss me out on my ass and relishing the thought. "Miraveena only came down after most of the worshippers were gone for the evening. And none but the acolytes were allowed near her." Her perfect eyebrows rose to cutting points. "Do you really think I would put her in danger?" she murmured in an undertone, too soft for Mira to hear.

"Thank you for—"

"Don't," was her unamused reply. "Watch your sister, Bal. I'm not her mother."

"Sorry." I winced the word, as her comment struck flesh. Shasheba wasn't ashamed of her position, and in the ever-contradictory ladder of Ashaarite society, she hadn't fallen all that far. But unlike Mira, Shasheba remembered my mother—well, remembered her prudish, noble aversion to earthy matters of the flesh. All Father save me, was I turning into my mother?

Guilt unfurled within me. Guilt, and more shame than I cared to acknowledge. My mother would have killed me for letting Mira come here, I thought, feeling my hands curl. My mother would have killed me for a lot of things I'd done over the past few years.

Shasheba saw something in my face that made her nod in a satisfied way. Her expression softened incrementally, and I ventured a smile. Despite the years, and Shasheba's undimmed anger at me for not taking her with me when I left Cothis, she could still read me like an open book. Her perfect nose wrinkled. "You stink," she said, tossing her waist-length hair over her shoulder. "I hope you were successful in finding your . . . associate?"

I blinked. The entire evening had gone completely out of my mind, but Shasheba always had that effect on me. "Yeah." I turned. "This is . . ."

Tass's hooded figure stood in the darkness by the door. The silent, alien menace I'd felt when she first appeared in my cell came rushing back. She took a step forward, but the shadows clung to her with greedy fingers, unwilling to yield her to the light.

The merriment of the men and women behind me guttered. The lights flickered. One of the acolytes gasped. Shasheba retreated half a step back, and without thinking I grabbed her hand.

"This is Tass," I said with a forced brightness that sounded foreign to my ears. "Tass, this is Shasheba Tal, the high priestess of the Cothis Temple of Nananthe."

Shasheba had recovered herself enough to smile and drew her hand away from mine. "Welcome, Tass."

Tass nodded absently, but didn't speak. Rather, she seemed to be looking at some point over Shasheba's head. I followed Tass's gaze past the still-entranced acolytes and scattered seating, to the opposite end of the long room.

An altar to Nananthe stood in a candle-laden alcove and was topped with an almost human-size statue of the goddess. She sat on a golden throne and was clothed only in long, flowing hair. Her hands were raised, hiding most of her face. A face so beautiful, it was said, that it could drive mere mortals mad. Only her mouth was visible, carved into an inscrutable smile—a smile that reminded me all too much of Tass's mask. I shivered.

"I see you've noticed our shrine," Shasheba said, her face and voice carefully guarded. "You are welcome to pray if you wish."

"Pray." Tass repeated the word like she was rolling a strange piece of meat around in her mouth and wasn't sure about the taste. "Is that why people come here?"

"We encourage many forms of worship," Shasheba said with a solicitous smile. "This is the Temple of Nananthe, after all."

"Is it?"

I winced as Tass's voice turned the question into an accusation.

Shasheba's face darkened. "Yes. It is." She licked her lips, composing herself with practiced ease. "What did you say your name was?"

"Bal gave you my proper form of address."

"Tass, yes, but no surname? I don't mean to pry," Shasheba said with a smile that implied the opposite. "But I do want to assure you that your privacy will always be respected within these walls. So there really is no need to hide your true self here. We encourage our worshippers to put down their fears and insecurities, and lay aside the masks they wear when they enter.

"Not that your mask isn't beautiful—it almost reminds me of something I saw while studying at the High Temple in Arisha."

Tass rounded on Shasheba, and although the strange woman didn't step forward, she loomed. To her credit Shasheba didn't look intimidated—not precisely—but she stopped rambling about the sanctity of her temple and the nonsense she learned in the capital. Tass had shut Shash up without saying a single word.

It was a neat trick.

Shasheba shot me an uncertain look, and I almost smiled simply for the joy in seeing her off-kilter . . . and looking to me for rescue. Instead, I cleared my throat. "There are cots set up for us in the attic if you're tired—"

"I do not require rest at this time." Tass's silver face turned toward mine. "I shall await further instruction at the shrine."

"Are you sure? We're all going to sleep now. It'll be morning before I meet with the others."

"That is acceptable." Tass glided forward, cutting between Shasheba and me. Then she stopped. Turned to Shash. "Thank you for your hospitality."

THE QUEEN OF DAYS   31

Shasheba's brows had drawn together. "You're welcome," she replied with a slightly hard note in her voice.

If Tass noticed it, she clearly didn't care. She crossed the room, ignoring the gaping acolytes. "Good night, Kai," she said, nodding to the big man. "Miraveena."

My sister's eyes, already big as saucers, nearly popped out of her head. She watched Tass walk to the shrine and kneel, back straight, palms open on her thighs.

Silence followed Tass, an entranced tension that colored the air and constricted the walls. I blinked, and the spell was broken. "Mira," I said, clapping my hands together so loud Mira flinched. "Time for bed."

Mira slid off the couch and made a beeline for the stairs with no foot-stomping or eye-rolling that such a command usually caused. I should have been relieved, but I saw fear in the stiffness in Mira's shoulders. A fear of Tass. Mira wasn't alone.

Once more I wondered if I was doing the right thing by taking on this job. By bringing Tass into our fold.

"Come on," Shasheba said through white lips, sliding her hand in mine. I gaped when she pulled me up the stairs and down the low-lit hall. She stopped at the door to her own lavishly appointed bedroom. An involuntary shiver of suspicion crawled down my spine.

"But Mira," I began, cursing myself internally. "I should make sure she's settled."

Shasheba's brows rose, eyes filled with silent laughter. "Surely she knows the way by now. Or are you saying she still needs a bed-time story?"

I grimaced at the thought. Mira would bite me if I tried putting her to bed. "No. You're right."

"I know," was the smug reply. She glided into her bedroom, eyes commanding me to heel, only to stop me with an open palm to my chest before I took two steps through the door. "Leave your boots there." Her lips turned down in a delicate moue. "And your clothes."

My mind hummed in warning that I didn't—couldn't—heed. I simply did as I was told, crouching with a groan to work the knots out of my bootstraps before kicking them off. Shasheba had gone to the window, her footsteps muffled by a carpet covering the intricate blue and white floor tile. She leaned over a hammered-copper tub and twisted the taps until water streamed out in a steaming gush.

"What are you doing, Shash?"

"Drawing a bath," she said, her voice noticeably frosty. "I told you, you stink."

"All right." I shook my head, swallowing the rest of my words before they could leave my lips. There had been whole years when I would have done anything Shasheba said only to spend more time in her glowing presence. But that was before. When I was still the future governor of Cothis and she was my soon-to-be bride. That life was gone. It died when I left Cothis in shame and blood, releasing her from our engagement in a vain attempt to save her reputation.

It hadn't worked. Shasheba hadn't moved on and married some other man. She'd devoted herself to Nananthe, chosen a different path. But Shasheba hadn't forgiven me. I knew it from the moment I knocked on the Low Temple's door and found her looking up at me with ill-concealed contempt.

In the week I'd been here, she hadn't touched me, not even to shake my hand. Hadn't even allowed herself to be caught alone with me long enough for me to apologize for leaving. Now there I was, in her bedroom. And she was drawing me a bath. And sure, listening to that niggling sense of suspicion would have been the smart move, but all I could think about was that this was it. A chance—my one chance to make things right.

"Shash, I want to—"

She tutted, impatience flashing across her perfect face. "Apologize. Yes, you've mentioned a time or fifty. You really want to talk right now? Or are you going to *take off* your clothes?" Perched on the edge of the tub, she issued the challenge with glittering eyes and a poise I doubted the empress could match.

She wanted this to be a battle of wills?

Fine, I thought, knowing Shasheba wouldn't tell me what was on her mind until she was good and ready. After that. I shrugged and shucked off my clothes. Forcing my shoulders back, I resisted the urge to cover my vital bits as Shasheba surveyed me. In a blink of an eye, her expression flickered from cold to smoldering. She straightened, motioning me to the tub with an open hand. I crossed the room on slightly unsteady legs and hopped into the scalding water. Stretching forward, I shut off the taps before I sloshed any water on her beautiful Arishan carpets—an unforgivable offense, I was sure.

I leaned back in the tub hoping the hot water would work some of the kinks out of my back. Shasheba retreated through the steam and sat with her back to me at her vanity. I couldn't quite make out her face in the mirror, but her shoulders were high and tense as she took off her heavy gold earrings and her many glittering bangles.

There was something comfortable about watching her wipe off her makeup and rub cream into her perfect skin. Painful too. A kind of homesickness, like looking into a life I should have lived.

The thought—*all thought*—fled when she stood and unwrapped her red-and-orange-striped dress, until all she wore was a thin shift of the palest pink I'd ever seen. The whole world around me went still.

A world that no longer included me—apparently, I thought, grimacing as a certain part of me very much stirred.

The little voice in my head warning me to be on my guard faded. In the golden light of the gaslit lamps, with her honey-colored hair dancing along the small of her back, I was sure she was the most beautiful woman I'd ever seen. Unfortunately, my body was sure of it too.

Heat flooded my abdomen and pooled there in a persistent strain.

I considered trying to cover myself for half a second, but Shasheba knew the effect she had on me. She'd only laugh if I tried to hide my reaction, and I didn't think I could take her mocking. Not now.

After a moment's indecision, Shasheba approached the brass stand beside the tub. She pumped what smelled like soap into her hand from one of the delicate glass jars and moved to the floor behind me. Her long fingers dug into my shoulders, kneading away the stress. I closed my eyes in spite of myself, then forced my shoulders to relax. I suspected Shasheba was getting close to speaking. She had always hated exposing her vulnerability. And almost always hid her face when she felt uncomfortable. Probably why I still never trusted a hug.

"Bal," she said slower than a charmer soothing a snake. "What have you brought into my house?"

I opened my eyes. "You mean Tass?"

She tutted. "Yes, I mean Tass. What is she?"

Shasheba was digging into one of my deeper knots, so I resisted the urge to shrug. "She's the Queen of Days, whatever that means. You've heard the rumors."

"Yes. And what I've heard worries me."

My lips twitched. The Shasheba I'd known hadn't been the religious type. Even though she was the high priestess here, I couldn't quite swallow the idea of her truly believing in the gods. "You aren't telling me you actually think she's a demon?"

Shasheba's silence turned brittle, and the urge to break it, to hear her laugh, was overwhelming.

"You're not jealous, are you?"

Shasheba shoved my shoulders down so hard my ass squealed against the bottom of the tub as I slipped under the water. I heaved up, ignoring the wave that crashed over the lip of the tub and pushed the hair out of my eyes. "Shasheba, I was joking."

She glared daggers into my face, arms coiled over her chest. "It's not funny."

I snorted and flicked water in her face. Predictably, Shasheba lashed out, aiming a slap at my left cheek. *Enough.* I plucked her hand out of the air and yanked her into the tub. Shasheba yelped as soapy water soaked her fine silk shift. She growled, her knees knocking into the metal sides as she straddled me. Admittedly, this caused a different kind of difficulty, but at least she had no choice but to look me in the face.

"What is wrong with you?" she snarled.

"Oh, I imagine you're about to tell me."

"This isn't a joke, Bal. You're playing with forces you don't understand."

I looked her up and down, or I tried to, but my eyes snagged on the peaks of her breasts, fully visible and heaving through her sodden shift. "I know."

"Not *me,*" she said, jerking my chin up to her face. "Tass. She's not . . ."

"Normal?"

"Of this world."

That caught my attention. I looked at Shasheba, really looked at her, at the tightness in her eyes and the pallor of her normally tan skin. "What do you mean?"

She shook her head, looking away for a second. "If you'd asked me yesterday if I thought the Queen of Days was a demon, I'd have laughed at you and said she was just another too-clever criminal. But now that I've seen her? Spoken with her? Been *close* to her?" A frown pulled down the corners of her mouth. "I learned things at the High Temple, things about the creatures of the Nethersphere."

I scoffed. "Things about creepy, masked women?"

"Laugh all you like; it proves you've always been a fool."

"Shasheba—"

"No, Bal. Go ahead and think me a superstitious idiot. But ask yourself why your patron insisted she join your crew. *Think.* You're about to steal the idol of Karanis. Not only that, but you're going to do it on the very day we invite the god into the city, offering the idol as host to his spirit. Do you really think it's coincidence that your patron wants a demon with you?"

I frowned, trying to parse her words but coming up short. "So you think Tass is supposed to . . . what?"

"I think she's supposed to help you all escape before the god kills you in front of the whole city."

In anyone else, such a display of naked fear would have made me pause. But seeing it in Shasheba's face made my heart flip in perverse pleasure. "You're worried about me."

Her eyes bulged in total exasperation. "Yes, I'm worried. I may be angry at you for leaving—an anger I fully intend to cling to for the rest of my life—but I don't want to see you killed."

"You say the sweetest things."

"Shut up, I'm serious."

I clasped her shoulders, made her look at me. "I know you are, Shasheba. I know. But this job . . ."

"I know, this job could bring back your lost fortune. Give Miraveena the life she deserves. You've told me already." Shasheba's voice was filled with so much bitterness it could've muddied the water between us.

"Not just Mira," I murmured, though it was suddenly hard to breathe. "You too."

She looked at me, her expression suspicious, haunted even. I forced myself to continue, braced myself. "I mean it, Shasheba. I was wrong to leave you here when I—"

"Fled."

I winced but accepted the word for what it was. "Yes. I thought I was saving you, but I was wrong. I understand that now, and I'm sorry for it. But I can't take it back. I can't undo the past. The future, though? Come with me, Shasheba. After the job is done, come with me. We can see the world, together, just like we always talked about." For a moment something hard flashed across her face. Greedy.

But then I blinked, and it was gone.

She was frowning now, her eyes were big and sparkling. Shy. "What? Fly around on that stupid airship with you?"

"Yeah."

"You've said this all before, Bal," she said, her voice soft, catching her lower lip with her teeth. Nananthe save me, this woman drove me mad. "How do I know I can trust you?"

My mouth went dry as the past came crashing down on my shoulders. "You don't. No one *knows* anything, Shash. But I'm saying it and I mean it. You gotta take the leap. Just take it with me."

She was quiet for a long time, like she was calculating my words—calculating my worth. All Father save me, how I wanted to be found deserving. The corners of her lips rose, and when her answer came, it wasn't with words. It came with the shining in her eyes, and the velvet press of her lips on mine.

3

BALTHAZAR

I woke to the feeling of fingers drawing circles in my hair and smiled. The room was bathed in soft red light as the morning sun filtered in through Shasheba's gauzy curtains. Her high windows revealed a day that dawned cloudy and gray. The sort of day that demanded stillness. I sent my thanks to the heavens, planning on staying in this very bed for as long as its owner allowed.

"Good morning," Shasheba purred from behind me.

"Morning," I said through a jaw-cracking yawn. Her hand paused its drawings on my scalp. "No, don't stop. That feels good."

"Greedy boy," she teased, but I could hear a smile in her voice.

We lay still and silent in the comfort of her room for a few perfect moments. I closed my eyes, trying to shut out the sense of duty sniffing at the door. I knew I should go out. Talk to Zee and Edik, introduce them to Tass, and go over the plan again. Should. But somehow none of it seemed all that important right now.

"Bal," Shasheba said, her fingers lingering at the base of my skull. "When did you get this tattoo?"

"Which one?"

"This one," she said, scraping one long nail down the nape of my neck.

My eyes peeled open as cold air slithered beneath the sheets. Adrenaline poured into my limbs, but dread held me fast. "What does it look like?"

"It's your tattoo."

"Indulge me."

Shasheba tutted, oblivious to the way my tightening throat turned the words into a strangled plea. "It's a sigil of some kind. I can't read it though. It looks like it's written in ancient Sorien."

Ancient Sorien. The words rattled around in my skull, shaking loose a memory. A memory of me striking a deal with Tass; of a mosquito biting the back of my neck as we shook hands.

Shit.

I threw the covers off and lunged for my trousers, yanking them on.

"What are you doing?" Shasheba demanded.

I didn't reply. Couldn't. My mind was too frenzied to form a response. Shasheba was as well educated as I was, as well educated as any noble in the kingdom. But not even the nobility thought it worthwhile to teach their children a language that had died out over two millennia ago. The only people who could read it were scholars, and . . . "Zeelaya."

"What?"

"I have to find Zee. Now. She can read Sorien."

Shasheba rose, every hint of softness leaving her frame. "Why is your tattoo suddenly so important?"

"Because I never *got* a tattoo."

Shasheba crossed her arms, pulling her robe closed as confusion and suspicion chased through her eyes. Damn it, I was ruining things between us. Again.

I seized her hand, willing her to listen to me even as my heart screamed to find the others. "I don't have a tattoo on my neck, Shash. Or I didn't until I met Tass last night. When . . . we struck a deal."

Blood rushed out of Shasheba's face, leaving her skin ashen. "Bal . . . What did you give her?"

Nothing. Just a stupid promise that couldn't mean anything. Except . . .

My hand went to my neck. I opened my mouth but couldn't get any of the words out. Time. I'd given her time. Mine and Kai's and . . .

I dropped Shasheba's arms and sprinted out the door.

"Mira!" My bellow echoed off the temple's wooden halls, shaking the dust off the doorframes. Panic tunneled my vision as I sprinted up the stairs to the attic. Tass said she wouldn't take any time from Mira, but . . .

But how could she take time from anyone?

I took the attic stairs three at a time and shouldered through the door. I registered Zee and Edik's surprised faces before my gaze raked across the dim and cluttered room to Mira. She was still sprawled and drooling on her cot in the corner. I sprinted, banging my knees as I dropped to the floor beside her. She yelped when I flipped her over and immediately bucked. I managed to hold her squirming body with one hand, pulling up her corkscrew curls with the other. Clear.

"All Father, thank you." I sagged to the floor, Mira's spitting anger filled my ears, but I'd never been so happy to hear it.

"Bal, what the hell is going on with you?"

I stood, turning toward Zee's annoyed voice. She and Edik were on the other end of the rectangular room, their breakfasts forgotten on the warped table Zee had commandeered to lay out our plans. Her eyes were narrowed over her hawkish nose. Wearing one of Edik's shirts, her dark hair still mussed from sleep, Zee glared impatiently from me to Shasheba, who had ghosted into the room behind me. She stood only a few feet away looking flushed and oddly glassy-eyed.

Kai took up the doorway, watching me with bug-eyed amazement. He held his shirt in one hand, his trousers still undone like he'd dressed at top speed and ran when he heard me shout. His latest pair of lovers were peeking over his shoulder, eyes bright with curiosity. A curiosity that withered and died when they spotted Shasheba and received a look so dark it made the young woman bow and retreat.

The man flat-out ran.

Kai watched them go with a growl of annoyance. "What in Ruekigal's four tits is the matter with you?"

Shasheba hissed. "Do not speak that name in this house. Not now."

Kai rolled his eyes at Shasheba's outrage. He'd never paid attention to religion unless it resulted in a good swear. I wasn't even sure he knew why Shasheba didn't want the death goddess's name spoken in Nananthe's temple.

"What do you mean, 'not now'?" Zee asked. As usual, she'd cut to the important part with frightening accuracy.

I walked toward my cousin, ignoring the kick Mira aimed at my shins, and braced my hands on the edge of the worktable, readying for a fight.

"When I woke up this morning, Shasheba saw a tattoo on the back of my neck. I need you to read it."

Zee's gaze narrowed. "Bal, you did not give me a heart attack over some drunken nonsense you and Kai got yourselves into."

"Zee, please," I cut in before she could work herself up to a real rant. "It's in ancient Sorien. You're the only one I know who can read it." Well, that probably wasn't true. Somehow I was positive that Tass was fluent in the dead tongue. Not that there was a chance in hell of me asking her.

Zee straightened when she heard Sorien and bustled over without further comment. Spinning me around, she brushed the hair off my neck. "Interesting," she murmured, her annoyance completely forgotten in the wake of the tattoo's puzzle. Zee leaned past me, grabbing a slip of parchment and a charcoal stick. She scribbled something down and shoved the drawing my way.

Shasheba had said it was a sigil, and I was inclined to agree. It was rectangular, with two rows of cramped text drawn in sharp gash-like lines. "It's definitely ancient Sorien," Zee said, as the others crowded around the table to get a look.

"Why is that important?" Kai asked, pulling his shirt over his head.

"Knowing you two idiots, it probably isn't. It's unusual though," Zee allowed as she gathered her hair into a knot on the crown of her head and jabbed the charcoal stick through it to hold it in place—a sure sign she'd sensed a problem to solve. "The Soriens were the first civilization to use any kind of written language and it started with these tag-like markings."

"Tags?" I asked.

"Yes, at least that's what the scholars on Kisan assume they are," Zee replied. Kisan was home to the only university in Ashaar. If anyone knew the mystery of the marks, it would be them. "They're often found at archeological sites affixed to goods. They seem to denote place names or ownerships, or even to mark a debt."

My heart fell. "What does this one say?"

Zee shrugged. "It will take me a while to decipher this part," she said, gesturing to the top line of text. "I think it's a name, but this bottom part is a number. Sixty."

I closed my eyes against the word but found no comfort in the darkness there.

"Sixty what, Bal?" Shasheba's voice was whip sharp. Her nails dug into my arm hard enough to draw blood. "What did you give her?" she asked as I opened my eyes, her face only inches from mine.

"Time."

Shasheba's hand dropped. She stepped back.

"Time?" Kai repeated, obviously confused.

Mira was looking at me like I'd lost it. At the moment I was inclined to agree. "What's that supposed to mean?"

"No," Zee said, cutting me off before I could open my mouth. "We're missing something. Start at the beginning."

I raked a hand through my hair, then shook my head at the stupidity of the gesture. Not like it would help me organize my thoughts. "Yesterday, Kai and I arranged to get arrested so we could make contact with the fixer—"

"Yes, the 'Queen of Days,' I know," Zee said, making impatient air quotes with her fingers around Tass's title. "Did you make contact?"

"I did more than that. I secured her services. Thing is, she didn't want money in payment for her help." I hesitated, saw Zee shoot Edik a look.

Edik gave his wife a quelling smile. The ice to Zee's fire, Edik was usually the only voice of reason among us, like age had given him wisdom. My eyes narrowed in on his hair, black and wiry and flecked with gray at both temples. *Grayer than yesterday?* I wondered, feeling slightly sick.

"What did she want, Bal?" Edik asked.

"Time," Shasheba whispered.

I nodded. "Thirty days. She wanted thirty days of our lives."

Kai scoffed. "What does that even mean?"

"It means we're all going to die thirty days sooner than we're supposed to."

The silence that met my words was like a great intake of breath, like the dead space between two heartbeats.

Kai laughed. The great booming sound was filled with too much bravado to break the mood. "Great Below, she's even nuttier than I thought. How does she expect to collect something like that? It's impossible."

"That was my thinking too," I said, well aware of the defensive note in my voice.

"So you *agreed*? For all of us? Without even asking?" Zee's questions peppered my face like the first stones of an avalanche.

"Yes."

She paused a moment, letting it sink in. And letting me feel how annoyed she was that I'd made yet another choice on her behalf. "And then your mysterious tattoo appeared?"

I forced myself to meet Zee's stare and nodded. Her lips disappeared into a thin line. She spun to Edik, putting her hands on his shoulders, and forcing him to crouch. Her eyes narrowed on the nape of his dark neck.

Zee swore. "There is a sigil," she said in a brittle voice. "Same as yours, but the number is thirty."

Zee released her husband, her face a distinct shade of green. Her hands dropped to her belly like she was going to be sick.

Edik's face fell, one hand twitching toward the medal of Janus hanging from his neck. He brushed the hair away from Zee's neck instead, dread lining his every move. "You have one too, love," Edik said, and drew Zee under one of his massive arms. His eyes rose to mine. Demanding answers.

I winced at what I saw in Edik's face. He was always our ballast, the one calm point in our crew's mess of difficult personalities. He wasn't calm now. No one was. Kai rubbed the back of his neck, his lips moving in a wordless prayer. Shasheba hugged herself, looking at the table like she was at a complete loss for words.

Mira bit her cheek; I could practically hear the gears of her mind spinning. "Theirs say thirty," she said, looking up at me. "Why does yours say sixty?"

Shasheba inhaled sharply. "You took on Miraveena's debt, didn't you?"

Mira's eyes went wide, for once she was too preoccupied to snap at Shasheba and insist on being called Mira. Her lower lip trembled as she watched me, her silence a demand.

"Yeah. I did."

"But not for the rest of us? You just let that—that *thing* take part of our lives without bothering to ask us first?"

Shasheba's face was flushed with a rage my brain was too slow to understand. Then I realized. She thought Tass had taken her days too. "Relax, Shasheba. You aren't affected by this."

Like a candle being snuffed out, her eyes went flat. "Why not?"

In the time it took me to scrabble for a response, another voice provided the answer.

"Because you are not part of the crew."

Shasheba's eyes flashed, and she spun toward the door. Tass stood on the threshold, one shoulder leaning against the frame, arms crossed. She'd removed her hooded jacket, but her hair was still covered by a black veil worked with silver chains and several dozen tiny silver bells. There was a slightly amused air to the way she lounged against the wall and listened to the crew's outrage. I couldn't help but be grudgingly impressed by her stealth. Despite all those little bells and both Zee and Edik facing the door, she'd managed to sneak in unnoticed.

"Who said I'm not part of the crew?" Shasheba demanded, nostrils flaring.

Tass didn't bother to answer. Then again, she didn't really need to. Shasheba rounded on me.

"Am I not putting myself—and my people—at risk for your fool of a mission?"

"And snaking a huge chunk of Bal's cut out of the deal," Kai drawled.

"*Kai.*"

"What?" he said, as I shot him a repressive look. "Not like she's doing it out of the goodness of her heart."

"She's getting us in," I said quickly, feeling the way Shasheba's anger rose off her in waves but not knowing how to defuse it.

Unlike us, Shasheba and the men and women of the Low Temple had been invited to the ceremony. Though the idol was being dedicated to Karanis, it was the acolytes of Nananthe who would perform the consecration. The ceremony was meant to usher Karanis into our world, after all. And the acolytes of Nananthe were midwives before anything else. It's what made her the perfect plant in Governor Paasch's operation.

Kai knew it. The damn fool just didn't like Shasheba.

"Look, Shash," I began, trying for a smile, "you're not upset that I didn't give away part of your life."

"No, Balthazar," she said, livid splotches breaking out on her neck. "I am not *upset* about that." She cast a disdain-filled glare about the cramped room. "You will excuse me, I have responsibilities to attend to."

She turned on her heel and marched toward the door. To her credit, she only faltered slightly when she passed an unmoving Tass, who turned her head to observe Shasheba storm down the hall. Watching in profile, I could swear that Tass's black painted lips deepened into a smile.

The impression broke when she turned back to me. "Are your mornings always so eventful?"

I opened my mouth to say no, but truthfully . . . "More often than not."

She huffed a slight chuckle and pushed off the wall, swinging the door shut behind her with one hand. She took two steps toward the table. Stopped. Her head tilted to one side, attention entirely on Edik.

One of his hands had dropped below the edge of the table. I could just see the handle of an army-issue revolver grasped in his meaty fist. Aimed at Tass. Edik's face gave nothing away—it never did, but he'd shouldered Zee slightly behind him. And Zee had allowed it. I wasn't sure what was more telling.

"Edik." I waited for him to look at me. At first he refused to take his eyes off Tass, but then I said his name again and he finally glanced my way. I shook my head. He didn't relax, and I knew why.

There was something undeniably *other* about Tass that put people

THE QUEEN OF DAYS   47

immediately on edge. It wasn't just the pistols strapped to her thighs, or the swords on her back. It was the way she moved. Despite the weapons and the dozen or so straps and buckles that seemed to hold her together, she walked with a kind of fluid grace that hovered on the edge of violence.

Shash had seen it right away. Mira, too. And now Edik.

Was I so blinded by this job that I had failed to recognize the wolf in our midst?

I grit my teeth, feeling that threat begin to boil over. Though Edik was the one holding the gun, I was afraid *for* him. I planted myself between Tass and the barrel.

"Edik, Zee, this is Tass. She has agreed to help us." I placed a not-so-subtle emphasis on the last two words, praying it would get Edik to put the fucking gun down.

"Are you magic?" Mira leaned against the table beside Kai. She looked up at Tass, oblivious to the tension that hummed between the adults.

Tass's face tilted to Mira, clearly considering the question. "Define 'magic.'"

Mira crossed her arms, brow furrowed in thought. "I dunno. Can you do things I can't?"

"Yes."

The hint of laughter in Tass's voice made Mira scowl. "All right, but that's not really an answer. You took *time*. How is that not magic?" Mira asked.

Tass's head cocked to the left. "I do not understand the question. The time was offered to me. I received it."

"But that doesn't make sense," Mira argued. "Time isn't a coin. I can't pull it out of my pocket and chuck it at you."

I glanced around the room and found that, by some miracle, Mira's curiosity had made the rest of the crew—not relax, but pause.

Zee had returned to the table, watching the discussion with rapt interest. And though Edik still clutched the revolver, he no longer had it aimed at Tass. Kai was still frowning, but he'd leaned his elbow against the table, letting it take most of his weight.

"Ah. I believe I understand the source of your confusion," Tass said. "You see time as an abstract, something vague and undefined. It is not. It is something you come into the world owning and leave the world having spent your share. You think I am magical because I was able to receive some of your family's time. This is an imprecise conclusion. Time may not be tangible in the way your coin is, but it is still a commodity."

Mira looked up at me, shaking her head in mute confusion. I shrugged.

"Just because a thing is intangible, does not mean it cannot be given," Tass continued, but when Mira still looked lost, paused, considering. "How do you give a person your trust? How do you give someone love?"

The questions hung in the air, but Mira had no answers. Neither did anyone else apparently, though perhaps we were the wrong group to ask about such fragile things as trust and love.

"So you can't do magic?"

"No, of course I can," was Tass's tart reply. She pivoted away from the exasperation on Mira's face. "Perhaps now would be a good time to tell me your plan?"

"Yeah, all right."

"No." Edik's voice cracked across the room, thunder-sharp.

"Edik—"

"No, Bal. *Now* is the time for you to explain why the fuck you agreed to this without consulting us first."

4

SEPTINIRI TASSIEL JANAE

Edik's anger was layered. It had a texture that Tassiel recognized. How many times had she felt the same indignance when her siblings made decisions on her behalf? But her sympathy in the matter would help no one.

Instead she watched as Bal fidgeted, looking every bit his young age beneath the glaring anger of Edik and Zeelaya. Their silence demanded answers. But Tassiel knew that nothing Bal said would assuage them. The simple fact was that he had not believed her when she told him she was taking his time—*their time*—in payment. Yes, he had taken on Miraveena's debt, but Tassiel felt that was more out of habit. The knee-jerk response of an older brother protecting his little sister.

Not something her siblings would have done for her, she thought, before discarding the sentiment as useless.

To people like Bal, magic was nothing more than an artifact of a bygone era. A time when people needed faith and religion to explain the world. A time when gods lived among men.

When the Ankaari ruled these lands with an iron fist.

Before Tassiel's time, yes, but her father had always spoken of those distant days with relish.

And longing.

It was the longing that had always worried her.

Tassiel shook her head and slid from the room on silent feet, giving the humans behind her the semblance of privacy.

But only the semblance. They would be more open with each other without her there, and she could hear them well enough from the hall anyway.

She looked over the balcony rail, surveying the temple below. The acolytes were already busy with their day, ushering worshippers to exam rooms or bedrooms as the ailment required. One pinched-faced woman was even walking slow laps around the room, praying that gravity would help bring forth the child curled in her belly.

It was an odd sort of place, this temple to Nananthe, but Tassiel could not fault the intention. The longer she remained here, the easier it was to see that this temple was created to care for the body with empathy and compassion. Nananthe would have approved.

"I remember you."

Tassiel managed not to flinch at the words—the last three words she expected to hear.

She turned in the echoing *snick* of the closing door and looked down at Miraveena Vadalen.

The girl moved to Tassiel's side, bracing her arms on the balcony railing. She surveyed Tassiel, her young face made younger by the memory clouding her eyes.

"I am surprised you are out here and not speaking with your family."

"Not like they listen to me anyway." Mira shrugged, the gesture betraying so much bitterness, Tassiel laughed.

"*What?*" the girl spat the word; pride bruised for the fear that Tassiel was laughing at her.

"I apologize. I did not mean to offend. I simply know what it is like to have older siblings."

The girl's eyes narrowed. "You do?"

Tassiel inclined her head. "I am the youngest of seven, in fact."

"Yeesh. That sucks."

Did it? Tassiel could no longer remember.

"Did they ever listen to you?"

"No, but I never expected them to. Respect comes from power, and I was the youngest—and the least—of them by many decades."

"Decades?" Mira frowned like she was trying to tally the math in her head. "How does that work?"

"My people are rather . . . longer lived than yours," Tassiel replied, dancing around words like "mortal" and "immortal" so as to not scare the girl.

Though why Tassiel cared to spare the child, she was not entirely certain.

"We were only half-siblings, after all," she said instead, as if that might explain things.

Mira crossed her arms. "Why does that matter? Kai's my half-brother and I love him as much as I do Bal." Her ears went pink at the word "love," as though its utterance embarrassed her.

"Love is not spoken of among my kind." Tassiel started the sentence smiling, but she could not hide from the sadness at the edges of her voice. Or the longing.

Which worried her, too.

Mira, thankfully, was clearly too preoccupied to notice. "Your kind? What does that mean? Where are you from?"

For a wild moment, Tassiel almost told her the truth. Almost. Thinking of her siblings had cracked something open within her, a homesickness that many long years of isolation had scabbed over.

But no. Some things were too painful. Even for her.

"Elsewhere."

Mira glowered at the nonanswer. "But you were here. Had been here before, I mean. That—that day, you were here."

Tassiel inclined her head. "I was. Although I am surprised you remember it."

Mira could not have been more than six the day the city went mad. Driven by despair and hopelessness, bloodlust had taken root where reason could not reach. A mob rose, spurred on by Paasch. And the old governor's family—Bal and Mira's family—were dragged out of their beds. Murdered in the name of Karanis to slake the sea god's wrath. As if her uncle had ever spared two thoughts to the lives of men.

"I don't," Mira replied at long last, her voice so, so small. "Not much anyway. But I remember running. And I remember you."

The blood of Mira's parents was still hot on the ground when a handful of servants had grabbed the children in an attempt to smuggle them to safety. Bal, Kai, and Zeelaya had gotten out easily, but Mira's rescuer fell, and in falling called down the wrath of the watching crowd. If Tassiel had not been there, Mira would be dead.

But she had been there, watching the spectacle unfold with complete uncomprehending disbelief. Humanity often confused her, but the madness that would cause grown men to attack a child? It was a level of barbarity that only the meanest creatures of the Great Below could match.

So she acted. She grabbed the child and sacrificed precious drops of magic to turn them both invisible, then delivered her to the safety of her remaining family.

"Why did you do it?" Mira asked. "Save me?"

The answer was longer and more complicated than Tassiel could hope to articulate. Reasons of abandonment and loss, yes, but also a yearning.

To belong.

"You needed help," Tassiel replied instead. "And so I came."

"You wore a mask then too. Why?"

Tassiel considered the question for a long moment. Decided on the truth. "The mask is ensorcelled to ensure that I remain unnoticed to people like me."

"And?" Mira pressed, sensing words unspoken.

"And my face is . . . different."

A pregnant pause stretched down the length of the hall.

"You're not human, are you?"

"No."

"Does Bal know?"

Tassiel felt one of her brows rise. "Would he believe it, if I told him?"

Mira shook her head. "No." Her shoulders seemed to sag under the weight of the conversation. She glared at the temple below, at the men and women preparing for the day. At Shasheba ordering them about from a chaise that her presence made a throne.

"And you're here now, too," Mira began, still glaring at Shasheba. "How? Why?"

Tassiel opened her hands in a half-hearted shrug. "I often find my clients in the cells below the Code Halls. The men and women there are usually desperate enough to work with me. To make the sacrifice I require."

Tassiel had spoken the truth, but Mira was shaking her head. "Doesn't explain why you picked us."

She was surprisingly astute for a girl of twelve. "I was told your brother would be there and that my presence was requested."

"By whom?"

"I do not know—your patron, I presume," she replied honestly. The request had come to her on a warm breeze, slipping through the wards about her residence in the talons of a gray falcon. It felt ancient. Like magic.

Like home.

"Why are Edik and Zeelaya so angry?" Tassiel asked before the girl could press her further. Before Mira could ask if it was the mere oddity of the request that had drawn Tassiel in or if it was the Vadalen children themselves who had piqued her interest.

It was not a question she was prepared to answer. Not yet. Perhaps not ever.

"Bal's never taken a job without talking to us first," Mira said slowly, as if afraid of exposing her brother. "We always vote on them as a family."

"Democracy," she drawled. "How novel. Why did he deviate from the norm?"

"The payoff," Mira replied, as if it should be obvious. "That much money—we wouldn't have to steal anymore. We could leave Ashaar. Go somewhere new. Somewhere no one has ever heard of us."

Tassiel just nodded, knowing too well how it felt to be crushed by the weight of a family legacy. "How is it that your family came to thieving? Did none of your relatives or friends step in to shelter you after your parents' fall?"

"No," Mira said, her voice too hard.

"Why?"

"Cowardice," Bal replied.

Tassiel turned to the now open door. Marked Edik and Zeelaya whispering to each other on the far side of the room. Marked Kai rubbing exhaustion from his eyes.

"Cowardice?"

"Yeah," Bal said, dragging Mira to his side. "They fed us to the wolves so they wouldn't be eaten too."

"I see," Tassiel said, something in her bridling against the fear in Bal's eyes—the suspicion at seeing her alone with Mira.

"You still wanna hear the plan?"

She nodded, following Bal back into the room. A room that ran hot with the tang of anger and the mounting pressure of time running short.

He cracked his neck, shuffling through the scraps of paper on the table, upsetting one of Zeelaya's mechanicals as he went. The young woman hissed at his carelessness, swooping away from her husband to save her contraption from harm.

Ignoring her, Bal flattened a map of Cothis in front of Tassiel, tacking the curled edges down with a few used cups and plates. "The new temple is here," he said, gesturing to the center of the island where the outdated map showed the outline of the former temple. "The new one is much larger than any of the previous temples, so nearly all of this park space is gone. Its base almost butts up to the road."

Tassiel nodded. None of this information was new to her, but she let him continue. She would learn as much about this crew of thieves by what they said, as what they omitted.

"The fact that it's so close to the road actually works in our favor," Bal continued when she didn't speak. "The old building was only used for worship and as a meeting space for the governor and his aides. The new building will house the governor's family, as well as the families of his principal advisers."

"Why is this good news?" Tassiel asked. "Will the presence of all these extra people in the temple not make things more difficult?"

"The place will be packed regardless," Bal replied. "But with so many toffs now living in the temple, many of the manors surrounding it will be empty. Only a skeleton crew of guards and servants will be there to protect and maintain the properties. This house here," he said, gesturing to the largest house on the eastern side of the temple, "will be our exit point."

Tassiel stared doubtfully at his finger. "This is part of your vengeance, then? Escaping through the governor's manse? The home that used to be yours."

"His former home," he replied. "Paasch moved into his new apartment within the temple last week. His mansion will be nearly vacant the night of the ceremony."

Tassiel simply waited, unconvinced.

"Look, the choice in exit point isn't just a way to stick it to Paasch.

Mira, Zee, Kai, and I all grew up in that house. We know it inside and out. Which means if we get separated, or have to scatter, we'll have a better shot at getting everyone out in one piece."

It made sense in a way, she thought, even if his need for revenge was clear as glass. "Very well. Please continue."

Bal pulled out an undoubtedly stolen set of temple schematics and spent the next hour and a half taking Tassiel through the plan. She peppered him with questions from start to finish, probing the plan for every weakness she could think of, testing every decision. Every step had to be sound, valid if they were to make it out both whole and alive.

Bal looked ragged by the end of it, but with Zeelaya's help, they explained away all of Tassiel's concerns. Amazingly.

"All right," Tassiel said. "You've gotten to the top of the temple, created your diversion, and stolen the idol." She looked between Zeelaya and Bal. "Now how do you get it out?"

Kai flashed a wolfish grin. "That, sweetheart, is where you come in."

"Oh?"

Bal smiled as she turned to him. "Kai and Edik will smuggle you onto the temple's grounds the morning of the ceremony. While the rest of us are inside the temple, you will be scaling the side."

Kai sneered when Tassiel did not reply. "What? It's not too much of a challenge for you, is it, demon queen?"

She flicked Kai's words away with an impatient gesture. "No. It can be done, but to what purpose? You said your exit point was in your childhood home, across the street from the temple. I assumed there were tunnels connecting the two."

"No." Bal braced his hands on the table. "Realistically, we'll have less than a minute from the time we grab the idol until someone notices it's gone. Speed is going to be more important than stealth when it comes to our getaway.

"We'll need you stationed here," he continued, pointing toward a set of windows on the eastern side of the consecration room. He nodded to Zeelaya and she bent, rummaging beneath the table for a battered-looking brown case that she set down carefully. "Once you get to the top, you'll shoot a zip line into the governor's manor."

"How?"

"With this." Zeelaya spun the dial on the lock and the case opened with a snap. She smiled lovingly down at the crossbow-size mechanism. "It's a grappling gun. Of my own design," she added with a smug shrug, sliding the case across the table.

Tassiel picked up the gun, hefting it in both hands as she tested its weight. It was a thing of beauty, she thought, inspecting the solid metal arrow loaded in the chamber. It had a length of wire, sinuous as a sleeping snake, coiled in the case.

"Once you get to the top, you'll shoot this into the wall of the governor's mansion," Zeelaya continued. "This catch here will keep the wire from getting away from you. There is a balcony on the top floor, aim for that. It's only two stories lower than the temple, so the fall won't be too hard."

"I shall remind you of that when you break your shins on impact," Tassiel replied with a slight laugh.

"You'll need to shoot a second arrow into the temple and attach the wire to it," Bal said, ignoring her. "Take as long as you need to scale the building, but you must be in position before we make the grab. As soon as we have it, we'll slide down the line and get away."

"All of you?" she asked, her face turning fractionally toward Mira.

"No. Mira, Zee, and I are going in with covers. We'll be going out the same way we entered so we don't come under suspicion. Well. Too much suspicion," he allowed with a cutting smile. "Kai and Edik will be going with you."

"And Shasheba?"

"Shasheba's the only one who got an actual invite. She'll be fine. And if things go sideways, she's going to stay put and pretend she's nothing more than another guest."

Tassiel nodded, privately doubting Bal's ability to leave Shasheba behind should everything fall apart. Especially if Mira was staying behind as well. Which she would have to do, since Mira would be hiding in plain sight, dressed as a novitiate—an acolyte-in-training—whose job was to shadow Shasheba and fetch anything that might be needed. And while she would certainly have her share of duties there, her main reason for going in with Shasheba was to open the windows so Tassiel, Edik, and Kai could make a clear escape.

After the heist, Bal would certainly be detained for questioning—a fact he clearly knew. And relished. Zeelaya too, given their history with Governor Paasch. But Mira would leave the temple with Shasheba and the rest of the acolytes. Neither Mira nor Shasheba had the most dangerous job—that would be left to Tassiel herself, of course—but they would both be standing just to the right of the mayhem.

Tassiel was silent for a moment, her face angled toward the map, judging the distance between the temple and the governor's manor. "This seems like an unnecessarily dangerous escape considering you own an airship. Why not simply fly it to the temple's peak and escape that way?"

Bal opened his mouth, but his reply seemed to get stuck in the back of his throat. She felt his mind racing backward, tripping through each word he had spoken to her. "How do you know I have an airship?" he asked, arms crossing.

She resisted the urge to sigh. How could she not know? "You have the smell of Zefira all over you."

"How can anyone smell like the goddess of wind?" Mira asked.

"How can anyone *know* what the wind goddess smells like? No—" Bal closed his eyes for a moment, as if a headache had begun to twinge beneath his skull. "Forget I asked."

"Don't let anything she says surprise you," Kai said, drawing away from Tassiel with obvious distrust. "She's no better than the

Bodysnatcher, is she? Rutting demon can probably read our minds just like him."

Enough. Tassiel felt like she was arguing with her brother Calien. He'd never respected her either.

"Why do you keep calling me this?"

"What—why do I call you a *demon*?" Kai's upper lip curled in a sneer. "Why do you care? Does it hurt your feelings?"

"No. But if it will make you feel better, I shall endeavor to resent you for it."

Mira giggled, an easing of tension that the others clearly felt, even if it made Kai's mouth snap shut. His face went red. "Laugh all you want," Kai said, glaring around the table, "but she never actually said she wasn't one."

"Kai. Not now," Bal said, gaze heavy as he turned to Tassiel. "We aren't using the airship for the same reason I can't be seen escaping the temple. It's too easy to identify," Bal continued quickly, like he was trying to draw attention away from Kai's embarrassment. "Paasch would know I was behind the heist."

"Is not his knowing the whole point?"

"The point of the heist is the payday," he insisted, too firmly. Shrugged. "I want Paasch to know it was me, I just don't want him to be able to *prove* it."

Tassiel did not need to express her doubt with words. She simply folded her arms, but Bal turned away rather than reply. Kai had begun gnawing on his nails—surely a bad sign. Going through their plans clearly made him nervous, and Tassiel knew her presence already had him on edge.

"Kai, why don't you and Edik go to your contact at the temple and pick up your uniforms for tomorrow."

He nodded, pushing away from the table and going to his cot to dig out a fresh vest from the pile of clothes on the floor—"fresh" in the loosest possible sense of the word. Tassiel could smell his stale sweat on it from across the room. Edik, already dressed and ready, brushed a kiss on Zeelaya's temple and holstered the pistol he had so foolishly aimed at Tassiel.

"C'mon, Kai," Edik said. "We'll pick up some food and coffee for you on the way."

"See, this is why you're my favorite," Kai said with a slip of a smile. "We'll be back in an hour or two." He shoved his own pistols into their holsters and headed to the door.

"Be careful out there," Bal called. "We don't want to draw any attention." Tassiel had the sense that Edik didn't need the reminder to behave, but Kai was, well . . . Kai was another matter.

"Don't worry," Kai said, shrugging off Bal's words. "I'll spend the whole time in quiet contemplation."

"Will you?" Tassiel asked in a too-innocent voice. "Then while you are gone, I invite you to consider the wisdom in insulting the person securing your escape route."

A huff of quiet laughter sighed from her lips as he blanched. Flipping a rude gesture, Kai turned on his heel and stomped out the door.

"You could be nicer to Kai," Bal said, running a hand over his whiskers.

"Yes," she allowed, accepting the criticism with resignation. "But I do not think he would appreciate the effort." Both Mira and Zeelaya snorted at her unintended joke.

"You could be nicer to Shasheba, too."

"Shasheba is irrelevant."

Mira had to shove a hand in her mouth to stifle her glee. Bal glared at his sister. "Shasheba is sheltering us. She's smuggling Mira into the ceremony—for us. She isn't irrelevant."

Tassiel straightened from the schematics, pinned Bal with a long look. Willing him to reconsider. "Perhaps she should be."

He shifted, though from her gaze or from her warning, she wasn't sure.

"Why?"

She almost didn't reply. Her brothers had never heeded her advice about women, but Bal? Perhaps. "Be careful, Bal. Shasheba wears a cloak of bitterness, the kind that breaks into betrayal."

Bal's face was heavy with guilt, eyes darting to Zeelaya. She looked down almost like she was ashamed. Tassiel could not help but wonder why. It was obvious that Bal and Shasheba had been lovers, but for Zeelaya to feel guilty? Perhaps they had been friends, before the Vadalens fled the city.

And left Shasheba behind.

An unwanted feeling of pity for the priestess bloomed within Tassiel. She crushed it before it could take root.

"If Shasheba is bitter about life, it's because of me. So, it's up to me to make it right." He swallowed hard. "Don't worry about Shasheba, just try to be nice. That goes for you too, Mira." He turned to Mira who was leaning on the table looking unabashedly ecstatic about this whole conversation. "Speaking of which: What are you still doing here? You should be downstairs."

"I'm staying here."

"No. You're supposed to be with Shasheba. You need to learn your role for tomorrow."

"Blegh," Mira said, pulling a face. "I'm playing her servant. She bosses me around and I obey. How much practice do I really need?"

Bal rubbed his temples, and Tassiel experienced an unexpected jolt of sympathy. Her upbringing may have been brutal, but she'd never had to negotiate with a child. The youth in her world feared their elders far too much to contradict them.

Perhaps brutality was underrated.

"There's more to it than that, Mira," Bal said, impatience brimming in his every word. "There are prayers you need to learn."

"I know the prayers, I'm not an idiot. Shasheba has been making me repeat them. All. Week. Long." Mira heaved a put-upon sigh. "Tass is right. Shasheba sucks. I'm staying here."

"Mira, please." Zeelaya's voice cut through the fight brewing between the siblings. Mira shot her cousin a mutinous look, but the older woman refused to bend. "Go."

Mira huffed. Shoving her hands in her pockets, she stormed out of the room in a cloud of anger. "She will be an interesting teenager," Tassiel observed.

Bal shuddered at the words, then thanked Zeelaya for her intervention.

"She should be in school right now, Bal. Not planning a heist," Zeelaya said, her worry evident in each syllable.

"And she will be," Bal bit back, and Tassiel sensed the well-worn grooves of a familiar argument momentarily shouldering between the two cousins. "After this job, we'll have more money than we ever dreamed of. I can set Mira up with the life she deserves.

She nodded, but Tassiel was not sure if Zeelaya believed Bal, or simply had no stomach to fight. "What now?"

"Now you take me through it again," Tassiel said, crossing her arms, feet wide, expecting a fight. For while Bal had told Tassiel his plan, she was sure he had failed to reveal *all* of it. "But this time we discuss contingencies."

5

SEPTINIRI TASSIEL JANAE

Her crate's wooden walls groaned as one corner clipped the edge of the curb. The wine bottles above Tassiel shuddered into each other on impact, crying out little shrieks of agonized glass. She exhaled carefully, counting out her heartbeats to keep time while Edik snapped at Kai to be more careful. She appreciated the effort Edik was putting into keeping his end of the crate steady, but Tassiel knew even before climbing into this wooden coffin that asking the same of Kai was impossible.

Perhaps she should not have jested with Kai about being offended by his demon talk. Her brothers always said her humor was too dry to be funny. And anyway, beneath all his bravado, Kai's fear was as sharp and acrid as sulfur. So was Edik's, for that matter, though he contained it better. Fear did not make Edik reckless, but cautious. Strange that he was involved with the Talion at all.

Through the sliver-wide gaps in the crate's wooden sides, she watched Edik walk; each step was a precise, three-foot march. Any nervousness he felt was carefully coiled along the rigid column of his spine. He was clearly military. Seasoned, for sure. He had nearly a decade on the rest of Bal's crew. Odd that he was . . . *slumming*? It with Kai.

Tassiel's upper lip twitched in distaste as she forced herself through the mental gymnastics of using Ashaarite in the interior of her own mind.

Spending the past day with Bal and his companions had forced her to confront how out of practice her language skills had become. *How long has it been since I've spoken to anyone? Not just to contract employment or issue commands, but actual conversation for the simple joy of it?*

Her mind provided the answer: an accounting of years so vast it threatened to open a long-closed but never forgotten wound in her chest. Her heart almost stumbled, and she nearly lost track of time. Nearly.

Tassiel turned away from the pain. Closed the door on it and locked it so tight even her father would have been proud.

No. That was not true. That was not what her father was like, and she could not forget that. She could not let time soften her mind, because the moment it did, she would be useless. She would not claw her way back from so many years of abandonment, reaping pitiable sums of time off these silly human children, only to shame her family's lineage by breaking along the way.

You may live among them, she thought, letting her attempts at Ashaarite fall away like the frail thing it was, *but you are not of them. Use them. And return home.*

"Damn." Edik whispered the oath, his voice taut.

"What is it?" Kai asked.

"That codie on the right. The sergeant. I know him."

She pressed her face to one of the cracks, scouring the crowd congealing outside the temple's servants' entrance. Men and women swarmed about, hurrying to and from the monstrous building. Their crimson temple uniforms made them look like some exotic species of bee buzzing around their hive on urgent business for the queen.

Edik and Kai were well disguised, she thought. With the excitement of the consecration humming through the air, Tassiel doubted that anyone would look too closely at the two men or the long coffin-like crate they carried. Uniforms had a way of doing that—of stripping away individuality for the sake of unity.

But would it be enough? And if it wasn't, if Edik was spotted, marked, recognized as a criminal, then both he and the burden he bore would be searched. Thoroughly. Tassiel would be discovered.

Her eyes snagged on an older, wiry man with a chest full of glittering metals and enough bars on his epaulets to make him a sergeant. He had a bristly mustache and cropped white-streaked hair. Standing a few yards inside the gates, he was conferring with some kind of overseer.

"What do you mean you know him?" Kai asked. "Does he know you're a—"

"No." Edik's voice cut through what Tassiel was sure was a very inadvisable end to Kai's sentence. "We served together in the army."

"What if he recognizes you?"

She could not make out Edik's face as he turned to Kai, but the pause that stretched between them was pregnant with dread.

"You adapt." Tassiel's muscles went taut with the unbearable desire to burst forth from hiding and take control.

Bal said they were professionals. Impossible. Even by human standards they were barely formed. How could they be professional at anything? No wonder their patron demanded her presence. As quietly—and calmly—as she could, she whispered, "Kai, take the lead. Get us through the gate. Edik, face down. There is too much soldier in you. Hunch."

"Hey. I don't take orders from—"

"Shut it, Kai," Edik snapped. "Do as she says."

Kai grumbled, but when they finally reached the gate, he did as he was told. Setting the crate down—harder than necessary— Kai pushed forward, blocking Edik with his body, as he reported to someone she could not see.

"Good day to you, sir. We've got a delivery for the kitchen."

"What are you hauling?" the servant asked in a harried voice.

"La'Zemian summer wine."

"La'Zemian wine?" The servant's voice rose an octave, and she could hear the quick shuffling of papers. "I don't see any orders for that."

All their plans teetered on the edge of a blade. Tassiel stretched her fingers, brushing the daggers strapped to her thighs. If needed, she could get them, break free of the matchstick box, and make it to the temple before anyone could react. But it would leave Kai and Edik with a lot of explaining to do, not to mention put every officer in the temple on guard. It all depended on how Kai played this.

Creation save them, they were screwed.

"To be honest I'm not sure that you did order anything, but Rima Jaal asked me to bring it."

"Rima Jaal?" She could practically hear the servant's back crack as he straightened. "You know the steward?"

"Yeah, we go way back. I'm Malakai Fanoak, by the way. I'm supposed to report to the senior under-steward after I drop this in the kitchens. That's not you, is it?"

"Oh no. No that's not me," the servant said, clearly thawing to Kai's brand of rough charm.

"But someday, right?" Kai laughed. "Well anyway, Rima said Lady Kanju refused to attend the consecration unless she could have her favorite drink on hand. So here we are with a crate full of the stuff. You need a look?" Kai asked, sounding more agreeable than Tassiel had ever imagined possible.

"Yes, please."

With a shove that made the whole crate list dangerously to the left, Kai and Edik pried the lid up and dragged it to one side. Gray light filtered down through the false bottom and for the first time in an hour, she was able to draw in a breath of air that was not thick with dirt and the malodorous stench of Kai's feet.

"This is all summer wine?"

"Yeah. Nasty stuff, to be honest. But Lady Kanju is the governor's aunt. She gets what she wants."

"Indeed," the servant said bitterly. He backed away, and Tassiel saw the dusty hem of his red trousers come into view. "Go on through, then. Kitchens are straight ahead. You can ask one of the cook's assistants for directions up to the under-steward."

"Thank you kindly," Kai replied.

She shifted to the left, trying to keep a wary eye on the sergeant, as Kai and Edik hefted the crate. He stood with both hands clasped behind his back like a soldier at ease, and though the overseer was still speaking, the sergeant's eyes peppered the yard. For a human he was quite vigilant.

As she thought it, his gaze fell to the crate. Then rose. Those canny black eyes took in Kai walking purposefully and Edik, still hunched at her instruction. Lingered.

She pressed her lips together, prayed for the sergeant to look away. Willing Edik and Kai to move faster.

The overseer was still speaking, pointing emphatically at the paper in his hand. The sergeant's face turned down.

Only to jerk back up toward them. To Edik.

Tassiel swallowed a frustrated growl. "Edik, you have been spotted," she hissed. "Move."

Both men obeyed, not quite running toward the white brick wall of the temple. They jostled to the front of the line, swinging the crate like a battering ram between them. For a moment she relished the feeling of weightlessness before gravity clawed her back down.

Darkness swallowed her as Kai and Edik surged through the servants' entrance. Electricity sizzled across her skin, making the small hairs on her arms rise. Raw potential roiled in her stomach, suffusing her vision with a heady purple glow. Power leaped into the metal pads implanted in Tassiel's fingertips, racing up the wire embedded throughout her entire body. But it was not coming from the magic stored in the nameplate branded onto her spine.

It came from the building itself.

"Tassiel?"

Her eyes snapped open, and she found Edik and Kai staring down at her. Over their shoulders in the low light of tallow lanterns, she saw the dusty outlines of hundreds of wine bottles nestled in honeycombed shelves. Edik and Kai had gotten to the wine cellar as planned. They were now supposed to separate, but . . .

"Something is very wrong."

Even speaking the words soured the high coiling in her veins. They grounded her with a fear that had been a long, long time coming.

Both men frowned, but before either could speak, the door opened. "Corporal Agodzi, is that you?"

Kai whirled. Edik froze. Blood drained from his face leaving his dark skin ashen. His hand fell slowly to his pocket, where she knew a small pistol was hidden.

"No." Her hands snapped forward, twisting through forms she had not used in ages; forms she hadn't had the energy to use, but now—somehow—did. Magic flowed into her with every inhalation. It burned down her spine and back up again as she forced it through her fingers, an agent of her own will.

All three humans froze.

It should not have been possible.

Magic was formed from unspent time—from the limitless potential unused time created. In the land of her birth, time energy was everywhere, but here? Here it was hidden, tangled inextricably with the mortals who called this place home.

The nameplate grafted onto Tassiel's spine allowed her to store the energy she had so carefully culled from men like Edik and Kai. And though it was a limited space, it had taken her decades to accrue even the half-filled stores she'd had walking into this hideous temple. Yet now it was full. Brimming over with energy just begging to be used.

Begging her to return home.

The idea filled her—a longing so deep she thought she might be swept away on the currents of desire. Tassiel shivered.

Home.

I could go home.

The thought propelled her to her feet. She vaulted over the edge of the crate, a desperate laugh shuddering out of her chest, so wild she actually lost her balance, knocked into Kai.

Tassiel seized his arms to steady him before his frozen body fell to the floor. She was still smiling when she saw it. A shadowy spider-web substance clung to Tassiel's fingers connecting her to him. Her laughter guttered, strangled as though a garrote had wrapped around her throat.

She flicked the dark strands of time off her fingers, watched them slide back into Kai as a nameless revulsion burned her throat.

And shame.

Her father would have broken her hands for this foolishness. For the moment of joy she had indulged in—all at the feeling of her nameplate filling with power. For the prospect of going home, she had blinded herself to the obvious fact that something was happening here. Something that *could not happen* in this world.

Time surrounded her. Tassiel could feel it slithering against her skin, singing to be used. But it was not natural. It did not belong here, did not belong to her. It belonged to them, to the three men standing frozen before her. With new eyes, she saw the seconds scraping off them, flowing past her face and sinking into the stone walls. It was an invisible theft that only Tassiel could see.

Or someone like her.

The thought should have brought pleasure, but she found herself shuddering instead. For all her people's power, for all their wisdom, they were not . . . good. They were not kind. Or benevolent. Despite her longing to return home, the evidence of her eyes could not be ignored. One of her people was reaping time from these helpless creatures, from every one of the hundreds—thousands—of people crowded in this giant tomb of a temple.

But how? Why?

She needed to go. They all needed to go. But first . . .

With half a thought and a few practiced movements, the sergeant took her place in the crate, hands crossed over his chest, eyes closed in a deep dreamless sleep. She bent, scooping out the backpack with Zeelaya's grappling gun and swung it over her shoulders. Contorting her hands in a little known and seldom used form, she wove a simple shield over her body—not to protect her, but them.

Time, once taken, could not be given back, but she would not be party to the continued pillaging of these men and women. Their lives were already so small, taking a moment of it without consent felt like murder. Her shield in place, she went a step farther.

Stepping back, she let another whisper of magic burn out of her spine, tear through her chest and out her hands. Though she would never be a great mage, she'd had many long years with little else to do than devise and experiment. Tassiel cast the spell over the three humans, but let the magic linger on Kai. She forced it into his blood and, through him, his bloodline—to Bal and Zee and Mira. It would protect them.

From her.

And from creatures *like* her.

Another weakness her father would never forgive, but she needed the Talion to find out what was happening in the temple. Kai and Edik could go places and learn things she could not. So even if they were only allies for another twenty-four hours, she would protect them just as any general protected her men. Tools were most effective sharp and well cared for, after all.

The imaginary father who lived in her mind did not believe her.

Tassiel banished the thought by unfreezing Kai and Edik. Kai jumped so violently he shouldered the edge of the wine rack next to him, making it tip dangerously on one edge before banging back to the ground.

"Great Below, woman," he exclaimed. "How did you get over there?"

"That is not important, Kai," she began resisting the urge to scratch her arms as time energy chafed her flesh.

"What did you do to Sergeant Tammon?" Edik asked, clutching the edge of the crate. "Is he hurt?"

"He will be," Kai said, taking a step forward.

"No," Edik cried, grabbing Kai's arm so hard his hand paled. "Tammon is a good man."

"He's a codie." Kai spat the word like it was the greatest insult.

"So he deserves to die?" She recognized the look of disgust on Edik's face, for she felt it cross hers as well.

Blood rushed into Kai's ears and neck. "I wasn't going to kill him," he said, his voice hot. "I was just gonna nail him into the crate."

Edik released Kai slowly, like he was afraid the other man might indeed do something rash. "We'll put the top on it, but we're not nailing him in. But first"— he rounded on her—"tell me he'll be all right."

She waved the comment away. "He is simply asleep, but as I said, that is not important."

"What do you mean?" Edik frowned as he and Kai slid the lid over the sleeping sergeant.

Tassiel opened her mouth to respond but stopped. She did not know Edik or Kai, not well, but she knew their type. If she attempted to explain the true nature of the world now, the stream of questions that would follow would be endless. And Creation defend him, Tassiel did not think Kai had the mental capacity to understand it all anyway. She required them to do their best—to help her get the idol, for she suspected that was at the heart of this mystery. After that, if they all survived, she would try to explain.

"Tass?"

"I am not entirely sure what is wrong," she said, unspeakably grateful that neither man could see her face. Her sister always said she was a terrible liar. "But something is amiss. Something is growing, building." She shook her head as the scent of their fear soured the air. "I will know more once I see the shrine, but I think it would be better if the idol were removed from this place."

"Well, shit, I could've told you that," Kai said, his simple face relaxing. "Let's get moving."

Kai shouldered past her, sticking his head out the door before leaving without another word, nor backward glance. Edik flashed her a tight smile. "Good luck," he murmured before he too was gone.

"Good luck indeed."

She drew the shadows from the corners of the wine cellar and pulled them about her shoulders. Slinking out of the room, she crossed one hall then the next, gliding past the small army of servants who all instinctively looked away as she passed.

Ribbons of stolen time flowed through the air, pulled to the temple's outer walls. She felt it being funneled upward, pooling at the top of the temple. The odd hammered-copper pyramid on the temple's roof suddenly leaped into her mind. In all the years she had lived in Ashaar, every temple built atop these towering buildings had been flat-roofed. Like everyone else, Tassiel had assumed Governor Paasch changed the design to separate himself from the city's past rulers, but what if that assumption was flawed? What if he had devised a way to store time energy?

But for what purpose? Humans could not wield time magic. The Ankaari did. If her people had a hand in building this structure, it could only mean they were coming. And Cothis might not survive their arrival.

The thoughts filled her with an alarm she had not expected. Was it possible, that after so many years of solitude, she had become attached to this cramped, smelly city and its often-foolish denizens?

She followed the trail of time into an unused office and swung the window open. Tassiel surveyed the city around her with all its fetid canals and tightly packed streets before looking down. She was about halfway up the temple's first tier. People swarmed the lawn below, crossing the crowded street on business or strolling along the banks of the canal. Her brother Calien would have jumped out of this very window to dive in the water below just for the joy of it.

Tassiel was not so recklessly minded. Not surrounded as she was by stolen time and the threat of one of her own kind breaking into this city. Her city. And that was what she truly feared, was it not?

Her people, the Ankaari, did not belong in this world. Half bloods like her could cross into this plane, exist here with relatively little effort. But for a full-blooded Ankaari to open a portal? It was like tearing through the fabric of reality. The energy requirement alone was staggering and had caused calamities of such devastating proportions, they'd nearly ended humanity in the past. And once they arrived here?

There was a reason humans worshipped them as gods.

And there were reasons her people forbade the crossing. The decree against it had stood for millennia. Her siblings—the Septiniri—were bred to enforce it. But her siblings were not there. Only Tassiel was.

There was only one option now. Make it to the top of the temple, reach the idol, and stop whatever ritual her people had planned before it tore the world apart. Bal and his payday be damned, she'd break the idol if she had to.

The sky overhead gave a hungry roar. It sounded like a challenge. Like a gauntlet thrown.

Like it had heard her threats and was ready to play.

She shook her head, pushing magic into her hands, knees, and toes before swinging herself out the window. Her body latched on to the wall, sticking to the stone where the magic pooled. So even though the energy there was enough to send her home, she started to climb, ignoring the plink of rain on her mask. She would discover who was attempting to make the crossing. Stop them. And *then* return home . . .

A hero worthy of her family's name.

6

BALTHAZAR

The overly perfumed air around us hummed with the noisy whispers of nobles gossiping about Zee and me—about the spectacle our presence would cause. I pretended not to notice the excited murmurs and pointed glares. Or the way some had edged away from us, like we were a foul smell they could outrun.

Escape was unlikely. For all of us were trapped on the temple's wide central stair. The steps were packed with nobles from every house in Cothis—and a few neighboring islands, all filtering into the shrine high above at a snail's pace. Servants in bloodred robes made their way up and down the line with food and drink for the impatiently waiting lords and ladies.

Bastards all of them. Bastards who'd stood by and done nothing while my family was butchered. The hate boiling inside me was almost unbearable. For Paasch who'd started it all. For the empress who'd done nothing to save us. They deserved worse than the small embarrassment of a spoiled consecration. And worse I would give them. I'd take everything away from them—from *him*. Just like he'd done to me.

Someday.

Somehow.

I eyed a tray of wine with longing but didn't call for a glass. I'd need all my wits about me if I had a hope of charming our way into the party. Turning away from temptation, I craned my neck over the stairs. After almost two hours of standing, I was near the top and could see down onto the jutting lip of the temple's main level. Its wide base was almost twice as big as the second tier, which in turn was almost twice as large as the temple proper on top. It was like we were standing on some great, overdecorated wedding cake.

Yet even as the size of the layers diminished, all three rooftops were big enough to accommodate terraces. The lower two were currently overflowing with workers—the men and women who helped build the temple and whose families were invited to celebrate the consecration—so long as they maintained a healthy distance from anyone that "mattered." The workers might think this was a sign of Governor Paasch's generosity, but I knew it was nothing more than the demands of tradition. A way the nobles of Ashaar kept their large and underpaid workforce happy, by pretending they were part of the ceremony.

Shame wriggled through my mind, chasing away my righteousness. It wasn't as if my family hadn't done the same thing—for centuries, even—when we governed the city. I pushed the thought down, letting my eyes skate past the workers.

Trees and flowering bushes crowded the edges of the lower terraces. Beneath their shade, I could see long tables of food and drink set out for the guests. The party was already in full swing there, much to the smirking enjoyment of the nobles looking down their noses at the common folk.

Gods how I wished I was with them. Cothis Island was the main trading stop between the eastern and western seas. Goods were constantly coming in and going out of the kingdom from Cothis's ports. There was money to be had, and the greed that ran society was seldom allowed to halt. This was likely the last good party anyone in this godsforsaken city would see for a decade. Even these overstuffed nobles would be getting in on the fun. Once the drinks really started to flow, countless priceless rods would slide out of countless rarified asses.

And with what I had planned? I smiled. No, there would be no dignity left once we took the idol. Not that these overstuffed peacocks deserved any, I thought, savoring the idea of their pearl-clutching outrage.

I glanced up at the heavy sky before anyone read the disdain on my face. A blanket of iron-gray clouds completely occluded the setting sun, as distant thunder purred across the heavens. A storm was coming. It was as if Karanis himself was growling his scorn for this ridiculous display of false piety.

The idea of the sky opening up to drench every last one of these uppity nobles made a silent laugh twist my lips. That would be just the thing. Dull down the garish dresses and suits that surrounded me.

"Kai is going to come out of this with some truly revolting clothing ideas," I muttered, eyeing a twig of a woman wearing a flowing lime-green gown with lavender beads worked into the hem. Zee shifted, bumping into my arm. I glanced her way, but she was looking at the floor, her brow knotted in a scowl. "Zee?"

I summoned a bland smile for the people around us, all working so hard to pretend that the sight of two Vadalen heirs was nothing to note. For born liars, they were terrible actors. Still, it proved that Shasheba was right to insist that Zee be my date.

She'd wanted to sneak in with the serving staff like Edik and Kai. But Shasheba had gotten her hands on the finalized guest list a few nights ago. The list included several former family friends of ours as well as Zee's onetime fiancé. The likelihood she wouldn't be recognized was zero, and no one would believe that Zee would willingly join Governor Paasch's staff.

Though Zee loathed these kinds of events with a fervent passion, she knew she'd have to either come along with me or stay home. The latter was out of the question. Twice the spectacle I supposed, especially when one of us was looking at the floor like a child caught stealing.

"Zee," I hissed.

"What?"

"Why are you looking at your feet?"

"I'm not looking at my feet. I'm looking at the floor."

I felt my smile slip and hitched it back into place. "Please stop. It's making you look guilty, and we haven't done anything wrong."

"The 'yet' that belongs at the end of that sentence is truly staggering," she whispered, dragging her attention away from the floor. A frown still pulled at the corners of her mouth. The people around us shot her looks when they thought we weren't watching, no doubt wondering why she looked two inches from tearing someone's head off.

Zee usually looked serious—it was just the way her face was—but this particular expression didn't mean anger. She was confused, though Zee usually attacked puzzles the way some people did mortal enemies.

"What is it?"

"Have you seen the stairs?" she asked in an undertone.

I looked down surreptitiously. The stairs were the same white granite as the rest of the temple, only they were decorated with three bands of bright copper line that ran from the ground to the cella—the square room that capped the temple, where the actual business of worship took place. There were similar lines on all four sides of the building. I had to admit it was a striking look, but nothing worthy of Zee's rapt attention. "What about them?"

"They're copper, Bal," was her impatient reply.

Whatever else Zee was going to say was lost as the crowd

shuffled forward, finally approaching the cella entrance. Governor Paasch stood in the doorway greeting his guests with a wide grin that showed too many teeth. He looked like a jackal sneering at its prey.

The high priests and priestesses of Cothis formed up in a loose group around him, fawning over the nobles and laughing sycophantically at everything Paasch said. Shasheba was among them, wearing a remote smile that gave her a radiant air of mystery. Like Tass, I thought, though Shasheba would have slapped me for the comparison.

She was resplendent in a diaphanous ruby gown and glittering gold jewelry, beautiful enough to draw the eye of every man who passed. My teeth snapped closed on the tip of my tongue as Paasch leaned over and whispered something in her ear. She laughed, a high, cold sound that seemed to belong to someone else.

Zee's nails dug into my forearm. I obeyed her silent command, looking away from Shasheba. She wasn't my . . . whatever. Today, Shasheba was a high priestess of Nananthe, our plant inside Paasch's temple. Catching Paasch's attention was all part of the plan. *My* plan. It meant Shasheba would be above suspicion when the heist was over. Her people—including Mira—wouldn't be scrutinized.

I craned my neck but couldn't see my sister in the gaggle of priests. Hopefully Mira was already inside. The thought of her being here was enough to make my palms sweat. I'd have given anything to keep her out of trouble, but Shasheba needed help inside the temple. She would be too busy whispering sweet lies into Paasch's ear to ensure the right window was propped open, so it was up to Mira.

She would be safe, Shasheba had said. No one would question an acolyte during the consecration. And if everything went to plan, Shasheba and Mira would sit tight and get released with the other guests once the dust settled. No one would be any wiser.

The knot of nobles in front of me swept forward, eager to enter the temple, leaving an empty space between Paasch and me. Twice as eager to ensure Paasch knew they had nothing to do with our presence. The governor's gaze met mine, and I saw a second of confusion pass to recognition. His eyes widened.

I smiled, sauntering up to Paasch with Zee in tow. The people around us drew in a breath as Paasch and I came face-to-face. I ignored them, just as I ignored the way six guards detached from the wall and posted themselves in the entrance.

Silence stretched taut while Paasch and I surveyed one another. As much as I hated to admit it, time had been kind to him. His dark hair, slicked back to the nape of his neck, had gone slightly gray at the temples as had the whiskers of his goatee. And though there were fine lines etched into his skin, they somehow didn't make him look frail. He stroked the hair on his chin, like it gave him an air of gravitas.

"Balthazar Vadalen. Is it really you?" Paasch's voice boomed in the cavernous entryway, bouncing back in my face with physical force. He threw open his arms. "Come here, my boy."

Heedless of the way his guards went for their revolvers, Paasch pulled me into a tight embrace, thumping on my back with a closed fist.

What I would have given for any of my knives. Or a gun, I thought, dreaming of his blood spraying across my face. I locked my jaw together, forcing my smile to stay put, though I knew it must look strained.

Paasch's eyes glittered as he pulled away. That pale green gaze, an unusual color for Cothis, was filled with malice and laughter. "This is a surprise."

"A happy one, I hope," I said, managing to smooth the anger from my voice. "When I heard about the consecration of this beautiful temple, I knew I had to see it. Though if you'd rather I leave . . ."

I let my words wander off. Edik would have called it a gamble. Hell, by the way Zee just sucked in a breath, I knew she thought so too. They were wrong.

Would Paasch love to haul me out of here? Of course. I saw the temptation shimmer in his eyes. But if he kicked us out now, the fun would be over.

If he let us in, he could torture us slowly in front of every noble in the city. Remind them of his power. In the end it wasn't much of a risk.

Paasch had always liked playing with his food.

His smile widened. "I'm so glad you came, my boy," he said, his voice so sincere any of the onlookers could be excused for believing him. Until he put his arm around Shasheba's waist, letting one hand sit on her full hip. Bile rose up my throat in a scorching wave. I tore my eyes away, but the damage was done. Paasch's body shook with laughter.

"Shasheba," I said with a small bow.

She looked me up and down, haughty and indifferent. It hit me like a sucker punch, like we'd never been in love. Though it went against every instinct in my body, I let the pain flash across my face. Let Paasch see my weakness. The crowd behind me congealed as people pushed forward, hoping to witness the sight of my shame.

A cold kind of pride solidified in my chest. Good. The more they looked at me, the more they gossiped and whispered, the less time they would spend looking at the idol.

"It's good to see you, Zeelaya," Shasheba said, giving my cousin the dazzling smile she'd refused me. "It's been too long."

"Yes," Zee replied woodenly. Acting had never been her strength.

Shasheba laughed, sharing a look with Paasch. Her eyes fell to Zeelaya's hem, two inches too short and several years out of fashion— at least that's what Shasheba had said when she'd given it to Zee. The two women had spent the whole morning in stiches planning out all the awful things they were going to say to one another.

It had been nice to see them together, rekindling their friendship. But here, with Paasch at her side, it didn't feel planned. It felt like Shasheba was ready to draw blood

"Do come to me, this evening, Zeelaya. I'd love to catch up. Perhaps I can be of service to you." Shasheba leaned in, drawing the crowd in with her as if they were nothing but puppets on strings. "With a little effort, I'm sure we can get you up to standards. We'll just have to work on your clothes and . . . your manners . . . and well. If nothing else your lineage might be worth something to some new merchant family." Her stage whisper echoed, and a susurrus of excited murmurs exploded around us.

Even though she knew the cut was coming, I saw Zee wilt beside me, her face going slightly green. None of this felt like playacting. Not to me. And not to Zee, who'd heard these words a hundred times a day in our youth. Never measuring up to the impossible standards of polite society. A society Shasheba had been bred to rule.

Paasch grinned indulgently at Shasheba before waving the guards away with one ring-clad hand. "Please do go in, Balthazar. I'm sure you'll enjoy yourself," Paasch said, his gravelly voice deepening with a hint of a threat.

It felt like a retreat, the way Zee and I entered the temple, cutting a swath through the crowd. I shoved the feeling away as my eyes drifted over the curious onlookers, taking in my surroundings with as much nonchalance as possible. I'd been studying the schematics for weeks now but seeing it in person was another matter.

The rectangular space was as large and lavish as I'd expected from Paasch—compensating for something, I was sure. The white granite of the building's exterior covered the floor and ceiling, but the walls were inlaid with huge lapis lazuli panels worked with geometric copper designs. Six alabaster columns stood at the opposite end of the temple, creating something of an artificial barrier between the main area and what must have been the shrine. I couldn't quite see it from where I stood, but I was sure the idol must be somewhere behind the columns.

I looked away, not wanting to seem too interested, and steered us toward the food and drinks tables lining the edges of the room. Two carefully hidden doors studded the walls behind the tables. Servants' entrances, according to the schematics. They would lead to staging rooms filled with spare dishes and cutlery as well as dumbwaiters to deliver food hot and fresh from the kitchens below.

The high, pointed windows on this side of the cella were cracked open, letting in a whisper of salty wind. The breeze was sorely needed; the party hadn't even begun and the air inside was already soupy with the stench of clashing perfumes. I wanted nothing more than to rub my nose, but countless generations of good breeding kicked in to stop me. Instead I fell back on that tried-and-true crutch of all noble lines: alcohol. I waved down a servant, accepted two glasses of colorless liquid and handed one to Zee.

She took it but was too busy frowning at the ceiling to actually drink.

I sighed. "What is it now?" I asked, following her gaze.

The ceiling, which looked like the inside of a pyramid, was crisscrossed by copper rafters. They were set into the sides of the roof in a grid-like pattern. Each layer, and there were at least six, was slightly off set from the grid below so that when you looked up it seemed like you were being sucked into the center of a particularly rigid vortex. I felt my brow wrinkle.

"More copper," Zee muttered. "But why? The building doesn't require rafters for stability, least of all copper ones."

Part of me wondered if Zee's fascination was to mask her own nervousness—her trepidation—at being here, but I knew better than to ask. Anyway, my knowledge of architecture could fit into the glass in my hand, so I shrugged. "Maybe it's for aesthetics?"

Zee grumbled something derogatory about artists and took a sip. "I can't believe I have to suffer through another one of these parties," she said, glaring around the room. "I thought this part of my life was over."

"It will be soon," I murmured, flashing a genuine smile that was just for her. "I promise, after tonight we never have to return to this hellhole ever again."

Zee just grumbled.

Unlike me, Zee didn't miss anything about our old life. Yes, she mourned for our family, but the truth of it was that the fall of the Vadalen line had freed her. Zee's was a once-in-a-generation mind, the kind that would have been squandered in the marriage our family had arranged.

Without the noble name to live up to, Zee had been free to stay in her lab and invent impossible things, like the grappling gun Tass was lugging up the side of the temple (I hoped), or the pair of incendiary earrings that dangled from her lobes. They perfectly matched the green jasper necklace she wore only with the added excitement of unstable chemicals. They looked so real; it would be impossible for an outsider to tell which was the fake and which was the heirloom passed down from her mother.

It was a real effort not to wince every time she moved her head. The earrings could probably blow a hole right through any one of these freaking walls. I fervently hoped we wouldn't need them, or we'd probably get impaled by two tons of falling copper. Still, the thought of making such an exit brought a smile to my lips. The patron might think Tass was our only weapon, well. She had nothing on Zee.

"Come on, let's try and get eyes on the others." I stifled a laugh when she groaned. "I promise I won't make you mingle."

We edged along the western wall, scanning the crowd for the rest of the crew. I spotted Kai first, looking impossibly polished in his red servant's kit, offering a tray with a perfectly straight face to a large woman in a too-tight dress. Kai's eyes glanced past the woman, marking us. Leaning away from the lady, he brushed the top button of his jacket with his thumb. It was a sign that we needed to be on guard. I took a swig of wine and looked away before my face betrayed me.

Zee nudged me with her elbow, gesturing carefully with her glass at Edik. He stood by a narrow door in clothes that matched Kai's.

Unfortunately, he also wore Kai's expression of worry. Had there been trouble getting in?

But neither man was signaling to abort, and—for that, at least—I could breathe a little easier.

It was a miracle, really, that they were able to score this job in the first place. A miracle made possible because Kai knew the governor's butler from when the man worked for my family. Kai had guessed that a party this size would require some extra help from outside staff. Combined with the glowing letters of recommendation Zee had forged from a noble family in Eshara, Kai and Edik were shoo-ins for the job. Maybe the codies at the door had recognized them—or recognized Kai. My friend wasn't exactly a stranger to the law.

So Zee and I moved with caution—but we did keep moving. We meandered forward, lingering by one of the columns to marvel at the idol—or at least pretend to. The idol was nothing more than a two-foot-tall statue of the sea god Karanis, patron deity of Cothis. The statue, and the altar it sat on, was on a slightly raised platform behind a corridor-wide gap between the middle columns. In that part of the room, the grid-like pyramid of the ceiling was inverted. A funnel of copper girders stretched down from the ceiling toward the altar. I felt my eyebrow twitch as Zee's contempt comingled with my own.

Who knew Paasch was such a fan of modern art?

The statue was slightly rudimentary to my thief's eye. Its face was worked into the barest semblance of human features. The god's wings were wrapped tight to his back like the artist hadn't the skill to make them stand out on their own. Though it did have one hand raised, fingertips grazing the edge of the pointed copper tip of the pyramid. Strangest of all, the idol's black surface seemed to be dusty. Odd. I'd have thought it would have been shined to perfection before the consecration. I leaned forward. Squinted.

And froze.

The statue wasn't dirty, it was covered in fine etchings. Words.

Words I didn't recognize. But I'd seen that script before. Thunder crashed against the temple, answering the worry slowly building within me.

Out of the side of my mouth I said, "Zee, the idol is covered in ancient Sorien."

Zee's face jutted to me and then to the idol. Her hand drifted toward the back of her neck before she balled it into a fist and jerked it down. "Bal, I don't like this. And all the copper . . . I don't think it's for decoration."

"What do you think it is?" I asked, but then I saw Mira and my world went dark on the edges.

She was in the far corner of the room surrounded by blue-robed acolytes. They knelt facedown chanting prayer after prayer beseeching the idol, and through it the god, for protection, peace, and prosperity. The acolytes surrounded the idol in orderly rows, leaving gaps at the back near the wall and in the center, where the high priests and priestesses would finish the invocation when the time came.

Though she'd never admit to being scared of storms, Mira started as thunder shook the building. She peeked her head up, looking around at the gathered acolytes, but no one else was paying attention to her. A nameless fear sizzled up my spine seeing her so close to the idol. I forced it away.

If Zee had answered, I hadn't heard her.

"Admiring my idol, I see." Paasch's gravelly voice thwacked into the back of my head.

I turned, just managing to smile when I found him standing arm in arm with Shasheba, a victorious sneer on his lips.

"Zeelaya," Shasheba said, when neither Paasch nor I spoke. "Why don't you come and walk with me? I'd love to catch up." She held out her hand to Zee who looked at it distractedly. She glanced back at the idol before sighing and taking Shasheba's arm. Zee nodded in Paasch's general direction before walking off with Shasheba.

I kept my attention on Paasch. Shasheba and Zee would make

their way to the back of the room and cause a scene while I did the same with Paasch here. Everyone would be looking at one of us rather than at the idol. Kai and Edik would have enough time to make the grab and get out through Tass's escape route. Assuming she made it, I thought, as rain lashed the roof with renewed ferocity. Surely mere weather couldn't stop the great Queen of Days.

"I see your cousin hasn't changed much," Paasch said, watching the women go. "Still an odd one, Zeelaya Vadalen."

"Zee has always been one of a kind." I didn't bother to correct Paasch with Zee's married name. He wouldn't have believed me if I told him she'd married a disgraced soldier.

I ignored that niggling sense of unease and tried to put the expression on Mira's face out of my mind. Everything was going exactly to plan. By the end of the night, Paasch would be the laughingstock of the whole kingdom, we'd have our money, and the gods—

Well, the gods would have to worry about themselves.

"Yes, unique little rosebuds. That's what all you Vadalen brats pride yourself on, isn't it?" Paasch spoke in a voice so bland it was almost possible to pretend he hadn't just insulted me. It was a real effort to keep from shattering the glass in my hand. Paasch smirked, taking a few steps forward, inspecting the idol with greedy eyes.

"Honestly, I thought you had better taste, Paasch. Isn't this all just a touch overdone?" I matched his airy tone, but my voice was loud enough for the men and women around us to hear. "Gaudy?" I paused, as if chewing on it. "Yes—I think that's the word I've heard bandied about tonight. But that's often the case with new money. I guess it just takes a few centuries for class to develop."

Paasch rounded on me, his face burning scarlet. His middle-class roots had always been a sore point for him. People turned toward us, no longer pretending they weren't listening. Their expressions were alight with fake outrage and very real delight. Shocked whispers rippled through the room in a slow wave of vindictive glee. Even a few acolytes peeked over their hands at us. Good. I needed all eyes on me—on us—so that no one would see Kai and Edik go for the idol.

I dared a quick glance when lightning flashed through the eastern windows, illuminating a slim figure. Tass crouched on the window-sill directly to the right of the idol. My smile deepened. Right on time, I thought, as she turned her head skyward to study the copper girders that had so bothered Zeelaya.

"Insulting me is unwise, Balthazar," Paasch bit out between clenched teeth.

"Oh? Why is that?"

"Because things are about to change in this city."

My hands curled, and my eyes snapped to Paasch. This wasn't the first time he'd uttered those words. I remembered him saying the exact same thing to my father the night before Paasch led an angry mob to our door. "And you love it when things change, don't you, Paasch?"

"Still so bitter," Paasch said, sneering. "Yes, I do love change. Why shouldn't I, when I'm the one directing it? What may seem like chaos to the small is nothing but the change of the tide."

I cocked an eyebrow. "Are you saying you can control the tides now? You were always full of yourself, Paasch, but this is getting un-healthy. You may govern the sea god's city, but that doesn't make you Karanis." I glanced over Paasch's shoulder, but Tass was no longer on her perch. Movement flickered at the top of my vision.

There. In the rafters above the idol, Tass stood. An inky spot of night against the shining copper.

What the hell is she doing? Kai and Edik were supposed to make the grab. She was only supposed to secure the exit.

A dark chuckle oozed out of Paasch. "Not yet."

My attention fell to Paasch. "What's that supposed to mean?"

"It means you still have a few minutes to beg for your useless life. Do be quick. The ceremony will begin momentarily."

A hundred insults fought to break through my lips, but over Paasch's shoulder, Tass dropped to the ground. She stood right behind the idol, head cocked. It took every ounce of willpower I possessed to keep from shouting at her.

What the fuck *is she doing?*

"Nothing to say? No clever insult to throw at your superiors?" Paasch brushed imaginary dust off his sleeve, bored now. "I guess you really have grown up."

I barely heard him. Time itself slowed as Tass picked up the idol.

Paasch scoffed. His body began to turn. I seized one of his arms, holding him in place. He pushed me away, outrage twisting his face.

For a second, my mind went blank. Panic squeezed my chest. All I knew was that I had to keep his attention on me. Keep him from turning to the altar.

"What are you doing, Paasch?" I asked, spitting out the first question I could think of. "Does it have to do with the ancient Sorien scrawled over the idol?"

Surprise widened his eyes. But then he smiled, genuinely pleased. The expression made me sick. "Very good, Balthazar. Your father would be so proud to know that all your education wasn't a total waste. But can you read it?" he asked, his words almost lost to the storm battering the temple's walls.

In the second that he paused to watch my face, I watched her.

Tass held the idol in two gloved hands. She had it. Great Below, why wasn't she running? Why was she still here? No one had noticed her yet—no one but Mira, who was now standing, staring at the strange woman.

Sit down, Mira, I thought, fear turning my stomach liquid.

Whatever the hell Tass was doing, she needed to do it quickly. She was the Queen of Days, after all. She'd single-handedly breached the Bastion, I thought, clinging to that rumor like it was a gods-damned prayer. She'd walked us out the precinct doors two nights ago—for all I knew no one else could see her. We could still pull this off. Tass still had time. All she had to do was—

"*No.*"

"'No' what?" Paasch asked, confused.

Her whole body tensed and I knew without knowing what would happen next.

Tass snapped the idol in two.

She dropped the two chunks of broken statue on the altar like so much trash. Turned away. Ignoring Mira who'd run forward in mute horror, Tass sauntered toward the window.

Paasch shook his head. "It's a pity you're still such a fool," he said. "You might have been the only person in Cothis who could have seen this coming." Paasch leaned toward me, but I was barely listening. All my attention was on Tass, who'd just destroyed all our plans.

And on Mira who had picked up the top half of the idol. "Not that it would have saved you."

A man's bellow pierced the air. Paasch whirled to the man—a sergeant—and saw his outstretched arm, his pointed finger. Everyone saw.

Slowly, as if the air was made of molasses, the crowd turned.

They saw Mira holding the broken idol.

7

BALTHAZAR

N o!" Paasch's scream raked the side of my face. The rest of his words were lost to the crash of lightning on the temple's roof. Another crash rattled down the walls. Then another. Another.

My mind blanked. Instinct took over. I surged forward; vision narrowed on Mira. I had to reach her before Paasch did. I made it two steps before a pair of strong arms seized me.

"Wait, Bal," Edik's voice filled my ears.

"Wait?" I hissed. "That's Mira—"

"Just wait. He won't hurt her in front of all these people."

Edik was insane. Fucking cracked if he thought I was just— I swallowed hard. *Wait, Bal. Watch. Follow the plan.* I glanced around, saw the crowd fixated on Mira and the idol. He wouldn't.

Would he?

Paasch sprinted to the dais, face wild with rage. He snatched the broken bottom half of the idol, a wordless howl twisting his mouth. Mira backed into the wall, lips trembling, clutching the top half to her small chest.

Paasch foamed at the mouth in fury, but his words were lost to a thunder that simply would not stop. The storm battered the sides of the building, almost hungry to break in. Wind rammed against the temple walls. Wood and metal moaned. Light flashed.

The doors slammed against their locks, and I heard wood splinter a second before they blew off their hinges. Shasheba and Zee dove to the side as the doors flew past them, barreling into the crowd.

I almost went to them, but then the pressure dropped. My ears popped. A deep bellowing sound—almost below the level of my hearing—screamed through the temple. It shattered every window, showering broken glass through the air. Rain and hail pelted us, and the thunder . . . It didn't so much crash as roar.

Skeletal fingers of blue lightning scorched the floor, leaping up to the rafters. Everyone screamed, but their terror was drowned in the storm's rage.

A great animal growl bounced off the walls, a physical force that pushed me to my knees. I shivered against the stone, unable to move as the rain-soaked ground frosted over.

Frosted. It was an icy rime that crackled across the floor, freezing my brain with it because it simply wasn't possible.

Just as I had thought when Tass first came into the Code Hall, Cothis had never been cold enough for frost. Yet possible or not, ice crystals crusted the granite floors with spear-like hands, racing to the altar. To the broken idol.

To Mira.

Paasch's back was pressed up against the altar. His lips moved, but I couldn't hear his words. He held up his hands, beseeching—no, begging, *pleading* with the lightning as if it were a sentient being. The thunder roared, so loud it reverberated through my bones, but impossibly I sensed words.

Mira, I thought as blue light, brighter than the sun built at the ceiling. *Now. While everyone is distracted. Get Mira.* I surged to my feet, ready to follow the only instinct that made sense to me. I had to save Mira.

I tried to move; the light got there first. A column of blue flame speared through Paasch's forehead and chest. His body seized. His mouth dropped open in a wordless scream. His eyes—there was nothing of his eyes. The empty sockets smoked. His clothes caught on fire. His gold jewelry melted to his skin. Through it.

My joints locked as I watched—as the entire room watched— Paasch consumed by the light. We waited, instinctively knowing that something—something terrible—was coming through that fire. No one moved. No one even breathed.

Except Tass.

Her ebony-clad body seeped out of the darkness behind Paasch. She seized Mira about the waist and sprinted to the window. Hope soared within me. Without slowing, Tass leaped through the sill and into the inky darkness outside.

She did it. She saved Mira.

"Noooooo!"

A voice that didn't belong to Paasch scraped out of his throat. His face contorted in inhuman rage. He spun to the window; hand outstretched. A bolt of blue lightning shot out of his open palm. It connected with the wall and blasted a carriage-size hole straight through the stone. The temple shuddered so hard a few metal beams crashed to the ground.

But Mira. Tass. Their zip line was supposed to be connected to that wall. Anchored to the stone that now lay crumbled and smoking on the temple floor.

No, no, no . . .

I lunged, struggling against Edik's greater weight. Blood and adrenaline and desperation pounded in my ears. The mooring. Oh shit. The lightning had shattered the wall—had it blasted through the end of the zip line? Did Mira fall? I had to see. I had to . . . *Mira!*

A second pair of hands grabbed me, hauling me back. My heels slipped against the frozen stones as Kai and Edik dragged me through an unfamiliar door. The details of the room beyond wouldn't stick in my brain. All I registered was narrow walls and the confined feeling of a tomb.

Sweat soaked my skin. Desperation turned my stomach. *Mira.* Her name screamed through me. Was I saying that aloud or just in my head? I was no longer sure. I fought blindly against Kai and Edik. A wordless moan keening in my ears. I had to get to her, to see if she was . . .

Zee's face appeared in my vision a half second before her hand connected with my cheek. Pain jangled through my jaw. "Bal. Stop."

After so many years of obeying my older cousin, my body stilled. "Mira," I said, terror shaking my voice.

"I know," Zee replied, her skin deathly pale. "But Tass got her out. There's still a chance they made it to the drop point, but we won't know if we don't get out of here."

My brain felt like mush as I took in the faces around me. Zee, Edik, Kai and—"Shasheba."

Zee shook her head. "No. She knows the plan."

"*What* plan?" Nothing about what just happened was covered in my plans.

But Zee was undeterred. "She's smart, Bal. She knows she must stay put. But Bal." I looked at her, and she waited until our eyes actually connected. Nodding, she said, "We have to go. Now."

I took a fistful of terror and shoved it deep down inside me. Where it wouldn't get in the way. And then I got the hell to work.

"Wine."

"They're over here," Kai said, sliding behind me to a stack of familiar bottles: La'Zemian wine. Untouched and unopened because that's how notoriously nasty the shit was. And this batch was twice as bad for the meticulous way Zee had altered it.

Kai tossed a bottle to Edik as I ripped off my cuff links. The two other men popped the corks, ready for my mark. I looked at Zee.

She was at the dumbwaiter. Two more open bottles rested inside, ready for her to drop her rings in. Her gaze went to mine. She nodded once.

"Now." My order cut through the small room. As one, Zee and I dropped the jewelry into the wine. The reaction started almost instantly. The chemicals coating the jewelry dissolved into the compound mixed within the sour wine. Smoke bubbled to the surface as Kai and Edik slammed the corks back on their bottles. Crouching low, both men ducked their heads back into the main temple, rolling the bottles across the floor in opposite directions. Distractions from the main event.

Zee rammed the dumbwaiter closed and pulled the lever, sending it spiraling down the temple's spine.

"One. Two. Three. Fou—"

Three explosions cut her off. The two from the temple were loud enough to shake my teeth. And though I knew they'd surely scare the already terrified crowd; I trusted Kai and Edik to know better than roll them where they might injure anyone.

The dumbwaiter was a goner though.

Zee opened the now smoking hatch, peered through. "Looks like the dumbwaiter exploded between the first and second floor. Should be enough rope to get us to the second-floor kitchens."

"Go."

We rabbited through the hole, one after another. My muscles screamed as I slid down the rope. Skin burned too, but I was glad for it—glad for the pain. It was the only thing keeping me from falling over the cliff of terror that loomed in my mind. Terror for Mira. For Shasheba, too. Even Tass.

But Mira.

I busted through the second-floor hatch, into the kitchen, nearly kicking Kai in the back as I did so. "What are you doing just standing here—"

My words rammed into a wave of bile as my stomach turned inside out.

Because if the lightning had caused chaos above, it had wrought carnage below.

The kitchen around us was covered in copper wire. It was inlaid in the floors and walls and twisted into crisscrossing patterns on the ceiling. Every inch of it blackened from the storm and stained with boiled blood and viscera from the people ensnared there. Caged in a lightning trap.

I couldn't even count the bodies. They lay in malformed heaps, skin melted together until the border between one form and the next no longer existed. The stench of burnt flesh was a physical thing. It reached out to me, clawing at my clothes and hair begging for a mercy that wasn't in my power to give.

"What in the ever-living fuck happened here?"

I shook my head at Kai, having no answer. No answer but one. "Back exit. Go. Now."

No one needed telling twice. We ran—Kai and Zee looking down, trying not to see what had become of the world around us. Edik scanned the edges of each room we passed, each hallway that stretched, waiting for more attacks.

I counted.

This was meant to be our emergency exit plan. Drop from the glitzy party upstairs into the raucous one below. The one that wouldn't be governed by order or pretension, but packed with people simply enjoying their lives. It would have been easy to slip through the crowds, get to the back staircase and out of the temple.

And it was easy.

Because everyone was dead. Every. Single. One.

Rain and wind lashed my face as we reached the back staircase. But no matter how the storm raged it couldn't shift the smell. The pale granite floor at my feet was black with burnt flesh and stained with charred blood. Where several hundred people had been party-ing a scant hour ago, only empty husks remained. The lightning had taken them all. And for what?

So Paasch could— I couldn't even finish the thought. It didn't make sense. None of this made any fucking sense.

We ran, sprinting faster. No speech was necessary. No speech was possible. We'd all seen what happened in the temple. We'd seen the lightning. We'd seen the bodies. What we hadn't seen was what had happened to Tass. To Mira.

And that's all that mattered at this point.

By the time we hit the street the rain had stopped, but the sky still swirled and growled, threatening a worse storm to come. The temple grounds were eerily quiet as we cut across the manicured lawn to a boulevard lined with tall and stately mansions.

My joints felt like broken glass as we ran down the street, cling-ing to the shadows even though there was no one to observe us. Every step was agony, a terror that this was the step that would bring me to Mira's broken body. But no. I didn't see her. Thank the gods.

Kai and Edik grabbed my arms, stopping me. We'd made it. I didn't quite know how, but here we were. *Focus, Bal. Panic later,* I thought, as Zee ran forward alone. She hurried up to the governor's mansion, tilting her terrified face up to the gaslight lanterns. "Help. Please help," she cried.

Right on cue, the two door guards hurried down the cobblestone walk and opened the gates for her. "What is it, ma'am?"

"Please help," Zee squealed. "The governor. The temple. The storm. Something terrible . . ."

The guards looked at each other with obvious doubt and confu-sion. But there was no denying the panic and horror in Zee's voice. And surely they'd heard the storm, if not seen a part of the temple wall destroyed. Both men hurried down from the front steps, so wor-ried for Zee they didn't see us. Edik barreled through the open gate while Kai and I leaped onto the guards.

My knuckles crunched as my fist connected with one guard's face. He slumped, falling prone to the sodden ground. Kai had tackled his target, dragging him down before hitting the back of the man's head with the butt of his revolver.

"Bal?" Zee murmured, something in her voice—

I spun. Zee's eyes were wide, filled with tears. She pointed down.

At her feet lay a snaking length of rope. It hung limp and useless from the side of the house, trailing through the front of the lawn and disappearing in the darkness toward the temple.

"*No.*" Part of me knew denying reality wouldn't protect me for long, but I clung to it. Clung to that last inch of hope, of sanity. Small and fragile, it was only an inch, but without it I would break entirely.

I snatched a pistol off the guard and ran to the door, pressing myself against the wall to the left. Kai was on the other side of the door, gun raised. I nodded. He clasped the handle. Turned.

We ghosted inside; pistols ready. At this time of night, and with no one living here, I'd known that the front of the house wouldn't be well lit. I was right. Only a single lantern lit the foyer from a decorative table across the room. It cast grotesque shadows up the high walls, transforming the entrance of my onetime home into the gaping maw of some terrible monster.

Edik followed, and Zee slid the door shut, cutting off the light from the lamps outside. I held up my fist, and the crew went still. My ears strained. There. I pointed up. Kai nodded.

Muffled voices were coming from up the stairs. We followed them, hugging the edge of one marble staircase and then the next, following the trail of indistinct words. I'd known it was unlikely that the guards wouldn't notice people sliding into the mansion from a zip line attached to the temple. They were bound to see it. And investigate.

My knees went weak with relief. I made out two voices from a bedroom down the hall. If the guards were there, so was Mira. She had to be. Somehow Tass had gotten her out before the line snapped. It was the only explanation.

The only one I would—I could—accept.

"Great Below, Estu. What happened here?" one of the guards, young by the sound of his voice, asked.

I nodded to Kai and Edik, not bothering to listen to the reply. Both men crept through the open door. Zee and I followed a second later, but by the time we stepped into the dust-filled bedroom, both guards were down.

My vision narrowed on the two figures lying on the floor against the wall on the other side of the room. Air whooshed out of me. *Mira.*

I rushed over, banging into an antique wardrobe as I fell to my knees. Mira lay on her side, with Tass's body curled protectively around her. My heart stuttered when Tass didn't move, didn't even flinch, as I shifted her arm off Mira's body. All Father defend us. Were they breathing?

I shook Mira's shoulders. Her dress was wet. Sticky. My throat constricted when my hands came away red. "Mira?"

Her eyes popped open. "Well, it's about time."

I choked out a relieved groan, gathering her into my arms, every muscle in my body sagging.

"Bal. Bal, we don't have time for this," Mira said, squirming.

"Are you hurt?"

"No," she said vehemently, pushing me away to grab Tass's arm. "Tass is, though. Bal, I think she's hurt real bad."

"Great Below, Mira. What happened?" Kai asked in perfect imitation of the guard he'd just knocked out.

I turned but Kai wasn't looking at me. He was looking up. At the hole in the roof.

"What the . . ." I took in the broken plaster, the splintered timber and shattered roof tiles littering the floor. Plaster dust covered the fine furniture and hung in the air, clinging to skin and hair.

The sky was clearly visible through the hole, churning in pent-up rage. Below the hole, the stone floor was staved in. Cracks ran along the slate in a five-foot-wide circle of buckled rock. It was like it had been hit by some great weight. Water pooled in the spiderweb design reflecting the sky above.

I turned. Behind Tass's back, the wall was buckled the same way, only the wall hadn't fared nearly as well as the floor. Part of the next room was visible through the lath where the plaster had crumbled.

"Mira, please tell me you didn't come through the roof."

Mira tsked. "Of course we came through the roof, Bal. Use your damn eyes."

Zee shouldered past me, kneeling beside Mira. "Go to your brother," she ordered, taking Tass's wrist and testing it for a pulse. "Explain."

Mira nodded, but didn't move. Her eyes were glued on Tass's face. "After . . . after the lightning hit Paasch, Tass grabbed me. She carried me out the window to the terrace outside. But she didn't bother with the zip line. It's like she knew Paasch was going to destroy the wall. She didn't even hesitate. She just . . . jumped."

My mind blanked at her words. I looked from my sister to the still-closed balcony doors. Through the glass, I could see the towering side of the temple. But even a street away, I could barely make out the top terrace. It simply wasn't . . .

"Impossible," Kai exclaimed.

Mira spun, lip curled. "Whatever, Kai. You weren't there. *I* was. I'm the one who flew from the temple through that roof. I don't know how she did it, but it *is freaking* possible."

Kai opened his mouth to argue.

"It's not important now," Edik cut in from the doorway where he kept watch.

"Not important? She's saying Tass *flew*—"

"Not important. We need to get out of here."

Edik was right. "Zee, is she alive?" I asked.

"Yeah, but—"

"Good," I said, not wanting to hear more. "Edik, carry Tass. Everyone else: move."

8

BALTHAZAR

The only good thing about the storm was that it forced the denizens of Cothis to seek shelter inside. It was a reprieve, but I knew it wouldn't last. We ran through the darkened streets, passing abandoned street-carts and empty carriages while crossing one canal after the next toward the Low Temple. Though I saw no one, the closed-up homes and shops seemed to watch us with wide, hungry eyes. We kept to the back alleys, tempering the need for haste against an equal need for stealth. By the time I eased open the Low Temple's side door, our clothes were almost dry.

I hurried everyone up to the attic and bolted the door shut behind us. Snatching one of Shasheba's stupid pink lamps from the nearest table, I lit it, ignoring the tremor rattling the bones in my hand.

Shasheba. Shit.

I headed up the stairs, my steps heavy in the temple's oppressive silence. Dread coiled inside me, clawing up the back of my throat. The plan was always that if things went sideways, Shasheba was supposed to stay behind while we escaped. But after everything we'd seen . . . I swallowed hard, clutching the railing so tight my joints ached. Never in my darkest dreams did I think things could go so wrong.

Plan or no, I was sure that if by some miracle we all survived this, Shasheba would never forgive me for leaving her behind. Again.

I pushed into the attic room, adding my lamp to the crowd of lanterns on the floor. They surrounded the cot where Tass lay. A loose halo of unanswered prayers. Zee was perched on the edge of the bed, working furiously at all the buckles and straps across Tass's tunic. I made myself turn away.

But the sight of Zee's bloodstained hands haunted me. I went to the workbench where Kai hovered with a grave expression. Edik had turned away from us entirely.

On his knees, head tilted up to the window, he murmured a soft prayer to Janus, Prince of Heaven. The words were worn. A soldier's prayer for peace after battles well fought but lost. The fuck he hoped to gain by it, I had no idea. Whatever had happened in the temple was no well-fought battle.

This was a total cock-up . . . and it started with the prone woman on the cot.

There was an undercurrent of fear beneath my anger—all the more bitter for my helplessness. I snatched a discarded towel from the edge of the table, raked my bloody palms across it like the rough weave could scour my hands clean. I knew a vain attempt when I saw one, but it steadied me somewhat.

Death's suffocating shade clouded the room, waiting to strike. After everything I'd seen tonight, the lightning, the bodies, that broken zip line . . . all of it was unbelievable. But the knowledge that Tass was probably going to die felt like one thing too many. Too much to fully comprehend.

Somehow, I'd never considered the possibility that Tass would be in danger. Even though hers was the most dangerous job, the idea that she might be wounded, that she might die, never even crossed my mind. She was a legend. The godsdamned Queen of Days. She'd pulled off so much worse than a simple heist. From the moment I met her, Tass had seemed so far beyond the worries of mere mortals. Invincible, almost. And now?

"Please tell me someone understands what just happened." Kai's hands were braced on the table, head bowed low between his shoulders. He looked at me, eyes bright with fear. "I mean, first she breaks the statue—but, why? Why would she do that?"

"I'm not sure." I shook my head, trying and failing to shake loose some kind of explanation. "Maybe she knew what was about to happen?" It felt like a long shot, but what other possible explanation was there? Either she guessed what Paasch was about to do, or . . .

Or breaking the idol *caused* it.

"But how could she know?" Kai asked, rising to his full height with a gulp of air. "And the light. What was that? It hit Paasch. But he didn't die? How is that possible? And you saw what happened when Tass grabbed Mira. A bolt of lightning shot out of his hand, Bal—a *bolt of fucking lightning*."

"I know. I saw." I struggled to keep my voice even, sensing that Kai wavered dangerously on the edge of panic. "I don't understand it any more than you do, but—"

"All those people." Edik angled his chin toward me, eyes open, but vacant. Like he was still lost in the temple, witnessing the carnage all over again. "Hundreds of them, left out to die in the storm. Were they—were they sacrificed?" The words hung in the air between us, demanding an answer.

Yes, they were. I swallowed the response, because I wasn't certain. At least my brain wasn't. But I knew in my heart that those workers were meant to die. It couldn't all be some hideous coincidence. And Paasch's final words to me rang in my ears.

Was this the change he'd been boasting of? All those people dead? I shook the thoughts away. The crew was too raw, too frightened to have this discussion. What they needed now was rest. Tomorrow we'd have to clear out. As soon as Shasheba returned, we'd

get off the island. Whatever had happened in that temple, I wasn't
going to wait around to find out. I could explain what happened to
the patron later . . . Oh shit.

The patron.

I winced.

He was going to be livid. He wanted that idol something fierce.
And not only did we fail to get it, but Tass had broken the damned
thing.

And the money . . .

The thought of all that money. Gone.

Yes, we were alive. That was something. But I was hard pressed
to feel good about it right now. Because when the patron found out
how profoundly we'd failed, being alive might not be an asset.

"Let's get some rest while we can," I said, weakness washing
over me.

"But what about Tass?"

I turned toward Mira's voice. She stood at the foot of Tass's bed,
hands wrapped about the strap of a black satchel I hadn't realized
she was wearing. She clutched it with white knuckles like it was all
that kept Tass alive. Tears dripped down Mira's full cheeks, tears she
didn't even try to hide.

I went to her, wrapping my arm around her shoulders. "Zee?"

Zee didn't reply. She'd pulled Tass's tunic open, revealing dark
skin drenched in blood and mottled with huge bruises, clear indica-
tors of several broken bones. But the most obvious wound was the
one that would surely kill: the jagged alabaster edge of a broken rib
had thrust through the flesh above Tass's heart.

I could only guess how many shards of bone had punctured her
lungs and heart. Blood pooled on the floor. So much blood, the
golden tattoos on her chest—beautiful geometric tattoos—had begun to look dull. Lifeless. Zee sat back on the mattress, abandoning
all attempts at triage. She just held Tass's hand. Held her hand and
waited for her to die.

My eyes turned to Tass's silver mask. Even now, with her broken body exposed, I still felt that she should be invincible. That a woman who could break into a jail and walk out the front door, who could take time, and jump nearly a hundred feet couldn't simply die in the cramped attic of some decrepit temple.

It wasn't right. Wasn't fair. But I knew better than to expect fairness out of life. Or death.

Tass took a shuddering breath. And went still.

Mira turned her face into my chest, her body shaking as she tried to contain a sob. I held on to her, letting her cry for me too. Though I'd known Tass for all of two days, and though she often scared and baffled me, something about her had drawn me in. A connection I still didn't understand, but that felt like friendship. Or at least the beginnings of one.

And that this was her end? It was like seeing all the great heroes of every tale I'd loved die in freak accidents. It shouldn't happen, and for an instant I wished I'd met her sooner, if only to see what crazy, inhuman, impossible feat she'd accomplish tomorrow.

"What the hell?" Zee jumped to her feet like she'd been shocked.

"Zee?"

With an incoherent cry, she seized my arm with one hand, pointed at Tass with the other.

"What is it?"

My eyes bulged at the answer. Mira gasped as the broken rib slid silently back into Tass's body.

The whole crew drew closer to the bed. We stood, awed, as the bruises on her torso swirled beneath her skin. Then dissipated like so much smoke. We watched the blood that pooled on her stomach and ran rivers down to the bed, retract. As impossible as water falling up a cliff, it seeped softly back into her flesh. Even more impossibly, her chest shuddered. Her lungs expanded in a single rattling breath. Then a second. A third.

Edik muttered a prayer. Kai, an oath. Shock rippled across Zee's face. "How can this be?"

The building around us groaned and sighed as if echoing my relief. I shook my head. "How is anything we've seen tonight possible?" I asked on a breath of laughter, the kind that skirted too close to hysteria.

Zee and I flanked the cot, kneeling on either side of Tass's body. Her chest rose and fell in slow, even breaths, but she didn't move or speak. It was as if she were simply asleep. Given what she'd just gone through, it was oddly the most natural thing I'd seen tonight.

With shaking hands, Zee probed the skin on Tass's chest, but no wounds remained. And her skin—it wasn't black. Not really. It was purple and blue, like the swirling space between stars. Not even a shadow of a scar marred the mound of her breast. And her tattoos flushed once more with life. They weren't gold. They were copper. Repeating ladder patterns inlaid down the flesh of her chest and stomach. Her unmarred, unscathed flesh.

I pulled my eyes away, cleared my throat. Her veil had come loose during the night along with a lock of . . . *hair?*

I picked it up without thought, letting the silky strand slide through my fingers. It was perfectly gray—and not the iron-gray or white of age. It was the gray of ash, the gray of a baby bird. The comparison hadn't come to my mind without reason.

"Is that a feather?" Mira asked in breathless wonder.

I shook my head, but then nodded, my lips too numb for speech. The lock didn't end in so many strands like every other person in the room. It ended in a black feather, not tied or fastened in any way that I could see but fused perfectly with the shaft of her hair.

Tassiel.

Her name had sounded familiar. Now I knew why. The tassiel falcon was a raptor native only to the mountains of Arisha.

What the ever-living fuck?

I'd thought the mask and veil was nothing but a conceit, a way for her to keep her identity secret. Now I knew better. Because if this was her hair—if this was her skin—then she wasn't simply hiding who she was. But *what* she was. Something as different and other and awe-inspiring as she was. I looked at the edges of her scrolling mask, fingers itching to take it off.

My hand rose of its own accord, sliding under one blunt edge.

Another hand flew up faster than my sight could register. It fastened around my wrist, squeezing so hard, my bones nearly bent. I stilled, looking down at the gloved hand and slowly up again to Tass's black-veiled eyes.

I grinned. "About time you woke up."

"Quite," was her clipped reply. I sensed her glaring at me from behind the mask, but I was so relieved she was alive, I couldn't care less. After a moment she snorted, shaking her head at my grin, and released me.

Sitting up, Tass swung her legs over the edge of the bed, ignoring the way the others . . .

Retreated. There wasn't another word for it. Kai didn't even hide his flight, as he all but ran to the other side of the room, keeping the table between him and Tass. Only Mira and I remained by her side, and Mira was watching Tass with complete shock on her tearstained face.

"But . . . But you were dead." Mira pressed a shaking hand to Tass's arm like she couldn't quite believe what she was seeing.

Tass did up the buttons on her tunic before looking at my sister. Whatever she saw in Mira's stricken face made her sigh. "No, little one," she said with a gentle voice. "I *mostly* died. It happens from time to time."

"You really are a demon," Kai whispered, his normally tan skin a sickly shade of green.

Tass *tsk*ed. "I am *not* a demon, Malakai. We have been through this before."

"Then you better start explaining what you are, because 'human' ain't on that list, darling," he said, all bluster and bravado now that he had some distance from her.

Tass planted a fist on her hip, shifting her weight so one leg was straight. I didn't need to see her face to know she was annoyed. Just about every woman I'd ever met had taken that stance before dressing Kai down. "Is my heritage really what we should be talking about now?"

"No. It's not," I said, sliding into the space between Tass and Kai.

Now that Tass was up and apparently unhurt, all the adrenaline in my body evaporated. My limbs felt oddly boneless, and I wanted nothing more than to curl up and go to sleep. Unfortunately, my cot was soaked from Tass's wet clothes.

Even if it hadn't been, Kai, Edik, and Zee all wore similar looks of astonishment and suspicion. They were more likely to attack Tass than go to sleep. Not that I blamed them. Even if she hadn't just risen from the dead, she *had* broken the godsdamned idol we were hired to steal and nearly gotten Mira killed.

It's amazing how quickly grief can turn to anger when the reason for that grief rises from the fucking grave.

I leaned against the table, looking hard at each member of the crew, willing them to calm down. "We've seen one impossible thing after another tonight. And if we're going to figure out what to do next, we need to know what just happened. Starting at the beginning." I turned to Tass. "Why did you break the idol?"

"Why did I break it?" she snapped. "Why do you think I broke it? You saw what happened, Bal. You saw the lightning."

"Yes, but *why* did it happen, Tass?" I held up my hands for peace when she crossed her arms. "Look at it from my perspective: You break the idol and then lightning starts destroying everything. Everyone. I don't *think* they're connected, but you have to see how it looks to us, right? I'm just trying to understand."

She hissed out a breath. "You people. You create these kingdoms, these cities which you dedicate to your gods. You make homes for them in your temples. You create idols to give them form allowing them to walk among you. Did you really think that none would ever try to come through fully? To claim what you so readily surrender?"

"So, you knew this would happen? You knew about the light?"

"No—I would never have taken this job if I knew what was going to happen. But when we arrived at the temple, I sensed something was off. I said as much to Kai and Edik after putting Edik's sergeant to sleep."

My mind stuttered over that last line and, by the sound of it, Tass's did too. She paused a moment, before shaking her head at some thought I couldn't read.

"The metal latticework added to my suspicion. All that copper—it made no sense."

I shot a quick glance at Zee, and even drenched in suspicion and shock, she still gave me an "I told you so" look as Tass continued. "Then I saw the idol and I knew. It was covered in inscriptions; ancient spells that humanity should have forgotten eons ago, enchantments to ease the opening of a portal from the Nethersphere and contain a living soul."

My mind tried to hold the word "Nethersphere," but it slipped through my grasp as incredulity clouded my brain. The Nethersphere was the world of the gods, containing the Heavens Above and the Great Below. I knew people—the religious or superstitious—believed it, but it wasn't supposed to be . . . *real*.

"All right," Zee said, pushing her hair out of her eyes. "Putting aside the fact that the Nethersphere isn't a real place"—Edik growled at that last part, but Zee silenced him with a pointed glare—"what is it that the spells were supposed to do? You said it opened a portal. Assuming, for a moment, that magic exists: What came through?"

"How can you deny the Nethersphere exists? How can you even ask this?" Tass demanded with no small amount of anger. "You *saw*."

"I saw light. I saw an electrical current," Zee said, bringing to mind one of our more eccentric tutors who ran experiments with something called electricity. It was all beyond me, but nothing ever confused Zee for long.

"No, Zeelaya. Or . . . perhaps yes, but what you saw was not simple energy. It was a sentient being which crossed over from the Nethersphere."

Zee's eyes narrowed. "Clearly your brain is still healing from that fall. Electricity can't be sentient, it's—"

"There was a voice," I said, cutting through Zee's doubt. She might be unconvinced, but I wasn't so sure now. "I heard a voice in the light. Though I didn't understand the words." Then again, I hadn't needed to. I more than recognized the rage.

"I heard it too," Mira whispered.

"The creature lacked form on this plane of existence," Tass continued. "That's why I broke the idol. I thought it would induce him to retreat."

"Him?" Zee's voice was sharp, beating me to the question.

"You know him, don't you?" Mira asked, and though she spoke softly, the question echoed. "He's Ankaari. Like you."

I spun toward Tass, my legs suddenly weak. "Ankaari?"

Her silence was its own kind of answer.

"Bullshit," Kai swore in flat denial. "I don't know what happened in that temple, but I know a load of crap when I hear it."

"Kai—"

"No, Mira. I don't care what she says," he began, stabbing a finger at Tass, "or whatever you believe, Edik. There is no magical race of gods watching over us. And even if there were, no Ankaari would want anything from a shithole like Cothis."

"Cothis could be a ruin and it would not matter. Total dominion is all the incentive he required."

"I don't believe you." Kai bellowed the words. "I don't believe a single thing you've said tonight. Ankaari? Magic? What next? Are you going to tell us that you're some legendary Septiniri warrior?

Half mortal, half divine? Like Calien the Bodysnatcher or Gul the Brave, sent here to protect us?"

"I do indeed believe I was sent here to protect you," was her soft reply.

I didn't need to see her face to recognize the hedge. Few things tripped an honest person up so much as a half-truth.

"Shut your—"

"Kai," I said, holding up a hand. "Enough."

"Come on, Bal." His eyes were pleading. "You're not really buying this, are you?"

"We're alive, aren't we?" I must have looked as tired as I felt, for Kai backed down. "So breaking the idol—robbing us of our payoff—was your idea of protecting us?"

"Yes," she replied simply.

"You did a pretty shit job, then."

"If money is all you care about then I am forced to agree," she said, disappointment edging into her voice. "If the creature had been allowed to inhabit the idol . . ." Tass's words trailed off. She shook her head. "The city would be lost. Which makes me wonder: Why did your patron want the idol in the first place? How did he know what would happen?"

It was a damn good question. I had no evidence he did in fact know, yet there wasn't a doubt in my mind that he must have. His requirements were just too exact, and there was something wily about the old man, a hint of otherness that reminded me too much of Tass. "I don't know."

"I want to meet him."

Under normal circumstances the demand would have rankled, but I was secretly glad she'd be coming with me. The patron's home wasn't a place I wanted to return to alone. Or empty-handed. "All right. We'll go at first light."

"No," Tass said with a sharp cutting gesture. "We need to go now."

I looked at her, incredulous. Mira was practically swaying on her feet, and to be frank the rest of the crew was beginning to flag as their adrenaline waned. But more than that, I needed a minute to think, to gain my bearings. "We need to rest, Tass, even if it's only for a few hours."

"We have already been here too long. They could come for us at any moment."

I didn't bother asking who the nebulous "they" were. No doubt Paasch, or whatever was left of him, would be looking for the person who'd broken the idol. Still, we would be fine here for a few more hours. Truthfully, I couldn't see we had a choice.

"Bal, think it through," Tass pressed, clearly seeing my resistance. "They saw Mira holding the broken idol. They saw me flee with her, but more importantly they saw her in temple robes."

My gaze cut to Mira. She was still in her blue dress, though it was slightly rumpled and more than a little stained.

"It won't take them long to make the connection to the Low Temple, if they haven't already."

"But this wasn't the only temple to send acolytes to the consecration ceremony. A Nananthean temple in Eshara also sent some. They were all wearing the same robes," Edik said, though his face was pinched like he was doubting his words as he spoke them.

I nodded, clinging to a confidence that part of me knew was unfounded. "Shasheba won't give us up." I glared at Kai when he snorted and Tass's stance shifted just enough to know she thought I was being an idiot too. "She wouldn't give up *Mira*." My insistence sounded feeble to my own ears, and Tass's warning about Shasheba rang in my mind.

"If that was the case," Tass began, her tone more than a little loaded, "if Shasheba denied knowing anything and successfully cleared the Low Temple of suspicion, then where is everyone? How much time has passed since our escape? An hour? More?"

"There's a storm," I said, the words feeble to my own ears. "And the plan was always for Shasheba to stay behind. We all knew that everyone would be questioned, and that kind of investigation can take hours."

"But nothing could have prepared her for what actually happened. She could be the best liar in the world, but can she withstand a true interrogation?" Tass shifted closer, willing me to believe her. "Just because she does not wish to give Mira up, does not mean she won't."

I looked at the people around me, my family. The silence in the temple below seemed to boil, gathering steam. Ready to blow.

Tass clasped my arm. "Bal, I do not know how much of Governor Paasch is left, but he saw you flee. He saw Zeelaya. It will only take him a moment to identify Kai. He may not know Edik, and maybe he did not recognize Miraveena, but he will not need to. He will guess that the girl he saw—the girl who is the right age to be your sister—*is* your sister. If you believe nothing else I have told you about the Nethersphere and the creature that came through the portal, then believe your own instinct and ask yourself this:

"How far would Paasch go to punish you for ruining his ceremony?"

My gaze rose immediately to Kai. He straightened, eyes widening with the same conclusion I was coming to. "Shit."

9

BALTHAZAR

"We gotta go."

There was a second of silence that followed my command. Then Edik pulled himself straight and clapped his hands twice, jolting everyone to action. "You heard the man. We evac in ten. Everyone, change out of your disguises. Your go bags are under your cots. Pack essentials only."

Thanks to Edik's foresight and extraordinary organization skills, we made it out of the Low Temple in less than ten minutes. Though the streets of the Middlemarch were still empty from the storm, that soon changed as we neared the harbor. This was the one day and night of the year that all the dockies and sailors had off. No amount of rain was about to stop their fun—a fact that electrified the air with the tang of frenzy. I kept a firm hand on Mira's shoulder as we wove through the crowd.

At least until she swatted me aside. "Quit grabbing me. You look like a creep."

"*Mira*," I hissed her name through my teeth. "This is a dangerous part of town."

"Then hold on to Kai's hand," she said, rolling her eyes. "He's the only one likely to wander off."

Which . . . okay. Fair. With the bars filled to capacity and the party spilling onto the streets I ordinarily wouldn't put it past Kai to take a stroll. But this was far from ordinary. "The only one who left their post tonight was you."

"I was following Tass," was her cold reply. "I don't see you yelling at her."

The fact that I hadn't begun yelling was apparently lost on her. "Tass can handle herself."

"So can I," she spat, her eyes welling the way they always did when she got angry. Which only ever made her angrier. "I'm not a kid. Stop treating me like one."

Mira ducked her head low and cut past me, planting herself between Edik and Zee. With her arms wrapped around her middle she looked even smaller than usual. More like the six-year-old she'd been, watching our parents die.

It took half a block to banish that image back to the recesses of my memory where it belonged. But I managed it, just as I dodged puddles of trash and filth. The cries of celebration raked against me. It was a lust for life that I could almost taste. It was like the people of Cothis were celebrating in defiance of the swirling sky, like they were determined to live before those skeletal forks of lightning came to claim them. Before the creature inside the temple stepped out to survey his new kingdom.

I tried not to look at it, tried not to acknowledge the way my gut twisted each time the lightning flashed. Tried not to glance over my shoulder. But I did. With each rumbling stroke of illumination, my gaze dragged inexorably back to the temple. It glowed starkly white against the night sky like a misshapen skull. A herald of more pain to come.

But not for me and my crew. I focused on our route, leading us through the night toward the sea and then skirting the coastline until we left the party behind.

By the time we hit the western side of the harbor, the wharves and warehouses gave way to modest homes and narrow lanes. It was far from the richest part of Cothis, but even though the row houses all slanted inward, and refuse congealed in the gutters, it wasn't the poorest part either. Eventually, even these neighborhoods petered out as we continued west, and the land banked upward.

The Western Hill, as it was so creatively called, was the only place below the Grand Canal that cut the island in two, where the land naturally reached out of the sea. It jutted from the water like a crooked knuckle of gray rock. Every few decades someone—usually some overeducated lordling from Sala—got the brilliant idea to build a house there.

On the surface it wasn't a terrible idea, but on Cothis the surface was almost always an inch from the swirling waters of a cold death. Nowhere was that more true than Western Hill.

Though the land was ostensibly higher, this lonely spar of rock was always hit hardest by winter storms, and scoured bare by punishing summer winds. Nothing man-made could ever survive. Even nature struggled to assert herself here. Only sparse patches of hardy scrub grass grew on the hill, giving it a slightly desolate feeling even in the middle of the day.

Now, with night sticking to our backs, it was deserted. Unnaturally cold wind picked at my clothes. It slipped its fingers beneath my collar, scraping at my skin. I pulled my jacket closer to my body and squinted at the earth, barely making out what once could have been described as a path. Now it could only charitably be called a dent in the ground.

Zee shouldered up next to me as we stumbled up the hill in the darkness. "I cannot believe you didn't tell me *he* was our patron." She spoke in an undertone, but in the silence, her words carried.

I gave her a flat look. "Who else would hire us for this job?"

"What were you thinking, Bal?" Zee's voice dipped low, like it couldn't bare all the disgust she felt. "No. Don't bother answering that. You weren't thinking. Not with *him,* not with giving our time to *her,* not with *anything.*"

I resisted the urge to close my eyes against it. To bow to guilt. Because the patron funding this job wasn't a man to be trifled with. The Curator only ever contracted out for the rarest of finds. The most dangerous.

And though Zee, Kai, and I had known the man since childhood, the one job we had done for him in the past—a bank heist on Rocanthe—had been so crazy, so risky, Zee had flat refused to work for him ever again.

So I hadn't told her. And yeah, I understood why she was pissed. But was now really the time?

Apparently so. "How could you trust him?"

"I don't," I snapped, anger pushing back the guilt. "But you know how much money was on offer."

"You still should have told us. His last job nearly killed us all. If I'd known—"

"You still would have said yes."

Edik took a step forward at the heat in my voice. "Watch it, Bal."

"No, you watch it," I said, rounding on him. Edik had done nothing but complain since we took this job. Since *I* took this job. First about the plan. Then Tass.

I was done with it.

"It's easy to be all high-minded in hindsight, but you know that a prize like this will change our lives—all of our lives. And I didn't have time to consult you all. He put me on the spot. I had to decide right there. So yeah, I agreed. Of course I did. Because this was exactly what we've been looking for all these years. I cut out the four days of bitching you'd have dragged us through and agreed."

"And look where it got us."

"Don't you fucking put that on me," I said, balling my fists. "There's no way I could have known—"

"Enough," Zee said, sliding into the narrow gap separating Edik and I. "We deserved to know," she said again, softer now. "But we can argue about it later."

"If we're still alive," Edik muttered. He let Zee tug him forward, but not before throwing me a dark look. A look that promised more words indeed.

I winced. Edik had an annoying habit of keeping his promises.

"Don't know why you're complaining, Zee," Kai said from the back of the line, his voice too-cheery for the tension running between us. "At least he likes you. He always makes me wash my hands when we see him. As if I can't be trusted to clean myself."

"*Can* you be trusted?" Tass asked, voice so bland it drew a laugh from even Edik's sour face.

"Hello?" Mira called, so annoyed she'd dragged the word into four extra syllables. "Other people are present. Would someone care to explain what we're doing here and who 'he' is?"

Zee gave me a quelling glance, and I managed to count to three and contain my exasperation before replying, "Our patron lives here, Mira. He calls himself the Curator. The Curator of the Archive."

"What's the archive?" Mira asked as we crested the hill.

"Not the archive. *The* Archive," I corrected with all the emphasis the Curator demanded.

"Is that supposed to mean something to me?"

"It's a kind of library," Zee panted, holding her arms over her head to catch her breath after the steep climb.

Mira stomped up to Zee and me. She turned in a circle and frowned up at us. "I don't see a library. I don't see *anything*."

"That's because it's underground." My gaze soared past the craggily earth and straight out to the cobalt sea. The waves were heavy, and even though I wasn't close enough to the edge to see them crash against the cliff face, I could hear them.

"We used to call it the Underbrary when we were kids." Kai gave Mira a playful nudge. "Get it? An underground library? The Underbrary?"

"It's a stupid name." The "and you're stupid for saying it" subtext simmered in her glare.

"Yeah," Kai agreed and heaved a sigh. "The Curator thought so too. Best not repeat it. Old coot holds a grudge."

Kai would know, I thought, my legs feeling oddly heavy. Funny, after everything we'd seen tonight, the thought of facing the Curator still gave me pause. My father brought all of the older Vadalen children here, Kai included, as often as he could. We spent many a hot summer day ensconced in the Curator's vast underground domain while my father peppered the Curator's encyclopedic brain with questions.

Too bad the Curator never asked why his protégé was so curious.

The wind seemed to hold its breath as Tass stepped forward. "How do we enter this Archive?"

"There's a staircase down to the entrance," I said, squinting into the darkness, my eyes combing the edge of the cliff. "There." I spotted the slight divot in the earth, where the land flattened out in a three-foot length of too-level stone.

I made my way to the landing and leaned gingerly over, gazing down. Narrow stairs were carved into the stone face of the hill. I could almost imagine a distant past when this winding staircase cut cleanly down the cliff, but time and water had eroded them to a crumbling mess of cracking, uneven steps. They descended a good fifty feet, completely exposed to the water below, before bottoming out in a second narrow landing.

The steps glistened in the moonlight, still wet from the storm and so, so fragile. It would only take one wrong move and they would crumble. This was why I wanted to wait for daylight. Wet steps combined with almost no light were an accident waiting to happen. If any one of us slipped, we'd be sure to meet a nasty death, dashed to bits on the rocks below.

"All right, the steps are wet, so everyone be damned careful," I said. Swallowing hard, bracing for a fight, I turned to Mira. "Climb up on my back. I'll carry you down."

She took a mutinous step back. "No way."

"Mira, this isn't an age thing," I said, sure she was marshaling her tried-and-true "I'm not a kid anymore" argument. "These steps are steep. Walking down them will be risky for everyone, but we have a height advantage. It's too dangerous for you to try, and if you fall here you will die." I paused, glaring at Mira like it could make her understand. "I don't care who carries you, but either someone does, or you stay here."

Mira scowled at me, coiling her arms together. She cast a baleful stare at the adults around her. Only when no one came to her defense did she turn to Tass. I choked.

"Will you carry me?" Mira asked, her words a tiny mumble that nearly tumbled away in the breeze.

Tass cocked her head to the side like she was considering the question. "I will." She knelt, allowing Mira to climb on her back. Once Mira was secured, Tass rose fluidly, as if she hadn't been mortally wounded an hour ago, and nodded to me.

It was slow going down the cliff stair. The steps were so precarious, I was loath to trust them with my weight. I ended up crouching on one leg, gently placing my other foot on the next step to test its strength before transferring my weight.

By the time I reached the bottom landing, my legs were shaking. I shivered as the wind licked the sweat off my face and tugged me toward the edge. A tremble wound down my body as that wind caught my limbs. There was a moment of vertigo, where all I saw was the scant foot of ancient stone separating me from a life-ending fall.

I forced my weight backward, tipping myself toward the slimy cliff wall into which a weather-beaten door was set. Its wooden planks were banded together with iron bars, like at any moment the wood might spring apart and plant roots. Beside the door's massive finger-length hinges, hung a velvet bellpull.

I pulled it down, and registered with some surprise that, despite the torrential rain and the sea snapping its heels, the velvet was perfectly dry. After a moment, I pulled down again. My ears strained, but the waves made it impossible to hear if the bell was ringing within the Archive.

A minute passed. Then another. Cool air shivered through my hair. Did the bell still work? Perhaps the Curator was asleep? Or perhaps he already knew what had happened in the temple and was displeased? He was strangely prescient that way.

Click.

Zee started at the sound of the lock turning. I glanced up the steps at her and she shrugged. Not the best encouragement I'd ever had, but I doubted the night could get any stranger. Urgh. I was an idiot for even thinking the words.

Cursing myself, I turned the handle and pushed open the door.

It always surprised me, coming here. The Archive's entrance looked more like a subterranean street than it did the foyer of a private library. While the walls were as rough and uncut as the cliff face outside, the ground was paved with perfectly square black cobbles. There was even a streetlamp burning up ahead to light the way.

The crew filed in behind me, and the door slid closed quite of its own accord. An ancient skeleton key turned in the door, locking with an echoing *snick* that made Kai jump. He rubbed the back of his head and shot me an angry look, like he expected me to make fun of him. "I hate this place," he grumbled. "Gives me the creeps."

"Yes," Tass replied, like Kai had asked her opinion. She strode to the lamppost, studying it with apparently rapt fascination.

Mira squirmed on Tass's back. "Um. Tass?"

"Yes, Miraveena?"

"You can let me down now."

Tass didn't reply immediately. The lamplight shone across the planes of her silver mask, transforming it into something swirling and liquid. "No, Miraveena. I do not think that would be wise at this juncture."

Her words sucked all the air out of the room. The light flickered. The walls seemed to close in. My hand went to the pistol at my hip, as my heart leaped into my throat.

"Curator?" I called into the darkness beyond the lamp. "It's Balthazar Vadalen. My crew and I are here to close the deal." My voice bounced off the cavernous walls, echoing back to me in a distorted cacophony of unintelligible noise. No response.

I took a slow step backward, prepared to flee.

A second lamp flicked to life in the shadows beyond the first one.

Kai loosed a long breath. My heart slowed. Every time I'd been to the Archive the lamps had been there to light the way to the Curator. I knew on an instinctual level that I did not want to be here when the lamps went out.

I let my hand fall away from the pistol, forced my shoulders to relax, and started walking. Tass joined me as I passed the first lamp.

"Please speak carefully while we're here," I murmured, glancing at her in the semidarkness between the lamplights. "The Curator doesn't tolerate insult to his collection."

Tass *tsk*ed. "I am always careful, Bal. Unlike you and your crew, meddling in places that do not belong."

I frowned, feeling like I should be insulted but simultaneously confused by her words. "What do you mean, 'places that do not belong'?"

She tilted her head toward me. "Where do you think you are right now?"

"Beneath the Western Hill."

Tass's chuckle was darker than the cavern's shadowy roof. "We are most certainly *not* beneath the Western Hill. This is not the world you know."

I wanted to ask what she thought it was, but my sister was still huddled on Tass's back. Mira listened to us with an open mouth. Her frightened eyes darted this way and that, but found no purchase in the gloom. I did notice she didn't loosen her grip around Tass's neck—if anything, she held a bit tighter.

"You're a real bundle of joy, you know that, Tass?" I shook my head and kept walking.

Each time we passed one streetlamp another lit up about ten feet away. A small part of me, a childish corner of my mind that feared the dark unknown, sighed in relief each time, drinking in the light. My crew's shuffling footsteps echoed off the walls, but I didn't look back at them, knowing there was nothing but darkness behind. We walked from one lamppost to the next until the wall on our right fell away, and the ground began to slope down.

Between the next two lights, the cobblestones beneath my feet transformed into lush red carpet. And between the next two, an arched and gilded ceiling appeared. On our right, the first of many massive bookcases emerged in the gloom. They were lined up at equal intervals like soldiers on inspection, following our descent into the earth.

Only the first few feet of each bookcase was visible in the low light, but I knew their shelves delved deep into the darkness. What would happen if we tried going down one of those aisles? Would more lamps flick to life showing me another path down? Or would the world ripple and fold in on itself? Circling me back to where I started?

I gave myself a mental kick in the ass, suppressing the urge to find out. After the disaster of the broken idol, I knew it was better to make our obeisance to the Curator first. As if that would help us. We were probably fools for coming here with nothing to show. Suicidal fools. But we were *here*. No turning back now. And I had the sickening sense that a person could lose themselves forever here. If the Curator wished it.

The path curled in on itself, turning us in circles from one level to the next. It felt like we were walking down a giant nautilus shell. Or an illusionist painting of hypnotic swirls—the kind that had no beginning and no end. And it was that last part that had the hairs on the back of my neck rising in panic. The sense of being trapped in the Curator's web.

After ten interminable minutes, the floor finally leveled out in what looked like a reading room. I paused at the end of the ramp where a pair of giant granite wolves stood sentinel on either side of me. Their snarling faces made for a menacing welcome to the heart of the Curator's kingdom. I used to have nightmares about them as a boy—half sure their stone eyes were watching my every move, like living beasts awaiting the order to kill.

The reading room was an enormous space, scattered with wide gleaming tables and unforgiving chairs. More bookcases crowded the edges of the chamber, arranged in a labyrinthine pattern that made it hard to see the far distant walls. Green-shaded lamps were lit on each table, though no readers sat using them. Several mammoth chandeliers hung from the ceiling, casting even more light around the space, leaving no corner free for darkness to gather.

Directly ahead of us lay a huge desk, its legs carved into beady-eyed griffins. It was perfectly circular with a large, open middle where someone could sit and do their work.

Where someone *was* sitting and working.

An old man sat in a wingback chair at the center of the desk. He was hunched over an ancient-looking tome, which had been lovingly placed in an angled bookstand to keep its spine from opening too far.

The Curator's dark skin was creased in a map of fine wrinkles. He had a curling gray beard that fell to the middle of his narrow chest. In my youth I often wondered if he kept it so long to make up for the fact that almost no hair covered his head. The thought made me smile as I opened my mouth to say hello.

He held a single crooked finger up, silencing me. For several unbearable minutes, we stood there while he finished his reading like naughty children waiting for punishment. *Damn it, Bal,* I thought, thoroughly hating my brain.

Eventually he laid a silky black ribbon along his page and closed the book. His eyes, when he looked up at us through his wire spectacles, were a deep dark brown and completely unamused.

"Good evening, Balthazar. Zeelaya, Edik." His keen gaze landed on Kai and then slowly down to Kai's hands. Frowned. "Malakai. You're early. Have you come from the temple?"

"Yes."

"Very good," he said, before I could say more. He gestured to the others. "Introductions, if you please, although I assume this is your younger sister?"

"Yeah, this is Mira and Tass." One of the Curator's wiry brows arched high on his forehead. I licked my lips. "Tass is the Queen of Days," I explained, wincing as my words hit the floor.

The Curator took one look at Tass and came out from behind his desk. He stopped only a foot away from her and peered deep into her mask. He didn't seem to be looking at it. But *through* it. The air in the room grew dense and charged as they surveyed one another. The candles dimmed. "Do you know who I am?"

"Yes," Tass replied, her voice packing too much emotion into such a small word. A long breath hissed out from behind her lacquered lips. "You are not supposed to be here."

At that, the Curator smiled, and the lights regained their strength. "One could say the same for you, my dear. But this is ancient history," he began, waving his hand airily.

"Welcome to my home," he said, and though he was smiling at all of us now, it was clear he was mainly addressing Mira and Tass.

"Please know that while you are here, you are welcome to peruse my collection and admire its countless artifacts. But be aware that should you try and take anything from my Archive without my express permission, I will rend you limb from limb and leave your body to rot in my halls as a warning for future guests."

His voice was genial, friendly even. But the threat implied in his speech echoed with a too-animal growl and a whiff of sulfuric wind. A tiny squeak escaped Mira's mouth. She ducked her head behind Tass with such obvious fear, the Curator's attention shot toward her.

"You are wise in your choice of protector, little one. But even this old warrior would struggle to defeat me in my own domain." He chuckled as if he'd told a good joke. "Come. You look tired. And hungry. We will sit while we speak."

He beckoned us forward with a careless gesture. We followed him past the reading desk and down a short corridor of shelves that ended in a decidedly nondescript door. The Curator ushered us through, and I found myself in what looked like the sitting room of a posh men's club.

Wood covered nearly every surface, from the dark paneled walls to the equally dark glass-covered curio cabinets. A pair of crimson claw-footed couches sat facing each other in the center of the room and flanking them were four overstuffed chairs. Just past this cozy sitting area, a fire danced merrily behind the grate of an oversized hearth.

I didn't think it would be possible for me to be hungry, but my gaze landed on the long coffee table nestled between the couches. Several overflowing trays of pastries, cheese, and cured meats lay on its top. Beside the food stood a delicate silver tea tray with just the right number of cups for everyone gathered.

"Please sit," the Curator said, circling the couches to take a seat nearest the fire.

Awkwardly, no one moved. Being the boss was a real bitch sometimes. I sat pretending that this was all part of a normal day's work. The others followed, though only Kai was bold enough to take any food. From the corner of my eye, I saw Tass set Mira down—hopefully a positive sign. Though the way Mira wedged herself into the corner next to Kai spoiled the thought. Tass, I noticed, remained standing by the door.

I turned back to the Curator and found him watching me over steepled fingers. "I can tell by your expression that you failed."

"Hey, it's not our fault you sent us in there without telling us a flipping portal—"

"Kai," I said sharply, willing my friend to shut up before pulling my attention back to the Curator. "We went to the temple and were in position, exactly as we discussed, but . . ."

"But?"

I scratched one of my eyebrows, and for a moment I couldn't bring myself to speak. I didn't know how the Curator would react when he found out Tass broke the idol, but happy wasn't high on the list. "The idol was broken," I hedged.

The Curator folded his hands in his lap, giving me his complete and considerable attention. "How did it break?"

I pressed my lips together. I really didn't want to roll on Tass. She'd saved Mira's life. But I sensed this was a question that I had to answer truthfully, or all my friends would die. "Tass broke the idol."

The Curator brightened. "Good."

Kai surged to his feet, the teacup in his hand crashing to the floor. "Good? What in the burning Great Below do you mean, *good*? She broke the damn idol."

The Curator nodded like Kai's hulking rage was nothing of note and took a sip of tea. "Yes, I thought she might."

Kai sputtered. His face went purple as he gestured wordlessly at the Curator and Tass and me. I glanced at Zee in time to see her roll her eyes. We'd evidentially reached that stage in Kai's anger where words were no longer possible.

"Kai, sit down," I said.

"No. Not until he explains why he sent us into a death trap with this . . . this thing." He stabbed his finger toward Tass.

"I sent you to steal the idol to prevent the city from being destroyed. I wanted Tassiel to accompany you to give you a chance to survive—much though I regret that now."

"The weapon of last resort," I said, recalling his words as I dug my fingers into my temples. "Is this what you had planned all along?"

"Indeed."

"Yeah, I'm sure you thought it was a brilliant plan," Kai said, finding his voice again. "Except the time-eating demon almost got Mira killed."

The Curator scoffed. "Please. Tassiel isn't a demon, you superstitious twit. She's a Septiniri warrior. You should be honored she agreed to help you. In fact—" The Curator straightened, confusion pulling at the wrinkles on his face. "Did you say 'time-eating'?" He looked at Kai, but my friend couldn't answer. At the word "Septiniri" Kai had sunk back into his seat, his face ashen.

"Seriously?" It was all my overcrowded brain could supply. Septiniri? Kai had once said it as a joke, but the Curator *knew* it.

The Curator cocked his head in Tass's direction. "What are you up to, my dear?"

Tass's answering chuckle poured into the edges of the room. She walked forward with what I could only classify as a strut and took the armchair across from the Curator. "Oh, you know," she replied with a regal shrug. "Just passing time."

The Curator tossed his head back and laughed. The fire in the hearth brightened momentarily. I squinted, but the illumination didn't offer an explanation. Neither the Curator nor Tass seemed inclined to comment further. Frustration welled up inside me, merging with stale fear until it became something I had no name for, but really, *really* didn't like.

Damn them both, I thought, feeling like I was drowning in a sea of things I didn't understand. Between everything that had occurred in the temple, everything Tass had tried to tell us at Shasheba's, and now . . . what?

When the Curator's laughter subsided, so did the extra light. "So. The idol. You brought me the pieces."

I winced. "No."

All the merriment slid off the Curator's face, drawing the light down with it. What remained was a wrinkled husk with too-bright eyes. "You mean you left the broken idol in the temple?"

I tried to swallow. "Yes."

"No." Tass's voice spoke over mine, and the Curator's attention snapped to her. "Or, not entirely anyway. Miraveena." She held out a hand to my sister who wriggled the black satchel off her shoulder and passed it to Tass.

"It's my fault. I thought with the idol broken, he would retreat. By the time I realized I was wrong, it was almost too late. I was able to recover part of the idol. Not all. But enough—for now, anyway." Tass shoved a black gloved hand into the satchel and removed the top half of a statue. She passed it to the Curator without further comment.

He held the statue to the firelight and inspected it with greedy eyes. From far away, I had thought there was something unfinished about the idol. Like it had been something of a rush job on behalf of a new sculptor. But up close I realized that the sculptor wasn't a novice, or they hadn't been. The idol was carved with heavily stylized features common in artifacts from old Soria and stained with the blue patina of age. It was ancient.

"Balthazar," the Curator said, still gazing at the idol. "Tell me what happened in the temple."

Recounting the story was easy. Gods knew I'd been going over it in my head nonstop all night.

By the time I finished, the Curator had set the idol in his lap and was looking at me with brows raised. "Don't you know what you saw, boy?"

I opened my mouth to answer but different words tumbled out. Words born of years, years of anger and hate and—

"Is Paasch dead?"

The look of understanding I received in reply nearly broke something in me. But I couldn't break now. I had to know.

"Yes, my boy. Paasch is dead. Though by the time this is all over, you may wish otherwise." He turned to Tass. "Didn't you explain it to them?"

"I tried," she said with a note of defensiveness. "They declined to believe my explanations. You know how times have changed." She waved a hand in Zee's direction. "Scientists everywhere."

"Indeed," was the dry reply as Zee ruffled at the derogatory use of "scientist." "Well, the main thing is that the idol is broken. Do you know who was trying to come through the portal?"

"Karanis."

"What?" My voice was ragged to my own ears.

"You're sure?" the Curator asked, ignoring me.

"Yes. I am sure," Tass replied, her voice dropping an octave.

"Hmm." The Curator scratched his chin, dislodging a few crumbs from his beard. "I don't remember Karanis being so courageous. He can't have been certain he would succeed. I'm surprised he didn't send a vanguard through first."

"Unless he *is* the vanguard."

The ceiling creaked high above my head. Like the unnamed dread her words caused had been given form and freedom to creep through the Archive.

The Curator's shoulders slumped. "Let's not borrow trouble, my dear."

"Karanis?" I asked, my eyes swinging back and forth as I tried vainly to keep up with their tête-à-tête. "You think the sea god, *Karanis,* came out of the Nethersphere to possess that idol?"

"Yes, Balthazar. Do keep up," the Curator said, shooting me a disapproving look.

"Karanis will not be able to use half an Idol," Tass said, as if she was trying to make me feel better. "That was why he possessed the governor, but he cannot survive long in a flesh form."

"That's about the only good news," the Curator grumbled, and even though I only understood a quarter of what they were saying, I was inclined to agree with him. "Still. Karanis will be vulnerable. His powers will be hampered, and he certainly won't want to risk burning out the body before he has the rest of the idol. It's not much in terms of blessings, but . . ."

The Curator seemed to sink into himself, consumed with his own thoughts. Eventually, he waved a hand in front of his face like he was clearing away cobwebs. "Well, there's nothing we can do now."

"Now?" I asked, instincts on high alert.

"Yes," the Curator replied. "You should all get some rest."

"What do you mean, *now?*"

"Tomorrow will undoubtedly be most trying."

Fuck everything, I thought, my whole damn face going numb. Just not numb enough to stop the next question. "What's tomorrow?"

The Curator flashed a wolfish smile. "Tomorrow, Balthazar, you kill a god."

10

BALTHAZAR

Edik made a strangled noise. "You cannot be serious," he
said, pressing three fingers to his forehead in a silent prayer.

"Why ever not?" the Curator snapped, his eyebrows
arching like bushy caterpillars on his forehead.

"It is rather dramatic, for one thing." There was a touch of re-
proach in Tass's voice, but none of the abject shock that was currently
bouncing through my crew. "Karanis is not a god."

"Semantics. He is to *them*," the Curator replied. "I am simply
attempting to increase their understanding by using their own ter-
minology."

"It is imprecise."

"Is it?" he challenged. "What must beetles think of mankind?"

"Enough." My voice scraped out of my throat. What little pride I
had left bridled at being compared to a beetle, but I pushed the feeling away. It wasn't important. All that mattered was the Curator's
assertion that we were somehow responsible . . . and that it was our
mess to fix. Bullshit. "It's not our responsibility to kill Karanis, god
or otherwise."

"It wasn't Karanis," Edik said with the wavering denial of a man whose faith was being sorely tested. "It can't be."

The Curator frowned at Edik's outburst but ignored it by turning to me instead. "I don't believe I said it was your responsibility," he said, "though as a citizen of Cothis—indeed as a member of humanity—it could be considered your duty. But if such things are powerless to move you into doing what must be done, then consider it a matter of self-interest."

"How?" I demanded. No way I was going to let him guilt me into a suicide mission. Whatever the Curator said, I was not responsible for Cothis, let alone all of humanity. I was responsible for Mira, then my crew, and then myself.

That was it.

"Karanis saw you and your companions break the idol," the Curator said. "He saw you take half of it—the half he now needs in order to survive. He will be looking for you. And don't think that it's only Paasch's face he took, but the whole of his experience too. Once Karanis has had time to peruse all those dark memories, he'll know exactly how to hurt you. I daresay it will be like the governor himself is hunting you. Albeit a version of Paasch soiled by madness and magic. What do you think will happen when he finds you?"

"Something colorful, I imagine," I said, sounding far colder than I felt, because the thought of facing Paasch again . . . it wasn't just terrifying. It was shamefully exhilarating. For in my heart of hearts I knew that watching him die wasn't enough.

But it would have to be.

Wouldn't it?

"Very colorful," the Curator agreed. "Mostly reds, I'd wager."

"Then he won't find us," Kai said, though without the bravado tinting his voice, it sounded oddly small. But it was enough to jar me back to myself. I coiled my bloodlust back into my chest as Kai continued, "We have the *Fortune's Fool*. We can get to it and get the ever-living fuck out of this kingdom."

The Curator turned to Kai slowly, disdain scrawled across his wrinkled face. "Would you really, Malakai? Would you really flee to your airship and doom your people to a life lived under Karanis's thumb? You saw what he did to reach this island, the people he sacrificed. Would you leave them to save your own skin?"

"But Karanis can't stay here for long," I said, willing my brain to move, to suspend the denial I so desperately wanted to cling to. Karanis couldn't be in Cothis. Whatever happened in that temple, whatever power Paasch now possessed, it couldn't be from a fucking god.

But . . .

But the Curator and Tass clearly believed it.

They couldn't be right. Could they?

"Karanis greatly weakened himself by taking Paasch's form," the Curator said, taking me in with glittering eyes. "So it really shouldn't be a great difficulty to kill him."

"Goody," I snapped. "Then *you* do it."

"Why should an old man move when I have you bright young things arrayed before me?" he said, gesturing to all of us like we were no more than a few books in his collection. He chuckled, the laugh curling maliciously at the edges. I refused to rise to the bait.

"You said he can't survive in a flesh form. Eventually he'll burn out Paasch's body."

"That is correct," Tassiel said, nodding.

"So either way, Paasch is dead," I said, more to myself than anyone else—as if speaking the words into the semidarkness could soothe the beast of vengeance raging in my chest.

"That's what you care about right now?" Edik demanded as if it wasn't a valid freaking point. As if the need to know, to be utterly certain, about that fact wasn't thrumming through me like a second heartbeat.

"Bal." Tassiel's voice was steady and solid as the foundation of the earth. "Trust me. Paasch is already dead."

That phantom heart went still. And I almost, almost felt relieved. Not the time to dwell on that emotion, I thought, turning back to the matter at hand. All twelve thousand of them.

"And without form, Karanis will die."

"He cannot survive without a form, you are correct about that." Tass leaned forward, bracing her elbows on her knees. "And yes, he will use up Governor Paasch's body in a matter of days. But he has plenty of other bodies to choose from, Bal—a whole city of them, in fact. So long as he conserves some of his power, he will be able to transfer himself from one human host to the next."

Against my will, my mind flashed back to the consecration ceremony, remembering that copper latticework. Remembering too all those terrified nobles crammed in that temple. Selfish people. Useless, overstuffed, entitled assholes.

"Balthazar." Tass's voice was sharp enough to cut skin. I looked up. Her mask's eyeholes threatened to swallow me whole. "Think about what the Curator has told you: Karanis knows everything that Paasch knew. He will know how to hurt you.

"And you left Shasheba behind."

I surged to my feet, pulse pounding in my ears. Though my knees felt like jelly, I made a beeline to the door. I got less than two feet before Kai snagged my arm and swung me around. "Oh, no you don't. I am not risking my life for that woman."

My hands shook as I pushed him away. "I'm not asking you to. I'll do it myself. Just keep Mira safe." My mind was too overwrought, too edged in exhaustion to anticipate the avalanche that met my words. The entire crew leaped up, crowding me, penning me in.

"Balthazar!" Zee exclaimed. "You can't go storming back there without a plan."

"If you'd stop thinking with your pecker for half a second, you wouldn't go back there at all," Kai said, looking like he'd like nothing more than to smack me.

"We don't even have a safe house to flee to, let alone somewhere to hide Mira," Edik added, a low blow in my opinion. "She won't be safe as long as we're on the island. None of us will."

"Silence!" The Curator's bellow contained the crash of thunder and everyone but Tass ducked.

The Curator rose, arms crossed. "The Archive is closed for the evening. No one in. No one out. So, while I admire your desire to rescue your paramour, Balthazar, you will have to suspend the mad dash to your quick and messy death until tomorrow."

"You said we should stop Karanis. You said—"

"I am aware of what I said, Balthazar, but I do not wish to see you commit suicide in such a spectacular fashion. You are tired and overwrought. Remain here for the evening. Rest. Plan as Zeelaya said. *Then* go and do what needs to be done."

My shoulders drooped without my consent as my body betrayed me. My head knew he was right, but my heart would not lie still and be convinced.

"Shasheba is Karanis's leverage against you. This makes her valuable," Tass said, her voice bracing. "He needs her too much to hurt her."

Tass was right. Shasheba was in terrible danger, but tonight at least she would be safe. It was enough, *barely*, to keep me from running headlong into the bowels of the Archive.

The Curator seemed to take my silence for the tacit agreement it was. The door swung open behind us. "If you would follow the light; rooms have been prepared. You are safe while you remain in my domain. Rest well."

I was safe, sure, but knowing Shash was in danger meant there was little way I was going to sleep, let alone well.

I had no choice, though, and I let myself be ushered out the door. The lights led back up the Archive's winding ramp to the level just above the Curator's reading room. We walked through the stacks, the smell of old parchment perfuming the air, until we finally hit an iron staircase. It led us to a balcony I hadn't seen from the ramp. One of many things I'd failed to see in this unending night.

A lamppost burst to life when we reached the top of the balcony. It stood by a lonely-looking door in the wall. I pushed it open and discovered a large sitting room. It was a perfect mirror to the one we'd just left, only this one was set with five additional doors.

A quick circuit around the space revealed that each door had been stamped with our names. One door each for Mira, Kai, and myself, plus another for Zee and Edik. The last door was stamped with a complicated sigil in ancient Sorien, which I assumed was Tass's name.

Assumed, but I couldn't ask her. She'd stayed behind with the Curator. As curious as I was about the history that obviously lay between them, I was too worn out, too sick of the strange and supernatural bullshit that had filled the rest of my night, to pry.

"How the hell does Tass know the Curator?"

I couldn't suppress a sigh as Edik's voice filled the room. My feet dragged against the floor as I claimed one of the overstuffed chairs by the fire.

"I don't know," I admitted, letting the plush velvet fabric envelop my body, wishing I could sink straight through the chair and avoid this conversation all together. "Does it matter?"

Edik crossed his arms. "How could it not?"

"He's right, Bal," Kai said.

"Please, Kai. You've had it in for Tass ever since she joined the crew."

"Joined because the Curator demanded it."

"Kai—"

"They're right, Bal."

Zee's words stunned me into silence. Zee was supposed to be the voice of reason that tempered Kai's heat. She wasn't supposed to agree with him. With *both* of them, I amended, watching Edik stare me down. His face was unreadable.

"Bal," Zee continued, forcing my gaze back to hers. "The Curator has single-handedly placed the responsibility of saving Cothis at your feet. And don't tell me you aren't considering shouldering that burden, because I can see the guilt all over your face. None of this is our fault, but that's beside the point.

"Because, Bal—isn't it starting to feel like the Curator was expecting us to fail all along? And if he was, then doesn't that put Tass's involvement in a new light?"

Kai stabbed a finger in Zee's direction. "See? Even Zee agrees with me. Why is Tass here? What does she get out of this? Aside from a chunk of our lives," Kai muttered.

"*Now* you all believe in magic?" I asked, eyebrows rising as I took them all in. "When it questions Tass's motives, you believe. But when faced with what happened in the temple, you'll bury your head in the sand?"

"I'll admit that what happened in the temple was . . . uncanny."

"*Uncanny*, Zee. Really?"

"She saved my life," Mira said, her face glowing oddly in the firelight.

Kai just scoffed. "She saved her own life. You just happened to be close to her when Paasch lashed out."

"That's not true, Kai, and you know it," I said quietly. The memory of Tass sprinting back into danger to save Mira was seared on my brain.

"That's not what I meant," Mira said, shouting over the sudden din of Kai and Edik's voices. "She saved my life before. The day our parents died."

All sound crashed to the floor. Silence. I was on my feet, past and present on a headlong collision in my mind.

"What are you talking about?"

Mira took a deep breath. "After they . . . after they died. When we got separated. The crowd—they found me. They would have . . . but she came. She was there.

"She saved my life."

The silence that filled the air hung. Was it possible? Mira was so little when our parents were killed. It's possible she was mistaken, or misremembered, or . . .

Except it wasn't. Whatever else Tass was, she wasn't forgettable. And the night we met, when she'd asked me about my past—about Paasch and my father—it hadn't felt like she was asking those questions out of ignorance. It felt like she was trying to tease out motives from my memory of the mob. Like humanity at its worst was a puzzle she could solve.

"What she did for you, Mira . . . it's not to be discounted," Edik said, kneeling so he was on her level. "But she's not your personal savior. She wants something."

"She wants a family, Edik. To belong. Just like you did." Mira coiled her arms about her chest as if it could contain her frustration. "And the fact that none of you see that? You should all be ashamed."

I could feel Edik's disbelief—disbelief in Mira's memory, in Tass and the Curator, all of it. It was easier for the older man. He hadn't been here that day. But for me?

I had to wonder if Mira wasn't right.

Kai shook his head in mute surrender. Rose. And disappeared into his room without a word or a backward glance. Zee gave only a tired smile before pushing open her own door. I turned to Mira, expecting to see her trudging into her room. Instead, she darted forward and wrapped her thin arms around me. I barely had time to hug her back before she ran away red-faced into her room.

"Bal," Edik said, stepping in my path before I could retire. Or retreat.

"Yeah?"

"What's the plan for tomorrow?"

I sighed, rubbing a hand over my eyes. "First thing is getting Mira safe, which means—"

"You're not going to try and convince us to fight the creature, are you?"

The steel in Edik's voice made me wince, because we both knew this conversation was a long time coming. I remembered how still he'd become when I told him I wanted to steal the idol, how the soldier's rage that forever boiled beneath his unflappable surface threatened to burst out of him.

He'd always been against this job. Said it was too risky—but then, Edik said that about most of our jobs. He was bound to be right occasionally. That didn't give him the right to look down on me the way he was now.

"Look, I know things didn't go as planned—"

"Didn't go as planned?" he asked, his voice rising. "Mira almost died. Tass did die, not that it stuck. And now Karanis himself is after us if you believe the Curator—and I don't. I won't," he said, hand going to the medal of Janus about his neck.

Unconsciously, I thought. And smirked. "If you don't believe it's Karanis, then what are you getting all worked up for?"

"Maybe because your actions are about to get us all killed," he snapped. "And why? All because you and Kai can't deal with the fact that Paasch screwed you."

Anger seared through my mind. Blinding me. All I knew was that we were barely holding our shit together. That we'd been running on adrenaline and terror for hours. And now—*now*—was when Edik wanted to pretend like Paasch hadn't destroyed my godsdamned life. That my vendetta against him wasn't well and fucking earned?

Reason evaporated. I lunged. His shirt was fisted in my hands as I drove him into the wall. Hard. But even with blood boiling in my veins, even with rage howling in my ears, I couldn't strike him.

"Don't try and make it sound like all Paasch did was steal some money from us. He murdered almost my entire family."

"And that makes it okay for you to put Zee and Mira at risk?" he spat through clenched teeth, eyes blazing. But he didn't throw me off. He held me closer. Forcing me to listen. "They could have been killed today. They might still be killed if Paasch-Karanis-whoever catches up with us."

"'Paasch-Karanis-whoever'?" I parroted his words back to him, my laughter all the more bitter under the weight of his contradiction. I shoved myself away, unable to stomach the proximity anymore. "Make up your mind, Edik. Are you going to be one of Janus's faithful in the Heavens Above, or will you be joining us godless heathens in the Great Below?"

"Don't you dare make jokes right now, Bal," Edik said, his voice a low hiss of rage. "I have every right to be confused. But you? These are our lives you're gambling with."

"You think I don't know that?"

"Do you?" he demanded, stepping up to my chest. "Because you've got that look in your eye that tells me you're going to try something insane."

"I've got that look in my eye?" I said with a sneer. "Please. You don't have any problem with my plans when you're cashing in on them. Don't get soft on me now, old man."

"I'm not getting soft. But I'm not risking my wife so you can try and save Shasheba." Edik's nostrils flared as he spat her name. "That's what you're thinking. Isn't it?"

I opened my mouth, only to close it again. The sudden sense of light-headedness made my stomach lurch in warning. We were on the edge of a cliff, Edik and I. One wrong move, one careless word and the delicate rope tying us together would snap. One of us would fall. The crew would fracture.

"If I figure out a way to save Shasheba, I'll do it alone."

Edik shook his head, turning away like he couldn't stand looking at me.

"I cannot leave her behind. Not again. You know you would do the same for Zee."

"Don't pretend that Zee and Shasheba are the same," Edik said, voice low and almost pitying. "Zee would give her life to protect any one of us. Zee is my partner. My wife. Someone I committed everything to. You can't say the same about Shasheba."

"Shasheba put her life at risk to get us into that temple," I said, knowing how soft that sounded compared to Edik's . . . declaration of fucking love. Still, I pressed. "Come on, Edik. Where did all your piety go? What would your precious Janus say about you now?"

"Janus commands us to protect the innocent. Shasheba has never been that."

"How convenient for you."

"Shasheba's a snake. She wouldn't lift a finger if it helped you. If you had bothered to think it through, you'd see it was a mistake to involve her in the first place. She probably sold us out the moment we left the room."

"You don't know that!"

"Neither do you!" Quieter, he said, "That's my point."

I raked a hand through my hair, trying to shut out his words. "It doesn't matter what you think. She's part of this."

"Yes. She is. Which is why it's time to get the adults involved."

"What?"

"How much of my life have I wasted explaining right and wrong to the Vadalen children?" Edik muttered, passing a hand over his eyes. "It's time to go get help. Real help."

"Who—"

"Alert the empress."

I gaped at him.

"You want to help Shasheba. Fine. But there's a right way to do that, Bal. You're out of your depth here. Outnumbered and outgunned. So call for reinforcements."

I laughed. I had to. What other reaction could I possibly have to this astonishing display of naivete. "What? You want us to just sail to Arisha and ask the empress for help?"

"Yes!" he said, as if I were the crazy one for questioning that.

"We'd be arrested on sight."

"I see. So it's worth risking *our* lives to save Shasheba, but it's not worth risking *your* freedom?"

"No," I spat, feeling my argument snarl in the net of Edik's anger. I turned away, stepping back from the fire as if it would help me escape the heat in the room. "Even if the authorities in Arisha believed me," I continued, calmly as I could manage, "we don't have time. Shasheba doesn't deserve to die because of a job we took."

"No, Bal. But she is going to die because of a job that *you* took."

I felt my eyebrows disappear into my hair line. "Is that what you're angry about? After all this time, you're angry that you're not the leader of this crew?"

"I don't give a shit about leading the Talion," Edik said, looking like he didn't recognize me. "But you always used to come to us with prospective jobs. Let us in on the plans, let us hear out the proposal before agreeing to anything. Instead you got us involved in something none of us understand, put us all in danger. And you're thinking of doing it again—all without any of our input."

"All I've heard the last ten minutes is *your input.*"

"But you still aren't listening."

"Hey, I didn't hear you complaining about the pay we have coming for this." Quite the opposite in fact. The money the Curator was putting down had made any risk seem insignificant at the time. Even Zee and Edik had gone dreamy-eyed at the idea of everything they could do with that much money.

"What pay?" Edik turned his hands to the sky as if he expected the coins to pour down like rain. "Did you see any money? Because you just gave the Curator all the idol he's going to get, and I didn't hear a word about compensation."

My mouth went dry. He was right. "Relax. I'll get the money tomorrow."

"Yes. You will," he said, eyes blazing. "And while you do that, I'm going for my stash."

I blinked. We all had hidden stashes on each of the islands of Ashaar. Stores of money and weapons to be collected as a last resort.

Or when we were ready to leave the crew.

"Wait. Hold up. You can't go running off by yourself," I said, stumbling over the words in my haste to grasp at any last straw.

"Zee and I need that money. So yes. I can."

"No, Edik," I said, my hands balling up into fists. "I can get us off the island, but if you go running off on your own, we will all be screwed."

"Why? Will it interfere with your nonexistent plans? Has it ever occurred to you that Zee and I might have our own plans?"

The ground beneath me seemed to heave a good thirty degrees. "What do you mean?"

"I mean that we don't want to be running around thieving forever."

"I don't either! That's the whole point of this job."

"The point of this job was revenge, and you know it. Well congrats, Bal. Paasch is dead. Doesn't change the fact that we failed." He looked at me, shaking his head in such a pitying way I could've punched him. "You really think we're getting paid, don't you. When did you become such an idiot?"

I jerked back, feeling like he'd kicked me in the teeth. My heart dropped, and something cold took its place. "You really mean it? You want to leave?"

"Of course we want to leave." Edik scrubbed his face with his hands, and for a wild moment I thought—I hoped—he was going to take the words back. But some things can't be unspoken.

"Look, Bal," he continued, softer now. Softer, but still immovable. "Zee and I want to go legit. We want to start a family."

"The Talion is your family!"

"Oh, grow up. You can't honestly expect us to keep children at home all while running around on the *Fortune's Fool* risking our lives with you and Kai."

My shoulders drooped and I was nearly overcome with the childish urge to clap my hands over my ears. I cleared my throat. "No, I know you can't."

Edik nodded, the corners of his mouth turning down with regret.

"I get it. I really do. I mean the only reason I took this job was to set Mira up with a better life. A real life. Not all this."

"So, you see why I have to get to the stash."

"I do, but Edik, you can't go running out there by yourself."

A mutinous look crossed his face, and I clasped his arm, willing him to listen. "Edik, *please*. I will figure out a way to get you where you need to go, but I have to find a safe house for the crew and secure a way off the island first. You have to trust me. Please. One last time."

A vein in Edik's temple leaped as he looked down at me, eyes hard. He nodded once and went to his room. The sound of his door shutting reverberated through my chest. I felt utterly spent.

Hollow.

I wondered if he and Zee would still be here in the morning.

11

SEPTINIRI TASSIEL JANAE

Tassiel let Bal and the others go ahead. They reeked of exhaustion; the kind that sleep alone could relieve. Their lives had been shaken apart. So simple a realization, yet something within her flinched at it. For it was an experience she was intimately familiar with. Only time could soothe that kind of wound.

Or so she had been told.

"You've been injured."

Tassiel's attention rose with her gaze. The old man studied her through dark eyes and a heavily wrinkled face. The frail body he wore was so at odds with the unimaginable strength she knew was hidden within. Bitterness curled on her tongue.

"I was. I will heal," Tassiel replied even as her ribs burned beneath her flesh. She could deal with the pain, but she knew the fusing process would take several more hours to complete.

He nodded in satisfaction, the firelight carving his wrinkles into canyons. Silence settled between them, not easy or companionable, but heavy and filled with loss. It sucked the air out of the room. She slowly straightened her spine, forcing herself to ignore the upsurge of emotion boiling within. In her mind, she could feel the carefully erected wall against memory begin to crack. Bit by bit, the wall was coming down.

She tried to fight it. Tried turning her mind to other things, like imagining the expression on Kai's face when he found out who the Curator was. Not an old man criticizing Kai's lack of proper hygiene.

But the All Father himself. Enkaara, King of the Heavens Above and Keeper of the Great Below.

And Malakai thought he was just a librarian.

The idea nearly made her smile. Nearly. But some heartaches could not be eased by humor, nor distracted by idle thoughts.

"What are you doing here?" The words slid out from between her lips on a puff of breath she could no longer contain.

His face sagged. "My dear child. You know what I'm doing here."

"But I saved you. I *saved* you and was left behind." Tassiel snapped her jaw shut, tasting blood as she caught her cheek between her teeth. The pitying way he looked at her, the terrible childlike tone in her own traitorous voice, made her want to scream.

He rose from his throne-like chair and edged around the table with a wince—like his human joints were aching—and sat on the couch beside her. "You tried to save me, my dear. You thought I was taken and stranded here by our family's enemies. But the true enemies were always within." A growl escaped his chest and for a moment the facade of frailty nearly melted away. His throat bobbed as he contained what was surely centuries of rage.

"It was your father who exiled me here. And that same father cast you out too."

Tassiel closed her eyes against his words but wasn't strong enough to close her mind.

Father.

That wall of guarded memory crumbled further, and she recalled the day she discovered his loss. It was the same day that Tassiel had gone to her gathered family and demanded that they save him.

"It was my idea to rescue you," she murmured. "I would not take no for an answer."

He nodded, looking at his hands. "You always were the voice of reason."

"And I suppose that if exile was good enough for you, it would be more than enough for me."

While the rescue mission was her idea, it was Calien, her clever half-brother, who planned it. Calien, who arranged to send Tassiel and their other siblings out of the Nethersphere on a doomed rescue mission. Calien, who had probably summoned the creature that had nearly killed her.

She could still feel the heat of those flames on her face. They had just reached the cave where Enkaara was being held when the creature emerged from the darkness. It was a monster of black scales and spiny tentacles and fiery breath. It had taken all her strength, all her cunning, to escape with her life, but when she finally broke free, they weren't there. Her brothers and sister were gone, and she was alone in a strange world, a finger-width from a true and lasting death.

And Father had ordered them to do it. All of them.

"You never made it back?" she asked with no real hope.

He barked out a laugh. "No. I burned through three human hosts just fighting them off. And I lost a fourth escaping. Your dear siblings, my own beloved grandchildren, left me for dead." He shook his head disdain scrawled over his features.

Tassiel smiled. She knew full well he was not disappointed that they had tried to kill him. It was because they hadn't had the good sense to finish the job. He'd taught them better than that.

"Eventually, I found this place," Grandfather continued, waving his hand at the room around them. "My own little pocket of space and time. Took me more than a century to make it habitable and many more to collect all these wonderful things."

"Why didn't you ever reach out to me?" she asked, barely managing to keep the hurt out of her voice. Barely. The weight of her loneliness bore down on her shoulders, making her bones feel oddly hollow.

"It was many years before I learned you'd survived. Or wasn't that the point of the mask you wear?" He cocked an eyebrow at her with a wry smiled. "Sarthaniel will be so pleased. She was sure that all those years of magic lessons had gone to waste."

She shrugged. Her aunt, chief mage of their kingdom, had not been her favorite teacher. But Tass had learned enough to protect herself against the enemies that had caused her exile. She just never imagined that those enemies were her own family. "But you sent Bal to find me. You must have realized who I was."

"I did," he said, not bothering to deny it despite the accusation coloring her voice. "I saw you from afar almost ten years ago now. But I couldn't be sure that you weren't still working with your traitorous siblings. So I kept discreet tabs on you. When I heard about a masked woman single-handedly breaching the Bastion prison . . . well. My interest was piqued. Then I learned that you were hiring yourself out to humans," he said with a laugh, shaking his head like it was the funniest thing he'd ever heard. "I knew then that you and I were in the same boat, so to speak."

She bowed her head, allowing herself two heartbeats to lament her family's betrayal and a third to come to terms with a past she could not change. When she lifted her head again, she was ready to move on.

And if her heart did not believe her, her head was willing to pretend.

"Were you expecting Karanis to cross into this world?"

He shrugged, and she felt her eyes narrow. Her grandfather was too ancient, too wily to have expected nothing. The fact that he'd hired Bal—hired her—meant that he knew something was about to happen. But what was going on? And why now? There were questions she needed answered.

"Don't give me that look," he grumbled, reading her expression through layers of metal and magic. "I didn't expect Karanis specifically. Certainly not first." A frown creased his weathered skin. "Karanis was never the greatest of my children. If I am honest, he is one of the least. Yet here he is. A vanguard, you called him."

"You think I am wrong?" Tassiel asked, hoping she was even though she knew it was pointless.

"No. I'm sure you're right. Just as I am sure Karanis was chosen to go first because his loss would be no great hardship to your father."

She winced at that, at the idea that her father had sent Karanis. That he and the rest of his siblings would truly decide to come here, and what? Rule humanity? "I cannot believe that they would come here simply to conquer."

Grandfather snorted. "No, you don't *want* to believe it. And why should you? Your father was so careful to only show you his best face. He only let you see his strength. He made sure you idolized him as much as feared him. Janus quietly, insidiously ensured that you knew your place in the Nethersphere was through his benevolence alone. And without his blessing, you would never belong."

He rubbed his eyes—an uncharacteristic display of regret, she thought, for things he had done. Or not done.

"My damned eldest son made sure you loved him. But you were never more than a tool to him, my dear. None of your siblings are. The truth is that since the moment we discovered this world, Janus has been obsessed with conquest.

"At first, it was easy to turn him away—humanity was in its infancy after all. There was nothing here that was better than the Nethersphere. But no longer. The kingdoms they have created, the world they've populated, and the weapons they've fashioned; humanity must seem like good sport."

"And none of the others had the slightest objection?" She could believe that Karanis was weak-minded enough to obey her father, but for none of her aunts and uncles to speak against this? It was unthinkable.

"How long have we been gone from the Nethersphere? How long have *I* been gone?" He huffed a dry husk of a laugh. "More than enough time to solidify his rule, don't you think? Time enough to convince the others that they are owed this world."

"So father sent Karanis to test the waters here."

"An apt analogy," he said, nodding. "Yes, and it is Karanis who we must now destroy."

She felt one of her eyebrows scrape against the inside of her mask as it rose. "We? I thought you wanted Bal and his family to take on that burden."

"I do," he insisted. "And they must."

"They'll die," she said flatly

"Not with you there to help them."

Tassiel tutted. "You have always overestimated me."

"And you've always underestimated yourself," he pressed. "To-gether, you can destroy Karanis and save the city, not to mention humanity."

No. They could not.

There were full-blooded Ankaari she could defeat in single com-bat, but Karanis was not one of them. If she was forced to fight him, she would die. As would Balthazar and his family. It was a simple fact.

As simple as the fact that her grandfather obviously didn't care. To him, their lives—her life included—was worth the chance at re-covering the rest of the idol. At stopping Karanis. Her face went cold. She wanted to feel betrayed, angry even—because there was a kind of solace in righteous anger. But he was right. About every-thing. She was born to be a tool. To be used. Defeating Karanis *was* worth her life.

THE QUEEN OF DAYS   151

She allowed a long exhale and moved away from an emotion she had no desire to examine. "And what will you be doing while we are off playing suicidal heroes? Not helping us, I suppose?"

"I can't, my dear. I don't want Karanis or any of his siblings to know I'm still alive. If they find out, there will be nothing to stop Janus from coming. Not even Karanis's failure. Anyway, humanity needs to prove that they can protect themselves against our kind. Destroying Karanis will prove that, and it will make my other children pause." His eyebrows lowered as his gaze narrowed on her. "Karanis isn't at his full power. And you, my dear Septiniri, should be more than a match for him."

The word "Septiniri" burned through her, hotter than salt water in an open wound. Tassiel leaped to her feet. She had to turn away from the surprise in her grandfather's eyes.

Septiniri was the name her father gave them, his seven children. His personal army. Born half human, half Ankaari, they had no real standing in the Nethersphere, no rights or place that could be occupied but as the lowest of servants. But her father's words lifted them up. He gave them pride of place in his family and put them on equal footing with his full-blooded children. Or so she had thought.

For all her life, Tassiel had taken such pride in that name. Pride to be called Janus's daughter. And now? "Don't call me that," she whispered.

"Why? Don't you think you deserve it?" Her grandfather slid one of his hands into hers, squeezed until she opened her eyes. "You are the only one who deserves it."

She exhaled long and hard. "Grandfather—"

"Do this for me," he said, looking at Tassiel with wide, dark eyes that seemed to see straight into her. The mask on her face could disguise nothing from him. "Do this and I will send you home."

A tremor ran down her spine. "Impossible. If you had a way back, you would have taken it."

A small smile curled the edges of his lips, and the tiny hairs on the back of her neck rose. Something unknowable shimmered behind her grandfather's eyes. Something too vast for her to comprehend.

"My reasons for remaining here are my own, child. But I confess, I'm curious to see how your father's plans play out."

She repressed the urge to shiver. Her father always said that grandfather played a long game. Long indeed if he was willing to wait centuries to see what his children intended. "But you'd just let me leave?"

"If that's what you want, and I can only assume that it is. Isn't that why you've been taking time from your clients?"

She allowed a grudging nod.

He chuckled. "Only you would request to collect time from humans. The rest would simply take it. It's why I know you'll do the right thing. And if, once Karanis is dead, you decide that you want to go home, I have the way."

Home.

The word struck a chord deep inside her chest, a chord of yearning she'd carried so long it seemed to have calcified her bones. For so long, she'd wanted nothing more than to tear open a portal and fling herself back to the Nethersphere where her siblings waited. Where her father waited.

But never, in all her years of exile, did she allow herself to wonder why no one had come back for her. She'd forced herself to believe that they thought she was dead. That was why they had not come. It had seemed so natural, but that was the deadly allure of denial. It let you twist the truth into a beautiful, foreign thing.

Now she knew better. She wasn't lost to her family. She'd been thrown away. And for what?

Anger snaked up her bones. She could go home, demand answers. But why? The home she longed for was gone. She would never get it back.

"I will consider it."

His smile was terrible to behold; filled with compassion and pity. "I understand, my dear."

12

BALTHAZAR

I awoke from a dreamless sleep, the kind that left my body re-
freshed. But my heart? I shook my head at the ceiling. I should
have been over the freaking moon right now. Everything I had
worked for, everything I had sacrificed, all of it was for this:
Paasch's death.

Why did the victory feel like a mouthful of ash? Was it because
Paasch had been replaced by something so much worse? Or was it
because I hadn't been the one to deliver the killing blow?

Edik would have guessed the latter. Then would have scoffed and
said vengeance would never slake the thirst I felt. Only forgiveness
could. Not that he'd listened to his own pious bullshit, I thought, my
mind running over every word of our confrontation even though I'd
have rather pulled out all my nails. No matter how much time I spent
trying to game out how I would react when I saw him next—and
what I would say—the words wouldn't come.

Back straight and ready for a fight, I opened my door, expecting to face Zee and Edik, but no one was in the sitting room. A
fire leaped and crackled in the hearth, and the comfy-looking chairs

seemed to beckon. But the idea of being alone with my thoughts was unbearable, so I kept walking. Perhaps I could find the Curator and get more information on . . . well everything.

The lamp outside the door was still lit, but surprisingly, so were many of the lamps dotting the stacks below my balcony perch. They easily illuminated the only person in the room: Tass. She sat atop one of the bookcases, leafing through the pages of a large tome.

"Shouldn't you be asleep?"

I hadn't realized she'd noticed me, but I wasn't really surprised. "I was sleeping. What about you? Did you sleep at all, or don't you need to?"

"No."

My lips twitched at the nonanswer. I walked down the iron staircase and made my way through the labyrinthine stacks like a moth drawn to a mysterious flame. I wandered the shelves until I spotted one of her feet kicking idly in the air beside a rolling ladder.

She budged over as I climbed up, giving me space to sit beside her. I looked across the lit bookcases with renewed respect for the Curator, for the sheer wealth of knowledge he had managed to gather. It wasn't something I'd been able to appreciate until now. My love of learning might have paled in comparison to Zee's, but still. The fact that all these books existed in one space was something to behold.

The bookcases gleamed as far as I could see, which admittedly wasn't very far. The lamps brightened our perch, but the darkness beyond their radius was thick and unyielding. Unsettling too, I thought.

I ran a finger across the top of the bookcase. No dust. Not even a single speck. Unbelievable. Though, the fact that this surprised me, after everything I'd seen, said more about me than about the Curator's magical cleaning abilities. I shook my head. Magic. Gods. Portals. What was my life coming to?

I glanced sidelong at Tass, whose face was bent over her book. "Are you really one of the Septiniri?"

"Does it matter?" she asked without looking up.

I frowned. Did it matter that she might be part of the cadre of warrior demigods? Did it matter that she'd been alive to see ancient worlds fall and new ones rise? It certainly made sense in a twisted, mystical, slightly impossible way, but I got the feeling that it was a complicated topic for her.

"Not really," I replied in as bland a voice as I could manage.

Her answering chuckle sounded like broken glass. "Yes. I was one of the Septiniri. Before I got stuck here."

"What do you mean?"

"It is difficult to explain." She was silent for a long time, and I began to think she wasn't going to answer. "You know who my father is?"

I nodded. Despite my remedial interest in religion, I knew. "Janus." The Prince of Heaven. Oldest and most powerful child of Enkaara, the Great Creator.

"It started out as an experiment, I think. He wanted to see what humanity could do when blended with the Ankaari. So he chose women from all across this world, fathered us, and when we were born, he brought us to the Nethersphere. There he molded us, trained us." She seemed to hesitate, and I sensed a struggle waging within her. "I am sure it sounds like a cold upbringing, and it was in some ways, but then again, it wasn't. Janus cared for us, saw to our every need, gave us all the advantages of any highborn, full-blooded Ankaari.

"For many long years, my siblings and I were the right hand of Janus. He fed us. Clothed us, schooled us and in return . . ."

Her voice trailed off, and in my heart, I didn't think I wanted to know what she was forced to do in Janus's name.

"Then something happened; a cataclysm that threatened to destroy the Nethersphere."

"What?"

She seemed to hesitate, like she wasn't sure how much she could or should say. "One of the Ankaari—one of our leaders—was forced into your world. My siblings and I were sent to recover him."

My eyes widened. "What? How?" According to legend, the Ankaari were the race of gods who ruled the Nethersphere, from mighty Enkaara and Janus, to Nananthe and Karanis. I'd seen the chaos Karanis wrought in coming through the portal. And now she was telling me there was another one here?

She twitched a shrug. "Happens more often than you would think. It is a good way to eliminate your enemies without the fuss of disposing a body."

"But if another god is here, they could help."

"They are not gods, Bal," she snapped. "Their native forms are strange to human eyes, that was why your ancestors thought the Ankaari were gods, but that could not be further from the truth. They did not create this world for humanity, and you do *not* owe them anything."

"What are they then?" I demanded. "Karanis was able to shoot a bolt of lightning out of his palm. You jumped eighty feet, died, and then healed yourself. The power you have, can you blame us for thinking you are gods?"

"Governor Paasch had more power than you; did you make the mistake of worshipping him?" I acknowledged her point with a bow of my head. "The Ankaari are simply a different iteration of life. An older one, true, able to harness energy in ways that your kind cannot. But give your people a few more millennia to catch up, and who knows what you will be capable of."

I pressed my lips together, trying to rearrange everything about the creation of the world I'd ever learned and reframe it based on this conversation. My brain resisted. The idea that the Ankaari created the heavens and earth and then, with love, created humanity was a tidy story. A neat one. The kind that my order-loving brain liked. But my heart knew that Tass was telling the truth, that however this world and humanity rose out of the primordial muck of creation, the Ankaari had nothing to do with it.

"What happened to you? Did the mission go wrong?"

"Yes. It went . . . sideways," she said, testing the word, "almost from the beginning. I was separated."

"And they left you behind." The words fell into the empty space between us, as my mind conjured images of Shasheba. "It was an accident," I said, not sure if I was trying to assuage my guilt or to make Tass feel better.

"Was it?" She snapped her book shut. "How can you possibly know that? Besides, if it was an accident, then why did none of them come back for me, the way you want to for Shasheba?"

"Maybe they thought you died."

Tass scoffed. "And not one of them wanted to verify that? If it were Mira, torn away from you, trapped in another world, would you not look for her? Even if everyone around you thought she was dead?"

I swallowed hard at the hurt in her voice but didn't answer. I didn't need to. We both knew there was nothing I wouldn't do for Mira. That Tass couldn't say the same for her siblings . . .

"Tass—"

"You do not know them, so do not bother defending them. They do not deserve it."

I nodded, ceding the point in silence. She knew them. I didn't. At this point was I really hoping I was wrong about her family? Or just praying that I had what it took to keep mine in one piece. That I could somehow stop Edik and Zee from walking away.

"Why did you stay here?" I asked at long last. "Surely if there's a way to come to this plane, there is a way to return to the Nether-sphere."

"And yet here I am. Culling time from the mortals who hire me. Did you never think to ask why?" She sighed. "I am trying, Bal. I have been trying to get back for a very long time. But it is not as simple as chartering a boat."

I knew it couldn't be that easy, but it was obviously possible. I thought back to the temple, to the copper wire that coated the stairs and the rafters, the storm that churned outside. "So how do you do it? Cross from one reality to another?"

She looked away, out onto the Archive's dark heart. "It requires energy. A great deal of energy."

"You mean like the storm last night?"

"Yes and no," she said, tilting her hand back and forth. "The storm last night contributed to the energy requirement, but it was more of a catalyst. Only an extremely powerful storm could rend a tear in the fabric of the universe, and I am not sure that kind of storm could exist without magical help."

"If it wasn't the storm's energy that opened the portal, then what kind of energy was used?" My brow creased. I already had the answer, didn't I? "Time."

Tass hesitated, as if steeling herself. "Yes. Time."

The patch of skin on the back of my neck tingled—the same patch that was inked with a strange tattoo.

Tass had asked for my permission before she took my time. Somehow, I doubted Karanis had been so accommodating. And something told me Karanis had needed a lot more energy than what Tass had taken from me and my crew. "How do you do it? How do you harness time as energy?"

"You must understand that while time exists in the Nethersphere, the Ankaari are not subject to it the way that life is here."

I blinked a few times as if that could help me process this information. "So . . . you live forever?"

"Theoretically."

"Why only theoretically?"

"We can still die, Bal. And anything that can die, does." She snorted at the blank expression on my face and shifted, folding her legs beneath her so she was facing me fully. "Imagine that you and Governor Paasch, with all your bloody history, had to coexist in this city."

"Okay. Easy."

"Now imagine that neither of you could ever live sure in the knowledge that eventually one of you would die. Time would never score lines onto your skin. Age would never render you weak or senile. There is no clock ticking away your minutes. Eternity stretches out at your feet."

"Sounds pretty good."

She nodded. "It does. Until you remember, that because time cannot touch you, it cannot *heal your wounds,* as your people are so fond of saying. You live every day with the same exact pain as you did the day Paasch killed your parents."

"I *do* live with that pain."

"No, Bal. You don't."

I opened my mouth to argue but managed to stop myself when Tass held up her hand. "Can you tell me the expression on your mother's face when the executioner's sword fell? Can you describe the exact color of your father's blood? Or how it smelled? Can you hear with perfect memory, the precise pitch of their screams? Of your own?"

I swallowed. I couldn't, not in such detail. Thank all the gods for that small mercy. "No."

"No," she repeated. "Because you are human, your memory is filled with ghosts. They may haunt you, but they cannot touch you. The past changes you, yes, but it does not *chain* you. This is a blessing, Bal, one that allows you to heal and sometimes even to forgive. The Ankaari do not have this gift.

"In a world where time is still, the past is never the past. All you would have to do is close your eyes, and you would be back there, seeing Paasch kill them in perfect, brutal detail. What would you do?"

Bile rose in my throat. "I'd kill him."

"Yes," was her simple reply, as if the molten thirst for blood and revenge coursing through me was the most natural thing in the world. "But you have eternity, remember. Eternity to marshal your allies and to plan your revenge against not only Paasch, but every single individual who helped him do it and helped him get away. But Paasch has eternity too. Can you see how quickly such a feud could become a war?"

That galloping need for revenge stumbled in my chest. "Yes." Part of me, a dark, not-so-small part of me, longed for such a thing. It was easy to push the thought aside, as the rest of my heart recoiled against the prospect of such violence. Because the world she was describing was the world every Ankaari lived in. And every single person, human or not, is wronged. Everyone wants revenge. "So Ankaari die in great wars?"

"Usually," she replied, shrugging.

I shook my head. "But you could live forever. Throwing that away seems . . ."

"Brutal?"

"Wasteful. Foolish. Outright stupid—take your pick."

Tass's answering laugh was a dark, bloodthirsty thing. "The Ankaari are powerful, I never said we weren't primitive. In many ways we are ruled by our passions: anger, desire, jealousy. Remember this should you go up against Karanis."

"I will," I vowed, tucking the information carefully away in my mind. "So, you're not subject to time, but it still exists in the Nethersphere?"

"Correct."

"So, you, what—mine it?"

She laughed. "Sure."

"Sure?"

Her shoulders shook. "Yes. If it helps you to think of time like the gas in a lamp, then sure. The point is that we can harness it and use its energy like any other natural resource."

"So, in the Nethersphere time is just lying about waiting to be used, but in this reality, it's wedded to the creatures living here."

"Correct."

"And that's why you ask for time instead of money on the jobs you do." She nodded, but I was still confused. "People talk about you like you've been ghosting around for decades doing jobs. But you're still here. How much time do you need to open a portal?"

"I'm a half-breed, so on a cosmic scale, it is a relatively small amount. The problem is that I am often called to complete the most foolish things, deeds that require a certain fudging of the natural order. Acts that literally waste my time."

I closed my eyes briefly. "Things like jumping eighty feet?" Or coming back from the dead.

"Indeed. Time is a malleable force. It does not simply open portals. It can also be used to make the impossible possible—to make magic. I often use up most of what I collect just getting the job done." She slumped. "Truth be told, fighting Karanis, even in his weakened state, will probably exhaust the store I have managed to collect—and likely won't be enough to defeat him on its own."

"Couldn't you just take it from people? It's not like most people would notice a few months gone. I didn't."

"You may yet," Tass said, drawing away. "Just because I can do something, does not mean I would do it. You all live such small lives; they end just as they've begun. How could I take even a minute of it from you without consent?" She shook her head. "There are lines that should not be crossed, Bal. You should know this."

I did know it. I also knew that her attitude was likely the reason she'd been abandoned here in the first place. Not that I'd ever say that out loud. "Well, I'm glad you feel that way. I'm sure not all Ankaari do."

"Karanis clearly doesn't," she said darkly.

My mind flashed back to the temple and the sight of all those charred corpses painting the floor, the acrid smell of burnt flesh. "The bodies?"

She nodded. "Hundreds of people, thousands of days, all taken to open a portal through which he could enter this reality. And it wasn't just their deaths."

"What do you mean?"

"I mean the temple itself was built to strip people of their time."

I blinked, my mind going momentarily blank. "Wait. What?"

"All that copper wire you saw, it was imbued with magic that stripped tiny increments of time from the mortals inside the temple. It funneled their energy into the pyramid at its peak, storing it to help ease Karanis's crossing. And when it wasn't enough, Karanis killed all the workers."

My lips went numb as her words sank into my brain. "But . . . but Mira and Shasheba, Edik and Kai—they were all in the temple for hours. Far longer than Zee and me. How much time did they lose?"

"Mira, Kai, and Edik? Very little. When I discovered the theft, I wove a small shielding spell over Kai and Edik. Since the rest of you share Kai's blood, the protection extended to you as well.

"I was unable to help Shasheba."

Unable or unwilling, her tone didn't quite make it clear which. Still, the fact remained that she hadn't had to protect any of us. Protected us again. Mira's words were still rattling around my brain—the knowledge that Tass had saved her not once but, time and time again. It was a debt I'd never be able to repay. "Thank you, Tass." It was all I could offer. And it was so, so inadequate.

She seemed to understand this, but inclined her head in acknowledgment anyway.

"I still don't understand why it was necessary," I said, gazing out onto the vast font of knowledge around me but finding no answers in sight. "You said that you could take time from your reality to open a portal to mine, and take time from my reality to open a portal to yours. Why did Karanis need to kill those people? Why couldn't he just use the time from your side?"

"You are forgetting that I am only half Ankaari. I am half human too, Bal. I can exist in either reality without the fabric of creation noticing."

I frowned. "What do you mean, 'noticing'? You speak of creation as if it's a sentient thing."

"Isn't it?"

My eyes bulged. "Is it?"

Tass held up a hand. "I think we are getting off topic. The point I am trying to make is that full-blooded Ankaari do not belong in this reality. Not without a price. While Karanis used energy from our plane to open a portal to yours, an equivalent portion of energy was required here to waylay the natural consequences of his presence, long enough for him to acquire a form that is more palatable to this reality."

"So he had to kill all those workers to give him time to possess the idol . . . or Paasch in this case."

"Correct."

It felt like there should be something to that, some kind of weakness we could exploit. "The copper beams," I said, mind churning over her words. "They were damaged when Karanis attacked you. Will that weaken him?"

She seemed to consider this for a moment. Shrugged. "It is possible, but the damage will need to be quite profound. At best it will make him cautious about conserving his flesh form."

"Not much of a blessing there. What I would give to do it all over again. Blow up the damned temple with Paasch inside it."

"As entertaining as that might have been, it would not have stopped Karanis from coming. He simply would not have had the required energy waiting for him here."

"What would have happened?"

"His unmasked presence in this reality would have set off a catastrophic chain reaction that would destroy this city, the island it sits on, and in all probability the kingdom it's a part of."

Oh, is that all?

"What? Why?"

"All life is energy. In your case, time energy. But the energy that makes up an Ankaari is completely foreign to this reality. In fact, it seems to be the antithesis of it, because the first Ankaari who came through died immediately, along with everything else for about a hundred-mile radius. All because reality rebelled and triggered a cataclysmic flood that nearly wiped out all of humanity."

I knew about that flood. Everyone in every culture told stories about the great flood. It was written into the collective memory of the species, and Great Below, it was caused by the Ankaari. "And after that, your people tried again?"

"They could not know for sure that the experiment didn't work." Tass shrugged, clearly unimpressed by my outraged reaction. "You are failing to account for the acute boredom that an eternal life causes. Exploration is an excellent way to alleviate this."

"That and war," I grumbled. "How did they figure out that they needed a different form in this reality?"

"Quite by accident," she replied, and I could almost imagine her grinning behind the mask. "One of our greatest explorers mistakenly opened a portal right in the middle of a battlefield—plenty of dying humans surrendering their energy. It delayed the oncoming cataclysm long enough for him to transfer into a human form, thereby averting disaster. It is also how our races first met one another."

"Oh?" It was as much of a question as I could manage.

"Yes. The explorer was Enkaara—who you call the Creator. When he realized his exploration was a success, he brought his children here too. They lived here for a number of years before duty drew them home again."

I scrubbed my face with my hands. Tass had a knack for saying really interesting things that invariably made me wish I'd stayed in bed. *No, Bal. The religions your people have been preaching for the last thousand or so years aren't in veneration to gods, but a race of terminally bored and bloodthirsty immortals from another reality.* And now one of them is in Cothis, wearing Paasch's body.

That almost made me laugh. The bastard deserved the hell of Karanis seizing his body. Great Below they were the same, weren't they? Both Paasch the dead man, and Karanis the stranded god. Both so entitled. So fucking sure they deserved everything. And Paasch had been so happy about the great change he was preparing for . . .

I let my hands fall into my lap. "Tass, Paasch knew Karanis was going to come through. He built the temple with all that wire, had all those workers brought in so they could be sacrificed. That means he knew Karanis wanted to come here. How could he know?"

"Paasch would have had to be in contact with Karanis through a half-breed intermediary." She paused like she didn't want to continue. "That intermediary was most likely one of my siblings."

"I thought the Septiniri only served Janus."

"They do." Her reply was heavy and bitter and edged in betrayal. "Which means that while Karanis was the first Ankaari to come through, he might not be the last."

I have to get Mira off Cothis, away from all of Ashaar. It was the only thought strong enough to break through the fear welling up within me. Trying to kill the creature wearing Paasch's face was one thing, but going up against the Prince of Heaven too?

As mighty as our legends of Karanis were, they paled in comparison to Janus. Second only to Enkaara in power, Janus was the right hand of the Creator. Clever and farsighted and mercurial to the hilt, Janus had raised whole civilizations.

Crushed them too, if the legends were to be believed. If Janus and the other gods were coming . . .

We wouldn't survive.

"Hey, what's going on?"

I followed the sound of Kai's voice to the balcony. He and the others were crowded around the lamppost looking down on Tass and me with unguarded curiosity. I wondered how long they'd been listening. Then I spotted Mira. The ghost of her arms around my waist crept into my mind. I'd never seen my sister as scared as she'd been yesterday. I swallowed, not wanting her to see my fear. "Nothing," I said, trying to sound as normal as possible. "Why, what's up with you guys?"

"Nothing," Kai replied, though I could see his eyes narrowing. "We were just talking in the common room when all the bedroom doors disappeared."

Goose bumps prickled my neck as he spoke. Below me, the floor lamps began to dim, Tass rose and we turned in a circle, watching the outer ring of lamps die.

"What is it?" I asked.

Tass looked over my shoulder and pointed. I turned in time to see new lamps lighting in the distance. "I believe the Curator is requesting our presence."

13

BALTHAZAR

We followed the lights down the ramp and back into the sitting room we'd been in last night. Only instead of tea and cakes there was a variety of breakfast food laid out on the table. The fire smoked behind the grate, and a chandelier I didn't remember seeing last night burned brightly overhead. The Curator wasn't there, which was a blessing. Seeing him after Tass's conversation would probably ruin what little appetite I had.

I let everyone file in ahead of me, but before I could follow, Kai caught my arm. "What was that all about?" he asked.

"What was what about?" I asked, trying to shake the distraction out of my head. Focus on what was to come.

"You and Tass."

I blinked. It was the first time Kai had said her name like it wasn't a dirty word. "She was just trying to explain about Karanis."

He nodded mutely at first, then said, "You sure you can trust her?" There was something contemplative in his words, like he wanted to trust Tass, but wasn't sure he should.

"I am. She saved Mira's life. And she's been protecting us since you first stepped into the temple."

"Yeah. Yeah, I heard that bit." Kai scratched his chin, looking unsure. "Why would she do that, you think?"

"I couldn't let Karanis take your time without your knowing, Kai. It wouldn't be right. So I shielded you. None of my kind will ever be able to take your time again. Not even me."

Kai and I jumped at Tass's voice when she appeared beside us. But instead of snapping at her the way Kai always did when startled, his widened eyes softened. He gulped. No doubt struggling to say thank you. Then he grinned. "Hey! You used a contraction."

My heart nearly stopped with everlasting surprise.

Kai knew what a contraction was.

He laughed, clapping Tass's shoulder. "We'll make you one of the crew yet."

"Creation save us," the Curator said from behind me, his voice tinder dry. "But before that happy day occurs, why don't we go inside, and you can tell me your plan." He flashed an amused smile, gesturing to the open door. "After you, gentlemen."

Kai rolled his eyes and did as he was told. He snagged a pastry and flopped down on the end of the couch, his legs sprawled so I had to circle the sofa and sit nearest the fire. Heat belched out of the hearth, the flames casting grotesque shadows across the walls.

The Curator reclaimed his seat from the night before. He folded his hands in front of his face, watching me, as the others helped themselves to breakfast. Tass had retaken the chair opposite the Curator and seemed to be watching him watch me. I forced my shoulders back, refusing to bow under so much scrutiny.

The Curator smiled as if he could hear this thought and opened his hands to the ceiling. "Well? What do you intend to do?"

There was only one thing to do; get Mira out of the city and rescue Shasheba. In that order. Everything that had happened with Edik, and all that Tass revealed about the Ankaari didn't change that. It just meant I would be going in alone. I was getting the others off the island. I couldn't let the crew take this kind of risk—a risk that would likely get them killed.

"Is it your choice to make?" the Curator asked, eyebrows raised.

I glared at him, wondering if he'd guessed my thoughts from my expression or if he could read my mind.

"Perhaps it would be best if you started by telling the rest of your crew what you learned from Tassiel," the Curator said when I couldn't find any words.

"We heard," Edik said, cutting me off before I could begin.

"All of it?"

"All of it."

I took in their faces, but my eyes lingered on Mira. Funny how often I looked to her when I needed to be strong. "And you believe them—the Curator and Tass. About Paasch and Karanis?"

Edik and Kai both looked to Zee, who was biting the inside of her cheek.

"I know it sounds crazy," I said when she didn't speak, "but I *do* believe Tass when she says she is half Ankaari. You've seen what she's capable of. And you saw what happened to Paasch. You saw the lightning shoot out of his hand."

Zee shook her head slowly. "I cannot believe that Paasch is a god."

"No," I agreed, my voice sounding soft but no less certain. "He's not. But he's not Paasch anymore either. He's Karanis now."

I looked at Tass and then to the Curator, but neither of them came to my aid. Not that I really expected them to. They'd spoken their piece yesterday and the crew had flat denied it. Even now, they looked at the Curator with suspicion that was no less intense for its silence. Now it was up to me.

"If you heard Tass and I talking, then you know that Karanis is here," I continued, my voice going husky from the weight of my words. "He's trying to take over the city."

Judging by their reactions, they didn't love hearing this a second time. Mira scooted back so far into the corner of the couch. It was like she was trying to disappear into it. Next to her, Kai was rubbing his hands on his thighs; either to calm himself or to dry sweaty palms. Either option wasn't good.

Across from me, Zee had closed her eyes and clasped Edik's hand.

"Ankaari or god, Bal," Edik said, and I detected a slight tremor in his voice, the tremor of a man losing his faith, "it doesn't matter. You can't expect us to fight Karanis."

"I understand that you people have spent the past two thousand years loving your patron gods, but the time has come to put that foolishness aside," the Curator said in a pinched voice. "Karanis is here. And if you want any part of this city to survive, you will do what you can to kill him."

"Even if we could, which I highly doubt," Edik said, his hand twitching toward the pendant before he stopped himself and crossed his arms instead, "I cannot."

Kai scoffed, snagging another roll off the tray. "I didn't know you were so devout."

Kai might not have known . . . but I did.

"It's easy to love the Ankaari like gods when they are safely tucked away in the Nethersphere. I guarantee you will find it much harder to love them when they stand before you, destroying everything you hold dear. No slave loves their master." Tass's voice was oddly heavy, and I had to wonder if it was easier for her to love her family when they were out of reach.

Edik shook his head. He didn't have to speak to make it clear he didn't want any part of this. And he was pissed. "This isn't a matter of devotion."

"Good," the Curator replied. "Believe whatever you want. The point is that he must be stopped. And stopped *now*, while he is at his weakest."

"And I don't disagree. My point is that this isn't *our* responsibility," Edik snapped. "We must alert the empress."

THE QUEEN OF DAYS   171

"I gotta say that I'm with Edik here. At least about the first part," Kai said. "According to you, Karanis, or whatever, won't be able to survive in Paasch's body for long. So let nature take its course."

It was the same point I had tried to make last night. "Karanis will undoubtedly switch bodies before Paasch's fails," the Curator argued.

"And when he does, people will know for sure that something's not right. I mean, if they don't know already," Kai shot back. "Look, the temple is crawling with codekeepers. They'll take care of the problem."

The Curator swatted Kai's words aside. "Karanis would destroy them before they got the chance."

"And he'll destroy us before *we* get the chance," Zee noted.

Kai pointed toward Zee, underlining her words. "And you don't know that the codies won't be able to kill him. You said that he needs the idol to be at full strength. And you have half the idol."

"The codekeepers don't know what you do. It is your knowledge that will make you successful where they will fail."

Kai shrugged. "Yeah well, my knowledge is telling me to skip town."

The Curator was looking at Kai like he'd love nothing more than to strike my friend. "You would really just leave your people in harm's way to tuck tail and run?"

"They're not my people," Kai snorted. "I don't owe them anything."

He wasn't wrong. These very people didn't lift a hand when my family was getting slaughtered. So why did the Curator expect we'd do any different? Why did I?

I shifted in my seat. This was why I needed to get my family off the island. They didn't want to get involved. They had no reason to get involved. I did. I had to save Shasheba. I owed her that much. I'd already ruined her life once. But my crew?

They had to live.

Kai turned to me like he could sense the way my thoughts were moving. "No offense to you, Bal, but Shasheba isn't my friend. She's not one of us. Yeah, she might be in danger now, but when Karanis realizes we've run for it, she won't be useful anymore."

"At which point, Karanis will likely kill her out of spite."

Kai balked at Tass's words, but didn't back down, didn't try to apologize. He looked at me, dark eyes drilling into my face. "I'm sorry, Bal. But better her than us."

"Kai—" Even this soft exclamation failed as the full impact of his words landed. I knew that Kai and Shasheba didn't like each other, but this . . .

This was exactly what I should have expected, what I did expect if I was being honest with myself. I couldn't ask Kai to risk his life for a woman who'd never treated him with anything but scorn. No matter how much I cared for her.

Without much hope I looked at Zee and found her watching me. Her brow was furrowed, lips pressed into a thin line. "I agree with Kai," she said at long last.

"Zeelaya." The Curator dragged at the syllables of her name like a parent appalled by their child's behavior.

She shook her head. "I'm not saying that he shouldn't be stopped. But the fact of the matter is that we are not equipped to do the job. We're short on weapons, on ammunition, and I have none of the supplies I'd need to formulate any kind of explosive. We would need all these things if we wanted to get back into the temple. And that's putting aside the fact that we don't have a way out. Even if we did have all our tools, you'd still be better off contracting someone else to do the job. We're too recognizable at the moment."

"I see." The Curator spoke the words like they left a bitter taste in his mouth, shaking his head as though he was utterly disgusted.

Then he smiled like a snake that had spotted a mouse. "If self-preservation and duty to your fellow man will not motivate you, then perhaps additional reward?"

He laid out the question like a line in the water, a hook baited and waiting for a bite. Kai went still. Mira leaned forward, and from the corner of my eye I saw Edik and Zee share a glance.

"More than the money you already promised?" I asked, oh so careful to keep my voice steady.

The Curator inclined his head. "Money, yes, but what I can offer you is far more valuable than simple coin. I know you want to start new lives. Those are lives I can facilitate. Do this and you won't just have coin, but clean identities too, lands somewhere far, far away from Cothis," he said, gaze lingering on Mira for a moment. Moving next to Kai. "And titles that no noble house could deny. I could even," he began, his dark eyes clapping on to my face, "write a letter of introduction to the Tulier Academie. It would all but guarantee Mira a place there."

I stifled the urge to whistle, but it was a near thing. The Academie was half a world away from Cothis, but it was renowned as *the* school for future queens and emperors. Not even my family's wealth had been able to secure a place for Zee and I there. But a letter from this old man and Mira would be in—and I had no doubt he had the juice to make that happen—and she'd be learning and living with the children that would one day rule the world.

It was beyond my wildest dreams—beyond any of our dreams, judging by the way Kai was practically vibrating with excitement. The kind of score that made my mouth water just thinking of it. That made my eyes squint for the brightness they cast.

New identities were one thing, but covers so good they came with noble writs? Don't get me wrong, I didn't miss having people bowing and scraping in my presence, but few things opened doors faster than the shine that came with a title.

Fuck me, the old man drove a hard bargain. He was good.

Too good.

I met Zee's eyes across the couches. Saw the same caution flying across her face. More than that really. The suspicion. We'd both been doing this long enough to know that a pot that sweet was probably laced with poison and rigged to blow.

"You reached too far there, Curator," I said, words bitter in my mouth. "You just tipped your hand."

Anger grew like clouds across his brow. "In what way?"

I shrugged. "If something sounds too good to be true, it probably is."

"I assure you; I am being deadly serious. All this could be yours—"

"If only we kill a *god*?" I asked, drawling the words with an indifference I didn't feel.

"Simply think of him as Paasch, newly improved. Afterall," the Curator began, a cunning edge to his words, "that's how the world will think of him, when he's sending his armies to find you."

"Bal," Edik's voice lashed across the room. "He's manipulating you. Don't let him. We are *not* doing this."

"Of course he's manipulating me! You think I don't fucking know that?" I shook my head, nearly accepting the new deal just to shut Edik up.

But I didn't. *I couldn't.* We'd gotten into this mess because I'd accepted the job from the Curator without talking it over with them. I wasn't going to do it again. Not when both Zee and Edik were so obviously against it. Majority might rule for most jobs, but not for something this big. Taking down Paasch—*Karanis*—needed all of us on board.

I turned back to the Curator. "You can offer us the flipping world, it doesn't matter. We aren't doing it."

The Curator opened his mouth, but Zee beat him to it.

"The prize doesn't matter," she said, immovable as a mountain and about as soft. "We already have everything we need."

The Curator looked down, studying the way her hand rested entwined in Edik's, and an understanding I couldn't trace passed through his gaze. He shook his head. Turned to me.

"So you're choosing to flee." Something deeper than disappointment carved fresh lines in the Curator's face.

"I don't want to," I said. "In fact, I think we'll be safer in the long run if we kill Karanis. But my first duty is to protect my crew. I have to get them off Cothis." And after that . . .

The Curator's eyes narrowed like he sensed what I wasn't saying. "And how do you intend to get off the island? I know you didn't bring your airship here."

"No, we left the ship on La'Zem," I said, referring to the island a few hours northwest of Cothis. "We'll have to charter a boat there."

"You intend to escape your sea god by fleeing over water?" the Curator snorted. "I thought you were smarter than that, Bal."

"Hey, it's your fault were being pursued by a godsdamned god in the first place," Kai snapped. "If you had been up front with us, we could have been prepared to fight."

"If I had been 'up front' with you, you would have run away like the terrified children you are." The Curator shook his head, gathering malice about him like a cloak. His eyes scorched my skin with the fire of his disdain. "Very well. Flee if you think it will save you."

My crew rose, they took a few tentative steps to the door before realizing I wasn't with them. I felt their eyes on my back, but I had locked gazes with the Curator. "Our payment?"

He growled a mirthless chuckle and reached into the folds of his robes. "Here," he said, slapping a heavy purse on the table.

I picked it up but knew right away it wasn't the number we'd agreed on. Not even close.

"I hired you to steal an idol. You only stole half," he said, daring me to argue. "Half a job. Half the pay."

Bastard, I thought, barely keeping the curse behind my lips. Pushing to my feet, I headed to the door. Surprisingly, Tass was by my side.

"What? You're running too?"

Tass turned, tilting her head to one side. "I was hired for three days' work," she said, parroting the Curator's words. "The day is not yet done."

The Curator laughed. "You always were a contrary creature, Tassiel Janae."

She inclined her head and walked out ahead of me. I was almost through the door when the Curator's voice rasped up my back.

"Oh, and Balthazar," he called, waiting for me to turn before flashing a savage smile. "It would not be wise for you to return here. The Archive is not kind to cowards."

"But it's okay with hypocrites?" I snorted mirthlessly. "I don't see you leaving to stop Karanis, one Ankaari to another." I doffed an imaginary cap at him with a mirthless smile. "Always a pleasure, Curator."

We made quick time through the Archive. Though the lights still led us up the ramp, I didn't want to count on them remaining bright if we tarried. The Curator's displeasure haunted my steps, and the darkness beyond the lamps was textured and seething. I remembered what Tass said about the Ankaari holding on to grudges and picked up the pace.

After a few minutes of fast walking, we reached the top of the Archive. Only the last lamppost wasn't waiting beside a closed door. It stood in a shaft of sunlight beside the bottom rungs of an ancient, rusting ladder. I looked up. And up.

Set in the ceiling, some seventy feet above us, was a grate—the kind of grate that lay in street gutters to keep them from flooding. Judging by the sound echoing down, the grate was in the middle of a busy road.

"How is this even possible?" Zee asked.

I shook my head. "Hell if I know."

Tass sighed. Looked at me. "Perhaps that last jibe was unwise."

"He deserved to hear it."

"Lots of people deserve to hear lots of things, Bal. It does not make it smart to tell them."

"Story of my life," I muttered, but I knew she was right. I slid to the front of the group and started up the ladder.

"Hang on," Edik said, placing a restraining hand on my arm. "Before we head blind into the city, we should know where we're going. What's the plan?"

My mind had been racing through our limited options all night long. I needed to get my people off the island. While many charter boats that traveled from one island to another, there weren't a ton I could count on to smuggle four fugitives. Five, if I counted Tass, but I was secretly—desperately—hoping she would come with me to save Shasheba.

"We need transport off the island without anyone knowing about it. Only one man on Cothis fits that bill," I said, throwing a loaded look Kai's way.

Behind me, Zee groaned.

"What? Who are you talking about?" Mira demanded.

"Tick," I replied just as Kai said:

"Tick the Dick."

"Tick the *Dick*?" Tass's intonation rose in confusion. "This is not a very auspicious name."

"He's an even less auspicious person," Zee muttered, even as Mira giggled, trying to hide it by shoving a fist in her mouth. I smiled in spite of myself, though it faltered when Tass leaned forward.

"Karanis will be looking for you. Are you sure you can trust this Tick?"

I grimaced. In my line of work, the only people I knew I could trust were standing beside me. And if Tick were here right now, I'd have had to revise the statement.

"No," I admitted. "But Tick is the best smuggler in Cothis. He's cornered the market in illegal transport from Cothis to La'Zem. And he owes me a fistful of favors."

"And will his desire to clear his debt with you ensure his discretion?"

I snorted. "Of course not. That's why I'm going to throw a bunch of money at him," I said, mentally counting up the coins in my pocket and kissing a chunk of them goodbye.

"Will money be enough to secure his loyalty?" she asked doubtfully.

"Money's enough for everyone but you, Tass my girl," Kai said with a laugh. "Though feel free to take as much of Tick's time as you'd like. I bet he'll piss himself at the sight of you." Kai shook his head wistfully. "Now that's something I'd like to see before Karanis brutally murders all of us."

"Karanis isn't going to touch us," I said sharply, glancing meaningfully from Kai to Mira and back again. Kai winced and mouthed a silent "sorry" at me. "It's all going to work out fine," I said with far more confidence than I actually felt.

"We'll need spending money," Zee murmured. "Small coins, not the ingots the Curator hands out."

I nodded. Tick's services wouldn't come cheap, but if he saw the payment we'd just gotten—the heavy gold roundels jingling in my coin purse—the price would triple. I swallowed hard. Turned to Edik. "That's where you come in. Me, Kai, and Mira will go find Tick while you, Zee, and Tass go clear out your stash box. We meet at Tick's joint."

"Is it wise to split up?" Tass asked,

My first reply was a half-hearted shrug. "Don't split your party" was practically rule number one. Except when you can't stop half your team from doing something stupid. Then you may as well lean into the chaos.

"A group our size is bound to stand out, and that's the last thing we need today." I looked at Edik, read the guarded approval in his dark gaze. "You got forty-five minutes—hour at the most. After that, Tick will probably stash us in one of his safe houses."

"We won't need that long," Edik replied, his soft voice heavy with broken promises.

"Let's get moving," Kai said brightly, oblivious to the tension between Edik and me. To the sure and present knowledge that our cobbled-together family was about to break.

Forever.

14

TASSIEL

Sunlight seared her eyes as she pulled herself out of the manhole. Tassiel blinked a few times, only to find herself in the middle of the road right in front of the Cothis Code Hall.

She cursed her grandfather's pettiness, as their sudden presence in the middle of the street caused an uproar from the carriages trying to get past. She ignored the red-faced drivers shouting from their carriage seats and helped Bal pull the crew onto the road. They needed to hurry. Things would get complicated if any codekeepers came to investigate the noise.

"Oi!"

As if her thoughts had summoned them, she spun and spotted a dozen codekeepers pouring out of the Code Hall, looking at them like they were insane.

"Shit," Bal swore, hauling Edik up while the rest of the crew sprinted to the sidewalk. "We gotta move."

"See you soon," she said, darting one way as Bal went the other.

Zeelaya and Edik were ahead, weaving through carriages and street-carts, their arms pumping to outrace the codekeepers. She lengthened her stride, easily catching up with Zeelaya and Edik as the street wound and curved in nonsensical loops. Typical Cothis, she thought. Creation forbid the humans lay out their cities in orderly grids.

Behind them, the shrill sound of a whistle cried out. The noise raked up her spine so sharply, her lips peeled back with a snarl. What was the point in whistling? Did the codekeepers really think they were going to stop?

She followed Edik around a blind turn and slammed into his back. He shuddered forward, nearly toppling, as Zeelaya skidded to a stop behind them.

Up ahead, six more codekeepers stood in a line, their eyes wide, as they sized she and Edik up, hands falling toward holsters. Perhaps the whistling wasn't pointless after all.

Edik seized Zeelaya's hand and dragged her sideways into a trash-lined alley. Tassiel followed, darting around molding food and jumping over puddles of sick. Once more she couldn't help but denigrate humans, swallowing down her own vomit. Having superior senses was usually a boon, but on hot Cothis mornings, she'd have gladly traded them away.

The alley let out not on a road, but on a canal—though most of the water had been drained for repairs. Ten miserable-looking workers stood in ankle-deep muck watching them with unguarded curiosity, their hammers and chisels frozen in midair. Edik all but ignored them, his head darting back and forth, no doubt tallying his options.

A spider's web worth of sidewalk hugged the edge of the building and fell in a slanting three-foot drop to fetid muddy remnants of canal water. Edik risked the walkway, and she followed, expecting to see the broad man fall at any moment. His nimble feet surprised her. He sprinted the length of the sidewalk behind Zeelaya without faltering.

It appeared like they were heading for the bridge up ahead—not that anyone deigned telling her the location of their destination. If they had bothered, she could have perhaps suggested an alternate route. They'd have to clamber up the side of the bridge and try to slide into the crowd of morning traffic to escape the codekeepers. She bit the inside of her cheek, frustration welling up inside her. Humans were an obstinate breed, but she doubted even they could ignore three people vaulting over the bridge's railing.

If they even made it that far.

She calculated the average height of their pursuers and the distance they had to run before reaching the end of the alley. The codekeepers would spot them in less than thirty seconds. And if they were smart, they'd be sending some men ahead to block any escape.

There was nothing for it. They'd have to hide.

"Under the bridge," Tassiel commanded, threading a tendril of magic into her voice. She felt both Zeelaya and Edik resist. Their minds wriggled against the order, but with their adrenaline so high their human brains were mostly running on instinct. And all animals knew when to submit.

As one, they slid down the canal's brick embankment and into the mud. They darted beneath the shade of the bridge, wedging themselves in the V-shaped junction where the stone foundation met the side of the road.

"What are we doing?" Zeelaya hissed, dragging herself onto the downward slope of the foundation. "They'll see us right away."

"No. They won't," Tassiel countered, crouching beside her.

"But—"

"Stay still," she snapped. "I am going to disguise us, but do not move. Speak if you must, but do nothing else."

She sensed Edik's assent right away. Despite his distrust, there was a core of him that was used to taking orders. Tassiel didn't wait for Zeelaya's. She wouldn't believe no matter what Tassiel said. Only results mattered, and if Edik was staying, so was Zeelaya.

Tassiel spoke a latch phrase in her mind and felt magic funnel into her chest. Pain, white-hot and molten, flared down from the base of her neck to the tip of her tailbone, as energy poured out of her nameplate.

She cut off the flow of time energy, savoring its coppery tang as it passed by her face and pooled in her hands. The metal plates beneath the pads of her fingers hummed with promise, itching to do something wonderful.

She raised both hands. Stretched her fingers into well-practiced forms and froze. Magic unleashed in a jasmine-scented whisper. It passed unnoticed by Zeelaya and Edik, surrounding them.

Light twisted and turned away. Shadows grew, and slowly, inescapably, the world beneath the bridge went dark.

The scent of fear reared up inside the barrier, as human heartbeats ran wild against fragile rib cages. She sighed and twisted one hand thirty degrees, allowing a trickle of light into their unseen bower. Enough for the humans to see past the barrier, while maintaining their hidden pocket of space from the hawk-eyed codekeepers scouring the edge of the canal.

So complete was the barrier that none of the men looked their way as they heaved themselves up and over the bridge's railing. She heard thumping footsteps thunder through the brick. It was the unmistakable cadence of codekeepers sprinting up and down the bridge like rats on a sinking ship.

She allowed the muscles in her back to relax as the last waves of pain ebbed out of her body. "You can shift now if you need to but make no large movements until I say so."

"All Father, save us," Edik murmured. "What did you do, Tass?"

"I cast a barrier around our hiding spot."

"But how?" Zeelaya asked, slack-jawed with amazement.

Tassiel swallowed. Her arms were growing heavy as gravity pulled her limbs down with an insistent, intractable grip. "I doubt I could explain it to your satisfaction, Zeelaya. But the All Father had nothing to do with it."

"Magic, love. This is magic," Edik said, taking Zeelaya's hand.

"You would say that, you superstitious nut."

Edik smiled at his wife with an indulgence that was completely foreign to Tassiel. It was so intimate, so full of love and— She shook the thought away before her mind started down a road she could not follow. Instead, Tassiel turned her attention to the two humans. The advantage of the barrier—aside from the obvious—was that Zeelaya and Edik were stuck and she could finally try to get some answers.

"Why are we really out here?" Tassiel asked. The question had been bothering her since Bal split the crew.

Zeelaya shot her husband a sharp look before her eyes darted back, saying, "It's like we said. We need to get all the weapons and coins out of the stash. Things are flowing off a cliff fast here. There's no telling when, or if, we'll be able to return."

Tassiel felt the corners of her mouth turn down. Lies, she'd found, had their own rhythm, their own scent and song. And sitting there, with the shield blocking out much of the world around them, she could hear Zeelaya's heart skip. Her words weren't untrue, not completely, but she was holding something back.

"You already have weapons," Tassiel said, nodding to the bags strapped on their backs. "And the Curator gave you money, so whatever is in the stash is not required for your escape."

"But as I said before we split, the coins we have are too big—too noticeable. We need money we can use now without drawing too much attention."

"You really think this 'Tick' cares what kind of coin is put in his hand?" She paused, waiting for one of them to speak. Neither did.

Impatience swarmed around her like invisible gnats, nibbling away her calm. "From everything I've observed, Zeelaya, you are not the sort of person who acts on impulse. You calculate and weigh your actions as precisely as you did those beads hanging from your ears. And Edik, you are the one who plans for the worst—like you did with the go bags you stored in the Low Temple. You know coming for the stash was a risk. Doubly so since the Curator pushed us out

6

of the Archive in front of the Code Hall. But you came anyway. So
what are you really after?"

"We told you, we're going for the stash," Edik replied, his face
going carefully blank. He reminded Tassiel of Luithus. Her brother,
the consummate soldier, never gave anything away that might be
used against him. Little wonder the comparison sprang to mind.
There was something martial about Edik, something in the way he
stood, the way he moved. Those square shoulders always seemed to
be waiting for the worst to happen.

"I know that." She gave them a pointed look. "And I told you why
it doesn't add up."

"It's money—" Zeelaya said

"Which is, again, irrelevant to our current situation."

Tass could feel Zeelaya trying to resist, but the admission came
forth anyway. "It's *our* money." A strangled sound wheezed out of
Edik and Zeelaya gave him a flickering smile. "We're stuck in this
bubble, love. And I doubt she'll stop prying," she added, tossing
Tassiel an annoyed look. "I don't see any point in hiding the truth."

Tassiel let the disapproval slide off her. "What do you mean, *your*
money? Does the Talion not share their spoils?"

"Of course. But unlike the boys, we've been saving our shares,"
Zeelaya replied.

There was something smug in the way she spoke, like someone
who had sacrificed much and was soon going to see their just des-
serts. "Saving for what?"

An uncharacteristically shy sort of blush rose on Zeelaya's cheeks,
and she glanced at Edik, who grinned. "For our future. We've plans
to open a shop."

"We're going to sell my mechanicals," Zeelaya added, embold-
ened. "Not just munitions, either. I have all sorts of ideas. I'm going
to build everything, and Edik will sell them. They have all kinds of
those shops on Sala."

Tassiel nodded. Sala was the home of Ashaar's inventors and

scientists. Funny that, considering Sala's patron god was Sarthaniel, goddess of magic and chief mage of the Nethersphere.

Their excitement coated the barrier in a pretty pink sheen. Through it, she saw four codekeepers clamber down from the bridge. They slid into the water, searching the shallow shoreline for clues, as if Tassiel and her companions were hiding beneath four inches of muck and rubbish.

"You're leaving the Talion." Tassiel didn't bother posing it as a question. She knew the answer. They had a future planned, and it wasn't the kind that included being chased by codekeepers.

Zeelaya's smiled faded. "Not right away. We still need to save some more money . . ."

"But eventually, yes," Edik said, and Tassiel felt him navigate them past the edges of a very well-worn argument between him and Zeelaya.

"Does Bal know?" Tassiel asked.

"I haven't exactly told him yet." Zeelaya's hand fell to her middle, like these questions were a blade she needed to protect herself from. "I mean he knows we can't simply run around robbing rich snobs for the rest of our lives. He should know."

Edik, Tassiel noticed, looked carefully away, his lips pressed into a thin line as his wife spoke.

Tassiel's brows rose. "People very rarely consider all the things they *should* know."

Edik slid and arm around Zeelaya's shoulders appraising Tassiel with hard eyes. "What's all this to you, anyway?"

"Nothing. I was simply curious." A sickly sweet taste covered her tongue as the lie left her lips. She stilled, confused by the truth her untruth revealed. What was it to her if Zeelaya and Edik were leaving the crew? She barely knew any of them, and once their contract was through, she would never see them again.

"Are you going to tell him?" Zeelaya asked in a small voice.

"No," Tassiel replied. "But you should. Sooner rather than later.

He'll need to prepare." There was nothing worse than being blind-sided by loss. Abandoned. Betrayed.

"Bal's a canny sort. He'll replace us right quick and soon forget he ever let a pair of geezers run with him."

Zeelaya smiled as if this sentence made sense, but as usual, colloquially spoken Ashaarite had defeated her. "What in the name of Creation is a 'geezer'?"

Edik snorted, an annoyingly common response to her ignorance. "A geezer is an old person," he explained.

"Old? You?" She shook her head. Zeelaya was in her twenties, and Edik could not be more than thirty. "Surely you cannot be a geezer. Even for your short-lived kind, you're young."

Edik shrugged. "Compared to Kai, I'm ancient."

"Hardly fair. Even Mira seems ancient and wise next to Kai," Tassiel argued, surprised by the fondness in her own voice. It sobered her.

Tassiel opened her mouth only to close it again. He was right. Compared to the others, Edik and Zeelaya did seem older than their years. Was it the life they lived that aged them? Or was it simply that having Kai and Mira for a contrast made them seem measured and mature. "All this does make me curious."

"You're like my wife," Edik chuckled. "Everything makes you curious."

Zeelaya swatted his arm. "There's nothing wrong with an inquiring mind. What was your question, Tassiel?"

"Why do you follow Balthazar? The two of you are older, undoubtedly more experienced, yet Bal is your leader. Why?"

"Ah. More experienced at life, maybe," Edik said, waving a hand like he was flicking her words away. "Bal's the one with a vision for things, a flair for how to get things done. The rest of us are just here to make sure it happens."

Zeelaya tutted. "You make me sound like dead weight."

"Fine," Edik chuckled. "Zee's here to make sure the plans Bal dreams up become reality."

"Then Kai's there to break things at the worst moment," Zee added, her obvious affection taking the sting out of the words. "And then Mira makes sure both boys come home in one piece. They'd never leave her in harm's way."

"And I guess I'm here to make sure you all don't forget to eat," Edik added.

"No," Tassiel said, her mind turning back to the evacuation plan. "You are clearly the one who ensures that everyone makes it out alive."

"That seems to be your part to play too, Tass," Edik said with a smile, though the expression seemed strained, as his eyes traced the outlines of her mask. It was almost like he was searching for something.

His gaze cut away as another codekeeper appeared on the bank of the canal. Edik sucked in a breath, one hand going to Zeelaya. An instinctual attempt to protect her, Tassiel thought, turning toward the bank. A very familiar sergeant stood on the sidewalk, arms crossed as he surveyed the scene.

"There is your sergeant again," she said, catching the thinning of Edik's lips from the corner of her eye. "Who is he to you?"

"His name is Xavier Tammon. He was my superior officer when I served in the Ashaarite Army, First Brigade, Swords of Janus."

A bitter chuckle slid from her lips. "We have that in common too," Tassiel said—her father called all of them his swords. That was all they were to him. Tools. She shook her head, pulling away from her own anger. "Odd that he appears twice in so many days, pursuing you. Is there some bad blood between you?"

"Bad blood?" Zeelaya scowled through the barrier as if she'd like nothing more than to slap the older man. "Tammon is the reason Edik got kicked out of the army."

"It wasn't Sarge's fault," Edik said softly, looking from Zeelaya to

Tassiel then out to the Sergeant. "There was corruption in the ranks. Money and weapons were going missing. I didn't have anything to do with it, but I knew who did.

"Unfortunately, when the investigation started to heat up, the bastards who were responsible all went to their highborn daddies and got everything swept under the rug. But they needed a fall guy, and I didn't have an influential family guarding my back."

A sharp, fluttery something wriggled in Tassiel's chest. Empathy, she realized belatedly. She and Edik were more than just swords of Janus, they were also the convenient victims of corruption. Used up and tossed away. "Sergeant Tammon discharged you?"

"No. He was supposed to arrest me, but he knew I'd been set up. He got a message to me before he and his men came by, giving me time to escape."

A good man indeed, Tassiel thought. Far better than any of her siblings.

"I wonder what he's doing with the Cothis Code Hall," Edik mused as the sergeant raised his whistle to his lips. He gave it two short blasts and rounded up his men.

"I wonder if he is still the good man you knew."

Edik's eyes narrowed. "What do you mean?"

"I mean that our allies are in short supply. We may need your sergeant before the end." Especially if Bal meant to go after Shasheba, which Tassiel was half sure he intended to do the moment Mira was safe.

Tammon made to turn to go after his men, but something caused him to stop. Look over his shoulder. Some ingrained instinct drilled into career soldiers.

Tassiel's eyes went to Edik. Edik who watched his commanding officer. Thinking. Weighing.

Hoping.

Edik shook his head. "I don't know."

"I wouldn't count on him," Zeelaya said, her lips going thin. "He was in the temple when the portal opened. He would have seen what Karanis did to all those innocent people. Yet here he is now, free as a bird."

She shook her head, face filled with scorn. "He must be working for Karanis now, trying to locate the missing half of the idol. Trying to find us. And you know what will happen if we're found?" Zeelaya squeezed Edik's hand so hard her knuckles went white, forcing him to look at her.

"We'll die."

A lie once spoken has its own taste and song. But lies don't need words to exist. They can arise in the lines of a body. In a husband's nod to a worried wife.

Edik lunged, pushing Zeelaya away. Stumbling through the bubble of protection, fragile as a spider's web.

The darkness would have failed had Tassiel been any slower. As it was, her fingers burned with liquid fire as magic and will forced the bubble to stabilize.

But outside the bubble . . .

She watched Edik stand tall. Watched his gaze meet Tammon's.

A heartbeat and years passed between the men before Edik finally brought his fist to his heart in a salute. The sight of it almost seemed to make Tammon smile.

He glanced about himself as if checking that he was alone before joining Edik beneath the shade of the bridge. Tension roiled off the older man's high shoulders. Tension and tightly held horror. "I had sincerely hoped I wouldn't see you today, Agodzi."

"That makes two of us, Sarge."

The word made Tammon wince. "The governor is looking for you and your friends."

Edik nodded and Tassiel nearly screamed at him to find out more. Instead she threw her whisper into Edik's ear. "Where is he now?" He blanched but repeated the question.

"At the temple when he let me go," Tammon replied. "I don't

know if he'll remain there. He did not deign to trust others with his plans."

"Then why are you helping him?" Edik demanded.

"I'm protecting my people," Tammon shot back, desperation shining in his eyes. "And I must insist you do the same."

"What?"

"Do you have a way off the island?"

"Do I—" Edik faltered, and Tassiel could feel their shared history writhing between them like a living thing formed of loyalty and betrayal.

"Yes. I do."

Tammon nodded. "Then I hereby deputize you a codekeeper of the Kingdom of Ashaar, servant of the empress."

Edik made a strangled noise of protest, but Tammon had already closed the distance between them, pressing a folded parchment into his hands.

"Get this to the empress. And this too," he said, forcing his badge onto Edik. "So she knows it's genuine."

"Sarge, I—"

"We need help. Reinforcements, and you're the only one I can trust—the only one he can't reach. Do this, Edik, and I have no doubt that the charges against you will be dropped. You won't have to run anymore. You can start over. Clean.

"Do this, and you'll be free."

Humans.

They never ceased to surprise her.

15

BALTHAZAR

Mira and I followed Kai blindly around the first corner. The sound of a codie's boots pounding on the pavement at my back sent adrenaline pouring into me. My body screamed to go faster. Instead, I willed myself to slow, letting Mira's shorter legs set our pace.

We dodged past carriages and wagons, wove through young men clutching letters and fruit-sellers balancing oranges on their heads—crowds of men and women busy getting back to work after yesterday's celebrations and the deluge that night.

A handful of people sipping coffee at a café watched us pass with narrowed eyes. Not. Good. We were being too conspicuous. Standing out would kill our chances of getting off the island—might kill us too. We needed to go to ground.

Kai ducked down a narrow alley up ahead. I let out a low whistle and as I turned the corner, saw him pull to a stop in the shade.

I halted beside him, flattening myself against the alley wall and peered back out into the street. "All right, we've lost the codies. Time to blend in with the crowd; we've got a stop to make before we head to Tick's."

"What stop?" Mira asked, brows knitting together.

I shot a sidelong glance in Kai's direction. "We're not too far from Aunt Nell's."

Kai huffed a laugh. Nell was his aunt by the furthest kind of technicality, a relation so distant not even the old woman herself was able to clearly trace it. But she was also the proprietor of Thistle and Bloom, a bank—albeit one that didn't trade in money—that fronted as a perfumery.

"You want to make a withdrawal?" Kai asked, catching on to the idea. Aunt Nell held one of our many stash boxes in the back room of her business—same as she did for many crooks in the city. Kai had opened an account for us a few years back, and now seemed like a good fucking time to use it.

"As much as I hate being the voice of reason, is that a good idea?" Mira asked, biting the edge of her thumb as she scanned the street. "What if she turns us in?"

"Don't worry about that, Mira. Aunt Nell loves me—we're family. No way she'd turn *me* in," Kai said, fastening the top button of his rumpled plum coat to hide the handles of his twin revolvers.

I gave Mira a bracing smile when she didn't look convinced. "Staying neutral is how Nell stays alive. And anyway, we're going to need the firepower."

Kai's eyes narrowed in my direction. "What for?"

I gave Kai the side-eye. "After yesterday I want some extra backup. I don't want to risk getting caught on our way off this shithole without ammunition."

"You don't trust Tick?"

"I trust him as far as I can throw him."

"So . . . yard and a half?"

A surprised laugh whooshed out of my chest. Great Below I loved

Kai. Always knew when to lighten the mood. "Please, I could make it at least two."

"Bet?"

I grinned by way of reply and padded to the alley's other end. No codies that way either. Good. Or maybe not. Had they all gone after the other three? My eyes scoured the crowd, as if I could force them to reappear simply by willing it so. Gods, I hated splitting the group. But Edik and Zee knew what they were doing. And they had Tass. She'd make sure they were safe.

Glancing over my shoulder, I spotted Mira shoving her hair into her cap, collar flicked up so that she looked like any other street kid. "I'm ready when you are," she said with a half smile.

I led the way back into the morning sun, the air thick and humid on my face. It would be a gift worthy of the empress to be safe on our ship right now, putting my feet up with a cool pint in my hand. But that wasn't to be. Not yet, anyway.

Not until I got everyone safe. Shasheba included, I thought, hating how close we were to the Low Temple right now. Hating that I wasn't using this time to go and look for her. But I couldn't. Not with Tass's warning still fresh in my mind.

No. I'd wait until the crew was back together. Get them to a safe house and secure transport off the island. Only then would I go after Shasheba. Maybe I could steal her away. I was a thief, after all. My reputation would be ruined if I couldn't find a way to sneak off with a willing woman.

Bolstered by my plan—rudimentary though it was—and my overweening confidence, I led Kai and Mira across the city to the Thistle and Bloom. The perfumery had been built in the continental style, eschewing the typical hodgepodge of red and orange brick for a creamy facade that Aunt Nell must have paid a fortune whitewashing every year. Dusty rose shutters framed the curving windows and a cheery white-and-sage-striped awning covered her door. If it seemed like an odd place to hide an armory . . .

It was.

Which was what made it so damn genius. The last place the codies would search for illegal weapons was the store where they bought their mother's last solstice gift.

The door chime shrieked to life as I pushed into the store, setting my teeth on edge with its false merriment. I squinted into the gloom, trying to squeeze the sun out of my eyes when a voice lanced out from the darkness.

"Take one more step and it will be your last."

I knew better than to argue with Nell when she used that tone. Gluing my legs together, I raised my hands, felt Kai and Mira do the same as I scoured the shop for its owner. She wasn't sitting behind the gleaming mahogany counter, or cataloging any of the thousands of perfume bottles arranged on the cramped shelves. Rather she sat perched in an upper balcony made of black wrought iron. A slingshot, of all things, braced in her hands.

She wasn't aiming at me, I noticed, rather belatedly. But rather at an enormous—and extremely fragile-looking—glass canister above my head. It was full of clear liquid, and I was damn sure it wasn't perfume. Probably acid.

"Relax, Aunt Nell," Kai called out, a bright smile easing across his face for the first time all day. "It's just me."

Nell took another second to glare at me before turning to Kai, her expression transforming. Not that she looked particularly kind, mind you. Unlike most women who reached the far side of eighty, Nell hadn't softened with age. She was a wiry slip of a woman, and tough as old boot leather—in both looks and temperament.

She rose without any apparent effort, gliding down the spindly staircase with a slight smile that threatened to crack her porcelain face. "Malakai, my darling boy. What are you doing just standing there? Come give your auntie a hug."

Kai went a little pink around the ears, but did what he was told, though the old woman was positively dwarfed by his size.

"That was quite the greeting, Nell," I said as neutrally as I could given that she'd nearly dropped a vat of acid on my face. "You expecting trouble?"

She harumphed, her glower returning. "When you've lived as long as I have you can smell when there's trouble on the wind. Trouble that sounds an awful lot like the Vadalen family."

The glare she leveled at me made Mira shift slightly backward like I was a human shield she wasn't above using. I couldn't blame her. Nell had never liked me. Never liked any of the Vadalens. Even when we were the brightest stars in the city. Or, maybe especially then.

"No trouble, Nell. Honest."

She cocked a doubtful eyebrow at Kai. "Then what are you doing here? Picking up perfume for your latest paramour?"

He huffed a laugh. "No, Nell—no one's good enough for the magic you brew."

I exchanged a deadpan stare with Mira. Nell might have gotten her start in perfume, but she made most of her money in poison. The "magic" Nell brewed was deadly, and any individual Kai actually liked should count themselves lucky to avoid it.

"Just looking to make a withdrawal," I said, cutting in before Kai and Nell made a whole day of it. Typical Kai. He spends the whole week in the city without thinking of Nell only to waste minutes we didn't have on chitchat.

"Still not one to bother with good manners, eh, Vadalen?"

This was patently untrue but there was no point arguing with Nell. "Afraid we're in something of a time crunch."

"Hmm." It was the only reply Nell gave and hell was it loaded.

We followed her behind the counter and through a back room filled with drying plants and oils and beakers and tubes and All Father only knew what else. Didn't matter. The important part of the shop was its basement. Behind a hidden bookcase was a staircase so narrow only Nell and Mira could walk down it comfortably. There in the darkness, where the air cooled with a mineral-smelling caress, was a catacomb-like passageway.

"Ever feel like all we do is go underground?" Kai asked.

I couldn't argue.

The passageway spanned the whole block in a spindly network of interconnected tunnels. An ant colony of human proportions that only Nell knew how to navigate. And only she could safely access.

Nell stopped us at our vault and waved a gnarled hand in my direction. I produced the key for her inspection. Which she did. At length. Eventually she placed it in the first lock. Kai's key went in the second. Nell's in the third.

The last hole in the door was less of an actual lock and more of a stopper. So small it would be easy for an intruder to miss, it was the perfect size, shape, and dimension of the Talion pendant I wore around my chest. I handed the sliver of metal over to Nell and tried not to fidget as she studied it, like she expected it to be a fake even though she'd known me practically my whole damn life. Finally she fitted the medal into the last hole, where it would stop the bomb rigged in the door from exploding in our fucking faces.

The vault swung open with a hiss revealing a ten-by-ten alcove packed with three dozen bombs, at least fifty guns, hundreds of rounds of ammunition, and one large ball.

I grabbed a rucksack from a hook on the wall, slapped it on the wooden table in the center of the room, and got to work. Kai and I filled the bag with guns and bullets and as many hand grenades as we dared. I passed the bag to Kai when we were done. Paused. Then grabbed the ball and handed it to Mira.

Something almost akin to worry spasmed across Nell's face when she saw it. Then she remembered Mira was a Vadalen and all that fear evaporated into anger. She rounded on me.

"Just what the hell kind of trouble are you in, Vadalen?"

"Who said anything about trouble?" I asked the question idly, but if Nell had heard anything about what happened last night, I needed to know.

"The fact that you're here for starters. You wouldn't need all this firepower if all you were up to was a simple robbery."

"I never do simple robberies," I said with a smile that died before it reached my eyes.

She let out a sound that might have been a chuckle. Probably just dislodging phlegm.

I weighed her words, considered pressing her for more, but . . . But I didn't really think she knew anything. Half of me wanted to walk out and leave her questions unanswered, but for Kai's sake I managed something like civility. "Some shit went down on our job last night. We need to get out of the city."

"You probably should too, Nell," Kai added, the low light giving his skin a sallow cast.

Nell's lips evaporated into a thin line. "There's nothing Cothis can deal out that I can't handle. If you're smart, boy, you'll stay with me."

That last line she delivered to Kai—and Kai only—and I didn't bother hiding my annoyance this time. It was the same refrain she preached every time we came by. Great Below, I wished we didn't have to do business with this old harpy.

"I can't stay with you, Nell," Kai said. "It'll only put you in danger."

"I can handle the danger," was her sour reply. Her cheek began to tick. Words seemed to build inside her, working up to the real source of all her anger. "Now you listen to me, Malakai. Your mother is a good woman, but she was a fool when it came to that Vadalen bastard. Fancied herself in love. Don't mistake me—she doesn't regret a thing where you're concerned, but don't think it didn't break her heart to see what that family did to you."

Kai's wince of embarrassment was almost visceral. Mira looked like she wanted to disappear into the wall, because hell—what kid wanted to hear about her dead father's mistress? As for me? I was tired. I loved my father, and he hadn't deserved to die. But to say he left behind a checkered legacy? Understatement.

"They didn't do anything to me, Nell."

"That's exactly my point. You've got as much noble blood running through your veins as those brats, but did he bother to acknowledge you? Raise you up and give you his name? Of course not. He shunted you off to the servants' quarters and did his best to forget about you."

"That's not true," Mira said hotly. "Father loved Kai."

"But he loved his own reputation more," Nell spat.

I curled an arm around Mira, holding her silent beside me. There was nothing anyone could say to Nell when she got like this. She was just a storm to be weathered and the less we said, the faster it would pass.

And the sad fact was, I couldn't really blame her, I thought, as guilt wrenched through my gut. Not like Kai's mother got pregnant on her own. Though she'd never revealed who Kai's father was, she was obviously . . . favored . . . by my father. So was Kai. Just never acknowledged.

It wore on my friend—my brother—in more ways than I could count.

But the Curator had seen it, I realized all of a sudden. The identities he'd offered hadn't just been clean. They'd been *noble*. Not because me or Mira or Zee missed the status. But because Kai had always longed for it. For the life that could have been his, if only my father had been a better man. A braver one.

"His son is no different, Malakai. Don't think for one second that he won't turn on you when things go bad."

"Nell, stop," Kai said, sounding angry for the first time. "Bal isn't going to betray me."

"He doesn't have to," she countered. "You get arrested, and his name will do all the work for him. Doesn't matter that the Vadalens are worth as much as mud these days, there's power in a name that old. He won't go down. None of them will. Only you will, boy."

"If we get arrested, prison time is going to be the least of our worries."

"We're leaving," I said, putting a physical period on the conversation by grabbing my key and pendant and heading for the surface. "Always a pleasure, Nell."

Nell continued to harangue Kai all the way to the door, but I stopped listening. They were walking in the right direction. That was all that mattered.

I shouldered out of the store, checking my pocket watch while Kai said his goodbyes to Nell. Time for us to be heading south to the Bo'sun's Whip. Hopefully the others had shaken off the codies and gotten to the stash. But even if they hadn't, I was afraid to wait any longer. Last thing I wanted to do was hunt Tick down at the docks. I didn't want to risk that kind of exposure if Karanis was looking for us.

And he certainly was.

Gods did it just figure that all Nell was good for was a lecture none of us needed. Would it have killed the old woman to actually know anything useful? Probably, I thought, glancing bitterly at the too-blank-to-be-genuine look on Mira's face. At the misery crowding along Kai's shoulders as we hit the streets.

It was a look that didn't quite ease as we crossed canals and neighborhoods, wending farther and farther away from the temple. But the threat it represented loomed.

"Quit that," I snapped, my nerves getting the best of me as Mira bounced the melon-size leather ball on her head. She obeyed, but not before she shot me a mutinous glare that did nothing to hide the hurt in her eyes. *Aww, hell.* But that ball was the last thing she should be playing with. We didn't keep it in a vault with guns and clockwork bombs because it was harmless.

Which wasn't to say a bomb going off in this part of town wouldn't *increase* property values. The closer we got to the docks, the shittier our surroundings became. A rot that went right into the foundations, poisoning the road beneath our feet. The ruler-straight cobblestones and wide sidewalks of the upper city gave way to clay and mud. Only the occasional brick poked stubbornly out of the earth like the last tooth in an ancient mouth.

Several generations ago, one of my ancestors had paved these streets, but the roads had since eroded. Time and storms and destitution had that effect on the world. It washed away all traces of my family's legacy like trash in the rain.

This area was the lowest point in Cothis, and on days like this, the sea seemed intent on reclaiming it. The street, while hard-packed in the hot summer months, squelched under my boots after last night's storm. With the road buckling beneath me, I left a trail of misshapen footsteps in my wake. It was why the rest of the city referred to the harbor-side denizens as mudtrackers.

Mudtrackers occupied the part of the city no one else wanted to be in. It was the first area to wash out and the last to dry. Because it was so close to the port, it was always filled with foulmouthed (and even fouler-smelling) sailors from all over the world. And there was nothing worse than a sailor for a neighbor; always raging for drinks and a warm body—both readily available from any number of street gangs. Between the mud, the sailors, and the ever-present stench of week-old fish that crawled into your clothes and burrowed into your skin, it was the clear opposite of high society. And hopefully the last place Karanis would search for us.

I kept a sharp eye as we made our way to Tick's favorite hole, the Bo'sun's Whip, but no one I passed paid us any attention. I frowned. I'd sensed tension in the upper city. After the disaster at the temple yesterday, the codekeepers should be scouring the streets in search of us. People should be cowering in their homes, hiding from their would-be master. They had no business being out and about. Hell, a god appeared in the damn temple last night. He killed over a hundred people.

How could everyone be going about their day like nothing had happened?

The obvious conclusion was that no one knew. And that in itself beggared belief. Wouldn't Karanis want to proclaim his dominance over his new home? Why wasn't he parading through the streets, declaring his rule to the masses? Unless he was waiting for something. For the rest of the idol, perhaps.

Thinking of Karanis made the skin on my back itch. As if I had summoned him, the weight of being watched blanketed me like clouds passing over the sun. I peeked over my shoulder, but no one was scrutinizing us. No one even looked our way. Still, a real and painful longing for Tass's otherworldly presence gripped me. I remembered the way we walked out of the Code Hall doors the night I met her. That kind of gift could come in handy.

"Why does everything seem so bloody normal right now?" Kai spat onto the muddy ground, his shoulders so high it was like he expected the sky to fall at any moment. All the shame Nell had shoveled on him now coated with six tons of fear.

"I don't know," I replied tightly, wanting nothing more than to ease the load. Carry the burden. "But if I had to guess, *he's* probably trying to keep things quiet for the time being."

Mira gave Kai what I'm sure was meant to be reassuring pat, but he just about jumped out of his skin when she touched him.

"Someone should have noticed it by now, though—that none of the workers returned, I mean," Kai said.

"I know," I muttered. Then again, if Karanis was trying to keep things quiet, maybe he released the rest of his guests. A terrible, painful kind of hope expanded in my chest. "I'm sure we'll find out more from Tick. He always manages to stay in the know."

Whether or not he'd tell us—and what it would cost—was another thing.

The Bo'sun's Whip sat on the tail end of a winding street that led to nothing but a pile of chipped stones that no one ever bothered to clean up. It was a squat building whose whitewashed walls had aged to a slightly gray and green patina of slimy, chipping paint. The door hung at a distinct twenty-degree angle to the rest of the building and the shuttered windows were all so warped they bowed outward like buttons straining to contain excess fat.

I shouldered through the door and paused to let my eyes adjust to the half-light. At this hour, when the bar was usually empty, only about a quarter of the lamps were lit. But even if the barkeep had lit all of them, I was sure the darkness would have won its eternal battle against the light. This wasn't the kind of tavern where people wanted to be seen too closely.

Only two other people occupied the taproom. One of them, an exhausted looking barmaid with dark circles under her eyes and an unfortunate pair of handprints staining her tunic, glared as we entered.

I forced even the ghost of a smile from my face and made sure to meet her eyes. "A pitcher of whatever's on tap, please."

She nodded, abandoning her washrag, and left us with the tavern's only other resident.

A tiny man was slumped over the bar. His hair splayed in a greasy black halo around his skull. I'd have worried about dirtying the place, but this was the kind of hole that could only be cleansed with fire. I glanced to Kai. Nodded toward the sleeping man.

Tick.

Kai grinned and sauntered up to the bar. He slapped a hand on Tick's back so hard the smaller man broke out into a fit of coughs. "My man, Tick. How did I know you'd be here?"

Tick raised his head, squinting first at Kai, then at me. His eyes widened with recognition, bulging slightly out of his too-narrow head.

"Kai! Bal! My friends, how are you?" He grinned but had such a severe overbite that his smile was mostly upper teeth.

"Flourishing, as ever," I said as the barmaid slid a pitcher of ale in my direction. Tick looked at it, licking his lips like a man in the desert. "Join us for a drink?"

"But it would be my pleasure."

Suppressing a smirk, I picked up the pitcher and carried it over to a dark table in the corner. I poured Tick a generous serving, sliding the mug his way. He drank it down in one long pull, tapping his mug in mute request for a refill before Kai and I even took a drink. Mira, sitting in the corner of the table—as far from Tick as she could get—watched him with open disgust. She mouthed a silent "eeew" when he belched then smacked his lips like he'd brought up something tasty.

With Kai egging him on, Tick launched into a story about some fight he'd gotten into last night. He spent a good ten minutes describing in excruciating detail how the other man was totally at fault, so Tick was perfectly justified in cutting the man's purse when it turned out his jaw was made of glass.

I smiled, making appreciative noises as Tick spoke. The story was sure to be a complete lie. Tick's little bones were so thin, a rooster could have taken him down. But it passed the time.

Just as Tick was getting ready to launch into another tale, the tavern's door opened and Zee, Edik, and Tass shouldered in. Mira perked up with obvious relief, waving at them as if they could miss us in the empty room. Zee nodded my way. Her expression was heavy. Tight even. But she tapped her fingertips along the straps of her pack signaling a successful pickup—so whatever was bothering her, it wasn't that. It'd have to wait, anyway, I thought as they joined us with murmured greetings.

I nearly laughed out loud when Tass slid into the seat beside Mira. She sat so ramrod straight her back put the slanting wall behind her to shame. Tass folded her gloved hands over one another on the tabletop, looking more like a fine—if strangely dressed—lady, than an immortal half-Ankaari gun for hire.

Tick stumbled over his story when he saw her. Tensed as if he was about to make a run for it, but Kai threw his arm around Tick's narrow shoulders, weighing him down.

A strange little giggle whistled out of Tick's lips while his eyes darted around, taking in the rest of the crew, before returning to

Tass's silver face. "I didn't know your whole crew was coming, Bal. . . . And a friend."

I didn't bother hiding my smirk this time. "Yes. This is the Queen of Days. Perhaps you've heard of her?"

Tick's eyes bulged so wide I was half sure they'd fall out of his head. "Nice to meet you miss—uh, my la—um, ma'am." His body folded in what I'm sure was meant to be a bow, but he was so short his face nearly hit the table.

Tass didn't reply, but I thought I saw a slight tremor of contained laughter run through her. I refilled Tick's mug, swallowing the urge to laugh along with her. "So listen, Tick," I said, turning my mug in my hand. "We need a way off the island. Today."

Tick glanced to me, and I saw something cunning flash across his face. "Today? I thought you were here for a job—you finish it already?"

I took a long drink, stalling for time while I took his measure. Tick looked like a nobody, but he was the most well-informed man on Cothis with a network that reached all the way to La'Zem. Even if he didn't know about the temple heist yet, he would soon. "We *are* here for a job," I said. "Or we were, but our patron has put us off for the time being." I shrugged at Tick's narrowing eyes. "Not that he bothered to tell us why, just sent one of his men this morning to tell me the job was off. That's nobility for you."

"Ah. A shame," Tick said, gulping down some more ale.

"Yeah. Anyway, we need an . . . unofficial way to La'Zem. Sooner the better."

"Why the rush?" he asked, one of his knees bouncing out an uneven rhythm.

I summoned a winning smile. "You know me, Tick. I always have more than one job on the burner."

Tick chuckled. "That you do, Bal. That you do. And a good thing too, because an export like that—and for all of you here—costs."

"Not gonna be an issue."

"You need a crew?"

"No," I said, evenly. "We know how to sail." One of many seemingly useless skills crammed down my throat in my youth. One I'd put to such good use now as a criminal, and between Zee, Kai, and I, we could navigate the strait between Cothis and La'Zem in four hours. Might be more like five if I wasn't with them.

Tick's greasy unibrow rose. "Well, all right then." He drained his mug and stood. "It'll take me a few hours to arrange. Do you want to meet me in the usual spot, or do you need a place to wait?"

"If you have somewhere discreet, I'd appreciate it."

"Discretion's my middle name." He smiled. "I always have a place . . . though it will cost you double."

Slimy little sack of shit obviously felt the anxiety rising off my crew and knew he could cash in on it. Asshole, I thought, even as I nodded my assent.

His grin deepened. "If you come with me, I'll get you all tucked away nice and cozy."

Tick led us out into the bustling streets and started heading south, as if he were following the sound of gulls to water. The closer we got to the docks and the grim-looking monolithic warehouses that lined them, the busier things got. Capitalism bowed to no one. Not even an immortal wannabe god.

"My patron's man was awful twitchy this morning," I said, lying as casually as I could. "Got the feeling something happened last night at the consecration. You hear anything?"

"Not a tweeting peep, my friend," Tick replied, patting down the front of his coat until he found the pocket he was looking for. "Not surprising really," he said, fishing out a crooked and slightly off-color cigarette. He shoved it between his lips and lit it with a battered silver lighter. "With the storm we had last night, it was like the sea god himself were coming to the ceremony."

My gaze snapped toward him, scouring his face for any hint of recognition. Did he know what happened? Or were his words just an unfortunate turn of phrase?

He thwacked my arm and laughed, sending a puff of acrid smoke into my face. "No need to look so sour. Maybe old Karanis squashed your man Paasch."

He didn't know. He *couldn't* know, I thought. Tick was a wily bastard, but not even he would be able to joke about what happened last night.

I forced out a smile. "And rob me the satisfaction of killing Paasch myself? He'd have hell to pay for that kind of insult."

Tick was still chuckling as he led us into a long warehouse perched right on the water's edge. About twenty men trudged back and forth from the pier to the building's open maw, offloading crate after crate of Great Below knew what. A brawny foreman with a face that was mostly chin cursed at his men to keep working when the sight of us caught everyone up short.

The dockies hopped back to work, but the foreman glowered at us as we walked past. As tough as he looked, he didn't comment as we entered the building. Just went to show how often Tick must've brought strange people through here.

Most of the warehouse was stuffed with crates. They were stacked in such high towers they carved artificial streets through the building. I knew better than to ask Tick what was being stored there. How he stayed out of prison with all the crime he had his fingers in was beyond me.

At the far end of the warehouse, tucked behind a leaning box tower, was a rusting iron staircase leading up to a door on the second floor. The room beyond was a large office-like space, complete with a very worn desk piled high with books and parchment. The disordered mess looked like it would blow away with a heavy sigh. A drooping couch and a pair of chairs took up most of the space in the room, though they looked ready to collapse beneath the next person who tried to sit in them.

"How will this do for you?" Tick asked.

The drab furnishings practically shivered with bugs, but at least the room had windows—three whole walls of them. Even calcified with all the salt in the air, they provided a good view of the warehouse yard. It would be damned hard for anyone to sneak up on us. "Perfect."

Tick nodded, rubbing one of his lapels between two fingers, as he hovered by the door. Taking the hint, I shelled out half his payment while my crew wandered about the office.

The coins disappeared into Tick's coat the second after they hit his hand. He gave me an oily grin. "Let me go see what I can rustle up. I'll check back with you by two. I should be able to getchya something by then."

I clapped Tick on the back. "Thanks."

Shutting the door behind him, I turned and found Tass standing so close behind me I flinched.

"What now?" she asked.

The building sagged around me. "Now we wait," I said, shouldering past her as I crossed to the north-facing windows.

Through the scaled glass panes, I could see the great temple of Cothis rise into a gray sky. From this distance, it looked tranquil—hell, it looked idyllic, like a godsdamned beacon declaring the glory of this shitty little city.

I couldn't honestly say why this surprised me. Had I expected the temple to be burning against a black sky? Or see legions of undead soldiers spilling out of it like bees from a hive? Maybe that would have been true had Tass not broken the idol. But she had. And the city just . . . continued. Like nothing ever happened.

Zee leaned on the window frame, arms crossed, watching me with a resolute frown. "You have that look on your face."

"What look?"

"That stupid 'I'm about to do something reckless' look."

Kai groaned from somewhere behind me.

"You're not thinking of going after Karanis, are you?" she pressed when I didn't respond.

"I don't know," Kai muttered. "That reward sounded pretty good."

"Shut up, Kai," Zee snapped. "It sounded good because it was a trap. A trap that will get us killed. Tell me you know that."

I did know that. But with Nell's anger fresh in my ears and the painful hope in Kai's voice. . . . Damn, but a ruthless corner of my brain wanted to reach for it. That con man in my head wanted to take control and use that hope against Kai. My oldest friend.

My brother.

I shoved the urge away and tried not to puke at how ugly it was. "I'm going to the Low Temple." I held up my hand, stalling the argument this would inevitably cause before it could really get going. "I'll do it alone if I must, but I have to get Shasheba out of this."

"Shasheba was in this before we came to the island, Bal," Kai said, clearly struggling to keep his voice level.

"He's right," Edik added from his perch on the desk. "She was always going to be in the Cothis High Temple for the consecration ceremony. Even had we not come here, she would have been there."

"And that's a reason to leave her at the mercy of Karanis?" I nearly shouted. Edik had lost his right to question me as far as I was concerned. His eyes narrowed at me, and I felt the fracture between us widen incrementally.

"Bal—"

"No, Zee." I half snarled the words. Half begged. "I abandoned her once. I won't do it again!"

Zee rocked back on her heels, eyes shining and hopeless. I could've smacked myself. Zee didn't deserve my rage. Shasheba was her friend, too—or had been, at least.

"Look," I continued forcing my voice to a more moderate tone. "I'm not asking you to save her. In fact, I want you to leave. Get off the island. Get to the *Fortune's Fool* and go. Run." *Live.* I didn't say the last word, but it hung in the air.

"So what's your grand plan, Bal?" Zee asked quietly, and quiet was never good where Zee was concerned. "You're just going to strut back into the temple and grab Shasheba from under Karanis's nose, only to be stranded in Cothis without any of us around to help you?"

"Something like that," I said, jaw tight from clenching it so hard, as if I could hold the shreds of a plan between my teeth and will it into fruition. "Though I need your earrings."

Her hand went to one of her ears, confusion riddled across her face. "Why?"

"The Curator and Tass both said that Paasch is getting his power from stealing magic off the people in the temple. That he planned to store it in the copper rafters—rafters he already damaged trying to kill Tass. I'm going to help him finish the job. Kill his power source."

"*Karanis.*"

I turned to Edik, not sure what I did now to earn the derision in his voice. "What?"

"You said Paasch. Not Karanis." Edik shook his head, face utterly devoid of warmth. "Great Below, Bal, when will it be enough?"

"Enough what?"

"Enough rage. Enough grief. Enough of the eye-for-an-eye Talion bullshit." Edik took a step closer, his eyes unreadable. "You said it yourself, Paasch is gone. He's Karanis now. *You* said it, Bal. but you don't want to believe it, do you? Because if Paasch is gone you'll never get your revenge—never mind the fact that no amount of vengeance will bring your family back. Let go of your vendetta before you get us all killed."

It wasn't enough to turn away from Edik. I *walked* away from him. Grabbed the coat I'd abandoned on Tick's desk. It wasn't about revenge anymore. It wasn't about the deaths I could never undo. The life I could never re-create. It wasn't . . .

Except it was. Because Shasheba was still out there.

"What are you doing, Bal?" Zee asked, her voice halting. Afraid. But I couldn't soothe her. Nothing I had to say was going to make things better.

"You saw the city," I said, voice low and foreign to my ears. "Things are calm right now. So, I'm heading for the Low Temple while we're waiting for Tick. Maybe Shasheba has been released. Maybe not, but I have to check. If she's there, I'll bring her back and we will get out of here as planned."

Zee rolled her eyes. "And when you find out she's not there?"

"I'll come back. See you off." I looked at Mira curled up on the couch, staring at me with wide eyes brimming with betrayal. "I will come back," I promised. I would say goodbye.

"This is insane." Kai's voice was thick, like he knew what I was thinking and was fighting down some strong emotion. He prowled across the room, pacing its length like a lion caught in a cage.

"Don't do this, Bal," Mira said. "Tass, tell him not to do this."

I huffed a dry breath that couldn't qualify as a laugh. As if Tass could stop me— Well, she probably could, but she couldn't change my mind.

"This is a matter of honor for your brother, Miraveena," Tass replied after a long pause. Her voice sounded tired. "I think this course of action is ill conceived, but it is beyond my power to change his mind."

"But he'll—"

Whatever I was going to do in Mira's mind was cut off with Tass saying, "However, I have decided to help."

"You have?" Mira sat up straight, her face filling with hope.

"You have?" My surprise was enough—barely—to keep me from walking out the door.

"I have," she said, and then shrugged. "If you recall, I was contracted for three days. So I will go to the Low Temple in Balthazar's stead. If Shasheba is there, I will bring her back." She took a few silent steps to the door and turned, looking over her shoulder at Kai and Zee. "You have until two to change his mind about the rest."

Kai nodded, and Zee said a quiet, "Thanks," which for some reason made Tass pause.

She looked back at Zee and Edik, an emotion I couldn't catch passing between them. "You should discuss all your options. Clear the air. While you can."

On that enigmatic note, Tass walked out the door. But the air seemed to leave with her.

"The fuck is she talking about?" Kai asked, eyes narrowing on Edik.

Edik, whose face had turned to stone. And Zee. Who wouldn't meet my eye.

I looked back at Edik—the friend who had become a stranger. "Edik?"

He widened his stance, bracing himself, it seemed. "I spoke with Sergeant Tammon."

"You son of a bitch," Kai swore, stalking toward Edik. "You sold us out."

"No!" Edik exclaimed quickly. "Never that. But he gave me a letter. Told me to take it to the empress. Call for help."

The news alone didn't tally. It didn't account for Zee's reluctance. Or the acrid stench of guilt in the room. "And you're just supposed to walk into the palace and hand deliver it, are you? Never mind the arrest warrants you've got over your head."

"We get immunity for delivering the letter."

"We?" I asked, spitting the word. "Or *you*?"

"Shit," Kai muttered, "I knew you wanted to go straight, Zee, but—"

"You knew?" I whirled on Kai, who winced, holding up his hands in surrender to an anger I shouldn't be directing at him anyway.

Slowly, fighting waves of grief and blunted knives of betrayal, did I turn to Zee. Zee who practically raised me. More like a sister than a cousin. She looked up at me, eye shining.

"I didn't know how to tell you."

"You can translate a dead language in under a minute, but you couldn't figure out how to open your damn mouth?"

"Bal—"

"Fuck off, Edik," I said, my voice too-flat. "This is a family matter. And you've made your opinion of my family very clear."

Zee's eyes flashed. "That's not fair, Bal."

"Fair? You want to talk fair? I—"

"I'm pregnant."

I fell backward, but there was nowhere to flee.

"I can't bring a child into this life," she said, inching forward, hands wringing together like she wanted to smother the emotion tightening the edges of her face. "Not another one."

My gaze fell on Mira. On the way she'd curled into the shabby couch. On the way she hugged her knees to her chest, clutching so tight it was like she was trying to hold the world together. On the fear and heartbreak scrawled across her face.

All my fight evaporated.

I went to the desk, snatched a scrap of paper, and started to work. Edik and Zee wanted out. Fine.

Fine.

Really. It was fine. It had to be.

They deserved it. The peace. The quiet. The happiness.

And it didn't really impact my plans. I'd never counted on them helping me rescue Shasheba and take down Pa—*Karanis*. But it did bring into focus the clear and present need for more allies. People with a stake in the game.

Now—thanks to Edik—I had one.

My hand raced across the page, churning out a letter in record time; a letter embedded with an old military code Edik had once taught me. I distantly marveled at how quickly it came together, but shit. Disassociating had to be useful for something.

I had the letter folded and ready before I looked up. Found the crew watching me. Waiting, like those creepy wolf statues the Curator had in his library. The fuck they expected me to say . . . ?

"Zee," I managed. "Your earrings?"

I detected the faintest wobble of her lower lip before she stilled it between her teeth. Slowly, heavily, she removed the earrings, holding them out to me in an outstretched hand. I plucked them from her palm, dropping them with the letter.

The envelope distended oddly around them, their weight the only indication that they weren't genuine. Real green jasper wasn't half so heavy, not that anyone but an expert jeweler—or expert thief— would have noted it.

"What are you doing, Bal?" she asked, breaking into the determined focus of my thoughts. Making a lie of their dispassionate bent.

"Sending a letter," I replied as I rose, not quite meeting her eye. "I spotted a courier stand up the street, and I—"

"Bal. Look at me."

I closed my eyes. In the right light, Zee's resemblance to my mother was uncanny, which should have been impossible since we were related through our fathers. But the similarity wasn't rooted in appearance; it was in bearing. In their strength of character. Their poise under pressure. The way they spoke. And hearing her now nearly snapped me in two. I couldn't do that. Couldn't risk breaking. Not now. Not when—

Her hand found mine, warm and solid and sure. "Bal, I—I'm sorry."

"Don't say that," I said, making myself face her. Making myself see her, not as one of the last remaining ties to the life I'd lost. But as the cousin I'd loved every day of my life.

"You have nothing to be sorry for. You're living your life, Zee. It's the one thing they would have wanted for you."

"For *all* of us," she said, the emphasis not lost on me, the same way that the "they" wasn't lost on her. Something in my chest caved, about where my heart should have been. Zee gathered me into her arms. "Come with us, Bal," she whispered, voice shaking.

"I can't," I said, my own arms tightening around her. I wanted to, at least part of me did. But my heart wasn't where it should be because it didn't only belong to me. It was Shasheba's too. Always had been. And if I didn't save her now—didn't try to find a way forward with her, then . . .

Then I'd regret it to my dying breath.

"I can't go. Can't flee. Not again. But you should. You have to. Deliver your letter to the empress. Take Mira and start over."

"Bal, *no!*" Mira's voice cracked beneath the words. "I don't need to be taken care of. I just need you."

I had to close my eyes, if only to pry them right back open. Mira, at least, was too young to understand. But Zee would. And someday, she would explain. If I couldn't. "I won't be me if I don't try."

A simple fact for an unchangeable fate. There was very little left in me that anyone could classify as good. But if there was anything saving my soul from Ruekigal's hellfire it was my sense of duty. My loyalty. My devotion to the people I loved.

Including Shasheba.

"You can still help Shasheba if you come with us," Zee said, comprehension dawning on her face. Not that it brought anything but misery. "But, Bal, please. You deserve more than this life."

"This life is the only one I've got. The only one I want." I tucked my hastily scrawled letter in my pocket, Zee's earrings thudding heavily against my chest.

She shook her head, marshaling arguments like she could debate the world into an order more to her liking. "Then don't throw it away. Live it."

"I have to do this, Zee," I said, slowly. Evenly. As if I wasn't silently fracturing for the loss—the end—awaiting us.

"I'll be back in a few minutes," I said, knowing the fact did nothing to ease the pain of what was to come. I pressed a kiss to her forehead.

And let her—and all the rest of them—go.

16

TASSIEL

Tassiel slid down the warehouse stairs, skirting the edges of the echoing space before darting into the crowd outside. The road squelched and steamed beneath the soles of her boots. Too much rain, combined with the oppressive heat of a Cothis summer, made the ground shimmer with evaporating water. Sweat trickled down her spine, and she was seized with the almost animal desire to feel cool wind slide against her bare flesh.

She sighed the urge away and kept walking, slithering into the small gaps between one person and the next, as she cut through the midmorning rush. It was too crowded, Tassiel thought. Humans hurried about on the pretense of work, of normality, but she tasted the iron tang of frenzy bubbling beneath the surface. Tassiel frowned, her skin sticking to the metal inside of her mask. The city wasn't anywhere near as oblivious to last night's events as Bal and his crew hoped. Not by a long shot.

Fear pooled beneath the pores of the men and women she passed. It was as if some near-forgotten instinct screamed a warning of the predator in their midst. And for once, it wasn't Tassiel's they were sensing.

Tassiel shook her head, trying to dislodge the scent of dread from her nostrils, and thanked the unending Creation that Bal hadn't insisted on joining her. The likelihood that the Temple of Nananthe wasn't under surveillance and heavy guard was nonexistent. A fact that Bal must surely know. But like males of any species, all his common sense fled with the thought of an attractive female. Idiot.

Bal reminded Tassiel too much of her brother, Gul. Cocksure and ever the hero, Gul would twist himself into knots to impress his latest conquest, only to forget the poor woman a day later. A smile she couldn't quite stop pricked her lips. She winced it away.

Gul. The name echoed through her mind, a sigh filled with longing and loneliness.

It had been years since she'd been careless enough to think his name—to think any of their names. Her siblings who'd left her behind. Betrayed her.

It was like she'd known, on some level, that they had chosen to abandon her. Both then and now. She was just too weak to admit it to herself. But now, with Bal, and with Mira and Kai, with Zeelaya and Edik, it felt like she was seeing her lost siblings again.

Almost.

Tassiel shook her head and jumped onto the railing of the bridge. The press of humanity was suddenly insufferable. The smell of sweat, of sickly sweet unwashed flesh baking in the unforgiving Ashaarite heat brought bile to her throat. She held her breath as she crossed the canal via the railing rather than swim through the humans bottled up on the bridge.

Hopping off the rail, Tassiel reentered the human swarm. Forced her shoulders down—willed herself to relax, but her mind would not be still.

She had always thought that her siblings were close, but they measured their affection by Ankaari standards. Standards that, she had come to understand, paled in comparison with human ones. They may have lived together, worked together, fought together, but each of them was an island. They guarded their weaknesses and coveted their strengths. Forged alliances with some, while dodging responsibility from others.

Tassiel couldn't imagine the Vadalen family behaving that way. And that was the point, she thought, winding her way toward Middlemarch. The Talion were a crew, yes. But they were family first. And even though Bal wanted to save his fool of a woman, and even though the others obviously didn't agree, Tassiel knew they wanted to help. She had no doubt that even as they tried to dissuade Bal, they were thinking up ways to save him from himself. Their devotion wasn't blind, but it was as unyielding as the stone beneath her feet.

Something panged in her chest. Her heart came dangerously close to fluttering.

Pay attention!

Tassiel pushed away the weakness she was afraid to define and straightened her shoulders. This part of the city, with its line of decaying temples, was even busier than the docks—a rarity in money-loving Cothis. She cut a zigzagging path through the crowd, watching people streaming in and out of the Temple of Enkaara. Men and women rushed through the temple's open doors, white-lipped and ashen-faced. She felt an eyebrow twitch. Nothing renewed faith as quickly as absolute terror.

She was sinking back into the mob when a low hum started in her ears. Tassiel paused. A soft breeze caressed her body and set the bells on her veil chiming. A few people around her turned, searching for the noise. Their eyes almost found her face, only to slide away again.

Something like fear echoed in her mind. The bells never rang from the wind, and people never saw or heard her unless Tassiel wanted them to. That was the reason she'd forged the mask: to remain unnoticed. Wearing it gave her the freedom of near invisibility.

It was a low magic, she was sure her family would say. True invisibility would have been something to brag about, but the mask wasn't powerful enough for that. It simply made an observer's eye glide past without recognizing her presence. And though it might be low magic, it was enough to keep her beneath the notice of human and Ankaari alike.

But the bells . . . They were her warning. They were her alarms, telling Tassiel that the mask *hadn't* worked. She had been seen. Noticed.

She sidestepped to the edge of the road and pressed her back to the wall of the incense seller across from the Temple of Enkaara. She searched the street, the bricks warm against her spine. The musky scent of frankincense clung to her nose as she counted the slow beating of her heart. One. Two. Three . . .

Nothing.

Nothing was out of place. No one was behaving strangely. No one even looked her way. But she'd felt it, that whisper of magic.

And the bells had rung.

Tassiel wasn't alone.

She inhaled slowly. Exhaled. But the tightness in her core didn't ease. Her gaze dropped to the canal where the gray-green water shimmered in the too-bright daylight. Water was always Karanis's specialty, and through it he could see very far indeed.

In the merest blink, Tassiel pushed off the wall and rounded the corner of the incense shop. A tight alley formed in the space between one building and the next, hiding her from the water. In the shade of the two structures, the feeling of being watched eased.

She reached up, feeling along the length of the brick until she found a spot where her fingertips curled. Perfect. Dragging her toe into the grit between bricks, she began to climb. It was slow, and by the time she was halfway up, her fingers and toes were screaming. Tassiel brushed it away. The need to get away from the water was far greater than mere discomfort. It would be harder to be seen from the rooftop, and stealth was paramount now. It couldn't be coincidence that she'd been detected only two streets away from the Temple of Nananthe.

She pulled herself over the lip of the building and onto its dusty roof, pausing only to stretch out cramped fingers before jumping the narrow gap between one roof and the next. Most of the buildings on this block were of similar heights, and either shared walls or were crammed in so close to one another that it made jumping between them child's play. Human foolishness, packing homes so close together—like there was nothing to fear from your neighbors—but it was lucky for her. She didn't want to summon magic unless she had no other choice.

The Temple of Nananthe was in her sights. Its rusty orange facade looked like a livid glowering sun against the steel gray sky. She stood on the roof of the boarding house across the street, watching the shuttered building for several long minutes. Nothing moved in the windows, and the front doors stood resolutely closed despite several worshippers pausing to bang on them.

As she'd guessed, neither Shasheba nor her acolytes had returned. Tassiel shifted her weight from one foot to the next, tallying her options. There was some time yet. She could wait, but she knew Shasheba wouldn't be coming. Karanis hadn't released her. He would never release her so long as she still had value. Which meant Tassiel should go and return to her—to the crew.

But the feeling of eyes on her back hadn't abated. Worse, it had grown, clinging to her face and clothes tighter than the mud coating to her boots.

There was an intimacy to the feeling, an intensity that made her skin crawl. It didn't feel like the far-sight of Karanis watching her through water. Which meant one of two things. Either Karanis was physically here. Or it wasn't Karanis at all.

Only one way to find out.

Tassiel stepped up to the edge of the roof. Her gaze swept across the crowd, searching for that finely coifed blue-black hair, perfectly cut clothes, and a manicured goatee. Her muscles tensed.

Karanis wasn't there.

But someone else was. A body on the far-right side of the crowd went still. A face tilted up. Eyes met hers. Electric-blue eyes.

Fear rushed up Tassiel's spine, freezing her in place, as an ancient and cunning sentience studied her from the face of a paunchy middle-aged man. He smiled a broad, joyful grin and blinked. When he opened his eyes, the sentience was gone, the man shook his head and continued on his way. Three steps ahead of him, a woman froze, looked up, smiled, shook her head. Then an old man.

One by one, the sentience hopped from one person to the next. Closer. Closer. A slow wave of borrowed bodies turned their faces to her, each wearing the same clownish smile.

Tassiel watched the last person smile up at her from the door of her building before ducking inside. A shudder clawed through her bones.

Steady! she commanded silently.

She sensed rather than heard the sentience coming closer and had to lock her knees together to keep from running. There were only two creatures in existence able to send their consciousness across realities with such dexterity, and only one of them was mad enough to meet her with a smile.

Calien.

Her brother.

The second-most powerful mage in the Nethersphere. The chief strategist of her Septiniri siblings and, in all likelihood, the architect of her exile.

And, clearly, the one helping Karanis take over the city.

Tassiel heard a trapdoor open behind her and turned in time to see a little girl climb onto the roof. She was a few years younger than Mira, maybe nine or ten, but they had the same slight, underfed frames and curly brown hair. The girl took a few steps forward, bouncing on her toes and beaming in perfect imitation of absolute joy.

Joy. Right. Like Calien hadn't taken this girl's body to ensure Tassiel didn't attack him.

"Creation save me, it's you, isn't it?" Calien grinned up at her, and she forced her neck to bend in the barest of nods. He crowed an elated laugh. "How did you escape the harrow fiend?"

Tassiel felt her mouth flatten into a thin line at the name of the creature that nearly killed her all those years ago. So typical of Calien to have no remorse for trying to kill her, only wanting to know the details of her escape, like it would be a good story to bring the others.

"The means of my survival are perhaps less important than the fact of it."

He sighed with his whole body, like he truly was the child whose face he wore. "Aww. Come on, sis. That was ages ago. Don't tell me you're still sore."

"Sore?" She couldn't stop her voice from rising. "You tried to kill me, Calien."

He tutted away her response with a careless wave. "You know how it works. We get an order from above, and we follow it."

"An order from above? You mean you got an order from father. He told you to kill me." Calien didn't flinch at the accusation in her voice. Only watched Tassiel, waiting. Her heart flopped feebly like a fish on land. "Did you even question it? Did any of you?"

He rubbed the back of his neck, but there was no regret in the gesture, no guilt. "Look, you know how strained everything was. Father had barely begun to take control and you come charging in demanding to bring grandfather back. How did you expect him to react?"

"I didn't know father was behind the disappearance."

Calien snorted. "And is ignorance ever an excuse?"

Wind howled across her face, screaming the answer. No. In their family one did not find shelter in ignorance. It was a personal failing. "You didn't answer my question. Did any of you fight the order?"

He crossed his arms. "Gul and Keir . . . objected. But they both knew better than to take it any further."

She took an involuntary step back. It was one thing to know she'd been betrayed, but hearing that the two siblings she'd loved best hadn't even fought for her?

Tassiel had to turn away. She braced her hands on her hips and forced herself to breathe despite the fact that her clothes itched and clung, despite the fact that her mask suffocated, and a scream welled up her throat.

After a few moments, the little girl appeared at her side. Her brother's puppet kicked at a pebble, arms rigid at her sides. "Let me make it up to you. Come back to me. I'm sure if you apologized—"

Her vision flashed. "*Apologized?* I have nothing to apologize for."

"You'll do it if you want to come home," he shot back. "You can start by apologizing for butting into matters that didn't concern you."

Tassiel cursed, but he just sneered. "Don't you understand that if you had just stayed in your corner, stayed the silent little sword you were raised to be, none of this would have happened? So yes, I think you should apologize to Father, beg him to take you back."

Her nails dug into the flesh of her palms; she balled her fists so hard. "Father. Right. As if he cares to hear anything I have to say. As if he raised us to be anything more than curiosities. His little experimental army."

Tassiel didn't know how she expected Calien to react, but laughter wasn't on the list.

The sound of it smacked her in the face. "You finally realized that, have you?" Calien asked, his voice filled with disdain. "You know you're a lot cleverer than we gave you credit for. Quicker than Melcoran, I'll give you that." Calien shrugged. "I don't think he'll ever figure out that we're nothing more than father's slaves. And once we are no longer of use to him, well . . ."

He flicked his middle finger against his thumb. "Look at what happened to you."

"And you're fine with that? You're happy being disposable?"

"Everyone is disposable."

The wrongness of that statement froze her. The only reason she was there at that moment was to try and save a woman's life. A woman who her friend didn't think was disposable. Yet there her brother was, telling Tassiel she was no more valuable than trash. She tried to imagine Bal ever saying such a thing to Mira but couldn't even conjure the image.

She exhaled, trying to blow out her bitterness and betrayal with it. "I take it you're here on Father's orders, then. Helping Karanis claim the city."

"Helping . . ." Calien shrugged. "I'm just keeping an eye on things for Father. He wanted to get a realistic idea of the challenges an Ankaari might face, and well . . . no one knows how to miss an opportunity like dear old uncle Karanis."

Calien laughed at his own joke, and she found herself shaking her head.

"What?" he demanded. "It's been a disaster so far. With you and your friends breaking the idol and then stealing half of it. Karanis has been in an absolute frenzy ever since he arrived. His body's going to melt right off if he's not careful. And he didn't even send anyone here to watch, he just—"

"Do you really mean you are not here to interfere?"

"Me?" He pressed one tiny hand to his thin chest, looking at her with wide, innocent eyes. "Never. Why?" He grinned. "Are you?"

"Why shouldn't I? As you said, I already stole half the idol."

"Yeah but . . . you were hired to do that. The priestess woman said so. Now that you know it's Karanis, you won't—"

"I will not let him take the city."

Calien's eyes sparkled with elated surprise. "Why not?"

"What do you mean, why not? Look around, Calien," Tassiel said, gesturing to the street below. "Look at all those men and women, at the child whose body you wear. They are innocent, all of them. They don't deserve Karanis. They don't deserve any Ankaari."

He waved off the words. "You're many years too late for this moral debate."

"Whose fault is that?" she snapped.

"Touché." But all he did was shrug.

"You really care nothing for their fate?" she asked, voice raw with exhaustion. "You are half human too, brother. You *must* care."

"Why? What has my humanity ever gained me?"

"Obviously not a conscience."

"I should hope not," he said, laughing. "Our little family already had one of those, and we got rid of her."

His words landed harder than a fist to the ribs. "Damn you."

"Now, now, sis. It's not too late to come crawling back to Daddy," he said, dancing back to the door.

"Calien," Tassiel called, his name scraping out of her throat. "Leave the city. Cothis is protected."

He looked at her, eyebrows arched high. "By whom? *You?* I know you can't be referring to your little human friends. By now, Karanis will have them well in hand." A slow smile spread across her brother's face. "Literally."

Tassiel's heart stopped cold in her chest.

"*No.*"

17

BALTHAZAR

Tick scuttled across the open yard in front of the warehouse a little before two o'clock. I pushed away from the window as I heard him shuffle up the stairs. "All right. You ready?" he asked as the door squealed open.

No. Not yet. Tass was still gone. "It's not two o'clock yet. Can we wait?"

Tick's oily smile drooped. "What for?"

"Tass's not back yet."

"Tass?" Tick's beady little eyes darted around the room, like he was counting heads. His attention seemed to snag on Mira for a second before he pulled his eyes away. "Is that what your queenie's called, then? Where'd she go?"

"She went to see if she can find the last member of our crew."

"Ah." Tick licked his lips, glanced at the clock on the wall, scratching his whiskered face.

Understanding made me roll my eyes. "Don't worry. I'll pay you your due."

"What? No. No problem, Bal. I know you're good for it."

"So we can wait a few minutes?" I asked with a frown, not loving how easily he refused to haggle.

"Oh. Um. Yeah. Should be fine. Gotta get out at two though."

My eyes narrowed. "How long of a walk is it to our exit point?"

"Nothing but a stroll," he replied, with an answering smile that showed too many teeth to be genuine. "Ten minutes tops."

Tick flopped onto one of the rickety armchairs, ignoring the way its twiglike frame groaned under his negligible weight. I returned to the window, crossed my arms, and kept one eye on the yard outside and another on Tick.

Tass's voice bloomed in the back of my mind, asking me if money would be enough to ensure Tick's loyalty. Watching him now, I nearly laughed.

Barely seated, one of Tick's legs began to bounce out a staccato beat. His squirrelly black gaze darted about the room, dancing from the clock to Mira and around again.

My sister glared at Tick when he looked her way for the third time. "What?" she demanded in a hot voice.

"Nuthin'." Tick crossed his arms, and then uncrossed them again. "Shouldn't you be with a governess or something?" he asked a half second later.

Mira's frown deepened. "A governess?" She hurled the word at Tick's feet like it was the worst insult she'd ever heard.

"Yeah. Isn't that what you posh noble kids do; have foreigners come and teach you your numbers?"

My sister snorted. "I wouldn't know. My family isn't noble. Not anymore."

Tick nodded absently, his beady little eyes going back to the clockface. "Still. Isn't this life too dangerous for a kid? Has to be somewhere safer for you to be."

I exchanged a meaningful look with Zee. It wasn't that I disagreed with Tick, I just never thought I'd hear anything like concern for Mira's safety come out of his mouth. It might have been touching if it wasn't so damn suspicious.

"Safer than with my family?" Mira scoffed. "Not likely. And I'm not a kid."

"And yet you wouldn't leave home without your favorite ball," I said, scooping the toy that was very much not a toy off the floor and plopping it in her lap. "I've told you at least five times not to leave it lying around. Drop it again and I'll shoot the damn thing."

Mira looked ready to spit by the time I was done talking, but quieted at the look I gave her. A look that all but screamed, "Now is not the time."

Amazingly she seemed to agree.

Tick nodded again as he got to his feet. "All right. Time to go," he said, something like regret pinching his face.

I held up my hand practically willing time to slow. Reverse. But I knew it wouldn't with the same certainty that I knew Tick was up to something.

"Tick, c'mon. It's barely two." He'd expect the objection, and I was more than willing to give it. To give voice to the anxiety roiling within me. Not at Tick's probable double cross. But at Tass's absence. Why wasn't she here? Was there trouble at the Low Temple? Had Shasheba not been released?

Or had she simply refused to come?

"No, no," he said, shaking his head. "I said I'd give your girl till two, and now it's two. If we don't go now, you're going to miss your chance of getting off the island."

Damn it. I should have gone with Tass, I thought, searching the slumping forms of the dockworkers below, trying to find a familiar face among them. No Tass. No Shasheba.

No Karanis either. *Small fucking mercy that was.*

"Look," Tick said, clasping my shoulder, "if your girl shows up, I'll arrange for her to follow you, but it's time to go."

I exhaled hard, like the decision was an impossible one, and nodded. "All right."

Tick sagged a few inches, relief washing over his face. "Follow me," he said, so willing to turn his back on the five of us. Like we wouldn't put a bullet in his skull if he so much as sneezed.

Which only meant he had backup.

A lot of backup.

We made quick time through the warehouses, following Tick west, away from the main heart of the harbor where the bigger seafaring vessels were docked. This part of the port was reserved for smaller, interisland ferries and fishing skiffs. Exactly the sort of transport I'd expect Tick to procure for us, since we were only heading for La'Zem.

In the distance, looming over the squat flat roofs of the shops lining the street, was the summit of the Western Hill. It seemed especially desolate today. Its jagged peak looked like a giant finger stabbed my way, calling me a thief. A coward.

I hope you're watching, Curator, I thought, mentally flipping the old man off. *The next ten minutes are going to get very interesting.*

My gaze dropped as an airship passed silently overhead, casting us in shadow. I shivered in the sudden shade. This part of the harbor was usually on the quieter side, comparatively speaking. Trade between the islands ran in a cyclical pattern of ships coming in on one day and out another. A fair number of vessels were docked, but I didn't see much in the way of offloading happening. Odd.

Or, perhaps not odd at all.

A long-honed instinct for suspicion had been itching at the back of my head from the moment Tick reappeared. Now I knew it was spot on. The holiday was yesterday. Not today. Today the bosses should be working the men like dogs to make up for any lost revenue. Should be.

So why were all these dockworkers milling about with no work to do? It wasn't as simple as a day off. No man who spent his life breaking his back at the harbor wanted to spend his liberty time loafing around on the docks.

One of the workers turned toward me. We locked eyes, and I saw it. A spark of recognition that was too intense, too focused. A dark urge to laugh welled up in my throat.

I forced my gaze away. Forced my face to remain impassive, like I hadn't noticed anything out of the ordinary. I cast my eyes upward, at the underbelly of that giant airship. "That is a thing of beauty," I said, adding an appreciative whistle.

A two-toned whistle.

I sensed rather than saw my crew bracing for action.

"Funny thing about Cothis is that there aren't many airships here. It's why I didn't bring *Fortune's Fool*," I said to Tick conversationally.

"Is that so?" he remarked, fidgeting too much to see the way my friends were inching closer.

I nodded. "Airships don't fare well on the open ocean, so most captains don't bother bringing them here. Better to sail along the edge of the archipelago and north to the continent."

"Interesting," Tick said, in a tone that clearly meant it was anything but.

"It is," I replied in a falsely merry voice. My left hand slid into my jacket pocket, and I felt the cold metal grip of a pistol bite my palm. Throwing an arm around Tick's shoulders, I drew him close. "It means that the only airship permanently in residence in Cothis belongs to Governor Paasch.

"Now why would Paasch's airship be at the docks today, eh, Tickie?" I asked, squeezing his neck in the crook of my elbow so hard his face purpled. "You didn't happen to make some new friends, did you?"

Tick sputtered, gasping. "No, Bal. Never."

"That's wonderful to hear. Means I won't have to use the gun I've got aimed at your balls. Nasty way to die, a cock shot, but I think traitors deserve hard deaths, don't you?"

Tick gurgled something that wasn't quite words. I grinned, doing my damnedest to look like we were just two old friends catching up on a good story.

"Now I'm going to let you go, Tick. But before I do, I want you to know that the rest of my crew has you in their sights. You do anything reckless, if you say anything to draw attention to us, or signal anyone in the crowd, we're gonna put you down like the feral dog you are and take our chances from there."

I released the pressure on Tick's neck, let him pull himself upright and suck in a few gasping breaths. We kept walking as if nothing was amiss, but blood boiled in my ears, nearly drowning out the sound of gulls screeching overhead. The weight of keen eyes raked across my back.

I'd have to have been blind to mistake these people for dockies and sailors. These were codies. They were men in Paasch's pocket, which meant, whether they knew it or not, they were working for Karanis.

But they hadn't descended upon us yet. They were letting us pass, herding us to somewhere. Or to someone.

"When is this trap set to spring shut?" I asked.

Tick licked his lips, and I could practically hear the gears of his mind turning, as he tried to decide where his loyalties lay; with me or with a governor-turned-god. He shouldn't have bothered with the trouble. I knew damn well that Tick's loyalties were always with Tick first and forever. And right now, me and my crew were his biggest threat to survival.

"Pier Fifty-Eight."

"Good. Where's the exit?"

"Bal," he said with his squealing, nervous laugh. "Bal, look I'm sorry I sold you out. I—I didn't have a choice. There are codies everywhere looking for you and your crew. The reward. Bal. A man can't say no to that kind of reward. A-and if I said nothing and he found out . . ." Tick shivered as real, visceral fear, chased across his face.

The question of how Karanis knew to squeeze Tick writhed within me. I had an inkling—Shit. I had more than that. It might make my insides twist, but if I was being honest, I *knew* the answer. I pushed it aside, hoping I was wrong. Praying. But praying to what, I didn't know.

"I see you've met the new and improved Paasch."

"Yeah. What the hell happened to him, Bal?"

"I expect you'll find out soon enough. Where's the exit?"

"There is no exit."

"Bullshit," I said, laughing at the lie. Knowing that Tick always had a backup plan tucked into his grimy pockets was the only reason I'd let my people follow him out of that warehouse. "You always have a bolt-hole, especially when you're dealing with bigger and badder men than you. Tell me where it is, or I let Zee shove one of her little toys down your throat."

"Or up your ass," Kai snarled.

Sweat broke out on Tick's forehead. He was well acquainted with Zee's many inventions, and her penchant for making things go boom. "Pier Twelve."

"Good. Lead the way."

"Bal, the codies are all over this joint. If we diverge from the main road for even a second, they're gonna know something's up."

"Leave them to us," I growled, wishing I was half as confident as I sounded.

I ran through a mental list of our weapons store, our ammunition. Our options. It wasn't that we didn't have the firepower—our stop at Nell's place made sure of that. It was the exposure on the open street that would kill us. But maybe, *maybe* we'd have enough if we could duck down an alley, funnel them. Dropped the ball . . .

I nodded surreptitiously to the narrow opening just head to the left. "Where's that alley let out?"

"Back yard of the Ta'aket Fishery."

"And from there? Where is Pier Twelve?"

"If you round the building and go out the front gate, the piers will be straight ahead." Tick licked his lips, fishlike eyes darting helplessly around in his skull. "Don't suppose you'll be kind enough to leave me here?"

I breathed a mirthless laugh, the kind that promised violence. "Sure thing, Tick. Wouldn't want you to slow us down. But don't think I'll be forgetting this anytime soon."

"Hey, no hard feelings now, Bal," he said, voice cracking. "It's just business."

I felt my lips peel back into a dark, vindictive grin. "Be sure to tell Tass that, when you see her again. And you *will* see her again. Paasch isn't the only strange creature in the city, Tick. Not by a long shot." The look of fear in Tick's eyes warmed my belly. I shook my head, utterly disgusted by this weasel of a man. And yet, I still said, "You got anyone you care about on this godsforsaken rock, you get them out. Today."

He nodded, his squirrelly face getting ready for a fall, but I wasn't going to let him trip. No, his lithe little form would be more use to me airborne.

"Hey, Kai," I said, eyeing the two plainclothes codies at the mouth of an alley. They sat on a pair of crates, doing a bad job of pretending to play cards on the top of the wooden barrel between them. "You still interested in that bet from earlier?"

Kai laughed. "Sure thing, boss."

"Good." I grabbed the back of Tick's collar. "Give Tick a boost."

Tick whimpered.

Kai didn't miss a beat. He took a massive step forward, both hands bunching on the back of Tick's pants. The muscles in my neck and arms screamed as we hurled Tick across five feet of empty space. The codies froze, their faces slack at the sight of Tick's squealing body careening toward them.

Tick's head smacked into the first codie's face with a sickening crack. The other codie got a pair of knees to the groin. All three men went ass over teakettle into the wall. It was a thing of beauty, but I'd have to savor it later. A cry went up through the street before any of the men hit the ground. My body tensed. Guns were drawn as I threw myself into the alley, arms pumping.

"Mira, now," I snapped.

The ball was in play. Five.

We were halfway down when the first bullet cracked above my head. I shielded my face with my arms as shards of brick pelted down.

Four.

I heard return fire, knew it was Kai or Edik bringing up the rear, but didn't turn to look—just kept running.

The alley opened in front of me.

Three.

I grabbed the corner in both hands and swung myself around it. A second later, Mira and Zee sprinted past. "Round the building. Pier Twelve," I yelled, urging them on.

Two.

Wrenching both guns from my hip holsters, I ducked back into the mouth of the alley, laying down cover fire for Edik and Kai.

One.

They barreled past me, a half second before the ball went off. Such a small explosion—wouldn't even burn the two men standing next to it. But the ball wasn't a bomb made of fire and brimstone.

Rather, it was one of *sound*.

A catastrophic wave of weaponized sound filled the alley, slamming into the walls, funneling and reverberating. Codies screamed in uncomprehending horror as their eardrums ruptured. They hit the deck, clawing at their skulls like they could stop the pain. Or at least I assumed as much.

I was already off and running after my crew.

The fishery yard was blissfully empty—I probably had Karanis and the codies to thank for that. We dashed across the open space and through the iron gates. The pier was directly ahead.

In the distance, I could make out a huge crowd gathered on the far end; near Pier 58, I presumed. Someone shouted, and the crowd turned our way. They surged toward us like ants over the earth. They wouldn't get to us in time.

Zee and Mira scrambled onto the boat docked at Pier 12. It was a decrepit looking fishing boat—barely seaworthy, but it had a slanted covered cabin on one end so we'd have some protection if the codies started shooting.

When they started shooting.

"Zee, get into the cabin," I ordered, hearing the fear crowding the edges of my voice.

This was going to get ugly. Mira was already ducking down, but Zee—*pregnant Zee*—was still in motion.

She raced to the boats on either side of ours, chucking what could only be more explosives on their decks. My mental clock started the countdown as Zee whirled toward our ropes, cutting the lines as Edik and Kai arrived.

They heaved the side of the boat away from the slip before jumping aboard with me hard on their heels. I leaped, my legs working in midair, and landed roughshod on the deck. Without pausing I slid my guns to Zee and Mira, then seized the oars.

Edik grabbed another pair. He counted out strokes in a low, breathless voice, sweat dripping down his face. On mine too. Every muscle in my back and neck screamed at me. My arms strained as I rowed with everything I had. The pier filled with purple-faced codies—their guns drawn with us in their sights. Bullets pinged around us before someone ordered a ceasefire.

There was a second of silence.

Then.

Boom!

The shock wave of exploding boats tore through the air and water, scorching our faces as it propelled our rickety little boat farther to sea. I breathed a laugh.

"You're a freaking magician, Zee," I crowed.

She flashed an arch smile my way. "Magic is for idiots. I'm a motherfucking scientist."

We were going to make it. The mouth of the harbor was less than three yards away. After that, their guns would be out of range. We just had to get out.

"BALTHAZAR VADALEN!"

A voice bellowed my name with such force, ripples shivered through the water. I didn't need to look to know it was Karanis. I grit my teeth and focused all my concentration, all my strength on rowing. One stroke. Another. Closer and closer to the mouth of the port. We were going to make it . . .

Bullets plinked into the water on my left, splashing my face. A different voice shouted at us from above, commanding us to return to the pier. The governor's airship had outflanked us, creeping up the coast in a silent aerial blockade. Edik stopped rowing, indecision scrawled over his face.

"No," I shouted. "Keep going."

Crack.

The boat's wooden deck buckled between Edik and me. Splintered shards of decking flew upward, and I swore as one of them sliced a hot cut across my face. Water gurgled in through a roundish hole in the floor—a bullet shot from above.

My eyes cut to the crowd gathered on Pier 58. A single figure came forward. I couldn't see his face from this distance, but I didn't need to. I knew it was the sea god wearing Paasch's body.

Karanis stretched a hand toward us like a child reaching for sweets. Power whooshed out from him, shuddering through the water. In its wake, everything went still. Our small fishing boat came to a stuttering stop. It was as if we were suspended in a huge lake of congealed mud.

Mira gasped as the sea around us lurched, yanking us back to land. Edik scrabbled at his oars, struggling in vain to free us from

Karanis's magic. But even Edik had to admit defeat when Karanis crooked his fingers, dragging us forward like we were nothing but fish on a line. It was like he'd created a narrow river in an utterly becalmed sea.

The blood dripping down my cheek felt like a tear. I swiped it away, cursing my hand for shaking. Swallowing hard, I pulled in my oars. Made myself stand. Water soaked the soles of my boots as I took my pistols back from Zee and Mira. Counted the rounds.

"What's the plan?" Kai asked, his eyes drilling into the side of my face. "Can I shoot him? Please let me shoot him."

"Kai, no. We're surrounded," Zee said, voice low, urgent. "If we go for Karanis now, we'll be butchered."

"She's right," I said, before Kai could object and do something that would surely get all of us killed. Especially when there was no way of knowing if shooting him would actually do anything.

Besides, I thought as our boat was gliding into the slip right at Karanis's feet. Not all battles were fought with weapons.

I pushed my way to the front, shielding the crew with my body. As if mere flesh could halt a would-be god. Smelling blood on the wind, I raised my chin. And looked up at the patron god of Cothis.

I expected to stare into a fine patrician face. Paasch, for all his countless faults, had been a handsome man. But this—this *thing* in front of me . . . It wasn't Paasch. Not anymore.

"Creator, have mercy."

The sun seemed to dim at what I saw.

Karanis wore Paasch's flesh like an ill-fitting sock. His body wrinkled and stretched in all the wrong places; too little skin around jutting cheekbones, too much skin folding up in gelatinous rolls down his neck.

If this sudden transformation didn't betray the fact that Paasch wasn't the man we all knew and hated, Karanis's eyes gave it all away. The skin around his eye sockets was still charred with burnt flesh from the lightning that had boiled Paasch's eyes away. Karanis's eyes took their place, if the burning blue light swirling from lid to lid could be considered eyes.

But why? Why did he still look like that? If he had already worn Paasch to such a degree, why hadn't he switched bodies? Unless . . .

Unless he'd burned through more of his energy than Tass had thought? Damaged the temple more than we knew. Unless he couldn't risk another transfer save his final one?

Karanis's lips parted into a feral smile. "Balthazar Vadalen."

"Karanis."

"You know who I am." His smile deepened. "Good. That will make things easier. You have something of mine. Give it to me."

"If you'll pardon me, sir. I have nothing of yours."

A dark eyebrow rose. "Oh? You mean to say that you didn't steal half of my idol from the high temple?"

"I can honestly say that I took nothing from the temple." Since this was technically true, I smiled.

A low chuckle danced out of Karanis's borrowed throat. He held out a hand, beckoning someone. "You were right, my dear. I didn't think him so bold as to lie."

"Bold, yes. And foolish."

I shivered at the ice in that voice. Shasheba glided forward and slid her hand into Karanis's. She looked down at me. Her face was cold and utterly impassive, but her eyes blazed with rage.

Zee had been right, I thought, as a strange numbness tingled across my face and down my arms. It was like I'd been struck by lightning. Shasheba would be fine. More than fine, judging by the beautiful new bracelets that encircled her arms.

"I really did think he'd try to rescue you," Karanis said, pouting out a too-full lower lip in a gruesome pantomime of disappointment. "Everything in Paasch's memory indicated that Balthazar would come back for you."

"Paasch was mistaken." Shasheba smiled through her eyelashes at Karanis, emphasizing Paasch's name, as if he were still alive to give bad advice. "Balthazar doesn't know the meaning of loyalty. He would never come back for me."

"I was coming back for you," I said, my voice low but far, far too weak to withstand her rage.

"Oh? By one of Tick's smuggling boats?" Her lips twisted. "Funny how much your rescue looks like retreat."

I wanted to close my eyes against the accusation in her words. The unfairness of it burned my core. We'd agreed that Shasheba would stay behind if something went wrong. *She'd* agreed.

But I could see none of that mattered. That all our plans were helpless against the anger and betrayal I saw raging behind her uncaring mask. I forced myself not to react. If Karanis knew that he could use Shasheba to hurt me, if he knew that I really did care, then she would be in danger. More danger, that was.

"Then he truly is a fool, my pet." Karanis pressed his bloated lips into the back of Shasheba's hand and looked back at me. "You see, dear Shasheba knows a lost cause when she sees one, Balthazar. When I emerged into my rightful kingdom, she was wise enough to pledge her allegiance to me."

"I'll bet she did," Kai said, spitting to one side. "Never could pass up an opportunity, could you, Shash?"

"Quite." Karanis chuckled, ignoring the way Shasheba bridled beside him. Or perhaps he just didn't notice. She had always played things close to the chest. "Regardless, she's been rather useful. She told me all about your little plan to steal my idol. I know you broke it. And I know you took one of the halves. Where is it?"

I swallowed hard thinking as fast as I could. If I told the truth, it could go one of two ways: He could decide he didn't need us anymore and send us to the bottom of the bay. Or he'd give us time to get it back. It was a gamble. But that was life.

"I don't have it anymore."

Karanis's head tilted to one side, a gesture that reminded me so much of Tass, it made bile crawl up my throat. "Is he telling the truth?"

"Yes, I think so, my lord. But there is a member of his crew missing." Shasheba frowned at me. "Where is your precious Queen of Days, Bal?"

"Queen?" Karanis spat the word, clearly annoyed by Tassiel's title. "Which one is that?"

"The odd one I was telling you about, my lord," Shasheba replied smoothly. "A masked woman known throughout Cothis as a thief. An assassin too, if the rumors are to be believed."

Karanis turned back to me, his face betraying nothing more than idle curiosity. "Well, where is this Queen of Days woman?"

"Gone," I replied evenly. "She's taking the idol to our patron. She's supposed to meet us on La'Zem with the payment."

Karanis's blue gaze turned to Shasheba. "Well?"

Her eyes narrowed on my face. I swallowed. Fear and desperation and, curse me, yes, even a little hope swirled in the space between us. Never had it felt like such a chasm. But distance didn't matter. Not where Shasheba was concerned. She could always read me better than anyone I'd ever known. *Please Shasheba. Please give me a chance to get us all out of this.* Together.

Her expression softened. The shadow of a smile passed over her lips. "That is a lie."

Karanis's blue-fire gaze brightened with excitement. "Interesting." He looked at me, licking his lips. "What shall I do with you, Balthazar Vadalen? Shall I pop off one of your legs to get you screaming truths? Shall I skin one of your crew?"

"No," I blurted out. The force of the word made the boat rock beneath my already unsteady legs.

"No?" he said with a grin, knowing he had me beat. "Surely you don't need all of them? How about that young man there, staring at me with such impertinence."

Karanis reached out, and I didn't need to look to know he was about to kill Kai. "Stop," I shouted at the same time as Shasheba said, "Wait, my lord."

He turned to her. Frowned. *"Wait?"*

Shasheba immediately looked down, hands folded before her in perfect imitation of utter obedience. "If it pleases you, my lord. Take a member of his crew hostage. Then he will give you the idol."

His lips pursed, filled with doubt. "From what you've told me, Balthazar is little more than a pirate. Such men have no concept of honor or loyalty. All I'd end up with is another slave. And I have so many of those," he said, waving a hand at the gathered codekeepers.

"Ordinarily, I'd agree with you, my lord," Shasheba replied, her voice unctuously sweet. "But not if you take the girl."

All five of us shouted at the same time. Terror tore through me, arrowing into my very soul. I spun and saw Edik and Kai push Mira to the end of the boat. Zee planted herself in front of my sister, eyes filled with rage as she looked up at Shasheba.

"See how they all protect her," Shasheba whispered in that sickly singsong voice.

"I do," Karanis replied, looking confused. "Why? What is the girl?"

"Miraveena Vadalen is Balthazar's younger sister."

"And this means something?" Karanis asked, genuinely surprised.

Something unsettled flashed across Shasheba's expression, but she shoved it away before I—or Karanis—could read it. "Yes, my lord. There is nothing they wouldn't do to keep her safe."

"How quaint." Karanis scratched his chin, and a patch of hair blew away in the breeze. "Very well. Come, child."

I raised my gun. A chorus of hammer cocks behind me told me my crew had done the same. I glared up at Shasheba, at the surrounding codies, daring any one of them to come down here and take my sister. I pulled back the hammer of my pistol, and the click reverberated across the becalmed sea. No one moved.

Karanis chuckled. "I thought you knew who I was, boy."

The words didn't even have time to land.

Mira screamed.

I whirled.

A tentacle-like shaft of water rose from the sea and seized Mira about her waist. I lunged, dropping my guns to grab her hands.

"Help me," I cried through gritted teeth. Kai and Edik seized me. We pulled with everything we had. Heaved.

Mira kicked madly. She writhed. Her small hands clawed at my arms, straining for purchase. But the water would not be denied. Not when the sea god himself commanded.

Mira shrieked. Her hands slipped in mine. I grunted, willing myself to hold on harder. But Mira's hands slid farther. Farther.

Karanis yanked.

"No!" The word tore through me as Mira was ripped from my grasp. There was a moment of utter stillness, where time seemed to freeze. The world itself paused. My eyes filled with the sight of her terrified face. The same horror that made the sun go cold. My heart stopped as she plunged into the water.

I lurched to the edge of the boat, helpless as Mira's tiny body tumbled across the harbor floor only to be belched onto the ground at Karanis's feet.

A low ringing sound began in my ears as fury and horror shuddered down my body. Mira was on all fours. Her arms shook uncontrollably as she retched up water onto the cobblestone. Shasheba—*fucking Shasheba*—sank to her knees and patted Mira's back.

Blood boiled in my skull. How dare she pretend to care about Mira after selling her out to Karanis?

Mira hissed, throwing herself at Shasheba. With one small, balled-up fist, Mira punched Shasheba square in the jaw. Shasheba cried and fell back onto the ground.

"Enough." Karanis snapped his fingers in bored command. Water funneled out of the harbor, wrapping around Mira's body in an orb from toes to neck. Mira twisted, screaming in incoherent rage.

"You will behave, child, or I shall be forced to drown your dear brother and all his little friends. And then I won't really need you, will I?"

Mira's head jerked back like she'd been struck. Her arms went limp. She looked at me, hair plastered to her face. Fear shone in her eyes as she mouthed my name.

"Good," Karanis said with a satisfied smile. "Now, here is what will happen—"

"Karanis. Let. Her. Go."

I followed the sound of Tass's voice. It sounded like hope. Like one last chance. She stood on the roof of a boathouse just behind the crowd. Sunlight shied away from her, bending around her body like a pocket of dusk the full strength of the sun couldn't reach. She drew her swords.

"Tass!" Mira cried.

As if in answer, Tass tensed. And leaped.

The gathered codies gasped as Tass sailed through the open space, leaping across fifty feet and landing in a silent crouch only steps away from Karanis.

"You," he growled, and for a moment I saw uncertainty in the swirling azure depths of his eyes. "It can't be. You're dead."

"If that were true, I would be hunting Ruekigal right now."

"And instead you're hunting me?" he asked, his voice brimming with outrage. "You presume much for an outcast, Septiniri."

"Do I?" Tass asked with a feral purr. "In this place, and with your flesh-body already sloughing off around you, I'd bet we're an even match. Care to see?"

She took a single step forward and the orb of water trapping Mira rose, planting my sister square in between the two ancient beings.

"Careful, outcast," Karanis said. "Your little friend has suddenly become useful to me. I'd hate for that to change."

Crystals bloomed around Mira's body as Karanis spoke. She flailed. With a gasping scream, her right hand hit something solid enough to make her yelp. Ice.

No. No, no, no, no. It could kill her.

The orb of water crackled as ice hardened around Mira. Her lips turned blue. Her breath heaved in panicked gasps.

Karanis smiled. "As I was saying: here is what will happen. You and your little friends are going to get my idol back. You will bring it to me. And because I am feeling so generous, I will give you, shall we say . . . twenty-four hours."

No one moved. Every muscle in my body went taut as I prepared to run forward. Mira. I could do it, reach her—but only if Tass attacked. Right now. As if she read my thoughts, Tass tensed once more.

"Now, now, Tassiel Janae,'" Karanis said, admonishing her like a parent would a naughty child. "You can only save one of them."

Tass's face jerked toward mine.

The sea around us shuddered.

"Save Mira," I cried as the water dropped out from beneath us.

18

BALTHAZAR

Water was everywhere. It pressed down on my chest and snaked up my nose. I twisted and writhed, searching the darkness for any hint of the surface. There was nothing.

No light.

No sound.

No help.

Blood pounded behind my skull. My lungs burned, demanding, begging for air.

My vision went dark . . .

Then daylight seared my eyes. Water surged up my throat. I rolled over, retching on the wet sand. My chest heaved, greedy for air. I made myself look past the pain, and I found my crew strewn along the beach, all of us gasping and drenched.

Except Tass.

Tass was crouched over Zee, pounding on her back with the flat of her hand. Zee coughed and heaved, spitting water out of her lungs.

I knew a second of terror on Zee's behalf. Terror for the life within her. Until Tass passed a hand over Zee's belly. Paused. Nodded.

Relief washed through me. Zee was gray-faced, but she'd live.

I couldn't say the same for Mira.

"Where is my sister?" The words scraped out of my throat, burning sea-raw flesh.

Tass sat back on her heels. Then she turned, her silver face tilting toward me. "By now, she is on her way to the temple with Karanis."

"So you left her?" I threw the words at Tass's feet, all the hotter for the guilt, the helplessness I felt.

"I had to, Bal. If I hadn't gotten you out of the water, you might have died. All of you might have died. How would that have helped Mira?"

"It doesn't matter."

"Matters to me, mate," Kai said, looking like he wanted to puke as he clambered to his feet.

"Me too," Edik said, holding Zee.

"Karanis has Mira." They were the only words I could manage; the only words that could even hint at my desperation.

"I know." Kai clapped a hand on my shoulder. "And we'll get her back. We will, Bal," he insisted, his dark eyes anchoring me. "But first we need to make a plan."

Zee snorted. "Get the idol back. Planning done."

Tass held up her hand calling for silence, her silver face turning to the waves. "We must move away from the water now."

"Why?"

She turned to me, the barest hint of exhaustion rimming her movements. "Think about what Karanis is, Bal."

I felt my brow furrow. What Karanis was? He was a monster. A bastard and a—

Comprehension smoothed away my confusion. I looked at the waves, crashing beneath a gray sky. "The sea god. Can he see us?"

"See us. Hear us. Track us. We must move away from the water," she repeated.

I nodded, longing for my airship with more intensity than I'd ever felt before. I pushed away the desire. It was pointless. We'd never leave this island. Not until Karanis was done with us, and even then . . .

We might not leave alive.

"We need a safe house," Zee said, reaching for Edik's hand, a silent plea for comfort. I understood why. We had safe places on all other islands, places we could bolt to if a job went bad.

But only Zee and Kai had done any work on Cothis, and when they did, it was Tick who found a place for them to stay. We didn't have Tick. We didn't have Shasheba, I thought, my mind snarling at her backstabbing name.

And now we didn't have Mira.

"We could ask Aunt Nell," Kai said, but I was shaking my head.

"We already played that card, Kai. Besides, Thistle and Bloom isn't a safe house—too many people go in and out."

I looked at Tass, cursed a silent prayer. "I don't suppose you have a place we could hide out."

For some reason, this made Tass laugh. "Yes, Bal. I do."

We followed her across the sandy bank, making our way back to civilization. It wasn't long before fine-looking houses crept up around us, and I recognized where we were. Only the northern shore of Cothis had beachfront properties nice enough to make even the gods jealous. Which meant that we were as far away from the harbor as we could get while still being on Cothis. The harbor. And the entrance to the Archive.

I slouched, walking desolately through the clean streets, past extravagant mansions that were only used for a few weeks in the height of summer by Cothis's upper crust. This time of year, they should be packed with nobles and servants and guards. The beach should be echoing with children's laughter, the lawns chiming with the clinking of glasses as one garden party slid into the next.

But the streets were empty, the houses silent. I wondered how many of the nobles who owned these homes were still trapped in the temple. A petty part of my mind thought they deserved nothing more for turning against my family. But in truth, my ability to hold that old anger was evaporating with the water that drenched my clothes. My boots squelched with every step, leaving tiny ponds in my wake, following me like a wet shadow.

The longer we walked, the feebler my heart beat. My mind whirled, going over every single detail of our confrontation with Karanis.

Why hadn't I just shot him? He'd been standing ten feet in front of me. A few rounds into his skull would have solved everything. Not even a god-Ankaari-whatever could survive that. Probably. And yeah, we would have been shot immediately by every codie on the island, but the fact didn't seem to carry the same weight as it had when I was standing in the boat. When I had Mira.

And now what? We'd go back to Tass's hideout, wherever that was, and dry off? While anything could be happening to Mira. Then we were supposed to go back to the Archive and get the idol back from the Curator? Never mind the fact that he threw us out and told us not to return. There was nothing in the whole of the Great Below that would convince him to give us the idol back.

He was obviously a powerful Ankaari himself. Even if we were able to break into the Archive, we would still have to steal the idol out from under his nose and escape. Then, all we had to do was take the idol back to Karanis, trade it for Mira, and get out.

Easy.

Because Karanis would never dream of reneging on a deal.

Desperate as I was, even I knew that the odds of our success were slim to none. I shook my head, straining for any scrap of calm. Desperation and panic wouldn't help Mira. Pessimism wouldn't save her. I could.

"Here we are," Tass murmured.

I squared my shoulders, raised my head, and stumbled to a stop. Uttered a curse. "What are we doing *here?*"

Tass pushed open a very familiar gate and walked a few steps onto a wide red-brick drive. She looked over her shoulder at us, standing in a loose knot, mouths hanging open. "Is there a problem?"

"A problem?" I looked past her, past the enormous foundation held up by eight stone lions, past the vaulted arches of a covered forecourt that reached toward us in a three-sided square. My eyes raced across the brown-tiled roof whose even lines were broken by the pyramid-like peaks of nine small towers. Not that I could see more than four of them from my position. But I knew there were nine because: "This is my house."

"This *was* your house," Tass replied, matter-of-factly. "Or, it was your summer home, to be precise. I purchased it several years ago, through intermediaries, of course."

"Oh, of course," Kai parroted, shaking his head with obvious disbelief.

"Come," Tass commanded, pulling us along in her wake.

I was unprepared to step through the door of my old summer home. Like a sleepwalker, I ghosted through the halls. Passageways filled with memories that refused to lie still and sleep. Tass took us through the grand, gold-and-blue-tiled foyer, winding past a few overstuffed sitting rooms to the dining room.

My dining room.

All of it, from the furniture to the paintings on the wall, had belonged to my family. It was like a time capsule. In the most soul-crushing way. Nothing had changed. If I listened close enough, I could almost—*almost*—hear the sound of my parents' laughter. Almost grasp the life that should have been. Should have. But wasn't.

Tass crossed the room, peering through a wide bank of windows overlooking the beach. After a moment she drew the curtains closed. Nodding to herself, she turned. "Please, sit."

I glanced at my crew, at Kai whose mouth hung open, and at

Zee who looked like she'd seen a ghost. They were glued to their feet with the same shock that numbed my whole body. Edik, not having known us back then, was the most at ease.

But then, why shouldn't he be? Zee was safe. And there were a half dozen boats docked in the private slips behind the house. He could steal one and be at our airship in a matter of hours. Hell, he could take that letter and run straight to the empress if he wanted. Instead, he grabbed a chair on one of the table's long sides and tugged Zee into a seat beside him.

"I would offer you refreshment, but I advised the staff to leave the island. Still, if you're hungry I could probably . . . figure something out," Tass said, waving her hand in the general direction of the kitchen.

"Maybe later," Edik said, with a bemused, if tired expression. "Do you really have staff?" he asked, making conversation while the rest of us struggled for words. While *I* struggled. Flailed to make sense of a world that had been broken in two.

Because it didn't make sense. Nothing did. Why was he sitting here wasting time on chitchat? Why wasn't he grabbing supplies and running? Leaving?

Tass nodded sitting at the head of the table. "I seldom have the time to maintain my properties. Staff is necessary to keep everything in working order."

"Why is everything so . . . Why is everything the same?" Zee asked as I dropped bonelessly into the chair across from her.

Tass shrugged. "This was how everything was decorated when I purchased the property. The butler said Governor Paasch had no use for it, which is why the house remained untouched. It was eventually put up for sale in the months after Paasch . . . took power."

"But why is everything still here?" Zee pressed when Tass failed to grasp the real reason for our dismay. "All our things, why didn't you take them down? Redecorate? Something?"

"Should I have?"

"Yeah. Tass," Kai's voice was soft, but no less incredulous. "This is weird."

"I don't see why. People have things," Tass argued, clearly confused by our reactions. "I've noticed. They collect, not just required furniture, but items; trinkets, decorations, pictures of other people."

"People keep gifts. We keep *things* as reminders, and pictures of people we love," Kai said, adamantly trying to make Tass understand where she'd gone wrong. He gestured to the wall behind me as if to punctuate his words.

I didn't need to look to know that my mother's portrait hung there, staring down at me in grief. In accusation.

"I suppose you are right about that," Tass agreed, and then after a moment, she shrugged. "I do not have any of these things. My memory is perfect, so I do not require a memento to recall something pleasant. I have never received a gift, so I've nothing to display. And I do not have people because . . . I'm not people."

Tass spoke in such a matter-of-fact way, with such a lack of emotion that it would be easy to call her cold. But I felt something almost bereft behind her words. Then I remembered all those brothers and sisters; that family who'd tossed her aside. Anger reared up within me all the stronger for how surprised I was for its presence.

Tass was weird, and yeah, she could be unnerving. And sure, I'd only known her for a few days, but I liked Tass. And I felt lonely *for* her.

"The staff thought it was odd too, but the butler eventually convinced them," she continued, when none of us could formulate a response. "He said your mother worked so hard to put the house together, that it would be a shame to take everything down."

"Your butler worked for my mother?"

"Great Below," Kai swore weakly. "Enon works for you?"

"Yes."

"But he must be eighty, if he's a day," Kai said, his voice high in disbelief. "He should be retired."

"True, his age is a concern," Tass said, bowing her head to Kai's point. "But he is very attached to this house; it seemed a shame to make him leave it. In any event, his mind is still sharp, and he enjoys his vocation, so I let him have it on the condition that he move into the downstairs bedroom."

"The downstairs . . ." Kai's words failed him. "That's the master's suite."

"Yes. However I require so little sleep, it seemed wasteful to dedicate an entire room toward it. And Enon's knees are not what they used to be. I couldn't have him climbing stairs. He disagreed at first, but I was quite insistent." Tass almost seemed to fidget under Kai's gaze, and I could have sworn she was nervous, having us there. Foolish impression, probably.

But I suddenly remembered Mira's words—her assertion that Tass had saved her . . . all those years ago. I hadn't truly believed it until she brought us here. Still saving us.

The why of it should have bothered me. Would have bothered me yesterday. But today the answer was obvious—though perhaps not to Tass.

Family.

She was longing for family. Like all of us. It was why we were in this mess.

"Well, that's just . . ." Kai couldn't finish the sentence. His eyes had gone misty. Enon had been like a surrogate father to Kai, and I knew the summers we spent here were some of the happiest Kai had.

"Yes?" Tass's lithe form shifted beneath the unfinished sentence.

"Nice," I said. "That was very nice of you."

"Is it?"

"Yes," I said, smiling for the first time in what felt like ages. "It's not something most people would do."

"No? Well, like I said, I'm not people."

"No," I agreed. I looked around the room and for a moment, I felt like I was home. For a moment, I thought I'd see Enon come through the door with a tray of tea and the candied oranges I always loved.

But he wouldn't. Tass had sent him away to keep him safe, and for that I was grateful beyond words. Because if Enon were here, I'd have to tell him I'd let Mira be taken hostage, and I don't think I could have weathered his disappointment. Not to mention Enon would have thrown away his life trying to save Mira. Trying to save us all from the mess I'd created.

Tass's head tilted to one side. "Mira?"

"Yeah." I swallowed hard, though the memory of salt water scraping my throat refused to wash away. "I have to get her back."

"How?" Kai asked, leaning forward in anticipation. "What's the plan?"

Karanis's orders echoed in the back of my mind like a bell that could not be stilled. Bring the idol, and Mira would be freed. "I'm going to get the idol back from the Curator." What Karanis would do with that idol, well . . . I couldn't let that be a concern. Not when Mira's life hung in the balance. "I have to."

Zee scrubbed her face with her hands. "The Curator kicked us out of the library, Bal. How are we supposed to get into the Archive without his consent?"

"We do what we do best, Zee. We break in."

"'We break in,' he says. Like we're boosting jewels off an old lady," Kai said, his sarcasm a frail mask for his fear.

"Is the attempt worth the time we have left?" Zee asked. "Or should we be planning to go all in against Karanis now? Take him out and be done with it."

There was something dark and bloodthirsty in my cousin's voice. I loved it. That ruthless thread I'd never heard before. And she wasn't wrong.

"We'll have multiple plans in play," I said, acknowledging Zee with a sharp smile. "But I'm going after that statue."

Tass shook her head. "Even if that was possible, the Curator is not someone you wish to anger. I've seen him hold a grudge longer than Ashaar is old. You wouldn't survive it, Bal."

"Mira might not survive Karanis if I don't," I snapped.

"True, but Mira will likely die even if you do succeed."

I balled my fist, slammed it on the table. "So you think I should just do nothing?"

"No, but you need to acknowledge the possibility. Karanis is duplicitous to his core. Changeable as the sea, you might say. Account for it now and act accordingly," she replied evenly. "Now, how do you plan on getting into the Archive?"

I raked a hand through my hair, suddenly smothered by the sense of déjà vu. The first time my father brought me to the Archive, we'd come alone. As we walked up the Western Hill, he confessed to having something of an obsession with the Curator and his vast collection. My father told me on that long walk that the Archive had existed for countless centuries, from the earliest traces of Ashaar. He believed that our people hadn't put down roots here by chance—that Ashaar had grown strong and wise from our proximity to that vast font of wisdom.

As a young boy, still many years from manhood, I hadn't believed a single word my father had said. It sounded too much like the ridiculous sermons the priests of Karanis always spouted. Even as a boy, I hadn't been one to believe in the impossible. Ironic that.

"In his free time, my father read everything he could about the Archive," I said at last.

Kai snorted. "What free time? Only time he wasn't working was . . ." His eyes went wide. "Over the summer."

"Exactly."

"What did he find?" Zee asked.

One of my shoulders twitched. "Not sure. I remember him complaining that, for the oldest structure he'd ever seen, there was a frustrating lack of information about the Archive."

Zee sagged. "So he found out nothing."

"Thing is, I don't think that's true. Zee, you remember how he would always doodle our routes and scribble out notes when he took us to the Archive?"

"Yeah," she said, her back straightening. She looked from me to Kai and back again, her eyes wide and hopeful. "And when we came back here . . ."

"He'd lock himself in the map room."

Kai muttered an impressed curse. "Was the old man mapping out the Archive?"

I looked to Tass. "Don't suppose you've ever looked through the map room?"

She shook her head. "The room has a pretty enough view, but I've never had need of its contents. Until now, that is. Shall we?"

Tass and I walked side by side through my onetime home, and even though I knew she hadn't changed anything, seeing it was . . . There were no words. It was like a shrine to my lost life. Ghosts crowded these halls. Not the restless shades of lost souls but specters conjured from my own memories.

I could almost see them, my parents dancing slow waltzes when they thought we were in bed. My aunts and uncles playing cards over pitchers of sweet tea. The warmth of my mother's embrace when she tucked me in at night. I could almost smell her perfume, roses and hyacinth and . . .

I shook my head. Was this how all Tass's homes were? I wondered. Did she skirt at the edges of other people's stories, as invisible as she was immortal?

"Did you know who I was?" I asked her in an undertone. "When you saw me in the Code Hall, did you know this had been my home?"

"Yes. I knew." She didn't say anything more for a few feet worth of steps. "I confess to a certain . . . curiosity, about you and your crew."

I felt my eyebrows rise and for a reason that I couldn't quite explain, I was flattered. "Wow. The mysterious Queen of Days curious about a humble thief."

"It is true. I am not often curious about humans," she replied, my sarcasm flying right over her head. "Your people don't usually live long enough to become truly interesting, but something about you and your family made me feel . . ."

Lonely perhaps? A desire to belong? Both things felt true, but I wasn't foolish enough to say them aloud.

"Curious," she repeated at long last, as if her vocabulary—or her heart—had defeated her.

The map room was in the northernmost tower, located directly above my father's study. A narrow iron staircase led us up to a trapdoor that opened on tight, squealing hinges. That tower was the highest in the house and covered in windows looking out onto the sea from the north, and across the entire island of Cothis from the east, south, and west.

A long table took up most of the space in the center of the room. Its top was still covered with maps of Ashaar, their edges pinned with dust-covered paperweights like my father was moments from returning. The dust—or the sight—made my eyes water just a bit, thinking of him standing here. It was the dust. Definitely.

I ran my hand along the edge of one of the maps, this one depicting the island of Arisha, the capital of Ashaar. No doubt it was evidence of my father's last obsession, though what that was I'd never now know.

I turned away from the table. Beneath the windows were built-in bookcases, and in these, my father had stored stack after stack of neatly rolled maps.

Kai was looking at me with a slightly helpless expression. "This could take all day."

"Then we'd better get started."

I walked a quick circuit of the room, trying to devise a plan of attack. My father had made small notes on some of the bookcases, a half-hearted attempt at organization, I thought. One case for each of the seven islands of Ashaar. I hesitated at the stack labeled "Cothis."

Zee and Edik were already crouched in front of it, unrolling map after map in search for any sign of the Archive.

It made sense to start there, but something was pulling me away. That was the thing about grifting. The theft always began in a target's mind. Maybe it was just that I knew my father best, but an unmarked stack across the room seemed to be calling me.

Unlike the other bookcases, this one only had a top shelf. Where a bottom shelf would have lain, a decorative panel was emblazoned with the Cothis city crest. A dozen hardcover books were lined up in orderly rows on the shelf. Their spines were covered in black leather and gleamed with embossed gold titles loudly proclaiming their subjects: sailing, water currents, navigation.

I smiled. If there was anything my father hated more than laziness, it was water. Ironic that, for the governor of a city that claimed a sea god for a patron. He was a terrible swimmer, and he'd only let any of us go play on the beach if we brought about two dozen guards. In hindsight, I recognized his fear, but back then all I saw was an overprotective old man who refused to let me go on a date alone with my future bride.

A low ringing sound began in my ears, like my anger had become a physical thing. A malady with symptoms that could be categorized and diagnosed. Shoving Shasheba out of my thoughts, I crouched.

My eyes traced the sun-bleached wood, mind buzzing to discover why I'd been drawn to this shelf of books. Books on a subject my father hated. No. Not just that. *Boring* books. The kind that no nosy kid would come up here looking for. Not even Zee would have disturbed these tomes.

Only I wasn't a nosy kid anymore. I was a thief. A thief who specialized in stealing priceless crap off rich fools.

I smiled.

One by one I piled the books on the floor, leaving the top shelf empty. I studied the bookcase with a practiced eye. It was well made. Not an antique, though father surely paid a king's ransom to make it appear like one. If I didn't know better, I never would have guessed that the missing bottom shelf wasn't missing after all. Just hidden.

But I did know better.

My fingers danced on the inside edges of the bookcase, creeping from front to back trying to find the catch.

Snick!

The engraved panel fell forward. Its hinges well-oiled enough that, after so many years, they gave way without protest. I shifted, laying the panel flat on the floor, eager to examine the hidden space. Only a dozen or so maps were rolled in this cubby, but their edges were worn and stained slightly gray, like the oil from my father's hands had rubbed off after so much use.

I slid one map out of the cubby. Unrolled it. The title sent a little shock through my body:

"The Grand Archive of the Curator."

"Here."

Everyone turned at the sound of my voice. I rushed to the table and splayed the map out for my friends to see.

Kai let out a low whistle. "Your old man was a genius."

I managed a smile. "That he was," I said. Such small words— too small to encapsulate all that he was. All that he had been. The kind of man who could rule a city of outlaws like Cothis. Rule it and tame it and make it a place worth something. That had been his dream.

But it was all ashes now. His dreams of plenty were all twisted and the city he'd given his life for was ready to fall.

Because of men like Paasch. And creatures like Karanis. Now the only people standing up to stop it all was a band of thieves.

Typical Cothis. This city didn't want law and order. Not really. Was it fitting that the Talion were its only defenders? You're gods-damn right it was. Let chaos reign.

I stepped up to my father's place at the table with a perverse kind of pride. He'd have hated what my life had become. But I was trying, wasn't I? Trying to save Mira—and the city with her? It counted for something.

Didn't it?

The map was divided into nine levels, one for each of the floors we'd passed, all the way to the bottom where the Curator kept his reading room. I shook my head at the fine detail of my father's drawings. He'd mapped the layout of each stack, each lamppost, each stairway that led to nowhere and door that never opened.

Yet despite all his long years' work, not a single level was finished. The drawings just petered out, disappearing into black and white nothingness like words left unspoken.

Tass stepped up to the table beside me. "Amazing."

"It is," Edik agreed, his face troubled, "but I don't see any way *into* the Archive."

"Hang on," Zee said. "There are more maps here."

The crew descended on the bookcase and in a matter of moments, the rest of the maps were spread out on the table's long surface.

I took a step back and studied the maps, feeling my brows rise. "This isn't possible."

The maps showed entrances to the Archive—or rather, possible entrances given the question mark my father made beside some of them. Only the maps weren't just of Cothis. Arisha, Rocanthe, Eshara, La'Zem—all the Ashaarite Islands were here. Each island had its own map and each map showed at least two dozen entrances to the Archive. It simply wasn't possible.

Zee frowned. "This can't be right. The Archive is large, but there's no way it can span the entire breadth of the kingdom."

"I do not think it does," Tass said. "But I do think it has many entrances."

I considered her words. "You told me the Curator was Ankaari. Does his magic allow him to sustain these . . . portals?"

"Indirectly perhaps."

Zee held up a finger. "I'm going to need you to explain that."

"I think the Curator built his Archive in what my people call a pocket realm."

"What's that?" Kai crossed his arms, looking like a schoolboy settling in for a lecture about something far too complex to understand.

"Exactly what it sounds like. It's a pocket of space," she replied making a circle with her hands. "Only it's slightly out of shift with the larger universe that surrounds it." She tilted her hands to one side to illustrate this. "They occasionally form in the wake of great cataclysms."

She looked at me when she said this, and I instantly remembered her description of the Ankaari's first forays into our plane of existence. I wondered if the Archives were just another one of those explosions waiting to happen and shuddered.

"How could you possibly come to that conclusion?" Zee said, not seeing the interaction between Tass and I, but clearly unconvinced. The confusion was bound to piss her off.

"You mean aside from the fact that the natural laws of this world didn't seem to apply as strictly in the Archive as they do in this one? Time," Tass said.

"What about it?" I asked.

"It flowed slightly slower in the Archive than it does in the rest of the city. Didn't you notice? We spent at least twelve hours in the Curator's collection, yet when we emerged from it only about four hours had passed."

Zee swore under her breath, rubbing her eyes. "She's right."

"How the hell didn't we ever notice?" I asked, feeling like a supreme idiot.

Thankfully, Tass refrained from replying to that. She just shrugged. "I believe that the deeper you go in the Archive, the slower time becomes outside it. It would explain how the Curator has maintained his flesh-body for so long."

I nodded. It made sense, Paasch's body wouldn't last the week, not at the rate Karanis was burning through it. "I don't suppose that means that the Curator has less magic to use, given the age of his body?"

"I would not count on that. Age does not equal infirmity among my people. And in any event, the pocket realm has allowed the Curator to build his collection and maintain it for the past two centuries. It may be more forgiving to the energy expenditure that magic requires and thusly harm the Curator's body less. Although . . ." She tilted her head to one side. "Time must approach normality the farther from the center, which would seem to indicate that his power will be at its weakest near the entrance."

"This is all fascinating," Edik said, with a voice that very much implied the opposite, "but I'll admit I don't understand a word of this."

"Oh thank the gods," Kai muttered. "I'm fucking lost."

Tass sighed.

"Is it possible to break in?" I pressed, angling for the only answer that mattered.

"It should be. Though the idol will no doubt be in the very heart of his domain, where he will be at the height of his power."

"Great," Kai mumbled.

"Not really," Tass replied agreeably.

"I didn't mean—"

"However," she said, ignoring him, "the time differential will give us many more hours to complete the task than we would have ordinarily."

I looked up, sharply. "Us? You mean . . . You still mean to help us?" I had hoped for it. Creation save me, I'd hoped for it. But Tass seemed to have a history with the Curator. I wasn't at all sure she'd agree to help steal from him. "Our three days together are almost spent."

She didn't reply for a long moment. "Our original agreement is irrelevant now. This goes beyond the bounds of a simple contract," she said finally. Softly. "This is about family now. I will help you get the idol back and rescue Miraveena. But you must help me kill Karanis before he uses it."

I didn't immediately respond. It was a big ask. No—that was an understatement. She was asking me to *kill a god*. But if it saved Mira? I nodded.

"Bal," Edik said, gaze so, so heavy. "Are you sure about this. Karanis isn't—"

"I know Karanis isn't Paasch," I said, cutting him off. But there was no heat in my voice. It was important for him to know I was truly done with that. "This isn't about vengeance. It's about saving Mira, and all the other Miras in this godsdamned city."

"Saving the city isn't our responsibility," he argued, but something suspiciously like respect was edging into his eyes.

I smiled, running my hand along my father's desk. Funny. I felt his presence more in this moment than I had in years. "I know. But that's the thing about duty. You don't always get to choose it. Sometimes it chooses you.

"Cothis may be a shithole. But it's our shithole. And it deserves more than a psychopath like Karanis."

Zee grinned. Tass nodded. Kai began to clap.

I shot him a look. "Seriously, dude?"

He stopped mid-clap and looked around the room. "What—we're not—"

"Way to make it weird, Kai," Zee said, swatting the back of his head.

"So we have a deal?" Tass asked, voice warm with approval.

"Deal."

"Very good. Then I suggest we choose an entrance and stock up on supplies. You and I must leave within the hour. In the meantime, your compatriots should prepare to rendezvous with Karanis at the temple. I have no doubt the meeting will be quite trying."

"Hold up one minute," Kai said. "This 'compatriot' ain't staying behind."

"No, Kai. She's right," I said, holding up a hand. "We can't all go to the Archive. If we fail, or if we don't make it out in time, someone needs to be topside to save Mira." Kai looked mutinous, so I clasped his arm. "Please, Kai. There's no one I trust more to save her. Please."

"That's a low fucking blow, man," he snapped, shrugging me off as he turned away. His anger and fear clouded the air, but I knew he'd do whatever was necessary to save Mira. She was his sister too.

I turned back to the others. "Assuming Tass and I are able to get the idol back from the Curator, we won't have time to put all the pieces in motion for the handoff."

"You have a plan?" Edik asked.

"I do. But . . ."

Edik and Zee looked at me, a question in their eyes. "It's just, I know you planned on going to Arisha with the letter. But that was before." I swallowed hard. "Will you help us? Help me?"

Zee's eyes flashed with equal parts impatience and worry. "Leave the plan with us."

Edik crossed his arms, his expression grave as he looked at me. Searching. But for what, I couldn't say. He didn't want to help save Shasheba, but Mira surely . . .

Finally he leaned forward, bridging the distance between us with the weight of his hand on my shoulder. "We're family, Bal. That means we're with you. To the end."

Something in my chest unclenched and I managed a grin. "Good. Because I need you to do something for me."

"Of course, you do," he said, blowing out a breathy laugh. Then sobered. "It's going to be ugly," he said at long last, something unreadable in his eyes. "Be nice to have some additional firepower."

"The armory is, of course, at your disposal," Tass said.

Zee perked up like a kid at the proverbial candy store. "We have an armory?"

Tass's palms flashed to the ceiling. "It was my one small addition. It's in the basement, beyond the wine racks. Everything you should require will be there. I also took the liberty of restocking your laboratory."

THE QUEEN OF DAYS   263

"You did?"

"Yes. Just in case we needed to come back here."

Zee's lips wobbled into a smile, probably the first she'd ever given Tass. A miracle in itself.

"That's absolutely brilliant, Tass," I said when words seemed to have escaped my cousin. "Zee, if you have the parts, I think we're going to need a mouse."

Her grin widened into a look of pleasure that made me distinctly uncomfortable. "I don't need to *make* one," she said, her expression all feline as she reached into her pocket and passed me the small clockwork contraption. "Anything else?"

My answering smile was sharp enough to cut. "I'm gonna need something that goes boom."

Zee nodded.

"I'll see you soon," I said.

"You'd better," Kai growled.

"We're getting Mira back. We're killing Karanis. We're saving the city."

"That's the ridiculously confident cousin I knew," Zee said, heading for the door, only to pause on the threshold. Reaching back, Zee clasped Tass's hand. "Thank you," she said, and ghosted out of the room. Edik patted Tass's shoulder and followed his wife out the door.

"I think you just made a friend for life."

"Have I? That's nice."

I couldn't see her face, but I could feel Tass smile. I grinned. Even though I knew she would never admit it, and even though we'd only come here because Mira had been taken, I was sure Tass had quietly hoped for an excuse to show us this place. Her home. *Our* home.

"Well. Which entrance should we try?" I asked, the "we" feeling more and more natural the longer we stood here. Strange that, how the rightness of it all just clicked into place. Like it was all meant to be.

She seemed to consider the map for a moment and planted one long finger on the parchment. "Here."

19

BALTHAZAR

Here" was the public gardens located a block away from the summer house. Built on the ruins of an ancient pre-Ashaarite civilization, the Sunken Gardens were something of a local curiosity. In a pit some ten feet below street level, the crumbling walls and streets of a lost kingdom had been transformed into a picturesque garden filled with climbing jasmine and brightly tiled fountains.

Which all made a lot of sense, now that I knew it might be the entrance to a freaking pocket of time and space.

Tass and I made our way along the path, tension rising with each step. In truth, I'd never much liked this place. Walking on the bones of a dead city made me feel out of time, penned in. Lost in some inexplicable way. And now I was about to dive headfirst into the damn place.

I smothered the sensation as we rounded the path and found the garden's twisting heart: a perfectly preserved door, complete with lintel and scrolling iron lock. Locals called it the Witch Door because it was flanked on either side by eagle-headed lions, pets of Sarthaniel, the goddess of magic. According to legend, no one had ever been able to open the door. Until—I hoped—today.

The lions were bigger than I remembered, or perhaps the door was smaller. It was certainly shorter than it should be, I thought as we reached it. The Witch Door was made of three slightly warped wooden planks covered in chipping, dingy green paint. The planks were banded together with a half dozen dull bars of thinly hammered iron. The same iron as the heavy lock. Only a few flecks of rust marred the edge of the lock—no small miracle given Cothis's humid climate and how often the garden flooded.

Tass bent, putting her masked eye up to the lock. She let out an annoyed tut and straightened.

"What's wrong?"

"Nothing. The spell laid on this door is so rudimentary, it is shameful I didn't realize this place was here years ago," she said, sounding slightly chagrined.

"What does the spell do?" I asked, my traitorous mind conjuring images of a hundred terrible ways the Curator might kill us for opening the door.

"It is a small occlusion spell to keep any Ankaari, or half Ankaari for that matter, from noticing the portal. It's the same spell I use on my mask. I hadn't the chance to inspect the door on the Western Hill, but I suspect it received the same treatment." She shook her head. "It would seem the Curator does not want any nonhuman visitors."

I heard the slightly wounded note in her voice, and managed a smile. "To be fair, he doesn't usually like any human ones either."

"Least of all you right now," she said dryly.

"Yeah." It was the best reply I could summon. Looking around I could practically feel the day waning. Stealing pieces of my twenty-four-hour time line. "Shall we go through then?"

"Just a moment," Tass said. "I need to put an enchantment over us that will mask our presence."

My heart rose at her words. "So the Curator won't know we're in the Archive?"

"That is my hope," she replied. "As I said before, the Curator's power seems to be weaker the farther from the heart of the Archive. I will attempt to mute our presence so he cannot sense that his border has been breached. I warn you this will only work while we remain on the outer fringes of his domain. We will not stay beneath his notice forever."

I nodded. I was a good thief. Getting in and out of places unnoticed was my bread and butter, but I knew I wouldn't be able to do that today. Truth be told, even getting into the Archive without the Curator knowing was more than I could have hoped for. Whether it worked or not, it was worth a shot. "All right, then. Carry on."

Tass nodded, squared her shoulders, and stood still.

I widened my stance and closed my eyes, preparing myself. After a minute, I opened them again. Shifted my weight from one foot to the other. Sniffed.

"All right."

"All right?" I asked, my mouth pulling down. "Are you done?"

"Yes."

This couldn't be right. I'd never been enchanted before, but it had to feel like . . . something. "But I didn't feel anything."

"I should hope not," she said, her voice pinched and slightly affronted. "I am hardly a novice, Bal."

"Touchy subject?"

She tutted. "What *exactly* would be the point of enchanting someone if they know they're being enchanted? Do you advertise your thefts before you pull them off?"

"Hey, it was my first time. I was hoping to be dazzled," I said with an unrepentant grin. Shook my head when she didn't react. "But I see your point. Are you ready?"

"Quite."

Tass placed a gloved hand on the door and traced a small curving design on the lock with her other. Without comment, she turned the handle and pulled the door open. Whatever lay beyond the threshold—if anything lay beyond it, I couldn't see. All that met my eyes was complete and total darkness.

She motioned me forward. I took a long breath, like I was getting ready to plunge into deep water, and stepped through.

The world wasn't any less dark on this side of the door. No streetlamp turned on to alleviate it, and the daylight behind me didn't—*couldn't*—penetrate the blackness. I felt something hard beneath my feet but couldn't see if it was earth or stone or something else.

I turned to Tass, watched her come through the door. The garden over her shoulder was impossibly bright, impossibly colorful for such a gloomy day. Like a dream of safety and hope. A dream every instinct within me screamed to run toward.

Tass shut the door with a decisive *snick*. Darkness descended thick and unyielding. The kind of dark that made even the thought of light hard to conjure. It had texture, that blackness. A scent. A caress that spoke, not of night, but of nightmare. My heartbeat sounded so loudly in my ears it was possible to imagine it echoing through the entire cavernous maw of the Archive. For it was a maw—a great open jaw of a beast I couldn't begin to fight.

"Tass," I whispered, but the whisper grew wings and flew. She didn't reply. Terror trilled up my back, and my stomach fell into my toes. *Pull it together, Bal,* I thought furiously. *You are not afraid of the dark.*

"I am here, Bal."

A tiny blue flame flickered on my right. I spun toward it, desperate for more. The light grew. It wasn't fire. It wasn't lightning. It was something amorphous, almost liquid. It grew into an orb of soft blue-gray light that illuminated Tass's silver face. She raised it higher.

"Thanks for the light," I managed to say around a suspicious tightness in my throat.

She bent her neck in a graceful nod. "Do you have the map?"

"Yeah." I reached into my jacket's inside pocket and withdrew one of the maps my father had made of the Archive. Unfolding it, I tilted the parchment toward the light, squinting in the semidarkness. "I can't really make out any of the details. Can you make the light brighter?"

"I do not think that would be wise," she replied, "but I can carry the map."

"Can you carry the map and the light at the same time?" I asked, hating the naked fear in my voice, but unable to curb it. I had the feeling Tass didn't really need the light, but Great Below, I did. There was just something about this roiling blackness, the not knowing what lay beyond it, that put my teeth on edge.

"No, but I was not planning on carrying the light." Her hand turned as she spoke. The orb rolled off her fingertips and fell in a lazy spiral to the ground. It hovered a few inches from what turned out to be the cobbled bed of a street—exactly like the entrance on the Western Hill. "Better the light illuminates what lies ahead," Tass murmured. "That way we won't walk off the edge of the world."

I waited for Tass to laugh at her joke. My heart fell when she didn't.

"This way."

"Hold up. I need to release the mouse," I said, pulling out a small clockwork contraption from my pocket.

Tass's head cocked to the side as I began to wind it, her doubt a tangible thing. "You are certain the mechanism won't damage the Archive?"

"I'm certain it will cause a distraction," I replied, with a jaunty smile I didn't feel.

"Your funeral."

"Yours, too."

"No, Bal. Not me."

Oh, right. Immortals and whatnot.

Still, I released the mouse and followed Tass through the darkness, trying to see my father's sketch in my mind's eye. I had no idea how many years he'd worked on his map of the Curator's domain, but my father had apparently discovered a path to the reading room that didn't pass down the nautilus ramp of the main hall. We walked in silence, down the Archive's street-like foyer, veering to the right when the cobblestones transformed into a carpeted hallway.

Bookshelves emerged after many more minutes, though they stood only on my left. The spines of books uncounted shone brightly in the light of the orb, like thousands of tiny eyes watching us from the shadows. The wall on the right was still craggy and cave-like and I found myself hugging close to it as we walked on and on, searching for the infernal door which would lead to the next stage of our journey.

Curbing my impatience, I focused on the orb, as it bounced and tumbled on the ground at our feet. There was something merry about it, something joyous that made a perverse part of my mind itch to kick it. I resisted the temptation even as I embraced the feeling. Anything, even this itching annoyance, was better than the bone-deep fear this place spawned within me.

I rolled my shoulders, flexed my hands as if the small gestures could excise my annoyance. Tass said time had little meaning here in the Archive, but Great Below if I wasn't aching to sprint, even if that meant running into the undulating blackness.

I was staring deep into the orb's swirling blue-gray center when it bounced off a wall in front of us and came to a halt. *Finally.* We'd found the door my father's map promised. I grimaced when I saw what that meant.

It was perfectly circular, with a tiny silver handle right in the center. But then, the handle had to be tiny, as the door could hardly be more than two feet across. I mentally measured my shoulders. It was going to be a tight squeeze.

I crouched, opening the door. The orb bounced through, hovering to a stop a few feet past the tunnel-like threshold. I couldn't make out anything of the room beyond, aside from the fact that it did seem to be a room, not a cave, though the only evidence that supported my conclusion was the presence of amethyst carpet beneath the orb's weak light.

"I'll go first," Tass murmured, and I shuffled back to make room for her, not objecting with some grandiose idea of chivalry. This was no fairy tale, but even if it was, Tass made for a better knight in shining armor than I ever would. She rolled onto her back, knees bent, arms raised over her head, and slid through the door with one smooth push of her legs.

As her feet disappeared, I hurried to follow suit, copying her movements as best as I could. Hardly my fault if I was less graceful, I thought, grunting when my shoulders caught on the doorframe. Gritting my teeth, I pushed harder finally popping free. I pulled myself upright, glad that the orb's weak light would hide the flush burning my cheeks.

"There should be another door here," Tass said, looking around the room.

I smoothed down my shirt and did a quick circuit. This chamber was yet another sitting room—*How many godsdamned sitting rooms did one man need?*—complete with a table and set of overstuffed green couches. Unlike the sitting room downstairs, there was no fire crackling in the hearth, no cases filled with prettily bound books. Instead, the walls were covered with dead bugs, mounted and framed on the silk wallpaper.

The sight of spiders with pen-size pincers and moths as big as dinner plates left a sour taste in my mouth, despite the fact they were behind glass. I had no idea what hell these bugs came from, but I was glad it was nowhere I'd ever been.

"I don't see any doors," I whispered, turning away from the spiders.

"Me neither." Tass planted her hands on her hips, the small orb of light still dancing at her feet. I looked down at it, at the purple and red rug that covered the carpet, and smiled.

"Help me move the furniture back," I said, nodding toward the rug.

Tass hefted the table off to one side as I pushed the chairs away. Within moments, we were rolling up the carpet. I looked down at a rectangular trapdoor set into the middle of the floor, a sense of triumph warm enough to make even this room feel less creepy.

"After you," Tass said.

I got the impression that this was her idea of a prize for doing a good job. I'd have rather had a shot of whiskey, I thought, my mouth going dry. Only the memory my sister's terrified face surrounded by Karanis's water could propel me onward.

The door opened with a wail of rusted hinges. I cursed, my ears strained in the echoing aftermath of the sound. Waiting. Praying we hadn't been heard. When nothing happened, I peered through the door and saw the first few rungs of an iron ladder bolted to the side of the door. Without pausing to think or second-guess myself, I moved.

The ladder went down, and down, and down some more. The orb bounced along at my feet, but I tried not to look at it too closely. In this much darkness even the orb's low light was beginning to burn my eyes. Above me, I heard Tass climbing down. Heard. But when I squinted up, I couldn't make out so much as the soles of her shoes.

My feet hit something solid, and a metallic thud echoed through open space. It was a platform. One whose metal was braided into a diamond-shaped lattice. No more than five feet long, it led to a staircase that descended into switchbacks deep into the Archive. Deep.

Tass dropped down beside me. She rose in a fluid motion. Paused, her silver face tilted toward the darkness beyond the stairs. Her fingers traced a complicated dance and the orb snapped into her palm.

"What is it?" Because Tass's body seemed to hum in shock and recognition. She'd seen something more than mere darkness.

"Look," she said. The orb flew out from her fingertips, and the darkness parted before the light. Until it didn't.

What stopped the orb wasn't the rocky cliff face of the Archive's entrance. It was too even a line to be stone. Too gelatinous. The orb's blue-gray light reflected off the boundary's surface in an opalescent sheen. It reminded me of a gigantic bubble.

"What is that thing?" I whispered.

"A border," Tass replied. "It is the border of the Curator's pocket realm."

The longing in Tass's voice was sharp enough to cut. I looked at her, my heart sinking. "What lies beyond?"

"The Nethersphere."

I had to look away from the sound of her voice. It was too bitter, too filled with longing, too raw. "Why does the border look like this?" I asked, using the question as a shield. Not for me. For Tass. For the emotion I could feel boiling off her skin.

I always imagined the Nethersphere as a different plane of existence. Like the universe was a cake and the Nethersphere was a different layer, invisible to me but still there on top of everything. This, though, was more like a sheering off of reality. A clean cut through space—perhaps even time—severing the Archive from the Nethersphere. But it wasn't solid, I could tell that much from here. It truly looked as fragile as a soap bubble—a border every bit as imaginary as lines drawn on a map.

She shook her head. "It is the nature of such pocket realms, that they can sometimes press against multiple realities. It's likely that the Curator disguises the border between the Archive and your world as a cavernous doorway. This is what it would look like in its natural state. It is a kind of thinning of reality where the Archive touches them."

I licked my lips. Swallowed, because if it was as permeable as it looked, then . . .

"Could you cross over it?"

"Yes." Her sibilant reply echoed across empty space, caressing the length of the bubble. "But I'm not going to."

My eyes snapped wide. "Why not? You've been trying to get home for so long. Don't you have the energy to cross?"

"I do. From this point, I could jump across the border with almost no effort. I could even take you with me. The border itself is so weak, the energy expenditure would be negligible."

"But you're not going to?"

"No."

"Why?"

She sighed, and the silence that followed her exhalation was laden by many things. "I saw my brother today," she said, her shoulders slumping.

"What?" My voice echoed into the void louder, much louder than I'd intended. I winced. "Which one? Where?"

"Calien. At the Low Temple."

Well . . . shit. It was easy to forget just who Tass was. But the way she so casually dropped—in my mind at least—the demigod's name put things in stark relief.

"How did he get here? Did he open a portal like Karanis?"

"Yes, but it would have been quite small. Calien did not bring his body with him, you see. He just sent his consciousness from the Nethersphere. He borrowed a body when he got here."

"Borrowed a body?" Even the idea turned my stomach. "So Calien Bodysnatcher is real."

"Bodysnatcher?"

"You've never heard that?" I laughed. "Calien the Bodysnatcher is a legend, a sort of bogeyman prank that kids play on their friends. Story is that if you turn out the lights and look into a pool of water while speaking his name three times, Calien will possess the person standing right next to you." Which had been part of the fun, I thought. I'd done it to Kai when we were nine and he screamed so loud every adult in the house came running.

Tass turned to me with exaggerating slowness, like she'd been momentarily struck dumb. "Promise me you will never play that game again, Bal. My brother has a twisted sense of humor. And he could indeed "snatch" your body. He would do it too. For no other purpose than the hilarity he'd find in scaring you.

"Names have power when spoken with such intent. Once you hit that bell, it cannot be unrung. Even if it does not make him act, it *will* make him listen."

"Seriously? Could he be listening right now?"

She shook her head slowly. "With all the layers of enchantment on this space, we are protected. But I would advise against speaking of my brother when we return to your plane."

"And all it takes is saying his name?"

She inclined her head. "My brother is one of the most powerful mages in the Nethersphere. He could take over the body of almost any Ankaari, so taking a human body is child's play. Worse, you wouldn't even remember it."

The sight of Paasch's eyes melting in his skull rose in my mind. "How could they not remember? Paasch couldn't have survived a minute with Karanis inside him."

"It is not the same sort of possession. Calien only sends a portion of his consciousness to this world and as such, can only remain for a handful of hours before he must return. Karanis came here to stay. He sent everything he is . . ." I sensed a great well of unhappiness growing within her as her words trailed off.

I licked my lips, bracing my hands on the platform's metal railing. "Did you get the chance to speak with him? Your brother, I mean."

"Yes." The word dragged out of her in a long sibilant echo. "He admitted to trying to kill me. Confirmed that our father ordered my death. He did not even try to deny it." Tass shook her head at the border. "Yet he was genuinely happy to see me, odd though that must sound."

My heart twisted. "Maybe because he regretted what he'd done?"

"No," she replied with a dark laugh. "Not even a little. According to my brother, I deserved to be executed for daring to insist that we save . . . one of our own."

My head jerked back like I'd been slapped. "Bastard."

"That is only the beginning. My brother said that if I apologize for my impertinence, I might be allowed back. Like things could simply return to the way they were."

"What a load of crap," I said, wishing I'd been there if only to punch Calien in the face. "You didn't do anything wrong. If anyone should be apologizing, it's them."

She just shook her head. "This entire situation troubles me. The fact that Karanis and the Curator are here suggests a deep and endemic wrongness in my homeland, the kind that could spell disaster for your world. So I can't leave—I have to stay until I learn more.

"Not that I would be allowed to return anyway," she added bitterly. "Now that my brother knows I'm alive, it is extremely likely that he will tell everyone else. And tell them I've been working against Karanis. I would probably be killed on sight."

"Extremely likely?" I asked. "You aren't certain that he'll tell everyone?"

"Certainty is a fool's gambit where Calien is concerned." There was something almost affectionate in her voice. Almost. But the marrow-deep sadness layered on top of her words was impossible to miss.

"I'm sorry." Stupid, simple words, really. But I had nothing better to say. Nothing could make up for the fact that despite centuries of searching, she'd found a way home only to learn her home wasn't what she remembered.

Instead I asked, "So your brother's working for Karanis?"

"*For* Karanis?" she said with a shrug. "Indirectly, perhaps. Though I'm certain he was the original intermediary between Karanis and Paasch."

"Does that mean he'll help Karanis if we try to kill him?"

"I do not know," she replied after a long moment. "Whatever his initial involvement, he made it sound like his orders were strictly to observe at this stage."

"But he knows you're alive. Wouldn't his orders have changed?"

"Maybe," she replied, all her attention on that opalescent border. "If he told anyone that I am alive . . ."

I swallowed hard, like that could push away the painful sliver of hope wedged into the edges of Tass's words. Her brother didn't deserve her. None of her family did—and if I ever saw any of them, I swore to the gods I'd—

I shook my head. There were no gods. Only Ankaari. Tass's own shitty family. And if she wanted to go back, who was I to judge?

I nudged her shoulder with mine. "Maybe he won't tell anyone. Maybe he really does miss you. Maybe you could go home."

"Doubtful." She shook her head. "Anyway, I will not leave Miraveena in Karanis's hands. And now that I know this is here, I can always come back. If things change."

Assuming the Curator let her return, I thought, though I hadn't the heart to say it out loud. I had a terrible suspicion that this stairway would not be here after we stole the idol . . . even more so if we failed. I shook those thoughts away as we turned from the border and started down the rusted metal staircase. Down to the next platform. And the next. And the next.

There should have been nine. The thought circled round and round in my head. The Archive was nine levels deep. And my father's map clearly indicated nine platform-like landings to this staircase. But I counted more as we walked in silence, making our way slowly down the scaffolding's edge of the Archive. Many more. Minutes slid into hours in that unyielding darkness. Hours that made our escape plan utterly useless.

Once we took the idol, we'd have to get out of the Archive fast. Sure, the mouse I'd released would keep the Curator busy. Keep his attention divided. But I doubted that mouse would capture his attention so long we'd have enough time to climb back up these endless stairs. Eventually he would realize the idol was gone. And then what? For all I knew, the Curator would simply make the scaffolding disappear, leaving us stranded at the bottom. Wherever the bottom was.

"We need to rethink our escape," I said, my voice pitched low.

Tass inclined her head, but failed to comment. Not a good sign.

"Any bright ideas?" I asked, hoping against hope.

"Not bright, no," she said, and I couldn't tell if she was joking or not. "The way I see it, we have two ways out. The first, and the one I hope for, is up the main ramp."

"Somehow I don't think that way will be open to us," I said, feeling futility drop like a lead weight in my gut. "It's not like the Curator will just let us walk out of the Archive with the idol."

"He may," she countered. "He always had something of an unpredictable streak and a deep fondness for humans. Perhaps he will take pity on your sister and let us go."

My shoulders sagged in the darkness. Though he and Tass obviously had a long history, I doubted he'd ever show me that sort of kindness. "That's a lot to pin on 'perhaps.'"

"People have attempted much more with far less," she said, leaving me to chew on that little gem for a few minutes.

Deciding I wasn't getting anywhere on that front, I asked, "Who is the Curator, anyway? Anyone I've heard of?"

"Should we make it out of here alive, I will tell you. However, it would be unwise to use his true name within his domain."

"Names have power?" I asked, remembering her words about Calien.

"Indeed. And he will be listening for his. Using it would certainly call attention to us and we've been doing such a good job of avoiding it thus far. Suffice it to say, the Curator is—even among the Ankaari—an ancient and terrible being of such renown that your ancestors knew his name and revered him as one of their greatest deities."

The respect in Tass's voice was enough to give me pause, even if the "terrible being" hadn't caught me up short. "And here I was hoping he was just the cosmic janitor."

She laughed. I didn't. After the past few days, I'd had quite enough of gods for a lifetime. The gods of Ashaar, even in our most ancient tales, were always a changeable lot, prone to vengeance and awful rages. And my admittedly limited contact with their Ankaari counterparts didn't make me hopeful for the Curator's mercy.

"I'd rather not go in counting on a mark's goodwill. We need a backup in place in case the Curator decides to kill us," I said, searching my memory of the map. "We'll need to head for one of the alternate exits." My father had mapped out several of them, but even one was enough to give me hope.

Until Tass shook her head.

"The paths to reach them are so convoluted it would be inadvisable to even try."

Hope dashed.

"So what is the second way out you mentioned before?"

She was silent for a long moment. Eventually her silver face tilted over her shoulder, glancing my way. "Something so foolish I do not even want to give voice to it, lest the necessity become real."

And on *that* ominous note, we reached the bottom of the Archive. I stepped off the last iron tread and onto perfectly even black cobblestones. To my right, the curved edge of the border bubble waited in all its silent magnificence. To my left was a closed door with a brass handle that shone dully in the orb's light.

"Beyond this door lies the Curator's reading room," she said. "The moment we open it, he will be aware of our trespass."

If he wasn't aware of it already. The unspoken thought writhed between us.

"Then we'd better be fast."

Tass nodded. "And hope that his desire to study the object will mean that it will be on the desk in the reading room."

Seemed like a good bet. The old man loved that desk. Every time I'd come to the Archive, I'd found him sitting there. "What if it's not there?"

Worse—what if *he* was?

Tass muttered an oath. "Hope it's there, Bal. My other methods of locating it will take more time than we are likely to have. Ready?"

"Not at all."

"Good."

20

BALTHAZAR

She opened the door and the light from the reading room raced through, searing my eyes. I barely had time to register the bookcase standing three feet from the door before Tass was off running.

I sprinted after her, down the long line of the bookcase corridor. I didn't bother with stealth. Couldn't. For every ten feet a new lamppost burst to life, tracking our movements better than any bloodhound.

Faster.

Must move faster.

The row of shelves ended in an open corridor of space only a few yards away. Tass reached it first. She planted her feet, looked around, and lunged to the left.

I wheeled around the corner, hard on her heels, and found the circular desk just ahead, a beacon in the center of the cavernous room. The Curator was nowhere to be seen, thank be the—*no, not invoking any gods right now*—but the idol was there. It sat on a cushioned pedestal on the far side of the desk.

Tass slowed. I didn't. In five long steps, I was there. The muscles in my arm stretched as I reached for it.

"Is that wise, Balthazar?"

The Curator's voice struck like a whip licking up my spine. I spun, banging my hip against the desk hard enough that pain jangled down my leg. The Curator stood on the ramp not twenty feet away. His diminutive form seemed to lengthen and loom, looking down on us from between the giant wolf statues. The air around us grew heavy. Hot with the stench of iron.

"Probably not," I replied, edging my body between him and the idol. *The mouse,* I thought, looking him over. *Had it even gone off?*

"Then why are you doing it?"

I swallowed hard. "Karanis took Mira."

Something flashed across the Curator's face. A flicker of regret, I thought. "That is unfortunate. But I cannot allow you to steal from my collection."

"I'm not stealing," I replied. "I'm borrowing."

"Are you now?"

"Yeah. If everything goes to plan, you'll have this back within a day. And the other half too."

"Will I?" One of his wiry eyebrows rose. "This is reckless, Balthazar. I'm disappointed in you," he said, his expression closing like the doors of some ancient fortress. "And you too, Tassiel Janae."

Tass stepped closer to me, arms loose at her sides. She didn't reply.

The Curator tutted. "How did he convince you to help in this fool venture? You have a duty, Tass. You're supposed to be killing Karanis."

"And I will. But I will save Miraveena Vadalen first. This is part of it."

"Is one human life now so precious you would risk this entire island saving it?"

"Yes," Tass replied evenly, and I saw something twitch across the Curator's face. Something akin to surprise. Any other day, I'd have sympathized with the old man. Too bad he was standing in my way today.

"And there was a time you would have agreed with me."

He batted her words away with a careless wave. "Times change. And now you have damned Cothis to ruin. Karanis will flit from body to body until a new idol can be made or procured. Your people will die."

"Not if you let us leave here," I insisted. My eyes widened, beseeching, willing this ancient, cranky creature to help me. Help *us*. "Please, Curator. Let us take the idol. Let us trade it for Mira. The moment Karanis thinks he's won is the moment we'll strike. He'll be distracted, vulnerable. We can do it. We can kill Karanis."

The Curator looked at me for a long moment. His glare abated. His frown didn't.

"No."

Hope died with that one word.

"I cannot risk Karanis restoring the idol. If he is allowed to rejoin the two halves, he will use it to create a new body—a body that cannot be destroyed by any but a full-blooded Ankaari. I will not give him that chance."

He sighed, every day of his vast age pulling at his face. "You both know I'm right," he said gently. "If it was anyone but Mira being held in that temple, you wouldn't be taking this risk. Don't let affection blind you to what's at stake."

"Affection?" I asked, feeling disgust ripple across my features. Like simple affection was what drove me. No. No, I was not giving up. Not when I was so close to saving Mira.

I turned, reaching for the statue.

"Balthazar, *stop*."

The note of command in his voice made my muscles lock. It wasn't possible. It shouldn't be possible, but not even my outrage was enough to deny the reality of his magic.

And yet his magic was nothing against my determination.

White-hot pain sizzled through my skull as his words wormed and burrowed deeper, and deeper, searching for a hold. I couldn't give him one. I wouldn't.

Sweat dripping down my face, I set my feet and thought of Mira. For her alone, I was strong enough to fight gods and men.

I looked back at him.

His eyes widened.

Mine did too . . .

Boom!

The curator whirled as an explosion reverberated through the Archive. The mouse had worked after all. And the moment his will evaporated from my mind—

Was the moment I seized the idol.

The sadness leeched out of his face. Something cold and cruel took its place. "You know the penalty for damaging—and stealing from my collection."

I'd hardly damaged the Archive. The mouse was little more than a smoke bomb. Not that I was going to tell him that. "Think of it as a loan?"

"Do you really think semantics will save you?"

"Probably not." I shoved the idol into one of my jacket's deep pockets. My fingers brushed the edges of something cold and metallic. I grabbed it. Bent my knees getting ready to run. "But I am hoping you have enough sense to let us leave."

"Or what?" he asked, sounding amused.

"Or I'll have to do more than damage your Archive."

"Are you threatening me, Balthazar?" He laughed, though it sounded like sandpaper scraping steel. "I suppose I am only an old man. You could certainly outrun me. My pets on the other hand . . ."

Pets?

He gestured. A simple flick of his wrist, and the onyx statues flanking him shuddered. The stone over their hearts buckled, sending spiderlike cracks racing across the surface of the rock.

Silence, like the sucking void between lightning strikes.

A deep growl rumbled through the air. Through my bones. My mind scrabbled for thought as the deepest, most panicked corner of my being begged, *begged* me to run.

Another corner was, somehow, *curious*?

What the hell was wrong with me?

The wolf statue blinked. And sheered away from the wall, its brother following a moment later. They shook their heads, shedding shards of gravel across the floor. They looked, for all the world, like giant impossible dogs.

"Now that's just cheating."

Tass tugged my arm back as granite snouts inhaled, sniffing the air. Catching our scent.

The growl returned. Lupine lips peeled back from six-inch-long teeth.

Tass pulled again, dragging me away from the wolf. Wolves.

I stepped back, still not quite believing that the Curator, a man I'd known since childhood, would set these nightmare creatures lose on me.

Summoning every ounce of courage I had, I looked past the wolves. And saw utter, inhuman malevolence on the Curator's face.

My lips curled. "Really? You're gonna stop us with pottery?"

Wrenching out my gun, I fired two shots into each wolf. Stone skin flashed with sparks as the bullets ricocheted and whizzed past my face. They collided with the desk behind me, spraying my back with splintered wood.

"Okay—he's going to stop us with pottery," I muttered.

The Curator's answering grin was a thing of terrible beauty. He spoke a single word, a command in a language I couldn't understand but that burned my skin nonetheless. The wolves bayed in assent.

Tass wrenched my hand, and we were off running. We sprinted in a mad dash back the way we came. Panic burned the edges of my vision. Panic—and terror—for this was a race we could not hope to win. The wolves were nearly upon us. Each bounding step they took made the floor moan and shudder. Closer. Closer.

Hot breath licked the back of my neck. I pulled the grenade out of my pocket and whirled in one motion. The wolf's open jaw was six inches from my face. Terrible sight. Absolute nightmare fuel.

And a perfect target.

I shoved the bomb in its open mouth. Jagged teeth grazed my fingertips. But who gave two shits about fingertips if I kept the hand. I shoved the wolf away, grabbing the edge of a familiar bookcase, and propelled myself around the corner just as—

Light and heat and rock exploded at my back. Sound shuddered through my eardrums. Smoke burned my eyes.

No time to stop.

No time for triumph. Because the other wolf was still in play.

I ran hard, my legs burning. But it didn't matter how fast I went. The bookcase corridor stretched out in front of us, ever lengthening the distance between us and the door.

No. Not seemed to. It *did* stretch. Like in a dream, I pushed myself, legs screaming to move faster. But the door wasn't getting any closer.

Tass cursed, shouting words I couldn't understand. Her hands slashed through the air and reality shuddered around us, reasserting with a snap that I couldn't hear but felt all the same.

I glanced back. The second wolf was gaining on us. Its giant face showed no emotion, as if its stony visage couldn't stretch to expression. But I was pretty sure it wasn't coming to ask for scritches. The bookcase corridor was too narrow for its massive frame, and its shoulders sheared the shelves as it leaped.

It landed hard, wedged in, but didn't stop. Granite legs churning, it pulled, and for a moment I was sure it would simply tear the furniture apart. Every step it took made the bookcase shriek against the floor. It would take only seconds before it burst free . . .

Or the case toppled over.

I covered my head with my arms, books pelting down on me. Kept running because, Great Below, I was not going to die like this. Tass flung the door open. I stretched out my arms, fingers clawing at the doorframe, and launched myself through. I turned. Saw the wolf's foaming maw yawn open. It lunged just as Tass hurled the door shut in the wolf's face. Its great head staved in the center of the door, but it held closed. For how much longer was anyone's guess.

I wasn't waiting around to take bets.

I flung myself up the first two steps of the scaffold only to have Tass grab my hand in a viselike grip and pull me back to the ground.

"We have to run," I bellowed, not sure my fleeing had properly communicated my "we shouldn't find out how long the door will hold" plan.

"We can't outrun it on the stairs," she shouted back, dragging me toward the bubble-like border that pressed against the Curator's domain.

A second before we reached it, I realized what she was going to do. "Tass, no—"

My feet locked, trying to drag her back. The door splintered behind us with an all-mighty crash. Rabid growls filled the cavern, reverberating in my bones.

I couldn't help it. I flinched.

And Tassiel pulled me into the Nethersphere.

21

BALTHAZAR

I tripped and barely had time to brace my hands in front of my face before my body connected with the grass.

Only it wasn't grass.

It was hair.

"What the fuuuu—"

I leaped to my feet, my mind rebelling against what I saw. We stood at the edge of the world. Just not *my* world. There was a cliff to my right. A vast ridgeline sloped downhill to my left, all of it carpeted in wiry black hair. It was as if someone had shaved a man's back and sewn it into the earth.

The sky was no less revolting. It roiled thick and red like a vat of blood ready to tip over at any moment. I turned in a quick circle, desperate to find the opalescent border that would take me back to the Archive—back to my family. To *Mira*. A strangled sound of shock clawed out of my lips.

It was gone.

"The border," I gasped.

"It's still there," Tass said quickly, like she could sense the panic bubbling under my skin. "It's just over the cliff. We have to go."

"Go? Go where?"

The cliff where we stood was but one side of a gorge, easily a hundred feet wide and several hundred feet deep. A dark green river flowed through the bottom. Shadows lurked in the murky depths—the long, sinuous forms of beasts I could not name and did not want to see up close.

I turned at Tass's muttered oath. In the distance, only a mile or two off, was a lonely tower sitting squat against the horizon. Just above its teeth-like battlements, a skeletal something flapped its wings.

"You know, we don't need to talk about this—we should go."

"We should *run*."

Tass grabbed my hand, dragging me forward. We skirted the ridge like she was trying to keep us close to the invisible border. But there was no pearlescent, bubble-like wall marking the edge of this realm and the beginning of the Archive. Only that red sky and the jagged edge of a cliff, and in the distance; a stand of trees glowering and impenetrable.

A crack sharper than thunder sent shock waves of sound ripping through my hair and clothes. My knees buckled, and for a sickening second, I thought I would fall. Catching myself, I willed my legs to keep moving. Face forward. Didn't look back.

A wolflike growl tore down my spine. I swore. The Curator's wolf had followed us through the barrier.

Overhead, something shrieked.

"We have to go back," I shouted, pumping my arms through a growing pain in my side. "If the wolf is here, then our way out of the Archive is clear."

Tass shook her head, pulling me onward. "We cannot expose the border to the patrol."

Patrol?

The tip of a membranous wing scythed through the sky, and I realized she meant the flying creatures. Or rather, the people flying them.

The beast wheeled in the sky. Its green-black wings stretched wide as it dove straight at us. The creature, more lizard than bird, opened its mouth, revealing two rows of pointed teeth and a black tongue that lolled in its mouth. A piercing, banshee wail erupted from its throat, so high goose bumps erupted on my flesh.

"Roll," Tass barked. She didn't wait for me to obey, dragging me by the hand to the ground.

Wind buffeted my back as the beast shot over us. Tass pulled me up in an instant, and we were running again, straight toward the tree line. We weren't alone. Only a few bounding steps behind us now, the wolf snarled. The noise reverberated across the nightmare landscape. I heard every one of its steps as it thundered toward us. I could feel its carrion breath on my neck, each slobbering exhale peppered with rocks.

A reptilian cry rent the air behind me. I felt rather than saw the wolf whirl and howl a challenge. A second later, the unmistakable sound of two bodies colliding cracked across the bloodred sky. The wolf was down on its side, while the lizard beast snapped at its exposed belly. A gash slashed open the wolf's onyx fur but instead of blood, pebbles gushed out, littering gravel on the ground.

Relief washed through me. The wolf was down. My legs locked, and I stumbled to a stop.

"What are you doing? We must keep going."

My head swam and my lungs felt thick. Surely we were safe. The wolf was dead. Tass could just speak with the patrolmen. "But the wolf—"

Tass loosed a low cry, yanking me forward a second before heat erupted on my heels. A circle of flame devoured the ground where I'd just stood. And above, a humanoid riding on the back of the flying lizard was pointing a wraith-like hand at me.

Must remember: *Talk later.*

Fuck this place.

I sprinted, Tass by my side. We zigzagged up the ridge in a desperate race to reach the trees. Fire rained down on us from the aerial guard as acrid black plumes of burning hair scalded my throat. I pumped my arms faster, pushing past the tiny tears I felt scarring my legs, past the sweat burning my eyes, and threw myself into the woods behind Tass.

She kept us running for a few yards, clearly seeing much better in the dank and dark space of the forest underbelly than I did. The trees thickened the deeper we went, becoming so dense their fingerlike branches scraped across my clothes. Their roots wriggled beneath my feet.

She was barely out of breath when she pulled me to a stop, scanning our surroundings. I doubled over, gulping in air with burning lungs. Black spots floated in my eyes as I wiped the sweat off my brow, willing my heart to slow.

"I'm not really a smash-and-grab thief," I said, gripped with a self-conscious urge to explain my exhaustion. Not my brightest impulse.

"It's been a long three days."

Couldn't argue with that. I took a deep breath and my vision cleared, but what I saw made no sense. The forest floor was littered with pale leaves that looked like giant cracked fingernails. The rocks and boulders looked too much like skulls. I recoiled into the nearest tree whose bark rubbed against the palms of my hands rough as a cat's tongue.

"Great Below, Tass. Where are we?"

A dark laugh slithered out from behind her mask. "Where else could we be *but* the Great Below? There's a reason your people call Ruekigal the Queen of the Damned."

My mind blanked for a second before I shook my head, trying to dislodge the shock. I didn't have time for it. "We have to get out of here."

She ignored my charming, panic-induced penchant for stating the obvious. "No. *You* have to get out of here," she replied, her face tilted up toward the sky. "I will draw the patrol away. Once they are gone, run back to the gorge. The border to the Archive won't be more than ten feet off the edge of the cliff. You should be able to make the leap."

"Off the edge of the cliff?" I held up a hand like that could stop her words. "You want me to jump off a cliff?"

"Yes."

"Have I offended you?"

". . . No?"

As usual my sarcasm had flown right past her. "Tass, no. I'm not going to leave you here."

"There is no other choice," she said, her voice too edged for the calm she projected. "You have to get the idol back to your world."

"Yeah, I know, but . . ." The leaves around us shuddered, like even they saw the folly in letting Tass go off alone. "Even if I can get home, I can't defeat Karanis without you."

"You can, and you must," she said tightly. "I will draw the patrol away from the border. You have to save Mira."

"Not like this. We can get out of this together. We have time."

"You don't know that, Bal."

"Tass, come on—"

She rounded on me, her silver face only inches away reflecting the pallor of my skin, the terrified, manic gleam in my eyes. "This is not the Archive, where time is predictably slower than your world. Time is variable in the Nethersphere, sixty seconds does not always equal a minute. I have no way of knowing how much time is passing in your world, but I know we're wasting it arguing."

Her words drenched me, washing away even the barest trace of hope. The idol suddenly weighed down my pocket, dragging me away. Toward Mira.

A branch snapped and I stiffened, sensing the patrol approaching through the twilight. Blocking my route back.

"It's all right, Bal," she said, gently this time like she could sense my need to get to Mira. "This is my home."

Tass reached a hand to my face. One glove whispered against my skin before she stopped herself short. Her hand dropped to her side, clenching into a fist. She turned.

"Damn it. Not like this." I grabbed for her arm in a strange pantomime of the night we'd met.

But unlike that first night, Tass didn't check her strength. "Enough." Her palms connected with my chest, and I was flat on my ass before I could blink. "It's only a matter of time before the patrol realizes who I am, and when they do, they will summon their mistress." She looked down at me, shaking her head. "Believe me, you do not want to be here when Ruekigal comes." She shifted her weight onto her back foot, ready to run. Paused.

"Good luck, Bal."

I sat frozen on the disgusting ground for a full minute, staring into the darkness where Tass had disappeared. She was right. I knew she was right. I had to get back to the border, fight my way through the Archive. Save Mira.

Like Tass said, this was her home.

And I had to get to mine.

I got to my feet, but my eyes snagged on the alabaster mound of a child-size skull giving truth to the lie in my thoughts. This wasn't a home. This was a dungeon where no one, least of all Tass, belonged.

And Mira would never forgive me for leaving Tass behind.

But Mira would live.

Damn it all!

If I got out now, I could get the idol to Karanis before the deadline. If I waited, time could pass me by. The real question was, if I gave Karanis the idol, could I get Mira and me out again alive?

Or was he just going to kill us anyway?

Tass said he was as changeable as the sea. And I knew in my gut she was right. Our hope for survival without Tass was no better than a coin toss. Question was, which way would the coin land?

Screw this.

I wasn't gambling my life—Mira's life—on a coin flip. If any of my plans were going to work, if any of us were going to survive, I needed Tass with me in that temple. Which meant I couldn't let her wander off and sacrifice herself now. Couldn't surrender her to the family that threw her away.

Damn it, she was part of the crew. My crew.

Now I just had to make her see that.

The sound of wings beating overhead froze me in place. This close to the edge of the woods, I might very well be visible from above. I didn't dare to look up, but my ears strained, trying to determine the path of the creature's flight. Was the beast coming this way or going the other? The sound was distorted, twisting my sense of direction to uselessness.

BOOM!

The earth shuddered around me. The ground heaved so hard, I hit the forest floor. Hot air gushed through the trees. The smell of fire curled up my nose. Behind me, someone screamed.

Tass.

I ran. Not toward the gorge as Tass commanded, but back into the forest's depths. I had just enough sense left to try and step lightly, but with my ears still ringing with the sound of Tass's scream, I had no way of knowing if I was successful.

The press of hot air intensified, burning my sweat-soaked skin. I slowed. Placing each step with care, I slid around the trees, creeping closer and closer.

Their voices reached me first: rasping laughter that instantly filled me with dread. I ducked behind the base of a thick tree and peered around the trunk. A clearing that I was sure hadn't existed a few minutes ago revealed a perfect circle of crimson sky. Splinters of broken wood piled along its edges, while the snapped-off stumps of dead trees sent tortured smoke signals into the air. Embers licked the broken splinters covering the unforgiving earth. Their glowing malice was all that remained of what must have been a terrible fire.

And in the center of the clearing, between the two lizard-beasts, was Tass. Her body prone and unmoving in the ash. I sank to my knees. Told myself it was to find cover.

But I couldn't hide from my own terror for long.

The dragons—for that was what they looked like to me, though I knew it was their riders who cast fire—stood on all fours, looking bored and hungry. They snapped at each other through the savage-looking bits cutting into their cheeks. Black blood dripped down their scale-covered chins. Their riders didn't bother to curb the violence but sat tall in their saddles speaking over Tass's unmoving body.

The riders were terrible to behold, like corpses in every sense of the word. Gray, desiccated skin stretched over protruding cheekbones that jutted out all the way around their eyes, only ending in stubby horns above their temples. Their eyes were dark pits like empty skulls.

The one who seemed to be giving the orders had a gash down his right leg. Livid red blood streamed out of the wound—from the wolf, I thought. Too bad the Curator's dog hadn't taken him out. I hoped it hurt.

"I'll take this one back to the watchtower," Gash, as I decided to call him, said. "You go and track down the other one."

His companion nodded, slid off his mount, and stumbled over a charred root. Despite his emaciated face, his belly was fuller than an overstuffed toad. He bent over Tass before peering back up at Gash. "I think this one's only stunned."

"After a hit like that? Impossible."

The other one—Toad—slapped the palm of his meaty hand against Tass's cheek. "I don't know. Seems like she's already starting to come around."

Gash swore and spat over the side of his dragon. "All right. Drag her up here. We go back to the watchtower together and get word to the garrison. We can let one of Lady Ruekigal's pets track down the other trespasser."

"Yes, sir," Toad replied. He dragged Tass into a sitting position and, with a grunt, slung her over his shoulders. Staggering over to Gash's dragon, the two . . . *men* pulled Tass's limp body over the lizard's back.

In a moment, Toad had mounted and both guards ordered their dragons into the sky. Their wingbeats sent a cloud of ash into my face, searing my eyes and poisoning my tongue. I blinked the pain away, watching them carry Tass across the blood-soaked sky, back to the tower.

Pushing my sleeves over my elbows, I checked that the idol was secure, and started running once more . . .

Toward the tower.

22

BALTHAZAR

I angled toward the forest's edge, where it was easier to run between the trees while still being sheltered by the canopy. The cover lasted about a mile before my luck ran out. The forest hadn't been allowed to approach the watchtower. Hundreds of blackened stumps dotted the ground from where trees had been cleared away from the hunched building. The longer I looked at them, the more they looked like soot-stained teeth, lost and wandering across this desolation.

Thank you for that mental image, Bal. Super helpful.

I stood in the shade staring across the open space. The tower was only four stories tall, made of dark gray stone that glimmered and winked in the low light. The dragons were penned in a shabby-looking wooden corral off to one side. I hoped they were hobbled somehow to prevent them from flying, but I couldn't make out the details from this distance.

My eyes strained in the strange bloody light, scouring the tower for a way inside. The sole door was closed, and I assumed locked, if not guarded. But windows dotted the tower's face. They were wide too, not the arrow-slit windows I'd seen on old fortresses. Thank Creation for that. The ones on the first floor were fitted with bars, but the upper windows were bare glass. Could that be my entry point?

Entry point.

The words sent a bell of indecision chiming through me. My resolve wavered. Seconds passed, scoring my skin as they slid away, too fast to be caught. The thought of Mira trapped in Karanis's grasp made each moment I hesitated utter agony. A traitorous part of my mind begged me to leave, to obey Tass and save Mira, but my heart refused. I couldn't save Mira without Tass, it was true.

But there was another truth too, hovering at the edges of my mind. I could still hear the sadness in Tass's voice when she spoke about meeting Calien—when he admitted to trying to kill her.

There was no way I could leave Tass to people like that. Add that to the inescapable fact that none of us—not me, not Mira, not the whole damn city of Cothis would survive if I didn't have Tass at my back when we next saw Karanis. My resolve firmed.

But would it have fucking destroyed Creation to allow just one of my plans to come to fruition? It had been one disaster after the next these past few days, and I was not normally the "run headlong into chaos" kind of criminal. I spat to the side. Enough mayhem. I might not have time to plan, but I was more than capable of thinking on my damn feet. Of following my instinct and moving on the fly.

And my gut was telling me that I had to make a move. Now.

I darted from the trees, sprinting full tilt across open space. Not daring to slow, I brought my hands up, absorbing the impact as I slammed into the tower wall. Pain jangled up my arms. I hissed it out through my teeth, flattening my back to the wall.

I didn't bother trying the front door—too much of a risk, and it wasn't my chosen entry point anyway. Instead, I inched around the tower aiming for the window I'd seen from the forest. The curling, hairlike grass had the same echoing crunch as fallen leaves, but I was used to that now. I didn't need to be some immortal Ankaari to know how to walk without making a sound.

I crept on, rounding the tower to where the dragons were penned. Both beasts were asleep, sunning themselves in the midday heat like monstrous reptilian cats. I gulped, and as quietly as possible, edged on. The dragon nearest me opened one eye the size of a melon, pupil dilating as it spotted me.

My limbs locked; heart stopped. I stared at the dragon.

The dragon stared at me.

Neither of us moved. Seconds ticked by. A minute. My hands ached from clutching the wall in instinctual terror. I forced them to relax. That small victory completed, I loosed a breath and inched my chin upward.

There, on the second floor, was an open window. My gaze darted back to the dragon and then to the window in a frantic dance as I weighed my options. I didn't have any climbing equipment, so reaching the window would be tough. Tough, but not impossible. I'd made hard climbs before.

The tower was made of rough-cut bricks. They were stacked together like fieldstones and joined haphazardly so the rocks weren't flush with one another. There were gaps and ledges where different stones met. I knew I could climb it, but it would mean turning my back on the dragon. No problem. The beasts were obviously trained—like horses or guard dogs. They would only move when ordered.

The thought had been more comforting from the forest. I looked at the creature, trying to gather my courage. It hadn't moved more than its eye in the few minutes I'd been frozen here, which would seem to confirm my hypothesis. Except for one giant "but" looming in my mind.

I knew shit about animals, especially giant ones. *Especially* ones that shouldn't even exist. Still, the dragon seemed more curious than anything, maybe it wouldn't . . . sound an alarm? Even in my mind, I sounded like an idiot.

"You leave me alone; I leave you alone. Deal?"

I took the dragon's non-reaction as a yes.

Though it was utter agony to turn my back on the creature, I willed my body into action. Spurred by terror and desperation, I scrabbled up the wall, sure that the dragon would change its mind and attack out of pure, monstrous spite.

My fingertips burned as I craned my neck over the edge of the windowsill. A smallish room waited for me, complete with a desk and a pair of uncomfortable-looking chairs. No corpse-like guard creatures, though. Perfect.

I pulled myself over the window ledge, rolling nimbly onto the floor without a sound. My muscles still tensed, both hands going to my guns as I waited, breathless, for sounds of anyone approaching. More precious seconds slid by, dripping past like the sweat beading down my neck.

When my heart finally retreated from my ears, I stood up, pulled out one pistol and crossed the room. I pressed my ear to the door, straining to hear anything. Nothing.

The handle turned quietly in my hand. I eased open the door, peering up and down the hall, eyes straining in the low light. No one was there, but I heard the muffled sound of voices coming from above.

I slid into the hall and paused. Though four wrought iron chandeliers hung from the ceilings—larger and sturdier than a carriage wheel—none of the candles were lit. The passageway was all shadow and gloom and it took a long minute for my sight to adjust to the mirk. Three doors lined the small corridor, all of them closed. Silence radiated from behind their wooden planks just begging to be broken.

Resolve, sharper than steel and twice as cold, settled over my shoulders. Gods, Ankaari, magic? I knew nothing about that shit. But breaking and entering? This was my bread and butter. A spiral stone staircase beckoned to me at the far end of the hall. I crept toward it, and the voices became clearer, louder. Nothing from below, though. Were Toad and Gash the only ones on duty here? If so, it was my first scrap of luck in three days.

I followed the voices up the stairs, ghosting across the uneven floor. I barely dared to breathe, willing myself into total silence. The staircase curved and the next landing flattened out ahead. Glancing around the corner, I found a hallway identical to the one below, and just as empty.

Toad and Gash must be above me somewhere interrogating Tass. Anger shuddered through me. Even the sky outside seemed to darken at the image my mind conjured.

You have two guns, I reminded myself, clutching the edges of my plan. *You can take them by surprise. Shoot both at once and get back to the border in the next ten minutes.*

"Time is variable in the Nethersphere, Bal," Tass's voice whispered in my mind, chiding me not to waste time standing around.

I pushed my legs into movement, up the stairs, onto the landing, and . . .

Thud.

I twisted toward the noise. Knew it came from one of the rooms down the hall, but not which. I couldn't just bull-rush upstairs, not without knowing what I was walking into. And no time to dash through one of the doors—would have been a gamble anyway. I sprang upward instead.

One foot connected with the uneven wall as I leaped for the chandelier. It swayed sideways from my weight, but this was a game I knew. Using the momentum as an aid, I swung myself onto the chandelier. Braced my body against the chain, stilling it just in time for Toad to exit the room at the end of the hall.

He muttered something under his breath, pulling at the collar of his dark leather shirt. With the rolling gate of a sailor, he walked down the hall, empty pitlike eyes trained on the floor. Under the first chandelier.

The second.

I could barely hear his steps over my heart as he walked underneath me, and for a wild second I nearly grabbed my gun and shot him. Restrained myself in time. Because if Gash knew there was a rescue attempt on, he'd likely kill Tass before I could reach her.

So even though my eyes drilling into his skull should have hurt him, I let Toad walk. Let him reach the stairs. And watched him pause.

He angled his face into the air, sniffing deeply through a flat nose.

Son of a—

A masculine voice shouted from above. Toad jerked his head in that direction, no more than a horse, broken and reined in. With a muttered oath he started up the stairs, the sound of his steps echoing in my ears.

Forcing my hand away from my gun, I gripped the edge of the chandelier and lowered myself back to the floor. Gave my stomach a second to fall back into place. And approached the stairs.

Sniff.

I spun. *What the—*

Toad stood behind me, his lips peeling back in a silent hiss.

Shit.

I went for my gun.

Toad was faster. He moved in a blur of speed my eyes couldn't track. I didn't even have time to brace myself before he slammed me into the wall. One of his scaly hands wrapped around my neck, pinning me to the wall. His other hand curled around my wrist, crushing each nerve into bloodless shock until the gun fell out of my numb hand. Toad leered into my face, his fingernails puncturing my neck. He took a long savoring sniff, like my blood were a fine wine, and exhaled into my eyes.

I gaged as the stench of carrion filled my nose and mouth. Instinct shouldered past thought, screaming with the need to break free. I balled up my free hand and swung it at his jaw. Connected, only to feel my knuckles buckle against his skull. Pain splintered up my arm and ricocheted back to my fingers.

"Foolish human," Toad said with a sneer, not even wincing when I kneed him in the gut. "So far from home. What are you doing in the Nethersphere?"

His hand tightened on my throat, making it impossible to answer even if I'd wanted to. Pressure built behind my eyes. The trapped blood in my skull leaped against my temple. My eyes filled with stars. Then darkness.

"How did you get here?"

My mouth worked in wordless desperation. Sound squeezed out of me in a useless gasp of used up breath.

"Oh, you need air, do you?" Toad asked with a malicious laugh.

He eased his grip and my knees lost structural integrity. I hit the ground with the sound of Toad's voice ringing in my ears.

"Tell me how you came to be here, and I'll grant you a quick death. Then, I suppose, you'll actually belong here." He laughed at his own joke, which sounded like the worst thing I could imagine being crushed by an even worse thing.

Mira!

"No," I gasped.

"No?" He made to grab me again and I jerked into the wall, hands raised.

"All right! All right."

I licked my lips as my eyes dropped to the floor. The gun lay only a foot from my hand. If I got it, could I shoot before Toad grabbed me?

Toad cuffed the side of my face. Pain exploded in my head as one of my cheekbones rocked against the rest of my skull. "Tell me!"

Damn it, I couldn't fight this creature and live. Not without Tass or the Curator or . . .

The idea hit me like lightning on metal. I looked into Toad's desiccated face as my lack of options piled up around me, corpse-like and fucking useless. I needed backup—it didn't have to be *sane* back up.

Names have power.

The memory of Tass's voice filled my head, so visceral it was like she whispered the words in my ear.

"Well?"

"Calien Bodysnatcher, I summon thee."

Toad's face twisted with horror. "No," he whispered, backing away from me. "Why would you—" He made it all of two steps before his whole body stiffened. His face went slack and the life went out of his liquid-black eyes.

To be replaced by an all too familiar blue flame. I grabbed the gun and pushed myself to my feet, pressing back into the wall as Toad's face rearranged. He tilted his neck to one side and then the other, making his spine crack in a crescendo of crushed cartilage.

He looked at me. Smiled. "Balthazar Vadalen, as I live and breathe. What are you doing here?"

Hearing my name coming from the Bodysnatcher's mouth made me want to run to temple and repent. Not that it would have done me any good, but old habits died kicking and screaming. "I've come to save Tass."

One hairless eyebrow rose. "Tass? She's here, too? Well, I'll be damned. I guess her, too, if you're all here. Get it?"

I didn't respond, and he sighed.

"So. Little sister grew a spine, did she?"

Though I had a hard time of thinking of Tass as anyone's "little sister," I nodded.

"Where is she?"

"Upstairs," I replied. Swallowed hard. "Please. I need your help."

"I see." Calien strolled back down the hall, opening the back window to peer out at the countryside. I wondered how much of Toad's memory Calien had access to. If Karanis had Paasch's, surely Calien had Toad's. He would know where we were.

Unless he was checking to see if reinforcements were coming. That bloodred sky roiled and churned as I remembered who owned this tower. Was Ruekigal herself on her way even as we stood here in silence?

Calien turned from the window and strolled back down the hall. He stopped a few feet away and leaned against the wall. Arms crossed.

"Why should I?"

I felt my eyes bulge with outrage. "Why? What do you mean, why? She's your sister. Or doesn't that mean anything to any of you?"

"It means something, just probably not what you'd like to think."

"Fine. Then do it because you owe her."

"Do I?" While Calien seemed unfazed by my anger, he seemed truly confused by my insistence on his debt. "How so?"

"You tried to kill her," I exclaimed. "So yeah, I'd say you damn well owe her. She's your family, your flesh and blood. You can't just throw her away. She needs you."

He smirked. "I think you'll find family means something different in my world."

"Bullshit. Tass is just as much a part of this world as you are."

"I never said she understood it any better," he said, laughing. "But you misunderstand me, Balthazar. I want to know why I should help *you*."

My mouth went dry. "What do you mean? I'm trying to save Tass."

"Why? Why does saving her help you?" he pressed, curious now. "If it's simply because you need a path home, I would be more than happy to take you. So you see, you don't need Tassiel. Are you sure you want to waste more of your precious time helping her?"

My legs nearly failed again at the thought of wasting time. I held firm, refusing to bow to the panic that he was so slyly trying to seed. Calien was a trickster, but I wasn't going to be fooled. "I'm not leaving her here."

"Why?"

"Because she's part of my crew."

He grinned. "Is she now? My sister, the great Septiniri warrior, part of a cutthroat band of thieves. Father will be so proud."

"Oh please," I said with a sneer, answering his derision with my own. "Why would we bother cutting anyone's throat when a bullet to the head is so much cleaner." I angled my recovered gun his way for emphasis, make sure he was paying attention. Making sure he knew how serious I was. "But it's more than that—not that I'd expect you to understand. My crew is my family."

Calien's languid expression cracked for the first time, revealing something dark below. "Tassiel is not, as you say, your flesh and blood. She is *not* your family."

"And yet now she's yours? After you betrayed her? She deserves better than the family that raised her."

He looked at me for a long, agonizing moment like he was tallying up all the reasons to kill me. Then something else shouldered in. A kind of understanding that made his mouth turn down in disgust. "Oh," he said. "You're not in love with her, are you? Because there's nothing more pathetic than—"

"No," I snapped, seized by the urge to give a very Mira-like eye roll. "I don't need to be in love with her to see her for who she is. Not a tool to be used, but a whole person worth a hell of a lot more than you and everyone else who cast her out. You don't want your sister? Well, that's your fucking loss.

"I claim her."

"Do you?" Calien's body went still, and the air between us seemed to hum with the intensity of his attention.

"I do. Family isn't just about blood."

The corners of Calien's mouth curled upward. "There it is," he murmured.

"What?"

"The reason she likes you."

I shifted from one foot to the other. My pulse pounding in my ears as the predator in Toad's body considered my words. "So will you help?"

"But you just claimed her, Balthazar. So she's not really my problem, is she?"

"I—"

Calien's smile broadened.

Shit.

23

TASSIEL

One. Two. Three. Four.

Tassiel counted the slow, even beating of her heart. In a place like the Nethersphere, it was the only way to mark the passage of past to present.

"Tell me your name," the guard snarled.

She didn't bother to reply. Tassiel hadn't spoken since she'd been dragged off the gurugu's scaled back and marched up to this desolate attic. The circular room was empty of everything but the wrist shackles from which she now hung.

"Who are you?"

Who was she?

Seventy-eight. Seventy-nine. Eighty.

She was someone trained to keep her heartbeat slow. Measured. Steady even in the midst of pain. Of fear.

"Have it your way."

The guard muttered under his breath—amateur—and hurled his hand into her solar plexus. Electricity sizzled across Tassiel's skin.

Muscles contracted and twisted. Bones shuddered. Her teeth shook in their sockets, and she let herself indulge in a low whine.

It was decadent, that groan. Luxurious even, the darkest of guilty pleasures. Her father would have broken every bone in her body if he'd been there to hear it. After the centuries he'd spent training her to resist interrogation, to endure pain, why he'd beaten the urge to scream right out of her.

Ninety-eight. Ninety-nine. One hundred.

Still, Tassiel couldn't be completely silent. The guard knew she wasn't just any Ankaari. The fact that he couldn't remove her mask taught him that much. It was a middling enchantment, something any competent sorcerer should have been able to break. Then again, dear aunt Ruekigal had always prized brutality over intelligence in her minions.

Thirty-three. Thirty-four. Thirty-five.

The second punch came on the edge of the first. Another wave of electricity crested over her. She whimpered. *Whimpered!* Tassiel couldn't remember ever having made such a sound. Like she was Miraveena, lost in the dark.

Miraveena.

Get out of here, Bal. Save her.

Eighty-eight. Eighty-nine. Ninety.

Tassiel could give Bal ten hundred beats. Close to twenty minutes of mortal time. Enough for him to get out of the forest and back to the gorge. More than enough, really, but she wanted to make sure he got out of the Nethersphere. After that, she'd have to break free. Kill the guards and go.

But where?

Where could she possibly go? Not home. Calien had made it abundantly clear that her only hope of returning to her father's house was to apologize.

Tassiel grunted. It was as close as she could get to a laugh. Apolo-

THE QUEEN OF DAYS   309

gize for what? For making Father order her execution? She let her head loll forward in an awful parody of exhaustion.

Or perhaps not. She *was* exhausted from running for so many years, from hoping for a future that would never be. She was bone-tired of wishing to belong, to be loved. It simply wasn't meant to be. Not for her.

Standing at the edges of Bal's crew these last few days had made her forget, for a moment, that she was alone. But Tassiel didn't belong with them, not really. And truth be told, only Bal and Mira had any real regard for her. Bal's regard was tinged with fear. And Mira's?

Mira simply thought Tassiel was something Mira herself would never be: invincible. Mira thought Tassiel was immune to pain and fear, to time and all that made humanity frail. It was a lie.

Tassiel wasn't immune to pain.

Even now, every nerve in her body was ragged and screaming. But after centuries of training, she knew how to smother it. How to keep weakness from showing on her face or in her movements. Centuries of torture robbed her of reaction, all so she could be the Ankaari idea of strong. So her heart and her resolve would never waver.

Ten. Eleven. Twelve.

What Mira, in her youth, did not understand was that everything that made humanity weak also made them precious. Their time, their limited and so often squandered lives, made them priceless.

. . . Twenty-one . . .

. . . Twenty-two . . .

. . . Twenty-three . . .

Tassiel had no time. She had *all of* time. And so she was doomed to be forever outside, forever lost and abandoned and left behind.

What was the point?

She didn't bother to pretend when the next two shocks hit. She let them worm up her spine, let the groans and grunts fly free. What did it matter if she cried and screamed like a lowborn servant? She wasn't Septiniri anymore.

She heard the door open but didn't bother opening her eyes until long after the last shock faded. The other guard had entered the room. He was walking slowly on her right, but it was a waste of effort to trace his steps.

His boots scuffed against the floor behind her, a casual, almost jaunty stroll. "Has she spoken?" he asked, his words wriggling up her tender flesh.

"No," her interrogator replied.

The other guard laughed and for a moment, the sound seemed almost familiar. "Typical."

"Don't you worry, I'll make her talk," the interrogator growled. "What are you doing up here anyway? I told you to send word to the garrison."

"I know."

"Well? Did you?" The interrogator demanded as the other guard meandered toward him. "Creation damn me if you're not the—"

His words dropped into confused silence. A bated breath.

"Hey now, what's wrong with your eyes?"

Tassiel's head snapped up in time to see the second guard's hands shoot out. He seized the interrogator's skull. Twisted. A juicy crack echoed through the room. The interrogator went down, falling forward on his chest, his sightless eyes aimed at the ceiling.

The silent shock in her mind was so complete the only words she could summon belonged to Kai:

"What the fuck?"

"Tass!"

Impossibilities stacked and doubled and for a moment Tass wondered if the interrogator hadn't damaged her after all. Because there was no other way to explain how Bal rushed into the room, tight-lipped and wide-eyed. He ran up to her but stopped short. His face paled as he looked her up and down, clearly wanting to help but not knowing how.

"What are you doing here?" Tassiel asked, her voice rasping out of her aching chest. A blotchy purple bruise stood livid on his left temple.

"I couldn't just leave you here." His dark eyes met hers, and she felt her heart expand painfully against her ribs.

"Awww. My hero."

Tassiel turned to the second guard, the guard who now had blue eyes. A gaze that burned electric with a dark hilarity.

Fear. Fear that the interrogator had been unable to spawn in her expanded around Tassiel, tingeing the air with the taste of blood.

"Bal. What have you done?"

His throat worked in a gulp. "I couldn't save you on my own."

"So you summoned *Calien*?" she demanded, anger burning through her tired muscles.

"Yes, he did." Calien laughed, the way he always laughed when he was up to no good. "And just in time too. Look at yourself: trussed up like a slaughtered pig. A Septiniri warrior, a child of Janus himself, captured by two lowly Qaarshki guards," he shook his head in gleeful disbelief. "Why, if I hadn't seen this with my own-ish eyes, I don't think I'd believe it."

Bal swallowed hard and looked at her with a guilt-ridden expression. "Let me help you down." He reached up to the chains, his pathetic mortal face creased with pity.

Tassiel clenched her hands as a fire hotter than any guard's electricity raced through her body. Time energy sizzled up her nameplate, filling it with burning potential. She yanked. Metal screamed against stone. The chain shattered. Tassiel shook the shackles off and shoved them at Bal, whose stupid face was slack with awe.

"I did not require help, you fool. I was trying to keep the guards occupied so you could escape."

"Oh."

"I tried to tell him."

"Yeah, and you're just a paragon of truth," Bal said, flipping a rude gesture that her brother elected to ignore.

"Not terribly bright, this one." Calien laughed again, his eyes going comically wide.

"Do not start, Calien."

"Hey now. I saved your boy's life."

Tassiel pinched her eyes shut for a moment before forcing them open again. Calien was the last person she should be unguarded around.

"You did," Tassiel said, though the words were like ash in her mouth. "Why?"

"Balthazar cleverly pointed out that there is something of a debt between us," Calien replied, his smile going sheepish. "Consider it paid."

"It's hardly paid. You tried to kill her."

If Tassiel was surprised by the heat in Bal's voice, Calien only looked bored.

"Do keep quiet, Balthazar, my boy. Or I shall have to show you exactly how squishy humans can be."

Bal's hands went to his holsters. "You think bullets won't damage that body?"

"Enough," she snapped.

Bal looked mutinous but didn't draw his guns. "Let's get out of here."

"You should already be out of here," she said, but this time he just looked back at her, defiant. She didn't quite understand that look, but it made her feel . . . something.

Bal started forward, but Calien shifted his weight, blocking the way. Tassiel snatched Bal's arm, dragging him back. Her eyes never left her brother.

Bal looked uncertainly between them. "Tass, we've got to go."

"I'm afraid I can't allow that."

Tassiel studied Calien's face but couldn't detect even the hint of a smile.

"Why?" Bal demanded, as if the answer wasn't obvious.

"You know why," Calien said, echoing her thoughts. He shook his head, face troubled. "You shouldn't have come back here. Not like this. You brought a human to the Nethersphere? Why? What could you possibly hope to gain? More of Father's wrath? He might have been willing to ignore your existence before, but when he finds out about this, you're dead."

She shrugged. "I was dead before."

"Yeah. Right," Calien said with a bitter laugh. "Well, it won't be any of us doing the job this time. It'll be Father himself coming for you. Or Auntie dearest, since it was her land you trespassed."

"Don't tell them," Bal said, urgently now, like he feared their father might appear at any moment. "It's not like we meant to—"

"Bal," Tassiel said, her voice sharp enough to halt his words.

Calien cocked his head, a slow grin turning his lips. "You didn't mean what? To come here?" His head tilted back as he filled the room with laughter. "Which means . . . you've found a stable portal between worlds, haven't you?"

She said nothing, but held on to Bal's wrist hard enough to make sure he knew better than to speak again. Likely too much to hope for, but miracles had been known to happen. Calien didn't seem to expect a reply, though. They waited silently—three points of a triangle. Beneath her fingers, Bal's heart danced a staccato beat, counting away the minutes of Mira's life.

Tassiel looked at her brother, knew he could read her face, masked or not. "Get out of our way, Calien."

"And leave you to kill Uncle Karanis?"

"Yes."

Calien grinned. "All right."

He took two steps right. Tassiel took two steps left, pulling Bal along in her wake. His eyes darted between them, the scent of his pity a sad cloying thing.

"You could ask him to come with us," Bal whispered, clearly not knowing how keen Ankaari hearing was.

The very words threatened to undo her as her weak, weak heart wished that Calien was the kind of man she could ask for loyalty.

"No. She can't," her brother replied from across the room, his face uncharacteristically sober.

"Why not?" Bal pressed. "I know some part of you still cares for her. If you didn't, you'd have killed us by now."

"I still might," Calien said, eyes glittering with violence. "Which is exactly why she won't invite me to join your little crew. She knows better than to trust me."

He was right. She could not trust Calien. Not his words, or his actions. She didn't even trust the guilt that flickered across his electric eyes. When a man had access to all the faces in the world, there was no way of knowing where the act ended, and he began.

"You should go," Calien said. "Reinforcements will be here soon. You know what to do?"

"Yes."

Tassiel pushed Bal into the doorway and stalked up to her brother, meeting him in the middle of the room.

Calien looked over her shoulder at Bal. "Save your sister, if you can. They're more precious than you know."

Calien looked down at her from his hideous borrowed face, and for a second, her mind conjured the memory of his true image from her distant youth. Those blue, blue eyes and a shock of black hair, wickedly handsome even as a boy.

"Goodbye, Calien," she said, but Tassiel didn't know who she was speaking to, that lost boy, or the man standing before her now.

Calien grinned the way he always grinned, ugly face or no. "See you around, sis."

He winked. The blue faded from the guard's eyes. Calien was gone.

She snapped the guard's neck before the spark of consciousness could grow in his face. It was the kindest death she could offer him, and he had to die. Unlike humans, an Ankaari could remember being possessed. That memory would put Calien at risk. And despite everything else, he'd helped them. Helped her.

Tassiel turned, and found Bal in the doorway, bouncing on the balls of his feet. "Ready?" he asked, grim-faced.

"Let's go."

They hurried down the stairs and into the slowly darkening crimson afternoon. They'd hardly stepped onto the grass before the high-pitched shriek of a gurugu pierced the air. Bal looked at the two penned lizards sleeping in the grass ten yards away and back at Tassiel. "Is that what I think it is?"

"Reinforcements," she replied. "This way."

Tassiel sprinted across the yard. Her body, still in the process of healing, cried out in raw rebellion. Pushing the pain away, she slid between the pen's wooden bars and hurried to the nearest gurugu. "Up, up," Tassiel said, clicking her tongue against her cheek.

"This is a bad idea."

"You still being here is a bad idea. This is how we make the best of your stupidity."

"'Thank you' would suffice."

The beast opened one giant eye, inspecting her for a moment before shaking its head and yawning itself awake. Luckily the fool guards had left the animal fully tacked. She hopped into the saddle, using its scaly haunch as a step up. Tassiel grabbed the reins. Turned to Bal.

"Come on."

Bal was a delicate shade of green as he slid into the pen and approached the gurugu like a man about to be executed.

She glanced behind them, spotted three more gurugu flying low on the horizon. "We need to get out, now."

The urgency in her voice didn't spur Bal to action, it just made him greener. Ridiculous. "You captain an airship. Do not tell me you're afraid of heights."

"Not heights," he said defensively. "Just dragons."

"As you should be, but this isn't a dragon."

"Is this really the time to argue semantics. I mean—"

Tassiel cut him off by seizing his bicep and pulling him onto the gurugu's back. She gave Bal just long enough to get seated before ordering the gurugu to fly.

The beast surged to its feet and, with a show of strength that belied its skeletal frame, it shot into the air. Its wings pumped, parting the air in smooth, easy down-strokes. Air rushed through the fibers of her clothes, and for a moment, she was lost in the song of the wind.

"They're gaining on us," Bal cried.

Her moment of joy shattered. She flattened herself on the gurugu's back. Bal did the same, leaning gingerly forward like he was afraid of touching her, the fool. Tassiel laughed at that, tugging his arms around her waist, and signaled the gurugu to dive.

Its giant wings shuttered, and for a second of pure wonder, they were in free fall. The hideous earth of Ruekigal's Great Below reached up, beckoning them to crash. They banked in defiance, gathering speed, as they raced to the gorge.

"We have to jump," she shouted over the wind.

"What?" Bal yelled, but it sounded so much like a yelp, she knew he'd heard her.

Tassiel couldn't help herself, she laughed again.

"Jump!"

24

BALTHAZAR

Tass's voice filled my ears, and my body obeyed without hesitation.

My mind thought this was the dumbest fucking thing I'd ever done and was sure I was about to end myself with a juicy splat into monster-infested waters.

Leathery wing sliced through my hair as I leaped into open space. My body hung weightless for a moment that lasted forever. It was over in a blink. A shiver rushed from my toes up my spine and into my panic-numb brain. My stomach rose into my throat, as gravity reasserted itself.

We were falling.

We fell.

And fell.

I opened my mouth to scream, but with my gut jammed in my throat, no sound escaped. I couldn't see the ground below us, only that red sky.

Light flashed, blinding me for the shortest second on record.

Red gave way to black. I barely had time to register our return to

318 · GRETA KELLY

the Archive for we were still in midair. The floor shone in the dim light of the bubble some hundred feet below. But momentum hurled us forward.

Cold air rushed across my face and my feet connected with the metal platform. The whole scaffolding groaned and screamed from the impact, listing sickeningly away from the cave-like face of the Archive. I barely felt the landing somehow which had to be a minor miracle. The collision should have turned me into a Balthazar-shaped puddle on the floor. I didn't dwell on that image, launching myself up the ladder, Tass on my heels, scrabbling for the green sitting room above.

I barely crawled onto the carpet before Tass was shoving me through the door. Her urgency was unspoken but terrible. Terrible because the Archive was falling. Collapsing on our heads. Rocks and boulders plummeted from the unseen roof, catching my arms. My face.

"Roll," Tass commanded, and again my body obeyed.

I tucked in my head, rolling hard on my shoulder and barely avoided a shelf of rock sheering off above us. I was on my feet again in a heartbeat, practically falling through the door in front of me.

Daylight, normal clear daylight, kissed my cheeks as I stumbled through the door. I fell face-first onto the garden's manicured lawn and marveled at the beauty of the simple green grass beneath me.

Click.

My chin jerked up and I found myself staring down the barrel of a codie-commissioned revolver.

"Balthazar Vadalen, I presume?" The man pointing the gun in my face wore a grave expression. His bristly brown mustache framed a mouth that turned down at the edges, and his warm brown skin was creased with a worry that would have seemed out of place. Would have. But didn't. Not today.

Tammon.

He wore a smart black uniform with an array of little silver stars lined up across his shoulders and chest. But it wasn't the shine that set him apart from all the beat codies I'd ever known. Something about his posture, even more than his rank, even more than the barrel of the gun in my face, made me think he wouldn't be someone to trifle with.

"Yes."

The man nodded. "We're here to take you and your friends to the governor."

I looked past the man at the word "we" and found at least a dozen more fully uniformed codies surrounding the Witch Door in a loose semicircle. Kai stood toward the back of the group sporting a split lip and a livid bruise on one cheek. The codies' guns were trained on me and Tass, though one man still pointed his at Kai's back. My heart stilled as I looked at him. And only him. He was alone.

Zee and Edik weren't there.

"Up you get, son."

I obeyed the order, climbing to my feet slowly with my arms raised so I wouldn't spook the codies. The officer holstered his weapon, glancing past me at Tass and the closed door behind us. "I've never seen the Witch Door opened," he murmured, his voice surprisingly gentle for a codekeeper.

"I'd wager you've seen a lot of things in the past two days that you haven't seen before," I said, carefully guarding my face—my voice—as I watched Tammon.

"True enough. But it's been three days since the consecration."

My eyes raced to Kai. "*Mira.*"

"Your sister is fine. The governor is waiting with her at the High Temple. You have what he's after?"

"Yes."

"Good," he said, the worry in his face making the word a lie. "Now, I'm going to have my men search you for weapons. I expect you to comply without any fuss. Do we understand each other?"

"Yeah. All right."

The officer looked to Tass. "What about you, miss? You going to give us trouble?"

Tass seemed to consider this for a moment. "No, Sergeant Tammon."

The sergeant's lips flattened—the only sign of his discomfort about Tass knowing his name. "Hak, Jamil—collect their weapons."

"Yes, Sergeant," a smaller codie said, coming forward with a third. With a few practiced movements, I was stripped of all my weapons. And I could have sobbed at the sight of Zee's lemon-size hand grenades lined up on the grass next to my favorite revolver.

Not surprisingly, the codie didn't dare to take the idol out of my jacket pocket, though his hand shook when he spotted it. I couldn't blame him for giving it a wide berth. It had given me nothing but grief since the moment I first saw it.

But what should have been a few moments of work stretched. The codie searching Tass reached into her pocket and found two knives, an old-fashioned flintlock pistol, a pair of brass knuckles, and what looked suspiciously like a garrote.

And that was just the *one* pocket.

By the time he was finished the mountain of weaponry on the ground could have reoutfitted the entire Cothis City Code Hall.

And most of the criminals in the city too.

The men around us watched Tass with expressions of fear-tinged awe. I was one of them. In fact if I didn't know her, I'd have been calling her a demon like Kai once had.

"Damn, Tass," Kai murmured, very much *not* looking at her like she was evil incarnate. No. His face was unsettlingly filled with— "Will you marry me?"

Her head canted to one side. "Probably not."

I nearly fell over, sure I'd misheard. "Probably not?"

"The future contains far too many variables to accurately predict every single eventuality," she replied, as if she was giving this serious consideration. Which was part of the issue. Because:

"*Probably* not?"

She shrugged. "I cannot discount the possibility. Traumatic brain injuries do occur."

Kai ducked his chin my way, looking far too smug for a man in handcuffs. "So she's saying there's a chance."

A slight shiver of contained laughter shuddered through Tass. I shook my head, turning to Tammon for rescue. "I'm ready to be arrested now."

A long boat was waiting for us at the nearest canal. The codies herded us on board. They shoved Kai, Tass, and me onto a bench in the middle of the flat-bottomed vessel before surrounding us, their guns still drawn. From the corner of my eye, I watched them load all our confiscated weapons into a canvas bag at the end of the boat. My attention lingered on the explosives, sitting there ripe for the taking. If only I wasn't surrounded by codies. Tammon spotted me looking and I sensed some vast internal calculation churning away in his mind.

Good.

"What happened?" I asked Kai as soon as we were under way.

Kai's lips twitched in a mirthless smile. "You mean aside from almost missing the deadline?" He shook his head, eyes dancing from me to the watching codies and back again. "Zee and Edik did a runner during the night." Kai's jaw worked hard, like he was chewing on a long, bitter story. He spit over the side of the boat. "That's loyalty for you."

My gaze slammed into the bottom of the boat as I bent, arms braced on my knees.

"Don't know what you expected from a crew of thieving rats," one of the codies said with vicious laugh, like he was hoping to see me puke.

A muscle in Kai's face ticked as he struggled to contain his reaction. I was more preoccupied with the whole "almost missing the deadline" situation.

"They aren't rats," Kai said, voice low like he could no longer keep the words behind his teeth.

"Kai—"

"My cousin is pregnant," he said, glaring up at the codies around us—at Tammon most of all. "No one should have to bring a child into this city."

The codies went quiet after that, but I saw a stricken look pass across Tammon's face. The idea that his old friend's unborn child had been caught in this web of destruction . . . well. Tammon would understand why Edik couldn't be here.

"I'm glad they aren't with us; they don't belong here," I said, my voice even as polished stone. "Zee should stay as far from the danger as possible."

"What the hell took you so long, Bal?" Kai demanded. "Edik said the Cur—said *he* probably killed you for trying to steal the idol back."

"He tried," I replied.

"Is that what took you so long? I thought Tass said time passes slower in the Archive."

"It does," Tass said in response to the pointed glare Kai shot in her direction. "Unfortunately, we had to exit the Curator's domain for a short while."

"What does that mean?"

"We crossed into the Nethersphere, Kai," I said in an undertone—one I knew would reach every single codie on this floating trash pile.

Sergeant Tammon was sitting next to Kai. His weapons weren't drawn—they didn't need to be with all his men standing around us ready to shoot—but he watched us with keen eyes. His body tensed at the mention of the word "Nethersphere." His eyes narrowed from me to Kai.

Kai looked faint. "Great Below, you didn't."

"Great Below exactly, Kai. It was an unforeseen necessity," Tass replied tartly. "It was the only way to escape the Curator's guards.

Unfortunately, crossing into the Nethersphere and back again corrupted our time line."

"What in Ruekigal's burning tits are you people talking about?" One of the codies, Hak I thought he was called, was staring at us with a wide, incredulous expression straining his simple face.

"What does it sound like we're talking about?" Kai shot back.

"Sounds like utter nonsense," Hak said, swatting the back of Kai's head.

"I wish that it was," I replied carefully. So carefully. Refusing to show an ounce of anxiety. Because it was impossible not to taste the helplessness that boiled the air around us.

Not from Kai or me or Tass—that would have made sense. It came from the codies. From the people who had promised to protect Cothis and who had failed, so utterly. And no—not all of them seemed affected by the change. That would have made things too damn easy.

But Tammon was.

I focused all my attention on the sergeant. It was his opinion that mattered. Maybe if I could just get him to believe me, he'd stop sitting on his freaking hands waiting for an empress who was never going to come, and actually do something. Maybe he already had. Despite everything, Edik always said Tammon was a good man.

I'd already set the test.

"You have to know something is wrong," I said to him. "Governor Paasch didn't just wake up one morning able to control water and shoot lightning out of his palms."

"They say Governor Paasch is blessed by Karanis now," Hak interjected.

"He *is* Karanis," I said as the wind howled a desperate cry across my face.

I stabbed my finger over the side of the boat. Above the muddy blue canal water, the temple loomed, its white walls glowed sooty gray in the murky sunlight. "Somehow he convinced Paasch to build that monstrosity. Karanis used it to bring himself through to this world. And he killed all those workers to do it. You must have seen that if nothing else!"

Some of the codies shifted uncomfortably. Some of them didn't seem to care. The sergeant's eyes never wavered from mine. It was how I saw all the sorrow contained within him. "What exactly do you expect us to do about it?" he asked after a long moment. "There's only two dozen of us left."

Just two dozen codies? The idea staggered me, and not in a good way, considering my feelings toward the lot.

"You want us to stand up to a god?" he continued.

"Yes." The word was so simple. And utterly inescapable. "He isn't a god, Sergeant. And he might be powerful, but he isn't invincible." I leaned closer, willing him to listen to me. "When we broke the idol—when we took this half of it—Karanis couldn't use it to create his true body. He was forced to possess Paasch in order to remain here, but Karanis can't squat in Paasch's corpse forever. He's vulnerable. But if he's allowed to get his hands on the rest of the idol, he won't be. We will be damned."

The sergeant's body went completely still, but I saw a shadow of fear shudder through his gaze. A shadow of something else too. "Paasch. Karanis. Gods. Men. Doesn't really matter, does it?" he asked nodding behind me. "We're here."

The boat thudded to a stop, the prow bumping against a small dock behind me. The temple's shadow fell across my face, and I shivered in the sudden chill. The codies jumped up, one of them slinging the weapons bag over his shoulder. They disembarked at top speed, almost like they were afraid to hear any more of my words.

Kai rose, clambering onto the dock ahead of me. Then turned, offering me a hand up. I clasped his wrist and felt the smooth click of beads under my hand. A very familiar green jasper necklace was roped around Kai's wrist.

THE QUEEN OF DAYS   325

"Zee left them for you. Said they were your mother's," he whispered, eyes shining in the strange light.

"Well. Who knew Zee was so sentimental," I muttered, voice lost in the shuffle as I slid the necklace off his wrist. I dropped it in my pocket before any of the codies saw it. The weight of the necklace seemed to pull me. Tug not just at my body, but my mind too.

Tass's arm brushed mine as she hopped off the boat. She looked up at the temple, light flashing like liquid mercury off the planes of her mask. A low rumble, almost a growl, reverberated from her chest. Her fingers twitched an oddly fluid set of twirls and I swore I caught the faintest whiff of her jasmine-scented magic.

"Get moving," Hak said, shoving Tass in the small of the back with his club.

I wouldn't have blamed her for snatching the club and breaking it over the codie's face, but Tass had more restraint than I did. She only glanced over her shoulder, making Hak blanch, before moving.

We rounded the long eastern flank of the temple and soon I was face-to-face with the grand central stair. With the codies still watching us, we started up. No one spoke. Almost like none of us could speak. And the air was heavy against my face. So heavy. Smothering. Even our steps were muffled. And though my legs burned, aching from so much running, the thought of Mira up there alone pushed me forward.

"Balthazar."

Hearing Tass's voice in my ear made me flinch so badly the edge of my boot caught the lip of the stair, and I wheeled forward. More than one codie cackled at my expense as I righted myself. Cheeks burning, I glanced backward, and saw Tass a few feet behind me bracketed by two codies with Tammon sandwiched between us. Too far away to whisper in my ear.

"No, Bal. We are mind to mind now. I apologize for the intrusion."

No freaking problem. I shook my head like the action could dislodge my confusion and surprise.

"Did you manage to retain any of Zeelaya's incendiary devices?"

"*Shit, I wish,*" I replied, trying to—I don't know—*think* loudly. "*The earrings are still in play, though. Gods—or whoever—willing they should be in the temple right now.*" I pried open the edges of my mind, showing her a memory from yesterday. From when she went to the Low Temple and I sent a letter.

"*Interesting,*" she murmured, and I felt her gaze slide off my back. "*Could you get to them?*"

"*The earrings?*" I bit down hard on the inside of my cheek, working through the calculus of my plan. "*No,*" I replied at last. "*But if everything goes to plan, the rest of the weapons will be available.*"

"*That is good.*"

A muscle above my eye ticked at the caveat wedged into her words. "*But?*"

"*But we must have a contingency in place.*"

I smothered the urge to smile. "*A weapon of last resort.*"

"*Indeed,*" she replied. "*But it will not be me this time.*"

"*What are you thinking?*"

"*I will need you to procure a gun.*"

"*Oh sure. No problem.*" I wanted to laugh but something in her tone made my mouth go dry. "*Why? You want me to shoot Karanis?*"

"*Not quite.*

"*I need you to shoot the idol.*"

I felt my brows draw together, confusion and dread coiling inside my mind. Because this was all sounding a lot like our original plan: Kai was going to rescue Mira. Tass was going to kill Karanis. I was going to destroy the idol—making damn sure that Karanis couldn't weasel his way out of death by seizing his final form at the last freaking moment.

And sure, the Curator would probably be pissed that we'd broken the damn thing even more than it already was, but, well. Fuck him. Plan was the plan. Simple.

Not easy. Not even that straightforward. But simple. "*What's going on, Tass? I was always going to destroy the idol—*"

"You were going to use one of Zeelaya's bombs to explode the idol," she said, like the verbiage made a difference.

Shit, did it make a difference?

I shook my head. *"I'll get to the bombs, Tass. Trust me, it's all part of the plan—"*

"But what if you can't reach them, Bal? If they are too far away, then a different course of action will be required. A backup plan.

"You will need a gun."

My fingers danced an impatient jig against my leg. *"What aren't you saying, Tass?"*

"That there is a difference between throwing a grenade and firing a bullet."

"Yeah, and what's that?"

"Proximity."

"Clearly you haven't been paying attention, Tass. I'm a hell of a marksman." And I was. No bragging needed. I could even give Edik a run for his money.

"Your aim in this instance is less relevant because a long-range shot will not suffice. To damage the idol with a bullet rather than one of Zee's bombs, you will need to be close. You'll need to wait until the two halves are almost fused. When that happens, the idol won't simply break. With all the energy being funneled into it, it will explode."

I nodded. It still sounded easy enough. Things were bound to go sideways—shit, I intended to *force* them sideways. Guns would be available. I'd just have to reach one. Take a shot. And damn it I wasn't lying about being a good shot, but . . .

But there was something unfinished in Tassiel's tone. Something that made the air feel charged with foreboding.

"How close?"

"Very close, Bal. Point-blank."

I closed my eyes against the answer. Because how the hell was I supposed to get that close to the idol? Not like Karanis would just let me stroll to his side like a favorite pet.

And then there was the other matter. The one that ended with me as nothing more than a pink cloud of vaporized flesh. *"If I shoot the idol point-blank it's going to explode in my fucking face."*

"And Karanis will never be able to possess it."

A choked sound caught in my throat, so pitiful it drew a worried look from Kai. *"You don't get it,"* I pressed, the voice in my head weak with dread. *"If I have to get that close, it will kill me."*

I took ten agonizing steps waiting for her to reply. *"I know. It is our only hope."*

My heart shrieked against my ribs, desperate for the life Tass was throwing away. *"If it's our only hope, then why don't you do it?"* I snapped, anger and terror rearing red and savage in my chest.

"I will be distracting Karanis. Unless you would rather face one of your gods in single combat?"

A petty retort hovered on the edges of my consciousness. Then her words clicked. Anger fled. The hollowness it left behind trembled. *"Distracting Karanis? Don't you mean* killing *Karanis?"*

Tass's silence had texture. It had the weight of an ancient sorrow, one that marched ever forward. Unstoppable.

"I will try," she said at long last.

"Try?" I clung to my anger, to the false bravery it fueled. *"Don't try. Just do it. Kill him and we won't need to destroy the idol."*

"I will try," she repeated slowly, letting her words sink in.

". . . You don't think you can kill him, do you?"

"No. I do not."

My mind reeled against those four simple words. Words heralding the end of an existence that had spanned millennia. The end of my own existence too.

The edges of my vision began to gray. I'd been counting on Tass to do the heavy lifting. To shoulder the burden. I mean . . . She couldn't die. Could she? *"But . . . but you and the Curator made it sound like it would be an even match. Like taking on Karanis was—not simple, but doable."*

"I lied."

"Why?"

An ancient, exhausted sigh blew through my mind. *"Because your world was falling apart, Bal. And Mira . . . she was so scared. You all were. And the Curator was trying to make you feel like Karanis's defeat was up to you, but that burden was never yours. I couldn't let you shoulder it alone.*

"I will fight him, Bal. For you and your family, I will fight him with everything that I am for as long as I can. But if your family is going to survive, you must *destroy the idol. I can't fight this battle alone."*

No. She couldn't. And I wouldn't let her. We would enter that godsdamned temple side by side and do what needed to be done. For Mira. For Kai. For Zee and Edik. For all those workers sacrificed for this horrific godling.

And for my parents, who had died for this island.

Pain stung my eyes as tears filmed my vision. Wherever their souls were now, I prayed—truly prayed, that they were watching, that they would be with me to the end.

"Bal," Kai hissed. "What the fuck is wrong with you?"

Kai always reacted to fear with anger, so I forced a smile even as I struggled to swallow the knot in my throat. "Nothing, brother. I'm just fine."

Kai's face paled, eyes going wide, but one of the codies guffawed before Kai could reply.

"Just fine, huh?" he said with a smirk. "I'll remind you of that when the governor's playing with your guts."

"Hak," Tammon snapped. "Enough. This is no time for pettiness."

And it really wasn't. Because we just reached the temple's first platform. I gagged as the wind shifted, sending the carrion stench of spoiled meat up my nose. The terrace was still set out for a party, but it wasn't the smell of rotting food that burrowed into my skin. Bodies lay on the stone, bloated and baking in the heat.

"Why hasn't anyone taken care of these people?" I demanded, glaring at the codies around me.

Most of them looked away, at the ground or up at the temple ahead. Some of them flushed with shame or turned green with revulsion. Some. Not all.

The sergeant's face remained impassive, but I saw his throat bob with tightly contained emotion. "I'm sure they will be taken care of soon enough. The governor has had other matters on his mind."

"Yeah, I'll bet he does," Kai muttered, looking like he wanted nothing more than to skin the guards alive. "What's your excuse? Defenders of the public good—isn't that what all your badges say? What are you gonna do for all those poor souls? For Cothis?"

"Just you focus on giving the governor what he wants," the sergeant said softly, sadly. "Call yourself lucky if you don't join them."

Luck.

The word snarled through my brain. Luck was a fool's game. A lazy man's prayer for Creation to fix his problems. As if the universe didn't have better things to do. Luck and fate were nothing but smoke and mirrors. I didn't need any of it. Only one person controlled my destiny.

Me.

The temple doors were open, waiting with ravening hunger to swallow us whole. There were no guards or codekeepers on the door. None were needed. Not with a god inside.

Not a god.

I practically growled the thought. The anger, the ferocity behind it pushed away the despair clouding my vision. Karanis was not a god. He was powerful, yes, undeniably so. But he was not invincible. And I wasn't alone.

Kai, Tass, and I crossed the threshold together, afternoon sun warming our backs in benediction. Our steps echoed across the vaulted foyer, coming back to us like three heartbeats thumping in sync. The idol bounced against my leg, heavier and harder with each step.

The temple's once gleaming copper rafters were burned, tarnished, and slightly green. The once bright walls sagged inward, bowing under the weight of so much misery. Or maybe that was just the two hundred people crowded and penned on the edges of the room like cattle ready for slaughter.

And the stench . . . Days of being trapped here in the heat and humidity surrounded by corpses and filth. Not even the gaping hole in the side of the temple—evidence of Karanis's rage—was enough to shift the scent. We'd have to tear down the temple brick by brick to erase that smell.

If we survived.

I saw all this, saw the light coming in from the high windows on the edges of the room. But the fact that I was noticing these things was just a way to postpone the inevitable. A way for me to cling to a shred of courage, to brace myself and prepare, before facing what came next.

Tammon snapped his fingers and gestured a wordless command. The codies who escorted us in took up posts in a loose semicircle along the columned entrance to the shrine. A wall of flesh between us and Karanis.

But they dropped the weapons bag first. Exactly as Tammon had ordered. Dumped it against an unoccupied pillar on my left. Not close enough to seem like a threat.

But close enough to me.

It would have to be. *I was not fucking dying today.*

The feeling of Karanis's impatience clung to my skin. Not a bad thing, I thought, my eyes skating forward. Impatience could make a mark confident. Cocky, even.

The frailness of that thought cracked when I looked at the acolytes. They stared at me with terrified, desperate eyes. They clung to the walls, clearly afraid to go near the altar on which half the idol now sat. Or perhaps they were afraid of getting too close to . . . to him.

I searched their faces a moment longer, trying to find that telltale flash of blue light. That cunning smile that could only belong to Calien. He had to be here somewhere. Watching. Waiting. But would he act?

Of course he would. He may not do something big, but he wasn't the type to sit back and watch. Not after the look he'd given me when I claimed Tassiel. The real question was this:

When the mayhem really started, whose body would he take? There were two options. Two people he could seize to inflict the most damage.

I knew the answer. Knew it. Hated it. But I'd use it.

Better get this the fuck over with. I swallowed the bitter taste of knowledge.

And looked at Karanis.

He lounged in a throne that had clearly been dragged out of some dusty museum and shoved against the base of the altar. One hand cupped his chin, the other was thrown carelessly over the back of the chair.

His skin seemed to be shedding; it was crinkling and cracking in strange places. He had lost his fingernails since I'd seen him last. His hair was patchy where it clung to his scalp, though more of it littered the floor around him than remained on his head. Not that Shasheba—who knelt at his feet like a well-trained dog—seemed to mind. I barely looked at her. She'd get what she deserved.

But Karanis? I nearly laughed. He must have used up a whole lot of his precious energy coming after us, I thought. Why else would he still be in Paasch's crumbling corpse?

Unless he was playing me. Unless he knew all about my history with Paasch and was trying to weaponize his body. Another one of Shasheba's helpful suggestions, I wondered?

Didn't matter. His blue-fire eyes scraped across my cheeks and dropped to my jacket. Like a hound scenting a hare, Karanis went still.

He straightened. A smile peeled back his lips. "You brought it."

My hand went to my pocket. I felt the idol. Felt the necklace too, the beads so smooth they were almost oily beneath my touch. Unnatural, almost. Kai's words came back to me.

I smiled, the plans in my mind rearranging.

"Where is my sister?"

Karanis gave a careless wave. A guard emerged from the edge of the room with Mira slung over his shoulder. He dropped her at Karanis's feet and hurried away, like he feared he too would fall under Karanis's eye. Hands bound and mouth gagged, Mira pushed herself off the floor and rounded on me. Her eyes brimmed with anger and relief; the emotions so strong they took the breath right out of me.

"Give her to me."

Karanis's head tilted, like a cat eyeing a mouse, ready to play. "What happened to the rest of your little group? Weren't there more of you at the harbor?"

I felt my hackles rise at the question. At the implicit threat in his words. At the knowledge that Karanis wasn't simply going to hand Mira over and let us go. "Yes."

Karanis nodded. "I thought so. What were their names?" He looked away before I could answer—not that I was going to. "Shasheba, darling," he called. "What were their names?"

Shasheba rose smoothly from the floor. Polished as ever, she dusted the detritus of Paasch's crumbling body from the folds of her dress, taking her place like she deserved to be there. Shasheba took a moment to smile and preen under his regard before turning to me, her eyes glittering with malice and cruelty.

"Zeelaya and Edik Agodzi."

"Ah, yes. Them." Karanis stroked Shasheba's face with one skeletal finger. "Sergeant, did I not command you to bring the whole of the Talion?"

Tammon came to attention. "Yes, my lord. Unfortunately, Zeelaya and Edik Agodzi fled the island before we apprehended them."

Karanis frowned, eyebrows rising. The skin in between stretched to near opacity in effort to convey his displeasure. "That is unacceptable."

Tammon bent in two, bowing almost to the floor in submission. He didn't offer an apology or explanation, for which I was grudgingly impressed. Given the fact that Karanis had let us go the day before without an escort, and magically banished us across the island, it seemed a large ask to expect the codies to find us again. Then again, after everything I'd seen, I didn't really expect to see sanity in Karanis.

"I thought you said the crew was attached to the child?"

Karanis shot that question at Shasheba, who heaved an elegant sigh. "Balthazar and Malakai are certainly. I do not know Edik Agodzi well, but he always struck me as the sensible sort. He was certainly not the kind of man to adore so plain and troublesome a child as Miraveena Vadalen. I admit, I thought Zeelaya would feel some attachment to her cousin, but there was always something distinctly reptilian about her. She obviously values her own safety over theirs."

I ground my teeth at Shasheba's description, at the callous way she called Zee unfeeling. My cousin was a hard woman in many ways, and wasn't someone who formed attachments easily, but when she did, they went deep. Shasheba had been Zee's friend once.

Karanis grumbled, seeming to release his anger in a single long breath. "I suppose that's no matter. I have the other three, and I can sense they have the idol. Tell me, Sergeant, where did you find them? With their patron, I suppose?"

"No, my lord," Tammon said, releasing his bow like a spring flying open. "This man here we found in one of the old Vadalen family residences," he said, motioning to Kai. "The other two we found in the Sunken Gardens."

The sergeant's pause was pregnant enough to make Karanis lean forward. "And?"

"Hard to explain, my lord," he began haltingly, like even this battle-tested old soldier quailed in the face of Karanis. "The gardens are built on ancient Ashaarite ruins. At their heart is what the locals call the Witch's Door. It's a locked portal that no one has ever successfully opened.

"Malakai here told us that if we wanted to find Balthazar and Tassiel that we should wait outside the door. We did, for several hours, and even though each of my men attempted to open the portal, none of us were successful. So we waited, thinking that once your deadline came and went, we could at least deliver one thief to you. And then the door just . . . opened. These two came sprinting out like their lives depended on it."

Karanis's gaze moved to me. I shrugged, easing back into feigned nonchalance and the long-honed confidence every good con man needed to survive. "We were being chased."

"By what?"

"Wolves."

Karanis's eyes popped wide. "Wolves? In Cothis? You jest."

"Nope," I replied, hooking my thumbs through my belt loops. "Though we weren't technically in Cothis."

"Where were you?"

"The Archive."

Shasheba gasped. She wasn't the only one. Karanis glared around the room, displeased that there was an aspect of his new kingdom with which he was unfamiliar. A slow smile spread across my face. Karanis didn't know because . . .

"Paasch didn't know about the Archive, did he?" I chuckled, mirthless as shattered glass. "I guess the Curator has some taste when it comes to houseguests."

"What is the Archive?" Karanis demanded, sounding like a petulant child.

"The Archive is a vast collection of books and antiquities that lies beneath the city," Shasheba hurried to reply when it became clear that I wasn't going to.

"That is imprecise," Tass said, and all eyes turned to her.

25

TASS

Shasheba's cheeks reddened as Tass's words slapped her across the face. Her embarrassment was like the finest of wines. Tass savored it, letting her body fill with savage pleasure.

"The Archive does not lie beneath Cothis," she continued.

"Like it matters," Shasheba snapped, her mouth turning down in what Tass was sure the woman thought of as an adorable moue.

Creation save her, Tass loathed this woman. She reminded Tassiel of Ruekigal. Or worse. Of Tass's sister, Malien. Beautiful, as if beauty could excuse bottomless cruelty. "I am sure you will always be a bitch, Shasheba. You do not need to be an ignorant one."

The look of sheer bliss on Kai's face nearly made her laugh, but she contained it when a childish squeal bubbled out of Karanis.

"Well, this is simply wonderful," he purred the words with insane glee. Tass frowned. Karanis had always been an odd creature, but his mind seemed to have crossed some invisible boundary since she had last known him.

"You will want to hear what I have to say, Uncle."

"I do indeed. The entertainment value alone is worth a few extra moments of your existence. Go on, Tassiel," Karanis said. "Educate us. Where exactly is the Archive if not on this island?"

She paused a hairsbreadth of hesitance. Grandfather didn't want his children to know he was alive. But then, he was willing to forfeit her life to save his own—and to kill her for taking a broken statue—so what did she really owe him? Anyway, when Karanis found out . . .

To say he'd react was an understatement. He would panic. And in that panic, Tass might, *just might*, see her chance to save them.

Tass smiled, folding her hands primly like a school child begging for attention. "The Archive occupies a layer of reality that lies directly beneath the one upon which Cothis exists."

Shasheba and the other trapped humans looked around each other in confusion. A confusion that passed into fear. For the effect her words had on Karanis was impossible to overstate. He straightened in his seat, his back arching so far, so fast she could hear his spine crackle. Power lashed around him in thin tendrils of blue flame.

"That is not possible," he breathed the words, a draconic growl reverberating in his chest.

Tass shrugged, knowing the nonanswer would drive him mad. His gaze flashed from her to Bal, like he could possibly have an explanation to cool the suspicion chafing Karanis raw.

"Let's pretend I believe you for a moment. Why were you in this 'Archive'?"

Bal's brow furrowed, clearly wondering why Karanis was asking such an idiotic question. "We had to get the idol from our patron."

"And who, exactly, is your patron?"

It was Bal's turn to shrug. "He calls himself the Curator."

"You people and your labels," Karanis spat. "I didn't ask for a title. I asked for a *name*. Who is the Curator?" He all but bellowed the question, straining forward in the chair, grasping its arms in two clawlike hands.

Tass tutted. "You know who he is, Karanis. You would not be getting all worked up if you didn't."

"Be careful, outcast," Karanis warned, voice dropping an octave.

"I'm not the outcast you should be worried about," she replied, her murmur was low, but it carried, nonetheless. "As you've no doubt surmised, there is another. The reason I was cast out in the first place. The one with enough foresight to anticipate what you were planning with Governor Paasch. He's the one who hired the Talion to stop you."

The blood drained out of Karanis's face. His firefly eyes flickered and dimmed like his soul was trying to escape back to the Nethersphere. But there would be no going back. Not for Karanis.

"No. He's dead."

"So was I." Tass purred the words, her body humming with the promise of violence. "No, Uncle. Only a fool would think that a millennium on this world could kill the Great Father."

Great Father.

The name hit the humans around her like a kick in the teeth. Tass saw Shasheba's hand fly to her mouth, stifling a strangled gasp. Bal blanched. Kai swore. More than one codekeeper wilted in shock, and Sergeant Tammon—her words seemed to rattle around in his skull, refusing to settle.

Good.

He and all the codekeepers should know that Karanis was working against the All Father. Enkaara, the Creator. The creature they worshipped as the King of the Heavens Above. Keeper of the Great Below.

Perhaps the one being in all of Creation powerful enough to deserve the title of god.

But would it be enough? Were her words shocking enough—shattering enough—to make some of them pause when the fighting began. Pause, and Creation willing, help.

Karanis surged to his feet. Electricity crackled around him, dancing a panicked jig to his uncontrolled fear. Shameful. No wonder her father had sent Karanis first. He was expendable. Tass would make sure of it.

"Give me the idol," he bellowed. The sky outside growled in warning. Electricity gathered in the air. Lightning ready to strike.

Tass nodded once to Bal.

She watched, the world slowing around them like time itself had stilled, as Bal withdrew the broken statue from his pocket. The statue.

And a necklace?

Confusion ran rampant through Tassiel's mind as Balthazar draped the necklace around the idol like the string on a present.

What was he doing?

He looked up at Karanis. Smiled a smile that didn't reach his eyes. "Give me my sister."

Karanis grabbed Mira by the back of her neck and lifted her off the floor. He held the girl at arm's length, one eyebrow arched sharper than the blade of a knife.

Mira whimpered, face contorted in agony. Tass's breath caught at how easily Karanis's long hand encircled Mira's throat—how easy it would be for him to snap the girl's neck. All it would take was a single savage whim.

Sergeant Tammon shifted, his face gray, as he held his hand to Bal. But Bal didn't move. His eyes were on Mira.

"Bal," Kai whispered. "Do it."

She could hear his heart pounding in his chest. Bal reached out. Paused.

And gave Tammon the idol.

"What is that he's put around the statue?" Karanis asked, words sharp enough to freeze Tammon in place.

Tammon looked at the necklace. Looked back at Bal. Something passed between the two men. Something Tassiel could almost, *almost*, read.

Tammon unwound the strand of beads, each chiming click echoing loudly through the temple. Too loudly she thought. Like the gems were far heavier than they appeared.

"A necklace, my lord," he said, holding it out for Karanis to inspect.

"Trying to bribe me, Balthazar?"

Bal shrugged. "Can't hurt to try," he said with a small smile. "Give it to Shash if you don't like it. She always did love my mother's jewelry."

Mother's jewelry? That wasn't right. The necklace looked like Zeelaya's earrings. Modeled on jewelry that had belonged to *her* mother. Not Bal's.

Which meant . . .

Shasheba snatched the necklace out of Tammon's hand. "I don't need your family's trash anymore, Bal."

She didn't even look at it, just tossed it over her shoulder.

Where it landed on the altar with an echoing thud.

"A valiant attempt," Karanis said with a low chuckle. "But it's far too late for flattery." The shadow of a smirk twitched across Karanis's face. He dropped Mira only to plant a foot in the small of her back.

And kicked.

Mira's whole body arched. Hands and feet still bound, she flew through the air. Bal moved before Tass could stop him. He skidded across the floor catching Mira in outstretched arms. Tass was a step behind him. She clamped down hard on Bal's shoulder, pulling him. They had to move. Now.

Silent tears fell hot down Mira's face as the three of them dropped back to where Kai waited. Mira whispered something as Bal untied her, but Tass didn't catch the words. Only saw Mira retreat behind Malakai.

"Balthazar," Tass murmured in warning, willing him to be ready—ready for what came next.

Karanis's eyes were glued to the idol, the peeling skin of his hands caressed its black surface. Something almost tender swam in his blue gaze. Then it was gone

Karanis looked up at her, baring his teeth in a feral grin. "Kill them."

The twelve codies between Karanis and Tass raised their guns. Twelve fingers squeezed twelve triggers.

But Tass was faster.

Magic rushed from her fingers, hardening the air before her in an impenetrable shield. With the next movement she pulled her swords out of her memory, forging them with a flash of light that was all but lost in the gunfire.

She whipped the blades out of the air with a flourish. Bullets crumpled against her shield, falling to the floor like rain. The codies froze with unbridled fear as they beheld her. No doubt they thought she'd used her swords to snatch the bullets from the air. Foolish humans, she thought, launching herself forward.

Trusting Bal and Kai to handle the codies on the left and right, Tass went for the four men in the middle. The first two died instantly, her swords sheathed in their chests. The third codie turned on his heel to run. She tossed a corpse at him for his cowardice. The fourth codie fired again.

Metal seared through her sleeve and flesh as the bullet tore through her left bicep. A growl ripped out of her throat. Tass batted his gun away with her blade. White-faced, the codie backed toward the altar, whimpering as his heels hit an invisible barrier blocking both of them from getting closer to Karanis.

Damn, she thought, hitting the terrified codie with the hilt of one sword. His eyes rolled upward, and he fell unconscious to the ground. She sheathed one blade behind her back, pressing her palm to the barrier.

Where her shield had been nothing but hardened air, Karanis's was ice. Hair thin and completely clear, the frigid substance bit through her glove, greedy to taste her flesh. Power hummed through the barrier, and Tass knew that no amount of force would make it break. Not even a bullet—the bullet they needed to destroy the idol—would shatter the shield. Only magic would bring it down.

Her nameplate was still three-quarters full from her sojourn in the Nethersphere. Enough to make Karanis's wall crumble. But unleashing that amount of power would leave her nearly empty—and in no state to fight her uncle.

Which meant that Tass had to go the long way around. Unravel the spell keeping the shield intact. But could she break through it before Karanis mended the idol? She swallowed hard. She'd have to work fast.

Through the ice's glassy surface, Tass saw Karanis stand behind the altar. Arms raised as if to glorify this moment—the idiot. Only the laziest of magicians needed such grand gestures to channel their magic.

Unfortunately, the idol disagreed. It began to glow.

Tass growled a swear that would have made Kai proud and poured her magic into the barrier. She felt along the spine of the enchantment, teasing out thread after thread of spell work that kept the wall whole. The spider's web of magic that supported the shield burned bright indigo as she picked it apart, but each snapped thread whipped back at her in searing electric shocks.

"You're wasting your time, Septiniri," Karanis cried with naked delight. "You'll never reach me. You don't have the power. You never did. It's why my brother threw you away without a second thought."

She let the pain of those words wash past her; a glancing blow she'd deal with later. If she lived. But right now, she couldn't let him goad her. She had to break through. If she couldn't, Bal would have no hope of destroying the idol.

"You have no idea what I am capable of, Uncle," Tass replied. The shield should have shattered by now. Creation damn it all, she was using too much magic. She was taking too long. "You have always been the least of us."

"You don't know what you're talking about. I am Karanis the Glorious, God of Water, the first in our line to take this world."

She genuinely laughed. "Karanis the Glorious?"

"I *am* glorious!"

He sounded like a petulant child and hope like a second sun warmed her skin. She was close. So close.

Beneath her fingers, the enchantment shuddered.

Cracked.

And held.

The urge to close her eyes was overwhelming. She had failed. Failed. *Failed.*

The word played a despairing dirge on her ribs. Because she couldn't break through the shield. She didn't have enough power. Not on her own.

Light and heat and sound assaulted her as the second stage of Bal's plan hit. She tasted fire in the air. Felt stone rain on her back. But Tassiel didn't move. Didn't even flinch. All her focus bent toward Karanis. Toward the barrier.

The idea that sizzled through her tasted like ash and dust. Tassiel smiled.

"There's nothing glorious about you, Uncle. You're nothing more than an idiot. A gullible fool," she crooned the words, voice all but lost to the cacophony of battle that filled the room. No matter.

She knew Karanis was listening.

"Did you really think my father let you come first to honor you? No. He sent you to see if you would fail—like you *always* fail. He sent you because losing you would be nothing to him." Karanis's face purpled.

This was it. She grinned, knowing she had him. "You've always been expendable. Even Grandfather thinks as much. He said—"

"ENOUGH!"

Karanis's face contorted with terrible, feral rage. He leveled one hand at her. Tass raised her sword in answer, bracing herself as lightning shot toward her. It hit the shield, shattering the ice into so much frozen air before connecting with her chest.

Electricity was everywhere, burning into her.

Through her.

She felt her toes leave the ground. Felt her body fly back. And crunch into the floor behind Bal and Kai. She rolled hard on her shoulder. Her nerves screamed for mercy and she swallowed a ragged sob. Not waiting for the pain to fade, Tass pushed herself to her feet. Laughed.

"Thank you, Uncle," she said sweetly, as Karanis's face slackened with the realization that he'd destroyed his own shield.

Nothing separated them.

Tass drew both swords. Ran.

26

BALTHAZAR

Karanis's command rang in my ears. The codies detached from the pillars and raised their guns. I fell back to Kai and Mira—like a paltry two feet could save my life. Kai went for guns that weren't there. Mira sniffed. Tass stepped forward.

Time slowed.

I saw a flash. The crack of all twelve guns reverberated through my skull. My heart shrieked with the desperate will to live, but I locked myself in place. Trusted Tass. Trusted the plan. Tass whirled, arms spinning so fast she was a blur of movement my eyes couldn't track.

When the smoke cleared, twelve bullets lay dented and misshapen at Tass's feet. Twin swords, which hadn't existed even a handful of seconds ago, were clutched in Tass's fists. Like a lioness sighting prey, Tass cocked her head to one side. She swished the blades through the air with a tight flick of her wrists and launched herself into the stunned codies.

This time I didn't hesitate. Kai pivoted right. I went left, bowling into the nearest codie before he had time to react. His jaw buckled beneath the crunch of my fist. He slumped, and I shifted, letting his weight slide off me. Pausing to pluck the gun out of his hands and the knife from his belt I whirled toward Kai.

"Kai! Get her out of here!"

He flashed a salute my way, sprinting back to get Mira out of here like we'd agreed on.

I kept moving, staying low as bullets whizzed past my head. Half the hostages surged forward in a desperate stampede, hell-bent on escape. The others were frozen by terror, having only the strength to scream. Some of the codies were helping these stranded few. Some. Not all. The rest had clearly thrown in their lot with Karanis, judging by how hard they were trying to kill us.

And Tammon . . . Where the fuck was Tammon?

I fired three shots in quick succession. Two of the three men standing between me and the would-be god went down. The third codie spun toward me. A panicked gleam glossed his eyes as he aimed. For a half second, we stood facing each other like two idiot gentlemen dueling over a woman's spoiled honor. The trigger squeezed easily beneath my fingers.

I *missed*.

The codie smiled. Then jerked sideways, blood spraying from his ear. He fell, following a chunk of his skull to the ground.

Heart pounding in my ears, I traced the bullet's trajectory back to its source.

Because there he was: Edik, crouched on one of the windowsills.

Rifle in hand, he picked off the codies one by one. Relief washed over me. *Right on time.* But what about Zee?

Edik saw me staring and glared over his gun's sight. "Bal. Move." "Where's Zee?"

One of Edik's fingers twitched upward. Fool that I am I looked up to the ceiling. Saw only rafters.

Which could only mean . . . *Shit*.

"Tammon!" I bellowed the man's name. Spotted him—finally—standing to one side of the temple. The same side that Karanis blew apart when he saw Tassiel flee that first night. The gaping hole still stood there, giving an unmatched view onto the city below. But I wasn't here to enjoy the scenery. Neither was Tammon. Because he was holding a lantern in one hand.

Two earrings in the other.

The sergeant's eyes met mine.

I nodded. "Now."

Tammon lit the earrings in quick succession. Lobbed them to the rafters.

"Cover!" I shouted, sprinting forward to follow my own advice. I rammed into one of the columns separating the altar from the rest of the temple. Clapped my hands to my ears.

Light speared through the temple as the earrings exploded. Stone shattered. Metal shrieked as three copper beams barreled into the floor. Beams that helped Karanis funnel his power.

And though it wasn't enough to bring them all down, the huge spiderweb of cracks weakening the roof would sure as hell give Zee somewhere to aim.

Speaking of . . .

I flipped the revolvers latch, counting the bullets. Two remaining.

Two.

Don't fucking miss, Bal, I thought, ducking my head around the column to get eyes on Karanis. Then on the idol.

Then on the necklace.

Gunfire and screams rocked through the shrine with near physical force. While the nobles behind me fled, the acolytes were still trapped behind the altar. They stared in frozen horror at Karanis. His voice boomed through the air, like some terrible conductor controlling a symphony of violence.

Karanis stood straight, arms raised despite the hail of bullets. The two halves of the broken idol lay on the altar, only a few inches apart. Karanis's skin glowed. He burned with flames that leaped across his clothes, limning him in blue light. It shot out of his palms and surrounded the broken idol.

The light sizzled against the dark stone, burning it a livid, molten lava-red. The two halves stretched and with gelatinous fingers, they reached for one another. Pulling closer and closer. Beginning to fuse.

Karanis's lips moved, but whatever he was saying, whatever was passing between he and Tass—who even now stood before him, hand outstretched—I couldn't tell. Karanis's face contorted with animal rage. He punched a hand toward her, hurling a bolt of lightning straight into Tass's chest. She flew past me.

This was it.

Lightning forked off the metal girders as storm clouds gathered within the temple. *Now.* I had to act now. Before the idol was whole. Before Karanis could use it. I threw myself around the column, bracing half my body against the stone to keep me steady, and raised the gun.

Aimed.

Fired once.

Twice.

Karanis didn't even look at me. Just flicked one wrist and the bullets hit empty air. Instinct made me lunge as the bullets ricocheted. They barreled into the column where I had been standing a half second before. Rock rained down on me, catching my cheek. Pain bloomed in my face. Small. So small compared to the carnage tearing through the temple. Something in me went still.

Shit.

A gun. I needed a gun. The weapons cache. I could still—

A black form streaked past me as I struggled to stand. Tass leaped over the throne, clearing the altar with her two silver blades glowing strangely in the light. She attacked Karanis head-on, forcing him back. Tass moved with such predatory grace, slashing, spinning, thrusting, stabbing it was like a dance. And with each step she pushed Karanis away from the idol.

Karanis's magic formed two swords, mirrors of Tass's, but made of crackling ice rather than steel. He clenched the blades in skeletal fingers, meeting her every attack, turning it back before she could do much more than slash his skin. Blood stained his robes, but it didn't slow him down. And he didn't need to stand at the altar to make the idol whole.

Weapons, Bal!

I slid around the pillar, ducking low sprinting for the next. Where our weapons had been piled up and forgotten. All our guns and bullets. All our bombs.

And they were at my feet.

Two tiny hands seized my arm. "Bal, we have to go. Please!" Mira cried, begged.

Her entire body trembled with every lightning strike. It boomed down harder and fiercer each second, making temple walls shiver. But I couldn't make myself move.

"Where is Kai?" I demanded, hating the tremor of terror that gripped me. The only way Kai wouldn't have gotten Mira out of here was if—

"I don't know," she cried.

Damn it.

I glanced back to the altar. The idol was almost complete. It glowed an angry, hellish crimson that seared even brighter than the lightning raining down from above. Bolt after bolt speared through the acolytes, fusing their ruined bodies to the ground. Smoke gathered around the altar, smoke and the stench of burning flesh. The flesh of men and women sacrificed for Karanis's greed.

To the right of the altar, Tass and Karanis's battle still raged. Magic or speed protected them from the lightning, but not from each other. Even from this small distance, I couldn't tell who was winning. Karanis's left arm hung useless from his shoulder, but Tass was limping. Her black clothes concealed any blood, but she was favoring her right leg as well as her left arm. It put her off-balance.

Karanis hurled a javelin-like lightning bolt at her. I shouted, wordlessly. Uselessly. Tass didn't block it in time. It rocketed through her right shoulder. One of her swords clattered to the ground.

"Bal!" Mira screamed my name so loud, it set my teeth on edge. "Please. We have to run. Now."

A frigid wind that only I could feel raked across my face. Fear poisoned the air with a nameless warning. Even the sun seemed to dim, but not in foreboding. Because I knew damn well what was happening.

I turned, pressing my back to the pillar. And looked down at my sister.

Her face was buried in her small hands, shoulders shaking with the weight of her sobs. She begged, pleaded with me to run away. Those pitiful little-girl tears turned my stomach liquid.

Because they were a lie.

Mira never cried. Never sobbed. Never ran away from a fight. Which meant . . .

"Bal, please. Get me out of here. You're supposed to protect me. You're supposed to—"

"Look at me," I snapped, each ragged syllable hurled harder than any knife.

Mira's sobs guttered. She simply hit a wall mid-sentence and went silent. Her tears vanished. Her hands fell from her face.

When she looked up, she was grinning, electric-blue eyes shining with madness.

27

BALTHAZAR

D amn," Calien swore through my sister's mouth. "I really thought I had you going. What gave it away?"

I wrapped my hand tighter about my gun's grip, felt it bite into my palm. "My sister might be afraid. But she's no coward."

"No," he agreed slowly. "She's not. I can still feel her, you know, wriggling around in here." He tapped his temple. "Feisty one, your sister."

"Get out of her head."

"No." The sound of his mad cackle erupting from Mira's mouth made my knees weak. "I think I rather like it in here."

"Why are you doing this?" I asked, though I knew the answer. Knew it was all pettiness and spite—the capricious heart of a trickster god. Didn't stop me from wanting to tear my hair out in mindless horror. "You let us go. You saved us, Tass and me. Why?"

Calien tutted, as if the answer was painfully obvious. "Well, you did claim my sister, Balthazar. I thought it was only fair that I claim yours."

"You can't do this. She's a child."

"Not for long."

"You fucking bastard." I raised my revolver. My vision flashed red in panic and desperation even as I remembered the gun was empty. Even as I knew this was always going to happen. From the moment I'd declared my friendship for Tass. It was all leading here. To this.

"I wouldn't do that," Calien said in a singsong voice. "You'll only hurt dear sweet Mira . . . But, maybe that's what you want."

I blinked. I'd expected a lot from Calien. But this? It didn't make sense. "You don't know what you're talking about."

"Don't I?" His laugh was all edges, cruel and cutting. "I think you're forgetting that I know everything Mira does. She knows how much you hate having to look after her. How you can't wait to shut her away in some school. She knows she's nothing but a burden to you, a weight dragging you down. She's the shackle holding you back."

"No, she's not," I said, willing not Calien, but Mira to hear me. To know I spoke the truth.

"She really is. I would know." Calien glanced at Tass, still fighting Karanis, their movements a blur to my eyes. "Just look at the mess my little sister is causing." He heaved a put-upon sigh. "Ah, she used too much energy bringing Karanis's shield down. Tassiel really doesn't have a chance now, does she? It's a shame. Her form really has improved."

"You little shit," I said, my lip curling. "Your sister is fighting for her life while you squat in my sister's body doing nothing."

"*Am* I doing nothing?" he asked, eyes going comically wide. "I thought I was keeping you here—stopping you from getting the idol back. That is why you didn't take the chance to flee with dear Mira, isn't it?"

"Are you stopping me?" I asked, parroting his words back to him with my own savage smile.

His head canted to one side. "If you aren't trying to steal it, then . . ." He grinned. "You're going to destroy it. And how do you imagine you'll do that? It's a chunk of half-molten stone at the moment. You think you can just smash it on the floor?"

"I'd say you'll figure it out," I began, my smirk was sharp as broken glass. "Too bad you snatched the wrong sibling."

Creation obviously wanted to punctuate my words, for a massive harpoon speared through the ceiling. The impact made the entire temple shudder. The roof groaned in terror. Then screamed in writhing agony as two tons of stone, plaster, paint, and copper were wrenched clean off.

Laughter exploded out of my chest as I spotted something through the newly minted skylight: an airship.

And Zee. Manning a giant ballista. In an eyeblink she cut the line from the first harpoon. Scrambled to attach the second. I shot her a salute that I wasn't sure she could see, smirking to Calien who watched with naked glee.

"Interesting—without the metal girding to store energy for him, Karanis will only have one chance to transfer forms," Calien said, so obviously impressed it was a little insulting. "But you knew that, didn't you?"

"Nothing quite like a plan coming together."

I turned on my heel, refusing to waste any more time on Calien's games. I needed to find a gun and end this. Now.

Lightning forked down from the ceiling, spearing noble and codie alike in indiscriminate rage. Didn't matter that the girding was damaged. Karanis was too far in to turn back now.

Exactly where I wanted him.

My gaze dropped to the altar. Not to the idol, but once again to the necklace sitting only a foot to the left. I had to end this. Now.

"Not so fast, thief."

The cold metal end of what could only be a gun pressed into the back of my neck. My eyes closed instinctively.

"Turn around. Slowly."

I pried my eyes open. Turned. The codie holding the gun on me was glaring with small pig-like eyes. The same eyes that had glared at me on the boat ride here. A muscle in his pock-marked face twitched in time with the crashing thunder. And then.

His eyes dropped.

"Back up," he snapped, forcing me to move at the point of his gun. He lunged faster than I would have thought possible, grabbing one corner of the canvas bag, and hurling it across the floor. All those weapons. The bombs. Gone.

And my last hope for survival with them.

"Hak. Isn't it?" I asked, grasping at the man's name while trying to ignore the look of pure hilarity rippling across Mira's face. Trying to ignore the screaming sound of my impending doom. "You gotta let me go, Hak."

"I don't take orders from you."

"Well, you shouldn't be taking orders from the monster behind me either."

Hak glanced over my shoulder just as Karanis let out a roar of what I hoped was pain. Hak's throat worked as he swallowed. "He's still the governor."

"No. He's not," I said as slowly as possible, like I was speaking to a horse that had been spooked past madness. "The governor is dead. You don't owe anything to the *thing* wearing his face."

"Sure he does," Calien said, face pinging gleefully from mine to Hak's. "Karanis could kill you with half a thought. But if you kill Balthazar Vadalen, you'll be rewarded."

"Shut it, girl," Hak snapped, glancing down and away again before freezing. With agonizing slowness, his eyes dropped to Mira's face—to the blue orbs of fire dancing in her eye sockets. Hak recoiled, his revolver swinging from me to Mira. "What the hell is wrong with your eyes?"

My heart shot into my throat. The temple around us went dim. The world could have been—perhaps was—ending and I wouldn't have noticed. The gun grew in my vision as panic brought my brain to a screeching halt.

Because it wasn't supposed to go like this.

"Hak, be careful."

"Oh. Are you going to shoot me?" Calien asked, head cocking to one side. "But I'm just a little girl . . . you worthless piece of shit." The tone would have goaded a saint to violence.

Hak was far from a saint.

The gun shook in his hands. "But—but your eyes. You've got the same eyes as the governor."

"Hak, please." My voice sounded weak to my own ears. "This is my sister. She's been possessed."

"'Possessed' is such an ugly word," Calien drawled. "I'm only renting."

"Shut up, Calien." I ground out the words, trying to edge between them. "Hak, look at me. Please don't shoot her."

"No. Shoot me. I *dare* you."

I wet my lips, eyes glued to Hak even as his were trained on Mira. "Just listen to me. I have a way to stop the governor. But I can't do that if you're pointing a gun at my sister. Please. Tie her up. Handcuff her. But don't hurt her." Screams punctuated my words as more innocent people died around us.

Hak's eyes shot to me and away again in a blink. "You sure you can stop him?"

"Yes. I am."

For the first time, Calien's smiled faded. His face—Mira's face—filled with ancient, terrible rage. "Balthazar Vadalen, if you take one step toward that idol, I will scramble your sister's brain and spread it on my toast for breakfast."

"You wouldn't." The words were all hope and prayer, too weak to stand against the cacophony of screams tearing the world around us. I didn't need to see Calien's answering grin to know I was wrong.

"You know I would."

"No," Hak rasped, a tremor running down his arm. "You have to stop all this."

"Hak," I said slowly, willing him to see past his terror. To see that neither Karanis, nor Calien were the most immediate threats. Not to him.

Because I would kill him first.

"You have to stop this," he said again. "All those people. I knew some of them. Just left rotting. I got family down there. So you have to do something. I didn't sign up for this, I—"

"Hak, please," I said, cutting off the desperate rambling of a man sworn to protect the public good. A codie begging a criminal to do the right thing? It should have made me laugh. But for the gun he had trained on my sister's head.

"What are you waiting for?" Calien said. "Don't have the sack to kill me?"

Dread welled up inside me, so heavy I thought I would crumble beneath it. My hand went to the knife in my sleeve.

Hak shuddered, a ragged voice saying, "You said you could save us. So go. Save us."

Calien's smile turned savage.

Hak's eyes widened. His finger twitched.

Blue light faded.

I lunged. Buried the blade in his temple.

Hak was dead before he hit the floor. I tore the blade free, ignoring the feeling of Hak's blood hot on my hand, and went for Mira. Before Calien could take her mind again, I hit her. She crumpled. *She's going to kick me in the shins so hard when she wakes up,* I thought.

The smile died before it even began. Because I wasn't going to wake up. Too late to mourn that fact now.

I grabbed Hak's gun.

And ran.

Rain pelted from the ceiling, became ice as it slashed across my skin. Lightning crashed all around me. Men and women screamed and died in the same breath.

I ducked and dodged past spears of lightning. Past the fly of bullets and the stampede of men gone mad. I pumped my arms, trying to go faster, faster as the two pieces of the idol slowly became one.

And I was there. Standing before an altar so hot, the hairs on my arms curled and burned from sheer proximity.

This was it.

The end.

I raised the gun. Aimed. The trigger trembled beneath my finger.

"Enough!"

Karanis's bellow hit me a second before something barreled into the small of my back. A moment of pain-filled weightlessness filled my body as I careened over the altar and into the back wall. I heard my bones crunch and fell in a heap to the floor.

My ears began to ring. My vision was dark. The smell of burnt hair filled my nose. I blinked and blinked some more. Sight returned by degrees. Sight but not sound.

I saw Tass first, her body prone and unmoving on the floor thirty feet away. Blood stained the column behind her. Her chest worked in hitched gasps. I couldn't see her eyes, but I knew she watched me. Waited.

She nodded. It was time.

I looked for Mira. Couldn't find her.

Good, I thought.

She shouldn't have to watch this.

And my shins would be safe, I thought with a rueful smile, heart twisting. Because I'd have done anything to see Mira again. To walk out of here with her. But that wasn't to be. And I was okay with that. Well, not okay but . . . but it had to be done. And for her, for Mira, well . . . I was strong enough for this.

Karanis appeared in my line of vision. Skin and muscle and sinew slapped against the floor, each step shedding more and more viscera until barely more than bone remained.

My eyes raced up this nightmare body. Almost nothing of Paasch now remained. Karanis had used too much magic. The flesh form was little more than compost.

Now. He had to die now.

Now, Bal.

Now.

I struggled to rise. Had to use the wall to heave myself into a kneeling position. It wasn't enough. I had to get eyes on the necklace—the necklace that would make well and bloody sure that Karanis died here. My lungs burned with every shallow breath. My ribs felt broken. Didn't matter. Last chance.

Though every movement felt like glass grinding between my joints, I willed my body to stand. Back to the wall, I watched Karanis lift the idol in one skeletal hand. His entire attention was consumed by the statue, his face grotesque with rapture.

He didn't notice Zee's necklace at his elbow.

Didn't see me standing at his back.

My eyes rose without my consent. The remaining girders burned blue, capturing the energy the lightning had stripped from the dead men and women surrounding me. I couldn't hear the hum of gathering energy. Didn't need to. I'd heard it on the night of the consecration ceremony, remembered how it made every fiber of my being rise in horror just before it struck.

I tensed, sensing movement on my right, but it was too late now to stop me.

I raised the gun. Aimed once more.

Finally fired.

For a moment—a single second that stretched into eternity— nothing happened. The bullet just hung suspended in the energy field a hairsbreadth from the necklace.

There was a spark.

And then.

There was light.

28

BALTHAZAR

I came back to the world with the sensation of a slight weight on my chest. Air whistled out of my lips. Pain lined every inch of my body. I lay still for a few long moments, savoring the darkness, but it couldn't last. I opened my eyes and found the sky looking back at me. Clear, cloudless blue sky shone through a jagged hole in the ceiling.

Dust covered everything, sinking into my lungs with each inhale. I coughed, trying in vain to sit up only to find I was still being held down by a diminutive figure.

A woman. Shasheba.

She pushed herself up, sitting slowly like she'd been hurt. Probably had, I thought, struggling to find my own seat. Huge slabs of stone lay on the floor around us, crushing the altar. A crumpled body lay at its base. The body of a man who was once so familiar, but whose now-desiccated face was coated in mounds of white plaster dust. Like the death mask of a forgotten king.

I watched him, searching inside myself. Trying to find it. That sense of righteousness, of vindication. The feeling that after all the blood and sacrifice and terror that I had won. Paasch was dead. I had my revenge, but then again, I'd known that a long time ago.

But seeing it, now, in the actual flesh—all I felt was hollow. It was a victory as empty as the sack of meat in front of me.

Because nothing would bring my family back.

"Are you all right?" Shasheba's voice was halting.

I dragged my attention away from Paasch, turning my head slowly. Unwillingly. And frowned. Because Shasheba was never hesitant, never afraid.

She looked up at me through her lashes with liquid, beguiling blue eyes and a tremulous lower lip. I managed to nod but had to look away.

She'd saved my life, there was no doubt about that. Shash had risked her life tackling me out of the blast zone. Didn't mean I'd ever forget the look on her face when she singled Mira out to Karanis.

"Bal, I had to give Karanis something," she whispered urgently, as if she could read my thoughts. "He would have killed you all. I was just trying to—"

"I don't care." My voice clawed out of my throat in a scratchy rasp that wasn't entirely due to dust or exhaustion. I swallowed hard, nearly choking on the taste of rage and soured hope that rose within me at her every word.

"But I saved you," she said, sounding almost stunned. Not that I blamed her. It had taken me the better part of a decade to grow a spine around her. She was bound to be off-balance.

"I knew when you shot the statue, it would explode. I saved you."

I smiled, stroking the side of her face with the tips of my fingers. "You're so pretty when you lie."

"It's not a lie," she hissed, swatting my hand away. "I knew—"

"I didn't shoot the statue," I said, cutting her off. "I shot the necklace. The necklace I gave to *you*, knowing you'd throw it away like it was nothing more than trash."

Blood drained from her face as she realized she'd been used. Anger sparked to life in her eyes, and I relished it. It was probably the closest thing to a genuine expression she'd ever had.

"Just so we're clear: I wasn't going to leave you here," I said. "Because that's really what this was all about; why you gave Mira to Karanis. You were punishing me for abandoning you. But I wasn't running. I just needed to get Mira off the island and then Tass and I were coming back. For you.

"Until you fucked it all up by not trusting me."

The pretense of a vulnerable, helpless would-be princess—the mask of the woman I thought I knew, shattered. Shasheba lifted her chin up, looking at me through haughty and heavily lidded eyes. "Why would Tass come for me?"

"Because she was too honorable to let me come alone. She's my friend."

"Your friend?" She barked a brittle laugh. "She's a demon."

"Then what does that make you?" She jerked back like I'd struck her, but I was beyond her reach now. "Look around, Shasheba. Look at all the people you let Karanis murder. *Your* people."

Her face purpled, but her eyes never left mine—not even to acknowledge the burnt and broken bodies of her own acolytes lying at her feet. "I had no choice. I was just trying to survive."

I laughed, mirthless and bitter and broken. "Then that was your choice, Shasheba. You chose you," I said, and rose. Leaving all our bitter history on the floor where it belonged.

"Bal, wait." Shasheba seized my hands, expression tight. Afraid. "Don't go. Don't you see? This is your chance."

"What chance?"

"Your chance to take the city." She licked her lips, pressing herself into me. "You saved Cothis, Bal. You can take it, make it yours. Live up to your family's legacy."

"Take the city?" I felt my mouth hanging open.

My eyes raked across Shasheba's face, across the naked greed in her eyes. I could admit that my intentions in coming to Cothis were less than honorable. I'd come for revenge as much as any payday. More than the payday. But *rule* the city?

"Is that really what you think I want?"

She frowned. "I know it is. Don't you remember when we used to sit in your family's garden and dream of how we would rule this place? You used to speak about it with so much passion, the future you were supposed to have. The future *we* were supposed to have. It's what you've always wanted."

Something ashen soured my tongue. I pushed her away. "No, Shasheba. It's what *you've* always wanted."

"What—"

"I just wanted you."

I turned away from her, from the *idea* of her, and picked my way through the rubble and the bodies to Tass. She was leaning against a pillar, her black clothes remarkably untouched by the dust. She almost seemed to be lounging as though the destruction was just part of a normal day for her. Kai—thankfully unhurt—was crouched beside her, holding Mira in a tight embrace.

I nodded toward Tass's arm, which hung awkwardly from her shoulder. "You need me to pop that back in?"

"No thank you," she said with a half shrug like she was doing her best impression of Kai. "It'll slide back in on its own."

Mira perked at the sound of my voice and tore away from Kai. I opened my arms, expecting her to rush in. Instead, she wound her leg back and kicked me in the shin. I groaned, doubling over only to find Mira's arms wrapped around my waist.

"Don't you ever do that again." Something in my chest trembled when Mira looked up at me, her dark eyes shining with tears. I blew out a breath, my relief palpable. Not a trace of Calien remained. "I'm part of the crew. So you better let me in on the plan next time."

Calien's words came back to haunt me then—and the truth. That Mira feared she was nothing more to me than dead weight. I pulled her into a hug, willing her to understand how much she meant to me.

"You got it, Mira."

Edik slapped a plate-size hand on my shoulder nearly making my legs buckle. "I thought we'd lost you there for a moment."

"You wish."

He gave me a look that told me I wasn't *completely* wrong, yet I smiled. That faltered when Zee appeared beside her husband.

"Zee," I exclaimed on a sharp exhale, hugging her tightly. "You were absolutely brilliant. Even though I was not expecting you to shoot a harpoon through the damn roof."

Zee shrugged, brimming with an almost feline smugness. "I don't honestly know why you would expect anything less. I certainly wasn't sitting this one out."

"I didn't want to risk her in the thick of things," Edik murmured. "And we all know she can deal out damage no matter how close she gets."

"There's the sweet talker I married," she said, pecking him on the cheek.

I cleared my throat before they got going. "Where's the ship now?"

"Anchored just outside the door," she said, pulling away to look at me. There was a certain tightness to her lips I'd come to associate with worry. She looked me up and down. Frowned. "I hope you're done trying to blow yourself up, Bal. You owe me money. It's bad form."

"You got it, cuz." A smile creased my face, though it must have looked as fragile as it felt, since both Edik and Zee gave me similar looks of confusion.

"I can't tell you how happy I am to see you two," I said, my voice tight. "Thank you. Thank you both for being here."

Zee swatted my words away. "Heavens Above, Bal. It was the plan. Where did you think we'd be?"

My eyes slid to Edik, who watched me steady and calm, all trace of our fight sliding away. "We gave you our word. We're family, Bal. We'd cross the world to save you."

"How could you ever doubt it?" Zee asked tartly, blinking rapidly as if to suffocate the emotion clearly rising within her.

"Is it crazy that I had a small hope you would have just run away and saved yourselves and the baby?"

"Yes," Edik said, while at the same time Zee said, "Now you tell us!"

I had to laugh at the absurdity of the love surrounding us.

Gruffly, Zee asked, "Now, what do you want to do with this?"

She held out her hands, offering up the broken remnants of a too-familiar idol. Whoever was left of the city's leaders would probably want it. So would the empress and her people, now that I thought about it. But I knew it was too dangerous to leave floating around.

"Only one place I can think of where it would be safe," I said.

"You sure you want to go back there?" Kai asked skeptically. "He sounded right pissed off at you two."

"Yeah, I'm sure."

"Enkaara seems to have a soft spot for you. He may show mercy," Tass said, reminding me that the cantankerous old man I'd known most of my life was the mythic creator of heaven and earth. Judging by the way my crew winced, they didn't welcome the reminder either.

"He set two stone wolves on me."

"But he could have sent *more*."

There was that. "C'mon. Let's get this over with."

"Fine," Kai grumbled, losing a few inches of height. "But I gotta find a washroom first."

I shot him a quizzical look, and he flushed a deep dark red. He mumbled something about his hands being dirty and walked away.

"Mr. Vadalen," Sergeant Tammon called, intercepting us as we reached the temple doors.

Plaster dust peppered his hair, making him look older than he'd been only an hour ago. Or maybe it was the haunted look in his eyes—one mirrored in everyone around us.

"Sergeant," I said, shoving the idol's broken shards into my jacket pocket.

"I just wanted to thank you—all of you," he added, sharing a heavy look with Edik.

"I think we should be thanking you," I said. "If you hadn't thrown the earring bombs—"

"I just did my duty."

I was hearing that a lot the last few days, but this was the first time it actually seemed to mean anything.

Tammon continued. "But I see that your day is not yet done." He chewed on the inside of his cheek, dark eyes going from Edik to the statue weighing down my jacket and then back up to my face. "After everything that's happened, the empress will be mighty interested in studying that idol."

I gathered all my remaining strength to my chest. The crew around me went tense. Ready for a fight. "She will."

Tammon nodded to himself. "You'll make sure it never again sees the light of day?"

Edik was right, Tammon was a good man. Good enough to know that the things an empress might want aren't necessarily the things she should get.

"I will." It was as solemn an oath as I could give.

"Good. The codekeeper boat is yours if you need it."

I shot a glance upward, and Tammon nodded once more. "We'll make our own way," I said, nodding my thanks to an unlikely ally and rushing out of the temple. Best to be away before anyone else thought to look for the idol.

A problem for another day, I thought, setting my hands to the rope ladder. Scaling the twenty feet between the temple and the sky ship was an exercise in burning glory. My muscles sang with exhaustion, but it was a good kind of pain. The kind that let you know you were almost home again.

Zee and Edik took command of the ship, sailing us away from the temple as fast as the *Fortune's Fool* could manage. But I don't think any of us breathed until we made it out of the temple's shadow. Tass and I slumped side by side against the rail, nursing our respective wounds. There was a rightness to having her there. Like she was a puzzle piece I hadn't known was missing.

It should have taken me by surprise, that feeling. The fact that it didn't, well . . . It gave me something to mull over, that was for damn sure.

We dropped anchor in the Sunken Gardens, knowing the streets were so empty that it would be a while yet before anyone complained about it being there. Not that there were many codies left to complain to.

No doubt we looked like the walking dead, lost among the manicured hedges. Fodder for tall tales that would surely sprout up about this adventure. It seemed impossible that the sun could be shining, but the proof was in the warmth on my face. Muggy waves of moisture rose in the air as heat burned away the tiny puddles gathering in the cracks of the cobblestones.

By the time we reached the Witch's Door, sweat beaded up beneath my shirt and exhaustion weighed down my limbs. Tass placed the flat of her hand on the door, murmured something I didn't even try to hear. She turned the handle.

The darkness across the threshold had texture. It had weight. Awareness even. There was a menace to it that made Kai rock back on his heels and Edik whisper a prayer. Mira, worn thin with too much fear, slipped her hand in mine. I held on tight and glared into that impenetrable dark.

"Karanis is dead," I called through the door. "We've come to return the idol."

The darkness seemed to swirl in a curious, considering kind of way. Like a great intake of breath, it drew back. A lamp burst to life.

"Good sign, you think?" I asked, angling my head toward Tass.

She shrugged. "As good as we're going to get."

"Figures."

With lamp lights leading us on, we entered the Archive the way we did the night of the consecration: together.

The Curator waited at the bottom of the spiral, hands clasped behind his back, standing beside one lonely-looking wolf statue. The other stone wolf was nowhere to be seen, it's pedestal rough and broken from where it had leaped to life. I wondered if it would ever return from the Nethersphere, or if its remains would lay forever in that land of nightmares. I shivered, pulling my thoughts back to the present.

The whole of the Curator's attention was latched on to my face. He wasn't smiling, but his lambent eyes traced my features like he was studying a map he couldn't quite decipher.

Tass slid up beside me—not a shield but a support. Reaching into my pocket, I dug out the broken shards of the idol. "Here."

He cupped the pieces in his weathered hands for a second, before tucking them away as if they were no more interesting than a used handkerchief. "I must admit, Balthazar, I did not think you would survive Karanis."

My answering laugh was bone-tired with exhaustion. "Funny. I seem to remember you saying it would be easy to kill the bastard."

"'Easy' is relative." A smile cracked the Curator's face and with a sense of shuddering unreality, I remembered who this ancient creature was: the Creator. The smile flickered. "I see Tassiel told you who I am?"

I nodded.

"Humph. I do hope you aren't going to start bowing and scraping now."

"No," I snorted, as that was the last thing on my mind. Did he really think I was the kind to—

Edik contradicted me by bending in the middle, head nearly brushing the floor as he bowed.

"Enough, my dear boy," Enkaara said, swatting away Edik's

obeisance with an impatient wave. "When my companions and I first came to this world, your ancestors had only just begun to *be* human. It was natural for them to think us gods. And if I am to be honest, natural for us to accept your blind devotion. But no more. If time is cruel to you and cuts your lives short, you have advanced anyway. While we, I believe, are in decline."

The Curator's sigh seemed to echo through the cavernous space like the ghost of a grief-filled wail. "We cannot be your gods, child. We cannot possibly live up to the responsibility."

"We are in decline," Tass murmured, repeating Enkaara's words with contemplative musing.

"What does it mean?" I asked.

"Trouble," Enkaara replied, but shrugged, his expression wistful. "But trouble that will wait. Go, Balthazar. Enjoy your victory."

I was all too happy to obey. Pocketing the very heavy purse the Curator handed to me, I started up the ramp. Judging by the way my crew trudged up the hall in front of me, I knew I wasn't the only one longing for sleep.

As I thought it, Kai heaved a jaw-cracking yawn. "Where to, boss?"

"Home," Tass whispered. "Your summer home," she continued when I shot her a confused look.

Kai patted Tass's shoulder. "Sounds perfect."

It did sound perfect. It sounded right. But as Tass and I walked side by side through the dark, my stomach sank. She was offering us our summer home, but what did that mean for her? Our three days together were more than spent. Was she going to disappear into the darkness, slipping away like smoke never to be seen again? Or was she going home too? Not that the difference mattered. She'd still be gone.

My eyes flicked up to where Zee and Edik were walking hand in hand. They too were already half gone.

"Bal?" Kai's voice echoed back to me, and I realized that I'd stopped walking three steps from the door. Zee and Edik stood in that sunlit garden watching me. Kai waited in the threshold. Mira stood between us, caught in limbo, unsure of whether to go or stay.

I shook my head, trying to clear my thoughts. "Why don't you guys go ahead. I want to talk to Tass for a moment."

Kai's eyes narrowed at me. He looked at Tass, and then back at me, comprehension making his mouth *click* open. Then, no doubt guessing what I was going to do, he shrugged and took Mira. For her part, Mira smiled, flashing me a quick thumbs-up before hurrying away.

I felt the weight of Tass's considerable attention on my back as I walked to the door and eased down on the threshold. After a moment, she joined me, elbows braced on her knees. "What is it, Bal?"

"Here," I said, struck by a sudden bolt of inspiration. I unclasped the pendant from around my neck. Handed it to her.

"What's this?"

"A present," I said, beaming at her. At the way she cradled the small slip of metal in her gloved hands like it was the most precious thing she'd ever held. Maybe it was. For the woman whose life had been measured in usefulness, in duty and debt. Who had never known what it was to be valued for the simple fact of who she was.

Who had never even been given something as simple as a gift.

"I can't give you back your time," she said, so quietly. Tremulously. "It doesn't work like that, I cannot—"

"Yeah, I figured," I said, shrugging that particular worry off for another day. "I wasn't even going to ask for that actually."

Her silver-planed face angled toward mine. "What were you going to ask for?"

"I was . . . I was just wondering what you plan to do now?"

"Now?" She took a breath. "Surprisingly, I think I'd like to go to sleep."

"That's not what I meant."

"No," she agreed. "You're wondering if I intend to return to the Nethersphere."

A cool breeze danced across my face. "Will you?"

She was silent for a minute that stretched into an hour. "No."

"No?" Surprise and hope made the sun feel warmer on my skin. "Why not?"

"Enkaara being here is wrong. But Karanis's attempt at conquest?" She shook her head. "It is a sign, Bal. A sign that there is something very wrong in the Nethersphere."

"And you don't want to find out what it is?"

She made a cutting motion with one hand. "Of course I want to know, but . . . but my heart tells me that I'll be better situated to confront the problem here."

"Here?" I asked flatly, and that brief moment of sunlight fled. "You think other Ankaari will cross into our world?"

She nodded. "Of the nine Ankaari who ruled the Nethersphere after Enkaara's exile, Karanis was the least in every way. I didn't lie to him when I said Janus sent him as a potential sacrifice. And failure, well-studied, can be just as illuminating as success. What he attempted; others will try. Especially when they hear Calien's report of events." Her face tilted up, toward some point I couldn't see. "A storm is coming for your world, Bal. The kind your people may not survive."

We had barely survived *this* storm. My body felt heavy, crumpling under the trepidation these words caused. Tass looked at me, nudged my shoulder with hers. "I would not worry about it too much, if I were you. Like I said, time does not touch the Ankaari. Karanis's destruction will make them pause. You'll probably be long dead before they move again."

"If *that's* the case . . . ," I said with a wry laugh, never having felt so relieved to be nothing more than mortal. Sobering a bit, I said, "It sounds like you're free."

"Free?"

"Yeah, free. Free to go live. Free to explore the world . . ."

I looked down, scared to see her reaction to what I was about to say next. But I had to know, and so I glanced up and said, "Free to join a band of disreputable thieves."

Tass's body went still. She turned, the perfect oval of her silver mask facing me. "What are you saying?"

"I'm saying that I want you to join me—join us."

"Why?"

I'd never heard any word so loaded with suspicion and doubt in my entire life. But then I remembered the Septiniri and how they betrayed her. It wasn't the kind of loss anyone recovered from.

I swallowed, choosing my words with infinite care. "Look, I'm not asking because you're some superpowered demigod who can get in anywhere and stop bullets or whatever. I'm not even asking because we work well together, which we do, by the way. But that's not it. It has nothing to do with what you are. It's *who* you are."

"And who am I?" she asked, her voice so, so small. Like she truly didn't know.

"You're family." It was such a simple word. But the simple ones were usually the best. I smiled, feeling my heart expanding in my chest, knowing hers did the same. "And I want you to stay."

She was silent long enough that an unbearable coldness began prickling my fingers. Then I felt her smile, soft and silken as a butterfly's wings. She slipped the necklace over her head. "All right."

They were the most beautiful words I'd ever heard. I grinned, rising to my feet. "All right."

"You coming?" yelled Mira, and I grit my teeth. *I love my sister. I love my sister. I love . . .*

Tass's laugh startled me, and I couldn't help but smile. "We're coming," I called back. And with the solid earth of Cothis beneath my feet, I offered her my hand. Tassiel slid her gloved fingers into mine.

And I pulled her into the light.

ACKNOWLEDGMENTS

It always amazes me that a book which began in the echoing silence of my own mind could ever reach the hands of readers. It is an enormous privilege to call this career my own, but I have cherished every moment of it (even the hard ones), and that, dear readers, I owe to you.

Enormous amounts of gratitude also go to the people who helped shape this book and give it a home, namely: Jennifer Udden, Stephanie Kim, Suzie Townsend, and everyone at New Leaf Literary. As well as to Elena Stokes, publicist extraordinaire.

Thank you as well go to my amazing team at Harper Voyager, including David Pomerico, Mireya Chiriboga, Jennifer Brehl, Evangelos Vasilakis, and everyone else who took this book in hand and helped mold and polish it into the raucous adventure it has become.

Also to my fabulous crew of writer buddies: H.M. Long, Genevieve Gornichec, M.J. Kuhn, J.S. Dewes, and Meg Bonney. This is the most bizarre career in the whole freaking world and if I didn't have you all in my corner, I'm more than a little sure that I'd have crawled into the woods never to emerge again.

It's little secret at this point that this book began with my love for Dungeons & Dragons and the tabletop games I've played with my best friends. This book would not exist were it not for the original crew of the *Fortune*: EJ, Claudia, Steve, Dan, Kate, Karl, and Aiden.

Thank you all for the adventures, laughter, and support. We may not all be family by blood, but our ties are forged in magic.

Speaking of family, Bal and the crew of the Talion gang would not be half so funny were it not for my siblings: Gretchen, Kurt, and Karl—who knew that all our adventures, arguments, and one-liners would end up in print one day. And also to Nic, Katy, Rich, Julie, Kate, John, and Rachael for being a part of my weird family and rolling with the insanity. You are all saints beyond measure.

For my dad who read this book on a fateful trip to Florida and has spent the last five years demanding a print copy. Your enthusiasm for this story carried me through many rounds of edits and impostor syndrome.

For my mom and her unflagging support of all my creative endeavors and who somehow managed to be impossibly proud of all my terrible artwork and nonsensical stories. Who could have guessed it was all leading to this? And . . . yes, I used a lot of naughty words in this one. I know, I'm grounded.

Last but not least, my favorite people in the world: EJ, Lorelei, and Nadia. You are my strength and the wonder I see in every quiet moment. You give meaning to the word "love." Simply put: You are mine, and I am yours. There is no where you could go that I will not be with you.

ABOUT THE AUTHOR

Greta K. Kelly is (probably) not a witch, death, or otherwise, but she can still be summoned with offerings of too-beautiful-to-use journals and Butterfinger candy. She currently lives in Wisconsin with her husband, EJ, and daughters, Lorelei and Nadia, who are doing their level best to take over the world. She is the author of the Warrior Witch duology, which consists of *The Frozen Crown* and *The Seventh Queen*.